The Reluctant Daughters

Veronica H. Hart

Uppity Woman Press
Ormond Beach, Florida

ISBN: 978-0-692498743
Copyright © 2016 Veronica Helen Hart

Cover design: Chris Holmes
Author photograph: Barbie Marland

Uppity Woman Press
1201 Scottsdale Drive
Suite A
Ormond Beach, FL 32174

This novel is a work of fiction. Names, characters, places, and incidents either are the product of the author's imagination or are used fictitiously.

Dedication

To my beautiful daughters

Marie Louise
Constance Ann
Nancy Victoria
Karen Louise
Fiona Lynne

Thank you for your constant support

The Reluctant Daughters

by

Veronica Helen Hart

One

Elisabeth Mary Riis, awakened in the wee hours of the morning by the sound of wheels on the gravel drive, listened to her granddaughters' conversation from the top of the stairs. It never occurred to the girls to look up. If they had they would have seen her there, squatting down like a child hiding at Christmas waiting for Santa Claus. She had fallen asleep waiting for her girls to come home. Though she knew Ledger was with them and would keep them safe, their antics often alarmed her. She would have to wait until breakfast to confront them and once again confine them to their room as punishment for going out without permission. Part of Elisabeth wanted to smile at their adventuresome spirits, but part understood they could one day find themselves in serious trouble, Ledger or no Ledger.

I'm tired. How much longer can I live? Those two will be the death of me. Barbara is a born leader. Perhaps I ought to send Lillian to boarding school where she'd be free from Barbara's influence. She began to pull herself up from her cramped position when she heard a familiar name.

"Do you think what Senator Pembroke said is true?" Barbara said from below.

"He was talking to his friends," Lillian answered.

"Because he's a politician and wants to run for president. He said he needs to get it out of the way so it doesn't come back to haunt him. What would be haunting him? Do you think he killed someone a long time ago?"

"He said the name Ackert, Barb. Grandma's company is Ackert. What would he have to do with Grandma?"

"He's worried about getting rid of something or someone. It has to be a scandal, but I can't for the life of me think of any kind of scandal Grandmother could be involved in. Maybe something to do with poor materials for a government building project?"

Lillian didn't respond. Elisabeth could imagine her shrugging.

"That couldn't be." Barbara continued. "She always talks about making sure employees are honest and keeping the reputation of her businesses unsullied by scandal. She fires people like she fires the household help. Looks random, but she has reasons."

"I like Annie. She's been here a long time now."

"Everything I've read about Senator Pembroke suggests he is a less than honorable man. No, I can't imagine Grandma ever being involved with him, so why would he need to make sure she won't ever talk about whatever she hasn't talked about in all these years?"

"You sound like a riddle."

"Let's go to bed," Barbara said.

Elisabeth's skin crawled at those words. *Senator Pembroke. Please don't let it be true. Senator Justin Chauncey Pembroke running for president. Of course, there had been rumors at the office. Does he really think he can win against McKinley? Surely Tammany Hall would not support him.* Tears welled in her eyes as she stumbled her way back to her second-floor bedroom. *Of all the people in the world, her granddaughters had to come across him.*

Elisabeth slipped back into her bed and tried to return to sleep, but thoughts of Justin Chauncey Pembroke rolled through her head like a stage play. It was eighteen sixty-four; she'd been so young then. Even now, so many years later, her face burned with humiliation.

Before the sun came up, she pulled the bell and asked Ledger to come across to the house.

"Is something wrong? Are you unwell?" Ledger asked as he entered her bedroom.

"There's plenty wrong, Ledger. You took the girls to the Albany Gentlemen's Club last night."

He sat on a chair near the window. "I did."

"Why?"

"They expressed curiosity about it."

Elisabeth snorted. "More likely Barbara was curious. She's been the troublemaker from the start."

"Don't be so hard on them, Elisabeth. Barbara's a bright girl and naturally curious about everything in life. I maintain the position she ought to go for a higher education or else let me bring her into the company and apprentice her to a manager."

"I am not hard on them. They needed discipline. When I found them living in the New York *pied-a-terre*, they were unruly. Abandoned by their mother, living as they pleased. No. It was necessary to be firm with them."

She could tell by the way he pursed his lips he disapproved. He had disapproved of the way she treated her daughter, Mary Ellen, as well. Well, there were limits to his authority. "What happened last night?"

"Mrs. Burch's husband is the chef at the club so he arranged for the girls to work for one night as maids. I don't know how many people we fooled, but at least they didn't break anything."

"This is not a laughing matter. Do you know whether Mary Ellen is still living in New York?"

"She writes to me occasionally. I believe she is currently in residence."

"You never said a word to the girls?"

"You asked me not to."

Elisabeth eyed her long-time servant and companion, examining him for any signs of duplicity. "Call for the carriage. We're going on a trip. And send Annie in immediately."

He pulled out his pocket watch. "She won't have arrived, yet."

"Then wake Barbara!"

"A little patience. The girl should arrive by seven."

Two

By eight o'clock, Barbara was awake. The seventeen-year-old studied her still sleeping little sister as the sun streamed in through the opened window and highlighted the girl's flaming red hair and freckled face. Since she had been out of school for nearly two weeks and outdoors much of the time, Lily's freckles had multiplied like the dandelions on the lawns.

Barbara threw her bedcovers aside and stood up, not particularly anxious to greet yet another boring day. Her life loomed ahead of her with no plan, no goal. Her grandmother refused to present her at a debutante ball. "You aren't a debutante. Get that through your head, young lady. You're an orphan and ought to be glad you have a roof over your head. Someday you might meet a suitable man, but he won't be from society."

When she had asked her grandmother to learn a skill so she might find work, the idea was vetoed instantly. "No granddaughter of mine will work as long as I am alive. I'm well able to care for you. You want for nothing."

Barbara sat up in the bed and yawned loudly, hoping she'd waken Lily, but the younger girl could still sleep like a child, oblivious to any sounds around her.

She thought about their adventure last night and couldn't wait to see Grandmother's face when she told her what they'd done. With the help of their cook, Mrs. Burch and Ledger, they'd gone into the Albany Gentlemen's Club and were

5

permitted to work as maids for much of the night. Mr. Burch, the club chef, took charge of them and showed them how to serve drinks and to remain invisible as they moved through the rooms.

She was excited when she came across a group of politicians, including Senator Pembroke, smoking cigars and drinking in a small lounge. Moving unobtrusively through the room, she picked up glasses and emptied ashtrays while they talked. She hurried to the kitchen to collect sandwiches and then returned to the room. When she wasn't needed, she stood outside the door and listened to their conversations. The smoke from the cigars burned her eyes. By the end of the night when the men either retired to rooms upstairs or left, she was exhausted but her curiosity had magnified. Now she knew what the inside of the placed looked like; now she wanted to know how a scandal connected Senator Pembroke to her grandmother. Perhaps this morning she would find a way to bring up the subject.

After running down the hall to use the water closet, she returned to pull on her petticoats and throw a cotton summer dress over her head. She donned house slippers and left Lily to sleep until Grandmother sent Annie up to roust her out of bed.

Skipping down the stairs to the first floor, the fragrance of coffee floated up to greet her. Good. That meant Mrs. Burch was up. Annie ought to have set the table for breakfast by now. She liked Annie, a young Irish girl who had been hired to replace Tilda a few weeks ago. Housemaids came and went as a matter of routine. It didn't take any of them long to realize Grandmother was a harsh taskmaster who refused to tolerate abuses of her household rules. An abuse could mean taking time for a cup of coffee or a glass of milk in mid-morning or missing a dust bunny under a bed. Curtsies and bows, polite speech and proper attire required at all times, sent too many young servants running.

The only constant in their lives had been Ledger, who lived over the carriage house, and Mrs. Burch, who shared the third-floor servants' quarters with them. She was the housekeeper and cook.

Barbara skipped into the kitchen. "I'm up, Annie. Will you let Mrs. Riis know so we can eat? Thank you." She poured a cup of coffee, prepared to take it out to the morning room where they ate their breakfast.

"Mrs. Riis hasn't come down yet, Miss Barbara." The slight girl appeared pale and nervous, hands twisting the edge of her apron.

"Where's Ledger? Send him up for her."

"I haven't seen him either," she said.

The breakfast tray was on the table, everything ready to carry through to the other room as soon as Grandmother appeared. Barbara didn't know what to make of it. Grandmother never strayed from her routine. "Never mind. I'll go wake her. Miss Lillian will not be down for breakfast."

"Yes, Miss."

Grandmother had her suite of rooms on the second floor. It included a private water closet and bathroom with an enormous claw footed tub. Barbara tapped on the solid wood door and then turned the knob without waiting for a response. If Grandmother hadn't come down for breakfast fully dressed and ready for the day, then something on the order of a serious illness had struck. Barbara couldn't imagine any other reason for her tardiness.

The room lay in darkness. It took a moment for her eyes to adjust to the gloom as she crossed the large space to pull open the nearest set of draperies. When she turned around toward the bed, it was obvious no one was in it, though it did look slept in. The covers lay pulled back, the pillows in disarray. More curious than concerned, Barbara headed to the water closet, her footsteps silent on the massive Turkish carpet. She listened for a moment at the door and then knocked on it. No response. The bathroom door stood slightly ajar, so she peeked in to find another room devoid of any occupant. Only the scent of Grandmother's French milled soap floated in the air.

"Well," she said, as she placed her hands on her hips and looked around the large bedroom again as if Grandmother might be hiding behind the armoire or maybe under her vanity. Grandmother did not step out of the shadows to chastise her for entering the room unbidden.

~*~

Elisabeth sat with her back straight as the train car swayed along the tracks toward New York City. She wore a white high-collared blouse under a long-sleeved pink cotton over blouse, topped by a deep rose satin vest. Her skirt hugged her still small waist and flared to just above her ankles, the fabric a muted, gray-brushed cotton. She wore her sensible travel boots which Ledger had insisted on polishing before he'd let her out of the house.

He hadn't appeared surprised when she rang for him in his rooms over the carriage house. He knew where he had driven the girls the night before and he probably sat dressed and waiting for the summons. By the time he had the horse and carriage at the front door, she had packed the things she needed and was waiting for him in the foyer. She sent him to pack a bag for himself. "I may need you in the city."

"I'm sure you will," he answered with a smile.

She sat on the right side of the first-class train car so she could watch the river as they headed south. There would be many stops along the way and time for a good lunch in the dining car.

Ledger took his place in third class.

She wondered what the other people on the train would think if she told them her plans for Senator Pembroke. Although, no doubt some would cheer her on and offer to help if they were smart, most of them would be against her. Some might even wish her locked up in jail or confined to a hospital for the mentally insane.

So many years and so much time had passed.

"Start over," she said to herself. "Figure it out carefully before you do wind up locked away forever. Think what would happen to those two beautiful granddaughters of yours." She laughed. "They'd probably be glad to be free of you, old woman. You're far too strict with them. Well, they do behave like young hooligans." Her voice startled her. Glad no one shared her compartment, she leaned back against the plush velvet seat, turned her head toward the window and let her eyes rest on the river. Sun sparkled on the water. The swaying of the car soothed her. For a little while she stopped thinking about Mary Ellen and Senator Pembroke. Justin. So young. So handsome. She drifted off to sleep.

The screech of the wheels on the track woke her at the same time she was thrown forward onto the seat opposite. Her heart jumped in her throat as she held on to keep from falling to the floor.

There was a knock on the door followed by a porter opening it. "Poughkeepsie," he announced. When he saw her distress, he stepped into the compartment to help her back to her seat. "Excuse me. Are you all right, ma'am?"

"I'm sorry. I must have fallen asleep. Please, don't mind me. I'm fine." Her mind wasn't fine, that much she knew. She was on a dangerous mission where success could free her and her offspring forever but failure could end in death for her and shame for them. She waved the porter away. "I'll have lunch in a little while. Please let me know. Thank you."

~*~

Skirts flying, Barbara dashed down the stairs to find Mrs. Burch and alert her about grandmother's disappearance. She passed Annie trudging up the stairs with her cleaning bucket and brushes. "Mrs. Burch! Mrs. Burch, Grandmother is gone!"

"Yes, Miss. I gather she left a while ago with Mr. Ledger. And before you ask, I never heard for how long she'll be gone."

Barbara slid to a stop at the kitchen table and dropped down on a chair. "No note?"

"No, Miss. Do you want breakfast now?"

"Coffee and some of Irish soda bread. Butter. Cheese," Barbara rattled off automatically. "Where would they go so early in the morning?"

Mrs. Burch shrugged her huge shoulders and waddled to the ice box to collect milk, cheese, and butter. She worked silently as Barbara used a fork to tap out a rhythm on the tabletop, pondering what her grandmother could be up to.

"She wasn't ill last night."

"No, Miss."

"Nobody came to call? No one with bad news?"

"Not to my knowledge, Miss. Here's fresh coffee. Have some food and we'll figure this out after."

"You know me too well, Mrs. Burch. After I eat, I'll feel better and then I can tackle this problem." She buttered a piece of bread and placed a chunk of cheese on it. "Have you worked for Grandmother as long as Ledger?"

"No, Miss. She hired me when she told me she'd need a cook and housekeeper because she intended to bring two little girls to live with her. I've been here six years."

"We've been here five years."

"It took her some time to find you and bring you home, darlin'." Mrs. Burch patted Barbara on the shoulder as she passed by on her way to the sink.

"And Grandfather Riis had been gone a long time. She must have been lonely."

"I couldn't know, Miss Barbara. But she was livelier and happier after you two arrived. You were such skinny little things."

"Twelve and eight. Practically babies."

"She's plenty proud of the two of you. Calls you her Happy Hooligans."

"We are bad, aren't we?" Barbara agreed with a grin. "It was hard coming here and suddenly having to live by rules."

"You did well enough in school."

A frown crossed Barbara's brow as she leaned her chin in her hands on the table. "The problem is what to do with the rest of my life! We can't go into society. Our parents are dead. Grandmother doesn't believe in girls buying expensive dresses to prove they're better than other people. What are we supposed to do? I mean, you could teach me to cook, but then who would hire a rich heiress to be their cook? There is absolutely nothing useful for me to do."

"I have an idea, Miss. If you'll forgive a poor servant presuming…"

"Don't be silly, Mrs. Burch. You're more a mother than anyone else has been in my life."

"You know I can read, don't you?"

"Good for you! I had no idea. Do you read the newspapers and everything?"

"I like to read novels and stories of faraway places and romance."

"Have you read Jack London?" Barbara asked, excited by this revelation of a woman she'd only thought of as a household servant.

"I have. But if I may tell you something else." Mrs. Burch sat down across from her.

"Grandmother might come in. You ought not to be sitting with me."

"Hush. We'll hear the carriage. I've read The Awakening by Kate Chopin."

By the look on Mrs. Burch' face, Barbara thought she ought to know the book, but it didn't register. "I have to confess to not knowing of that one."

"Perhaps you shouldn't, but it's about a woman who might be much like yourself. Except you have more advantages. Her name is Edna and she refused to live life according to society's rigid structure. She married, refused to have children, and even took – well, never mind that part. She became an artist."

"You think I should become an artist? I was kind of thinking I'd make a good reporter."

"No. Listen to the title of the book. The Awakening. A woman finds her own soul. She doesn't let other people tell her how to live her life. She lives it as she chooses. The book was frowned on by the critics, but I found it decidedly profound."

"Good Lord. Imagine that. You and Ledger. We have the most educated servants in the state, I should imagine."

"Perhaps you could write of your experiences when your poor mother was alive. Tell about your travels. Do you remember your father?"

"Yeah. Jacob von Bek. A little bit. He and mother often disappeared and left us in the care of people I'd take an oath were gypsies. They'd come back days later, delighted to see us again. He was such a small part of my life. Write about them? Who would care? Besides, I remember Seamus more."

"You might be surprised at how many young women look forward to their fate with dread. Society ladies as well as the poor. No matter what we do, it's dependent on the men. It's their money, their world."

"Grandmother says we have our own money."

"In a way you do, but believe me, any trust funds are being managed by men. Never mind that. Finish your breakfast and go wake that lazy sister of yours."

Barbara smiled before stuffing the last piece of buttered bread into her mouth. "She's on the front porch sketching," she said in a muffled murmur.

"Humph."

"We read Louisa May Alcott, Jane Austen and the book by the lady who went to work as a teacher in Siam. Anna somebody. You're right, Mrs. Burch. All those women were guided by wanting husbands in their lives. I could be a teacher, couldn't I? What if I went to live in some exotic place? Maybe a king would fall in love with me."

"I think not, Missy. Go get your sister."

The sound of wheels on gravel announced the arrival of the carriage. Barbara jumped up and headed for the front door, but by the time she reached the vestibule, the carriage was already disappearing around the house toward the carriage house. Somebody was home. Somebody who could explain Grandmother's unusual behavior.

The person turned out to be an old man Ledger hired to return the horse and carriage to the house. Mrs. Burch fed him while Barbara tried to pry information from him, but all he knew was, "the big black man gave me money to bring the buggy here and promised the lady would feed me."

~*~

As the train rattled closer to New York City, Elisabeth continued her reverie, thinking of picnics with her father when they enjoyed a couple of boiled eggs, a loaf of bread and drank fresh spring water from the creeks and equally wonderful days sitting beside him in his office as he explained his vast holdings. "The secret is to keep a low profile, my dear. Though we own buildings, ships and have investments in shipping and railroads, I do it under a corporate name. I am a man of influence behind the scenes."

Unfortunately, not so much influence he could get his daughter accepted in society.

Three

"Harlem! Harlem!" the conductor shouted in the passageway.

It wouldn't be long before they reached the Grand Central Terminal. She prayed Mary Ellen would be at home and not in some opium den or off on another scandalous journey.

Disembarking from the train, Elisabeth stood waiting for Ledger to find his way forward. "We'll hire a cab to take us to the townhouse, Ledger. I'll be inside waiting."

Ledger tipped his cap. "Be right back, ma'am, as soon as I fetch the luggage."

Her foot tapped independently as she stood inside the glass doors and watched Ledger scramble through the throngs of people scurrying to and fro on the sidewalk. Horses and buggies vied for space with the electric taxi cabs. The city that excited her in spite of the grim purpose for her journey. Perhaps she would take time for entertainment; she had not been to the theater in years. Her entire life had been taken up with supervising the various businesses her father had left her, arranging her daughter's life and caring for her granddaughters. Ledger hurried back and held the door for her to pass through.

"It's the second one, there, ma'am." He sucked in his breath so she could pass him without touching him. Elisabeth, holding a delicately perfumed handkerchief over her nose to cover the city odors, marched purposefully toward the waiting vehicle, and let Ledger once again step ahead to open the door for her. After giving the man directions to the Park Avenue residence, he hopped on top of the luggage stacked and tied at the rear of the car.

She would enjoy a refreshing bath first and then confront Mary Ellen. The girl–the woman–would have no choice but to agree to her conditions and terms. Senator Justin Pembroke had to be stopped.

The narrow little taxi nearly tipped over on two wheels as the driver accelerated into a u-turn on the busy avenue. Elisabeth grabbed the sides and waited for them to set a steady rhythm. Despite her frayed nerves, she still enjoyed looking at the sights, the clothing styles. Why had she exiled herself to Albany after Jim died? What had she proved to anyone? She abandoned her only child and then later, her two granddaughters, though she had spent the last five years doing everything in her power to make it up to them.

They moved along. Policemen on bicycles tipped their hats as they passed by. A horse-drawn omnibus filled with passengers crept along, slowing a trolley behind it.

They pulled up before the limestone brick mansion where she'd developed three elegant flats. Hers was on the top floor where the noise and stench of the city didn't intrude. She climbed the steps and then turned to view the park across the street. Still vast, still impossible to believe it lay in the center of one of the largest cities in the world. She had enjoyed many walks through Central Park. Her little girl rode the ponies in the summer and skated on the pond in the winter. Now, what did her little girl do?

The walk up the three flights of stairs winded her. Removing her key from her purse, she handed it to Ledger as she gazed about the beautiful foyer, unchanged since she last had it decorated when she took the girls from Mary Ellen. The vase on the credenza created the only sour note; no fresh flowers.

When she entered the living room it was easy to tell Mary Ellen was in residence. The place was a sty! Clothing lay draped over the furniture, plates with left–over food remained on the tables and ashtrays with cigarette butts littered the room. Elisabeth closed her eyes and took a deep breath.

"Mary Ellen!" she sang out, trying to sound cheerful so she wouldn't scare the girl right away. "Mother's come for a visit!"

She turned to Ledger. "Put my things away and then please see to this mess. After you've had a moment to settle in yourself, of course."

He bowed. "Yes, ma'am."

One elegant little chair at the side of the room remained free of clutter. Elisabeth chose to sit there to await her daughter's appearance. The stale odors of cigarette smoke and whiskey hung in the air; she couldn't be far away.

Within minutes she heard the girl singing before she saw her enter the room through the opened double doors across the way. The doors led to the bedrooms and bath. Mary Ellen walked naked into the room with a bath towel wrapped around her head giving her the appearance of an Egyptian queen. Long, lean she could have been beautiful but for the sallow gauntness of her features. A bruise stood out on her upper right thigh.

"Hello, Mother. It's been a long time." She shoved clothes aside and stretched herself on the chaise near the marble fireplace. "How are my lovely little girls?"

"If you wanted to know, you might have sent a letter."

Mary Ellen picked up a cigarette.

Elisabeth's eyes scanned the room, taking in the fine artwork she and Jim had so carefully selected over the years.

She was relieved Mary Ellen cared little for her surroundings and had left the paintings, porcelains, and sculptures in place.

Avoiding looking at her daughter, she said, "Could you put some clothes on? Ledger is here and will be coming to clean up in a few minutes."

"I'm sure Ledger has seen me naked before, Mother. Everyone else has." She laughed, a deep throaty laugh. Elisabeth wasn't sure she wanted to see what color her hair was now. At one time it had been a lovely auburn, but last time, five years ago, it glowed a horrendous shade of yellow.

"Nevertheless," Elisabeth continued as she stood and crossed to the sofa to pick up a brocade coverlet. "Cover up, then get yourself dressed so we can go have some dinner."

"I was planning to go out with friends later." Mary Ellen stretched and yawned. "What brought you here anyway?"

"We have unfinished business. I'm here to bring you home." She dropped the coverlet over Mary Ellen.

Mary Ellen's heavy-lidded eyes shot open. "Home? This is home. This has always been my home. It was yours, mine, and Daddy's."

"Now it isn't. Get dressed. And try to look respectable."

Ledger entered the room burdened with cleaning utensils. "Ma'am, this is surely going to take a while. How much time do I have?"

"Hello, Ledger." Mary Ellen stretched out her long, naked arm to the man. "I've missed you."

He bowed. "Mary Ellen. Have you been keeping well?"

With a quick, fierce glare at her mother, she said, "I never lack for anything. You ought to know that. If you'll excuse me, I must dress for dinner."

Ledger stood close to Elisabeth and watched Mary Ellen saunter down the hallway, the coverlet dragging along exposing her thin shanks. "I shan't be long," she called over her shoulder.

Elisabeth sank down onto the sofa. "Oh, Ledger. What did I do to that poor child?"

"She is not a child, ma'am. If you'll forgive me, you gave too much to her. That's all that's wrong. Now all she can be is a taker."

"But the drinking, the smoking. Other things, too, I suppose."

"No use blaming yourself. You had help when Mr. Riis was alive. Now, come along. If she's dressing for dinner, I have about half an hour to do some cleaning then we'll have a drink ourselves before dinner."

"I don't suppose there's any hope she's retained a cook or there's even any food in the kitchen." Elisabeth looked up, pleading.

"You suppose correctly. My old room is exactly as I left it, Mrs. Riis. I wouldn't mind coming back to live here now. Long time since the war was over and educated Negros are being treated with more respect these days."

"I don't think so, Ledger. We've had enough troubles with you being a free man all these years. Don't you ever want to go back to Europe?"

He paused in his emptying of dishes and ashtrays. "I sometimes think about it, but it's been too many years. Now I have my own family with you and the girls. I have my books, my friends in Albany. Still some I communicate with here, too. No, when I chose to come work for you and Mr. Riis, I knew I'd be leaving Europe. Happy to do so."

"Delmonico's for dinner?" she asked.

He grinned. "I have my good hat with me."

"Mr. Ambassador." The two of them laughed, sharing their private joke.

"I might as well help you while we're waiting though I must confess a bath and a nap would be preferable. When we return, you can change the linens in my old room. We'll go back by the earliest train tomorrow."

"If you say so." He picked up a newspaper and after quickly scanning it, he shoved it into the wastebasket.

"What was that?" she said.

"Nothing, ma'am. An old newspaper."

"Something you don't want me to see. You don't fool me."

"About putting electricity in the houses in New York City."

"I've thought about having it done here but can't really see the value." As she spoke, she crossed the room and retrieved the paper from the basket. At first nothing of significance met her eyes, but then, on the inside was a photograph of Senator Justin Chauncey Pembroke of Albany. Beneath was the story.

Will the Senator Throw His Hat into the Ring? Time is running out for the Senior Senator from New York. Senator Justin Chauncey Pembroke, a Democrat, has not yet announced his decision but voices from Albany are talking and they are saying he is contemplating a run against our Veto President, Grover Cleveland. "I will make my announcement when I have my affairs in order so that I may take time from my otherwise busy life in order to take on this most important position in the world."

Elisabeth almost laughed aloud at the last comment. The Justin she knew wouldn't recognize an important issue if it slithered up his leg. She looked accusingly at Ledger. "You didn't have to hide this from me, Ledger. This is the very reason we're here. I'm going to see he never has the opportunity to run for president."

Ledger's eyes grew large. "How do you plan to do that, ma'am? And perhaps more importantly, why would you want to?"

"Maybe we can discuss it at dinner. I will go and wash up before we leave. In fact, now I've made up my mind what needs to be done, I feel like changing my dress, too. I'll see you shortly."

~*~

Two hours later, the evening being balmy, the three of them sat at an outdoor table at the Delmonico's on East 14th Street and 5th Avenue. Elisabeth had been surprisingly pleased to see Mary Ellen appear in a fashionable gown of green silk moiré with her hair, a dark brown, pulled back, topped by a small, feathered hat. Although she still looked far too thin for her own good, her natural beauty glowed through the powder and rouge.

When they first arrived, the maitre d' barred their way at the fence separating the tables from the sidewalk. "Excuse me, madam, but servants are welcome to eat in a separate area." He spoke softly so as not to embarrass her.

"My good man," Elisabeth began, puffing out her chest and pulling back her chin. She wished she had a lorgnette to peer through at him. "Do you not recognize the Ambassador of the African country of Madagascar? How dare you suggest he sit with servants? We will take our seats over there." She pointed to an empty table where a potted palm swayed in the evening breeze, an indication of a comfortable table. "You may send the waiter over immediately. We've had a long and tiring journey today." She leaned closer to the maitre d'. "I hope he didn't catch your English clearly, sir. We mustn't have an international incident. You understand."

While the man stood flustered, she turned to Ledger and spoke to him in French, explaining it would take a moment for them to set the table.

With a twinkle in his eye, Ledger suggested she ought to have introduced him as her husband. That would have stopped them.

She smiled and led the way behind the maitre d' to the table. Mary Ellen glared at the two of them, apparently not comprehending their game.

Once seated, Ledger took control, ordering sherry for three in halting English to be followed by the first course of cream of artichoke soup Morlais. They would give the waiter the rest of their order shortly, but meanwhile he hoped they still had a decent wine list.

The maitre d' left quickly.

Elisabeth leaned back in her chair and smiled widely. "You see, Mary Ellen, there is nothing you can't overcome if you put your brains to work. Ledger and I have been doing this for years. Even when Mr. Riis was alive, we took Ledger with us every place. Isn't that so, Ledger?"

"We have had much fun and I have had a good life, that's true. Though, my good lady, I confess to certain sentiments which are better left unspoken," Ledger said, his dark eyes focused on hers.

Elisabeth raised a hand as if to stop him from coming closer. "And will remain so."

"Excuse me," Mary Ellen said. "Can we get to the reason why you've suddenly appeared in my life after five years? You took my children away from me. You can't pretend to care what happens here." She fiddled with the utensils at her place. "Do you even know where I went or what I did once they were gone?"

"That's not why we're here, dear. Though I heard from friends you spent some time in the South of England."

"Brighton. The air was pure; the people didn't care where I came from or who I was."

"Most people don't care much about others. Has it taken you this long to figure that out?"

"Then, if that's the case, I ask you once again, why are you here?"

"Something has come up which makes it essential to bring you back into the fold. I haven't discussed it with the girls, yet, but I do hope they'll be pleased. They've turned into wonderful independent young women with extraordinary minds of their own. You ought to be proud."

"I had nothing to do with it, and you know that as well as anyone. What did you tell them about me, about why you took them away?" Mary Ellen's eyes never focused on her mother, instead she scanned the area, probably for acquaintances.

"I didn't have to explain much. You'd been gone from the apartment for quite a while. When I told them you had died, they were temporarily grief stricken, but quickly recovered."

Mary Ellen gasped. "You told them what? How could you be so cruel?"

"Don't sulk. We're here for a good reason and you should be happy."

"I should be whoever I am, not who you want me to be. You suppose I could have a cigarette?" She reached into her small, beaded bag. Moisture appeared on her brow. Patting it with her handkerchief she said, "What will they think when they learn I'm alive? They'll hate me altogether."

Ledger spoke up. "Ladies do not smoke in public. Do not embarrass your mother now."

Mary Ellen tugged at the strings and shut the bag. "Embarrass my mother?" She glared at Elisabeth with tears filling her eyes. Opening her mouth to protest, she instead slumped, looking down at her lap. "I wish they'd hurry with our drinks. Has to be sherry, huh? Ladies' drink?"

"A proper drink before dinner, dear," Elisabeth assured her. "You may have wine with dinner and, provided all goes well, perhaps we'll have a celebratory champagne after. Now, Ledger, Mr. Ambassador, what shall we eat?"

"The steaks are the best here. Shall I order for the three of us?"

"Steak is good for men. You have the steak. We'll have the lamb cutlets. Whatever they prepare here is excellent. No question."

A waiter appeared and silently set out three glasses of sherry. "Would you like your soup now?"

"Give us five minutes, young man," Ledger told him.

The waiter bowed and left, but not before raising his eyebrows at the colored man speaking to him.

"Ledger, you were born in the wrong time and the wrong place, but I'm so glad I met you."

"And I you." They raised their glasses to one another, gazing into each other's eyes almost like lovers.

Mary Ellen raised hers before swigging down the sherry. "That's better. Another, please?"

Elisabeth exchanged glances with Ledger. She knew he disapproved of her treatment of Mary Ellen, yet she often deferred to his judgment on matters concerning her. His eyes flickered; he gave a quick nod.

"Of course, my dear," Elisabeth said. "As soon as the waiter comes back with our soup, unless you'd rather have a nice white wine with it."

Mary Ellen drew a deep breath. "An opium den is more fun."

Elisabeth leaned across the table, her hands rigid on her handbag lest she reach out to slap her daughter. "You will behave yourself tonight. It's not often that we meet. We have important things to discuss."

Ledger then did something he had only done a few times in their thirty years together. He took her arm and pulled her back and then patted her hand gently. "Be calm, little mother. She is still your child and the product of her life. You have just informed her she's been dead to her children for the past five years. We must be patient."

Elisabeth scowled at him, but her fierce expression dissolved instantly when the waiter appeared with a tray laden with a soup tureen and three soup bowls.

When the waiter left, Ledger laughed at her. "Do you know how lovely you look when you are trying to be angry?"

"Don't be impertinent! I know very well my jowls sag and my skin is sallow. I've seen the creases and wrinkles around my mouth and eyes."

"A French roll?" He held out a napkin lined basket of hot dinner rolls, his eyes twinkling.

"I could stand up and call for help and have you arrested. You do understand, don't you?" She glowered at him as she took a roll and placed it on her bread-plate.

Ledger chuckled. "You know you'll never do that. Whatever you say or do, won't change the way I felt about you the first time I saw you struggling with that heavy invalid chair at Biarritz. You looked so helpless and fragile yourself. And the little girl hanging on to your skirts, making your chore ever more difficult." He smiled at Mary Ellen.

Elisabeth tested her soup and found it the right temperature. They ate in silence for a few minutes while she recalled their first meeting. Mary Ellen had been six years old. She and Jim dragged her around the world visiting specialists and spas, spending whatever was asked in an effort to find a cure for his spinal injuries.

When her bowl was nearly drained, Ledger added another half to it.

"You were a life-saver, Ledger. I don't know how I would have survived without you. Whatever or whoever placed you in my path that day, had my best interests at heart. I don't know what was in it for you."

"A man without a country needs a home. You've given that to me and I am always grateful. Though of late you've become a might snippety. I am not your Negro slave now any more than I was back then. I have always been a free man, able to make my own choices."

"I know, Ledger, as long as you were in a country where race and color didn't matter. But now we have to think of dinner. I've changed my mind and shall choose a boneless ribeye steak along with new potatoes and French peas." She turned to Mary Ellen whose eyes appeared glazed over. "And what will you have, darling?"

Mary Ellen shuddered as if someone had walked over her grave. Her eyes refocused. "Whatever you're having, Mother. Did you know father's distant cousin, Jacob Riis, is here tonight?"

"And so?" Elisabeth questioned.

"Don't you want to speak with him? He's famous, you know."

"We don't need famous relatives in our lives, dear. Here comes the waiter. Let's have a lovely dinner and some wonderful French wine with our steak. Ledger, would you select the wines, please?"

"Delighted."

They continued their dinners in relative silence with only an occasional aside from Ledger or Elisabeth. Mary Ellen glanced at them suspiciously from time to time but poked her way through her meal without comment.

"Did we ever tell you how Ledger got his name?" Elisabeth said after finishing her wine. The waiter swooped over and cleared her place.

"Probably a million times I don't particularly remember. He kept Daddy's books?" Mary Ellen seemed even less interested in Ledger's name than she did in her dinner which grew cold and congealed on her plate, only a small bit of meat missing.

"No. Because he kept my accounts in his head when we traveled so your father would never see how much we really spent on our junkets. Your father, wealthy as he was, could be the most frugal of men. I had him convinced I was thrifty as well, always claiming to have found items on special offer or received them as gifts from my lady friends."

"Who were you kidding? You never had a lady friend in your life."

That stung. Elisabeth's eyes snapped to Mary Ellen's to see if the jibe had been deliberate. But there was no guile in Mary Ellen; she was tipsy, tired and unconcerned with anything other than her next drink, drug or cigarette. She studied her daughter's dark green eyes briefly. Thick black lashes surrounded them. Full brows framed them. The eyes were the most beautiful part of her daughter. At one time, Elisabeth thought it would be her mind. She had been such a bright child. Something happened in her formative years to change her. Something that drove her into a shell from which she had never returned. Elisabeth had decided to give her more of an advantage than she herself had had by sending her away to a Swiss boarding school where she would receive the finest of educations as opposed to the simple finishing school where Elisabeth had learned to darn, embroider, play the piano, and speak French. One semester and Mary Ellen never went back.

"Are you ever going to get to the point of why you are here?"

"Dessert?" Ledger asked as a trolley rolled by laden with cakes, creams, and other confections piled high with whipped cream. His body nearly followed his eyes as the cart continued past to another table.

"Perhaps dessert and a little cognac," Elisabeth said. "Yes. You're coming home with me, as I said earlier. We have a mission to accomplish, you and I."

"You and I? As in mother and daughter doing something together?" Mary Ellen tilted her head in disbelief. "This sounds like a scheme to force me into a hospital. That's what it is, isn't it?"

Without warning, Mary Ellen shoved her chair back and ran from the table out onto the sidewalk. She dashed across the avenue in a panic, looking neither right nor left.

Four

Elisabeth and Ledger remained at the table another half an hour sipping cognac. She hoped Mary Ellen would return but didn't believe she would. The girl said she had plans of her own this evening.

"Would you like me to send someone in search of her?" Ledger asked.

Startled from her thoughts, it took a moment for her to recall that her plans for Justin included her daughter. "We can wait for her to return. We have a couple of weeks before I must make my move." She finished her cognac and set her glass on the table, her mind now clear on what she would do to stop him.

There was no question in her mind Justin Pembroke was an evil man and needed to be stopped. That it would be her own drug-addicted alcoholic daughter who would be the instrument of his destruction didn't bother her so much – the girl was lost anyway – but that her granddaughters would know, created pain in her heart. The girls had nearly forgotten their lives before Albany. Living in the splendid apartment yet in squalor; traveling on board ships First Class but neglected and cared for by the crews of those grand voyagers.

"Ledger, why did you really stop to help me that day in Biarritz?"

"I've told you so many times over, Miss Elisabeth, I couldn't bear to see you struggle to the beach with such a heavy burden every day. I knew there would be no cure for him in the sea."

"He'd become horrible by then." She twirled her glass on the table, studying the reflection of the electric light bulbs strung along the perimeter, helping to separate the dining area from the pedestrians on the sidewalk.

"He was a man in pain."

"You were always too generous. My daughter adored him. She wanted nothing more than to sit in his lap and have him tell stories."

"You don't have to go through all that again. How many times can you relive those days? He's gone. You have a good life with Barbara and Lillian. They are lively crackers, those two. Why don't we take them to the south of France again this fall? They love Nice and Cannes. They'll brush up on their French and play in the sunshine. Picture the bougainvillea, the azure sea."

"Picture nothing to do all day but watch the azure sea."

"Stop feeling sorry for yourself. It doesn't become you. You can take up painting again. You showed promise."

She took a sip of her drink. "I used to be very young and desirable. Now people see a dumpy old woman. Do you know what it's like ..." She stopped herself before speaking of unspeakable things with her friend and manservant. They had crossed the lines so many years ago, often she forgot his position in her life.

He pulled his pocket watch out, flipped it open and then said, "I think they might want to close the place.

She sighed. "She'll come home when she's good and ready. Shall we make plans for tomorrow?"

"I'd like to visit the Statue of Liberty. It's been there over a decade already and we still haven't taken the ferry out to see it. We can have lunch out and then I'll do some shopping and bring in something for dinner."

"Why don't you speak with the doorman and arrange for a cook, a cleaning girl and a housemaid for at least a week?"

"Are you sure? You want to leave the girls alone at home for an entire week?"

"Mrs. Burch and Annie are there. They may not like me much, but they do care for the girls. They'll be relieved not to have me around for a while. Let's take some time for ourselves to get Mary Ellen straightened out enough to see her daughters again."

"You always did like beating your head against stone walls."

"Perhaps, Ledger, but I did knock some of them down, didn't I?"

He laughed. "Like taking me on and traveling with me. I thought I'd be lynched a few of those times. Yes indeed, you broke down some walls. Unconventionally."

"Just like I'm going to defeat Justin Pembroke. Unconventionally."

"What is it that makes you hate him so much, Elisabeth? In all these years, never a word from you, except your mean, slit-eyed glare when his name comes up."

"I'll tell you this, if women were allowed to vote, he'd never get near a government office again."

"That explains a great deal." He cleared his throat. "I'll have a waiter hail a cab for us. It's too late to be wandering around city streets."

"Which reminds me. Have the doorman hire two hardy looking souls to escort us on our adventure tomorrow. I think you'll continue to be the ambassador while we're here."

His face lit up with a grin. "I do like your sense of humor. My pleasure. And you will think about France in the fall?"

"Only after my mission is accomplished and Senator Justin Pembroke is lying with his face in the mud."

Ledger took her arm as they exited the restaurant. The waiters bowed them out, wishing them a good evening, before scrambling to clear the table and close up for the night. Although there was a chill in the air, Elisabeth asked if they could walk for a few blocks before getting into the taxi.

"It might be time for you to know the complete story, Ledger. You may want to remove yourself from my presence, from my life, once you understand what I have in mind."

"That will never happen, Elisabeth. We've been together too many years to separate because of a personal disagreement. If you are about to do something of which I disapprove, you know I shall try to discourage you, to convince you otherwise. Failing to change your mind, I shall carry on with my work at the office and then withdraw to my rooms until you return to your senses."

"Meaning until I see things your way," she said.

"Indeed. You will have to come to me to apologize." They walked on in silence for a few minutes. "For all we've meant to one another over the years, you've never once come up to my lodgings."

"I've heard how wonderfully European you've made your library and parlor. The girls have told me; they love going to visit you in the evenings. I believe they find you far more entertaining than I." She paused to look at him. "Where did you ever find a mahogany desk?"

He chuckled. "In one of your attics." He helped her down a high curb and across the street as they headed north, the hum of the electric taxi following nearby.

Without preface or warning she said, "You know, of course, Mary Ellen could not possibly be Jim's daughter." She kept her face averted from his now, eyes straight ahead as her heart thumped irregularly from the unexpected exercise and the tension of finally, after so many years, exposing her secret shame.

"I rather understood that from the beginning. These are not things to be spoken of lightly, you understand." He cleared his throat as he hurried her past a group of children sleeping in a doorway.

She saw them and her hand automatically reached out before she even realized she had done it. The children were asleep and didn't notice her almost comforting effort. "Jim knew. He wanted to be able to name a son after himself. Sadly, he only had one opportunity for a child and that is Mary Ellen. He named her. Although she was mine, I never liked the child; I never wanted her."

"That, too, was clear from the beginning. I'm not judging, so don't look at me with such disdain," he said when she turned to him. "The child adored her father and I took right to her. She wasn't totally deprived of a caring family."

Elisabeth sighed. Her heart ached. "Let's get in the cab. I don't think I can make it all the way home. These shoes hurt my feet," she said, changing the subject.

Ledger stopped the cab and helped her into it, this time he took the seat next to her.

~*~

Sixteen and alone. Frightened and pregnant. 'With child,' they called it. She wanted to be *without* child. The day she had to confront her father was the most horrific day of her life. Shamed, humiliated, unable to face him, she wrote a note asking to meet with him in his study after dinner. Amber brought a return note to her room, "You are always welcome, my sweet darling. See you at eight."

The note shattered her. Flinging herself onto her bed, she cried herself to sleep, only to be woken by Amber a few minutes after eight. She missed dinner that night.

"Your father is waiting for you, Miss Elisabeth."

"I have to do this," Elisabeth moaned.

"What, Miss?" Amber approached her but Elisabeth held up a hand to stop her from coming closer.

"I'm going downstairs now, Amber. Will you please pull out my travel trunks and be prepared to help me pack?"

Amber's face lit up. "Well, Miss Elisabeth. I didn't know you were planning a trip. No one ever said a word! Of course. Shall it be for a sea voyage? Where are you going?"

"I haven't figured everything out as yet. Thank you."

Elisabeth brushed her hair from her face and then headed down the stairs to confront her father with the awful truth about his daughter. Would he fly into a rage? The thoughts raced through her mind as she approached the closed doors to his study. Back straightened, shoulders squared, she tapped on the door and then slid them open when she heard her father's muted, "Come in."

He'd had a tea tray with small sandwiches brought in. The tray sat on a table between two comfortable burgundy leather chairs. He stood from behind his desk and waved her to a chair. "I thought you might be hungry. You know you've been looking a bit peaked lately. Amber says you're not eating much at all. Missing school, are you?"

His voice grated in her head. He should be quiet and wait to hear her out instead of covering silences with stupid comments. "No, Daddy, I'm not missing school."

Five

The taxi stopped in front of her building and Elisabeth wearily climbed down with Ledger's assistance.

"I think a hot tub followed by peppermint schnapps. What do you think, Ledger?"

The night doorman saluted them and opened the door.

Her legs felt leaden as they climbed to the third floor. Again she thought about the possibilities of adding electricity to the building.

Inside the apartment, Ledger hurried to draw her bath and lay out her night clothes before he prepared tea and schnapps.

No evidence indicated Mary Ellen had been home.

Elisabeth disrobed and climbed into the bathtub, the steaming water soothing her aching bones. Within half an hour she was wrapped in her long cotton nightgown, resting on raised pillows in her bed. Ledger arrived with her nightcap.

"Sit with me a few minutes, will you?" She pointed to the rocking chair next to the bed.

"Pour yourself a nightcap as well."

He pulled up the chair, prepared to join her and filled a small liqueur glass with the clear mint liquid. "Here's to privacy," he said, raising his glass to her.

She glanced around the room. "Yes. Well, almost."

"I can read to you, if you like." He set his glass down, prepared to go in search of a book.

"No. I want to know you, how it is you came to be who you are. Tell me again, Ledger. I'm sure you leave out the most exciting parts of your story."

"Just an aging Blackamoor working to keep my mistress happy." He relaxed back into the chair and rocked slowly back and forth.

"You were such a baby when they took you from your family. Can you remember your mother or your father at all? Do they come to you in dreams? Sometimes I see my mother but she disapproves of me. She's disappointed in the way my life turned out."

"I don't think I could talk with my parents, even if I could see them. Besides, they're surely long dead. I figure I'm sixty years old now. That would make them in their late seventies or maybe even eighties. I had two older brothers and a sister. I was just old enough to start working in the fields with them, but the day I was meant to begin the overseer woke my family before dawn and said we had to go with him into the town. We were crowded onto a cart with two other families. I remember the crowds and noises and dust from the wheels on the road. The older people said our owners lost a lot of money so we had to be sold. My mother cried. I didn't understand. We lived together on one tobacco farm, we'd most likely live together on another.

"It didn't work out that way."

Elisabeth held out her glass for a refill.

"Mr. Weston Darling bought me, separating from my siblings and parents. He introduced me to his brother, Angus. I remember his exact words to this day. 'Come along, my little experiment.' I didn't know what the word meant, but he and his brother shook hands as if they'd just made a deal."

"Weston Darling," Elisabeth repeated the Englishman's name and wished him well. He, too, would be at least in his seventies if he still lived. "Imagine if you had been sold with your family, we never would have met. You might be working as a sharecropper with lots of children and grandchildren in Alabama or Georgia. Did you ever think of that?"

"Miss Elisabeth, at the time, I was terrified."

"I've seen the pictures of the little colored boys in the English parlors. I can't imagine dressing you up in such a ridiculous little suit and making you play page boy to those women."

"Some might call it humiliating; I called it an education. Angus was a businessman and Weston, a student of anthropology. Weston wanted to prove to his brother a Negro had as much intellectual capability as any white man. His brother believed otherwise, but never interfered with my learning."

"You were probably an adorable child."

"I was a scared one for a long time until I realized no one would come to take me away again. Mrs. Darling, their mother, made sure I had plenty of warm clothes for the winter. She was kind. Very kind. Even the other servants in the household remained nice to me while I sat in the kitchen and learned to read and write. They considered it nothing but a waste of time."

"So you became a scholar." Her heart had finally settled into a comfortable steady rhythm and she felt like now she could sleep.

"A scholar, and when they figured I was twenty-one gave me a small but adequate annuity and sent me on my way. That was shortly before your war, so I headed to Spain, France, Germany, and Russia. And now, Miss Elisabeth, you've heard my story for the hundredth time at least. Sleep well. We'll have a busy day tomorrow. Remember, we have new servants, and we're going on an outing while we wait for Miss Mary Ellen to come home."

"I remember seeing you coming up the walkway in Biarritz. Mary Ellen had refused to go play with the other children. She wanted to be with her father in the water. How tiresome she was. He was worse, complaining about every bump and shift of the chair. I wanted to hire an attendant, but he insisted I was strong enough and we didn't need to waste our money on unnecessary expenditures. Now, between his fortune and Daddy's, my girls will always be comfortable."

"That's right, Elisabeth. You have much to be grateful for."

"I am." She lay her hand on the top of the blanket and he covered it with his. She sighed.

"Different times, Ledger."

"Different times."

"He was suspicious of you, did you know? He asked me every night what you did during the day when he wasn't present. He kept fishing for any indiscretion. Even the day you and I went into the village and bought fresh fish at the market for the chef to prepare for him, he disapproved. No matter that Mary Ellen was with us; no matter that we only had his best interest at heart. No matter."

"You are becoming maudlin, Elisabeth. Go to sleep and plot your schemes. I confess to a strong curiosity about your plans for Senator Pembroke. The man is a vulgar fraud and I would not like to see him rise to any more importance than he already has."

Elisabeth felt a smile of relief. So, Ledger at least would not condemn her. "We may not be able to vote, you and I, Ledger, but there are many ways to affect an election."

Six

Mary Ellen Riis Von Bek rested on her left side, her hip pressed into the soiled silk chaise as she lazily watched a stream of smoke float away from her face, from her mouth, from her nose, resisting the urge to giggle as the smoke tickled her nose.

Her partner snored behind her. Mary Ellen had to twist her neck to remind herself whether the partner was a man or a woman. Sometimes she forgot, like tonight. On her first visit to this opium den she had been assigned a bunk in a dimly lit room where other women smoked, crooned and drifted in their own fantastical worlds. The bunk felt claustrophobic but once the manageress understood Mary Ellen's wealth, she was given a small room with the chaise to herself, and anyone else she chose. The ancient Oriental woman in charge of the female room sat in the doorway, hands folded, inscrutable.

Whenever Mary Ellen entered the den, the stench made her nauseous, but she knew if she forced her way to her personal spot, she would soon take delight in the magical visions, the soaring crescendos of glorious music and the touch and feel of hands on her body. If she missed anything in life, she decided, as her mind drifted, she missed someone holding and loving her. So many people here became eager and willing replacements.

Jacob von Bek had been a pig, his lovemaking close to rape. As soon as she could, Mary Ellen dropped him, yet out of the union had come the surprisingly beautiful and intelligent Barbara. She saw von Bek now in her mind's eye, or was his face really floating before her? She reached toward his face, to scratch out his eyes. She should have done that before she left with the baby.

She and Barbara traveled throughout Europe, the dear little thing learning languages as quickly as a brilliant parrot. There was nothing Barbara couldn't do. Except love her. Barbara remained an aloof, wide-eyed waif.

Mary Ellen giggled out loud, disturbing her partner. Ah. It was a man. Expensive clothes. Good. At least he might not be diseased. How she survived all those years...she sighed. *Tonight is to forget, not play memory games.* The man's hand reached out and pawed her naked breast. When did part of her clothing disappear? She half-heartedly pulled her blouse over herself only to be stopped by the beefy hand. What did it matter? She rolled her body over and pressed into the man. Something smelled bad. Did he stink? Or was that her?

She reached down to see if he was up for some fun, but his member remained curled in a small corner of his drawers. Too bad for her. The pipe ceased to smoke. She sucked on it, hoping for more, but didn't have to worry. A small Chinaman crawled up from behind and refreshed it.

Unlike many guests in this parlor, the operators knew they didn't have to worry about Mary Ellen's funds. She always paid, paid generously.

She threw her head back and laughed loudly as the fresh narcotic filled her brain. "I pay for what I want! Do you hear me?"

"Shut up, woman," her partner grumbled. "Can't a man get no rest around here?"

"That's *any* rest, sir. *Any* rest." She shifted so she could shove him off the chaise. He tumbled onto the floor and promptly went back to sleep.

She considered searching through the room to find someone else with whom to share her unlimited love, but then the memory she wanted to forget came back, striking her. My little girls think I'm dead. Am I dead? I could be dead.

"Will somebody please pinch me? I don't want to be dead!" she cried out. "Here. Here's my arm. Pinch my breast. Here, bite my nipples. Make me know I'm alive."

Her hair had fallen and hung in strands across her face and shoulders. It reached to her waist. "I was beautiful once," she told a passing girl.

"Yeah. Me too," the girl answered with a sniffle.

"You crying?" Mary Ellen asked.

"Why not? Nothing else to do. None of these stiffs has any money left. No more for me, lousy hipsters. Might as well get back on the street." She whirled around at Mary Ellen's touch on her thigh.

"Join me. I just got rid of my escort." She tugged at the girl's hand and pulled her onto the chaise. "You smell sweet."

"It's the opium. So do you."

Mary Ellen tried to focus on the eyes only inches from her face but the dimness of the room prevented her from seeing the color. "I think your eyes are blue. What do you think?"

"I like blue eyes. What color are yours?"

"Green. Green like the moss on trees."

"Green, like the mold in a grave," the girl responded with a cackle. "I don't like green eyes. Let's pretend yours are blue like mine and we can make little babies with blue eyes."

At a nod from Mary Ellen the China man appeared like an apparition and filled the girl's pipe.

"We'll have a lovely time. My name is Surreal," Mary Ellen offered. "What's yours?"

"Nothing weird like yours. Rita. Rita all right with you?"

The two women finished their pipes and then wrapped their arms around one another.

At around four in the morning the little China man covered them and then chased out the rest of the night's clientele. Mary Ellen Riis was always good for a generous tip.

Seven

Barbara reclined in the rocker on the front porch reading the newspapers, not something she did often, but she hoped to find a clue to why her grandmother and Ledger had traveled by train to New York City. Yesterday a stranger had returned the carriage, placed it in the barn, cooled the horse and mucked out his stall before coming to the house to bring her a message from Ledger – not Grandmother.

"I am escorting your grandmother to the city. We shall stay at the apartment and notify you of our return henceforth. Please be obedient to Mrs. Burch and kind to Annie. The messenger has been duly compensated for his labor. Ledger."

"Obedient to Mrs. Burch," she had shouted at the poor man, who cringed, hat in hand. "Never mind. You can go." She turned to Mrs. Burch. "Why would she go to New York City? That doesn't make any sense."

Mrs. Burch had no response other than to ask what she wanted for lunch.

Barbara rocked in the chair as she studied the newspaper while her mind still focused on her missing grandmother.

The news talked about politics, what else? They lived in the capital of New York State. Justin Pembroke hinted he might run for president. She didn't care; she couldn't vote anyway, but her heart lurched when she thought about the men's conversations the other night in the club. What had started out as a lark, had ended up with a great deal of mystery for her and Lily. Justin Pembroke, nasty old man, had a secret love child and the other men were determined to find her and get rid of her so she couldn't cause any trouble for him in an election. The fathers of "love" children were tolerated, even praised; the young mothers were blamed for being bad girls and shunned by their families for "getting in the family way." Mrs. Burch was right about one thing, it was a man's world and unless a woman took a stand, it would always be that way.

The cool morning breeze stirred her hair and cooled her face while Lily remained upstairs in bed, unconcerned about Grandmother's disappearance.

She studied the small news items – a boy was struck by a passing motor vehicle and taken to hospital with a broken leg, a man attacked his wife with a butcher knife but her life was spared by a passing stranger, *praise God for passing strangers,* and the ladies of the Flower Society would be holding a tea at the Governor's new mansion in the fall. The graduating class of the Albany Academy for Girls were to be presented this Friday. She sighed. Same news every day. An advertisement caught her eye. *Tired? Syrup of Pepsin might be all you need to perk up and stay bright. For members of the family who might suffer from irregularity of the digestive system, Syrup of Pepsin is available at your local pharmaceutical establishment.* Grandmother had appeared peaked lately.

Barbara folded the paper and left it on the rocker then headed upstairs to her grandmother's rooms. She first went into the washroom where a cabinet on the wall held Grandmother's personal washing items and her medications. Sure enough, there was a bottle of Syrup of Pepsin next to mustard for plasters, ipecac, bicarbonate of soda, chlorodyne, *whatever that is,* tincture of digitalis, citrate of caffeine, compound tincture of cardamom, tincture of cereus grandifloris. *My Lord! Grandmother is dying and doesn't want us to know.*

She slammed shut the cabinet and ran for a note pad from her room to write down the odd names of medicines. It occurred to her Grandmother hadn't taken any of these medications with her to New York. Why not? Maybe she had more, had duplicates. Barbara knew digitalis had something to do with heart disease. She wished Ledger could be here to answer her questions.

She sat on the floor and, as she copied the names, a plan formed in her mind. She finished with Calomel and shut her notebook. If only the Girls Academy had been more scholarly like the Boys Academy, she might understand this more.

"What are you doing?" Lily's sleepy voice asked from behind.

"Checking up on Grandmother. She's been gone two days already."

"Only one night." Lily yawned and flopped back onto Grandmother's bed. "What are you so worried about?"

"She's never done this before. I think she's sick and doesn't want us to know."

Lily rolled over, chin in hand. "Then we shouldn't snoop."

Barbara glared up at her. Her little sister often took her by surprise. The girl seemed so unlike the rest of the family, with those Irish looks Grandmother often mentioned even though the last full blooded Irish person in the family was Grandmother. But it was more than that. Lily lacked the intuitiveness, the insights, the quickness of Grandmother and of herself, if she admitted it. She was a sweet, simple young girl eager to participate in any of Barbara's adventures. With both a Dutch father and grandfather, one might have thought they'd both have plump, rosy cheeks and thick blonde hair.

"Come on," Barbara said as she pushed herself up from the floor. "Let's go have breakfast and talk to Mrs. Burch. She might have some ideas."

"I don't like Mrs. Burch."

"You don't have to like her, you have to obey her. At least while Grandmother's away."

"Think we can have some ham with our breakfast today?" Lily asked as they headed down the stairs.

"Delicious. Ham and porridge. Could be." Before they entered the kitchen, Barbara pulled Lily aside. "Pretend you know what I'm talking about when we get in there, all right?"

Lily looked up with innocent eyes. "Of course. I always follow your lead." And then she burst into giggles.

"We might have another adventure on our hands or it might be something serious."

"Good morning, young ladies. How are we today?" Mrs. Burch greeted them.

Barbara spotted Annie heading out to the breakfast room with their tray. "We're both fine, Mrs. Burch. How is it you can get up so early, prepare for the day and then slip down the stairs without ever waking either one of us?"

Lily slid onto a chair and folded her hands on the table.

"Your breakfast is in the other room." Mrs. Burch pointed. "I won't be hearing any of your flattery today. Not with our Mrs. gone and you being my responsibility."

"But I'm impressed, Mrs. Burch. Do you have any children of your own?"

"'Course I do. My girl married six years ago and she and her husband decided to go west. They wanted to farm. My boy and his wife are living in Chicago. Any other personal questions you want to ask before your coffee and eggs get cold?"

"We have eggs this morning?" Lily piped up. "What's the occasion?"

Mrs. Burch snapped a towel at her. "Don't be fresh. I know you become bored with your grandmother's idea of a good breakfast. Porridge. Porridge. Porridge. I'd get sick of it, too. Let's call this a little vacation When she returns, it'll be the same routine again."

Barbara folded her arms across her chest. "My, oh, my, Mrs. Burch. There is a bit of the Irish devil in you after all. Kindness is one thing but mutiny is quite another." She dropped onto a chair. "Will you tell us one more thing?"

Mrs. Burch took a defensive step backward. "Depends on what it is."

"It's simple. Do you have any idea why Grandmother went to the city?"

"I do not."

"Is Grandmother ill?" Barbara studied the woman's face for a reaction.

"Not so far as I know. She eats well. Gets a little tired in the afternoons, but then don't we all? What makes you think she might be ill?"

"I'm worried about why she would go to the city apartment for no apparent reason and the only thing I can think of is that she is ill."

Annie stepped into the room and cleared her throat. "Excuse me, ma'am?"

"What is it, Annie?" Mrs. Burch snapped.

"Should I be bringing their food back in here?"

"Please!" Lily begged with hands clasped. "I'm starving and I love eggs."

When Annie left the room again, Barbara continued. "I went up to her rooms and checked in her bathroom cabinets. Do you know she has about every tincture of something and syrup of something else for who knows how many diseases? I plan to look them up later. I think she's hiding a serious illness from us."

"You don't say." Mrs. Burch joined them at the table, her face creased with concern. "Most I've ever seen her take is a bicarbonate of soda or a little mint for her indigestion. Do you really believe she might be seriously ill?"

"I'll let you know what I think after we eat and I've had time to look up those medications. I'm sure there are books in the library that will explain them. If not, I'll have to go to the public library."

"I wish she'd send us a note to let us know when she's coming back," Lily sighed as Annie set her plate of food before her.

"You can't be missing her already. It's only been one night."

"I'm thinking about Mrs. Burch doing more for breakfast, like maybe strawberries and cream or blueberries or—"

This time Barbara reached out to give her a thump on the back of her head. "Idiot. We're genuinely worried about her health and you're worried about your stomach."

"I'm sorry I can't be as genuine as you, Barbs." Lily grabbed a fork and knife to attack her plate of scrambled eggs with ham and toast with cheese and butter.

Later, in the library, Barbara looked up most of the items from her list until she convinced herself her grandmother suffered from a serious heart condition. She would have to go to New York City, to the apartment, to be with Grandmother in her time of need.

Eight

Elisabeth rose after a restless night, donned her dressing gown and headed to the sitting room where Ledger had already delivered the morning newspaper. She heard his voice in the kitchen as he directed someone on the use of the gas stove.

The fragrance of coffee perfumed the air and she was glad to be alone in the morning without the responsibility of the two teenage girls or her middle-aged daughter. Having had a day and night to consider her choices, she and Ledger could now relax for the rest of the week while she developed her plan for Senator Pembroke. Election news headlined the paper. McKinley and Theodore Roosevelt were running for the Republicans. William Jennings Bryan and Adlai Stevenson for the Democrats, though there were other contenders, it was generally accepted those would be the candidates following their convention. The people believed McKinley had helped the country out of a deep depression last time he served; they now hoped for continued prosperity with him in charge again.

Justin Pembroke belonged to the Democrats. There had to be something in their methods that attracted him. Something that could make him richer and more powerful than even the czars of Russia or Queen Victoria.

An article caught her eye on the bottom of the page – Mr. Winston Churchill, the war correspondent from England, had been captured in South Africa. His venue was the Boer War.

Elisabeth had seen enough of the results of wars during her years married to Jim Riis.

The item beside it caught her attention and made her sit up straight. "A set of stands under a circus tent collapsed in Chicago, injuring dozens." She hoped Mrs. Burch' grandchildren hadn't been present. More than that, she hoped Mrs. Burch wouldn't read a newspaper for a few days and then fret. Her cooking turned sour when she fretted.

Something scraped the outside door. She dropped the paper and waited to see who would enter. If Ledger was in the kitchen, then no one ought to be coming in.

"Ledger!" she called.

Before he appeared, the doors burst open. A burly man wearing a bowler and in need of a shave carried a key in one hand. A woman's body dangled over his right shoulder. Her clothes and the now familiar hair sent a sense of dread through Elisabeth.

The man, on seeing Elisabeth, dipped his head in a brief bow and reached up with the key still in his hand to tip his cap. "Morning," he mumbled as he turned right toward the hallway to the bedrooms. Obviously, he'd done this before.

Ledger arrived in time to see the retreating figure.

"You called?" he said, still staring down the hall.

"Mary Ellen is home." She pushed the newspaper aside and closed her eyes. "I half-hoped she'd stay away for a few days. This trip was beginning to feel like a holiday. I suppose we have to see to her now."

"I've made arrangements and we now have a cook and two housemaids." Ledger said. "As to Miss Mary Ellen, her behavior goes on whether we're here or not. I see no reason to interfere with her routine until we have to. I'm sorry, Elisabeth."

"It's one thing when I don't see it," she said more harshly than intended. "It's quite another to witness a stinking stranger invading our home carrying my daughter in a complete state of dishabille. He knows where her bedroom is!"

She pushed up from the chair, holding out a hand for Ledger's assistance. "I will go to her."

The stranger barreled from the bedroom in a rolling walk. "Sorry to intrude, missus. Leave her be and she'll be up and around by evening." He tipped his hat again and left – with the key.

Ledger and Elisabeth looked at one another. She moved first, heading toward the bedroom, while Ledger went the other way to inform the new staff of their extra duties.

The sight of her daughter, dumped unceremoniously on top of her bed covers, sent waves of sadness and pain through Elisabeth's already weary heart. For a brief moment she accepted the guilt, the responsibility of what had become of her only child; a wanton, drug-addicted lost woman.

Picking up a nearby quilt, she pulled it gently over Mary Ellen's inert body. The action caused Mary Ellen to stir. One hand wiped the hair from her face and then she snorted, sounding like a man rutting. Elisabeth turned cold eyes on her and left the room.

"The man said she'd wake up this evening. Let her be," she informed Ledger when she returned to the living room.

Two rosy cheeked young girls stood behind him fully outfitted in proper maid's outfits, crisp cotton pinafores covering black dresses. They even wore caps. She'd have to talk to Mrs. Burch about proper attire for the maids at home.

The girls appeared happy enough to retire to the kitchen.

Ledger's eyes drifted from the hallway back to Elisabeth.

"What is it, Ledger?"

"I thought..." He stopped.

"Don't think. We planned an outing for today. I shall dress. We'll have breakfast here. Did you manage to find groceries?"

"Things are under control in the kitchen," Ledger answered coolly.

"Good. Arrange a taxi. We'll lunch out. Ask the cook to make something healthful for this evening. I think roast chickens and the assorted things that go with them. A jolly dessert would be nice. Now, send a girl to help me dress."

"And Miss Mary Ellen?"

"As you have reminded me, she can awake in her own filth which she's been doing without our help. Perhaps she'll be up in time to join us for dinner. I do have to talk to her, and to you, of course, about my plans. Did you read this morning's paper? Life is certainly different here in the city. Faster. Rougher, but far more exciting than in Albany."

"Yes, Miss Elisabeth."

"Don't sulk, Ledger. You'll still be the ambassador when we go out."

"Yes, ma'am."

"I mean it. We will have a good time. Once my scheme is completed, Mary Ellen can resume her life here uninterrupted by loving family." Elisabeth glared at her daughter's closed bedroom door as she marched across to her own rooms.

Anger pushed her through her morning ablutions and by nine o'clock she was seated in the dining room being served sausages, eggs, tomatoes, and steaming coffee. Biscuits with butter and jam completed breakfast.

"Our security will be here at ten o'clock." Ledger wiped his mouth with his napkin. "I'll meet you in the living room."

"Of course you will." Elisabeth's eyes rested on the portrait of her father that dominated the wall opposite. She'd forgotten about the picture and didn't notice it last night when they arrived. "Oh, Daddy, Daddy, if only you could be here now."

She retired to her room to pin her hair up for the day and then selected a straw hat to protect her from the sun while they rode the ferry to the island where the Statue of Liberty had been planted, determined this would be an adventurous and lovely day.

~*~

"What is the difference in the Democrats and the Republicans?" she asked Ledger when he appeared dressed and ready for their outing at ten o'clock.

He raised his eyebrows. "What makes you interested in politics? You planning to be another Carrie Nation?"

"That battle axe? I hope that's a joke. No. I'm trying to figure why a man as wealthy as Justin Pembroke would want to be president. The Republicans are credited with the financial successes of the past four years, but he's a Democrat." She held out her arms for him to assist her with her light wrap.

"You look charming, Mrs. Elisabeth."

"Thank you, Mr. Ambassador, but you're not off the hook. I want to know. He's already wealthy."

"Firstly, I am not particularly pleased with the Democratic party leaders who are against all the positive changes the Republicans have made these past few years. I approve of the Republicans changing our currency to the gold system. Our country has the best credit rating in the world. The Republicans have increased trade to our benefit. Democrats think the Republicans are too imperialist. They don't like the government taking charge of the Philippines, Hawaii or Cuba. And they are against the Chinese."

"I didn't ask for *your* opinion. What would a man who owns much of the shipping industry in this country gain from becoming president? More than he could gain by remaining a senator."

Ledger shrugged before opening the main door. "Power."

Elisabeth pinched her lips. "He has plenty of that already. He's even willing to risk exposure of a past indiscretion to run for the presidency."

"What indiscretion would that be and how do you know about it?"

She hesitated before forming her answer. "Something I learned when I was about Barbara's age."

They headed down the stairs where two well-dressed, muscular men awaited their arrival. Both tipped their hats and then each one held a lobby door open for them. Two cabs stood at the curb.

She enjoyed the ride down Park Avenue as they headed toward Battery Park where they would catch the ferry to the statue.

"I've heard there are a few of these automobiles in Albany."

"There's a steam powered one. I haven't seen others as yet. It won't be long the country will be clogged with these things and the horses will be food and glue."

"Disgusting," she said. "Yet the automobiles don't smell as bad as horses." Elisabeth paused for a moment. "Ships," she said. "How would being president affect Justin Pembrokes' shipping lines?"

"If you'll give me a few days, perhaps I can come up with an answer. Right now our country depends on the rest of the world for our shipping, except for maybe ten percent. I believe your Senator Pembroke holds nearly fifty percent of that. That might be a motive, but I don't want to say until I know better."

"Those Pinkertons you hired. Are you comfortable with them?"

"Of course. Why shouldn't I be?"

"I'd like to hire them for a little longer. At least until the party conventions are over. I want them available. I may have some extra work for them."

They aren't henchmen, Elisabeth. They won't kill anyone for you."

"I was thinking more of protection."

"Who might want to kill you?"

She laughed. "Not me. But someone we know. You were right, it is a glorious day."

"I think you said that earlier."

Nine

"I'm going." Barbara stood to her full five-foot seven-inch height, arms folded, daring Mrs. Burch to stop her.

"You can't, Miss. Please don't do this. A young girl cannot travel alone," Mrs. Burch said.

"Lily will come with me."

Lily looked up from where she busied herself drawing a picture of Annie who sat on a stool across the room listening to the unbelievable conversation. "Not me. I'd be terrified. All those people."

"You liked it well enough when we lived there," Barbara said, disappointed at her sister's betrayal.

"I was little. I like it better here. If Grandmother wants us to know about her being sick, she'll tell us. Maybe she went to buy new clothes."

"In the middle of the night without telling us? Hardly likely. Annie, go get fresh linens and a clean dress for yourself. We're going to New York City to see Mrs. Riis and find out what's going on."

"I don't think so, Miss. Do I have to, Mrs. Burch?" Annie's face turned beet red as tears formed in her eyes. "Besides, I still have lots of cleaning to do here and I don't have lots of dresses like you. Supposing Mrs. Riis comes home while we're traveling? She'd be awfully angry."

"She'd be even more angry if she knew you let me travel by myself."

Annie looked from Mrs. Burch to Barbara.

"I can't, Miss."

"Annie is in my care as much as you are, Miss Barbara. This would be a fool's errand. I will give you permission to send a telegram to her at the apartment. If you don't hear from her by tonight, we can rethink the situation."

"She could be dead by then."

"Why do you keep saying that about Grandmother?" Lily whined.

Now Barbara gained stronger ground. "Haven't you noticed how tired she is all the time lately?"

"We wear her out. Stay still, Annie. And stop crying. You're ruining my drawing." Lily bent her head over the paper until her face was inches from the surface.

"It's more than that. I found too many medicines in her cupboard related to heart illness for it to be a coincidence. I don't like her being alone down there without us. If we hadn't been so foolish and gone out the other night, she might have taken us with her."

"She has Ledger, what's she need with us?" Annie whined.

Mrs. Burch clapped her hands sharply. "That's enough. You are not going to New York City. You only want to go because you're bored. You need to find a purpose to your life or you'll wind up--" She stopped abruptly and turned away.

"Wind up what, Mrs. Burch?"

Mrs. Burch fussed with an empty pot on the stove.

"Wind up what, Mrs. Burch?"

"I heard you."

"Like my mother? Dead in some foreign country with no one to claim me or bury me? Maybe she's not really dead. Did you ever think of that? Maybe she was like your Edna and didn't want to live a conventional life. Maybe she's in darkest Africa teaching the natives to read."

"Who's Edna?" Lily asked.

"Mind your own business," Barbara snapped.

"I don't have to go with her, do I, Mrs. Burch?" Annie whined again.

Mrs. Burch faced the three young women. "If it were up to me, Miss Barbara, I would go with you myself. I do understand you believe she's seriously ill. I'm that concerned myself, but I can't leave the household and I can't simply pack you lot up and take you to the apartment not knowing what we'd find there. So there'll be no more talk of it. Go get some fresh air until lunch is ready. Annie, quit hanging around. You're no artist's model. Clean the fireplaces."

"We ain't used them in two weeks."

"Then clean the dust out of them. Get busy doing something!"

Mrs. Burch seldom raised her voice. Lily scrambled to collect papers and pencils. Hugging them to her chest she raced to the front hall. They heard the screen door slam. Annie gathered cleaning supplies.

"So, that's it, Mrs. Burch?" Barbara continued after the younger girls had gone. "We'll leave Grandmother to her own devices? She has nothing more than a black manservant to care for her. That is not exactly proper either, is it?"

"Don't use that mouth on me, young lady. You're in my care and you'll do as I say. If I send you to your room, you'll go there as well. Now, leave it alone for a few hours and I'll think of something. Prepare a telegram and we'll send it together. The four of us can walk down the street and buy a lemonade later."

Barbara would not be appeased so easily. She relaxed her arms and leaned on the table. "Thank you, Mrs. Burch, I'll go upstairs and start writing my first book."

"Don't be fresh."

Barbara headed up the stairs, her plan in mind. She found Annie doing a cursory sweep of the third-floor halls and

58

beckoned her to follow her into her bedroom. "I have an idea, Annie. An idea I think you might like."

Barbara sensed Annie's trepidation, but ushered her into the room anyway. "How long have you been with us, Annie?"

Annie stood at the foot of Barbara's bed, keeping her eyes downcast as she fidgeted with her apron. "You know, Miss. About six weeks."

"Do you like working here?"

Her narrow shoulders barely shrugged. "I guess."

"You seem to work well with Mrs. Burch."

"Yes, Miss."

"Where is your home?"

Annie looked directly at her young mistress. Barbara examined her closely. Annie's eyes were a pretty green hazel. Barbara realized she hadn't ever really looked at the girl before. In the right dress, she could pass for another sister.

"My home? I guess it were in Washington Heights for the longest time until my father took a job working on the river. He moved us to Albany a couple of years ago." She paused to clear her throat. "Miss."

"Washington Heights? That's near Manhattan, isn't it?"

"I believe so, Miss."

"Didn't you ever long for some adventure instead of cleaning other people's homes?"

"There ain't nothing wrong about the work I do. I earn my keep! What is it you want from me, Miss?" Tears again glistened in her eyes.

Barbara smiled to ease the girl's distress. "I always thought it would be nice to have a lady's maid. Would you ever want to be a lady's maid?"

"Never thunk of it. What's it mean?"

"A bit more money. And then you help me choose my clothes for the day, make sure everything is kept neat and tidy

- not sweeping and dusting, but ensuring my personal items are where they belong. Help me at night. Draw my bath."

At that the girl's eyes grew larger than Barbara would ever have thought possible. "Draw a bath? What's that mean?"

"When I want a bath, I call you and say, 'Annie, please draw my bath. I'm going to the concert in the park this evening. I'd like to wear the plaid dress with the green ribbons.' Something like that and then you make sure the water in my bath is the right temperature, you layout my dress and the accessories to go with it. Make sure my shoes are clean." Barbara sat on the bed and leaned toward Annie. "What do you think?"

"How would I know all what to do? I don't know an accessory."

"I'd teach you. It would raise your station. What do you think?" Barbara watched Annie as she debated this unexpected opportunity. A flash of suspicion crossed the girl's face.

"There's something not right. Who would do my work if I got to do everything for you that you can do for yourself anyway?" Her pale face relaxed into a sullen expression.

"Oh, Annie. You're only a year younger than I but by dint of our birth, I'm rich and you're poor. I'm trying to help you and I also want to make myself feel like I belong in society. Everyone, even people with far less money than we have, has a lady's maid. A personal servant. Grandmother brought us here and put us up in the servant's quarters, but I don't want to live like this. I talked to Mrs. Burch about it yesterday."

"About me being your maid?"

"No. About doing something with my life. I'll soon be eighteen, then nineteen. Some man might want to marry me because he knows I'm wealthy, but I want to do something with my life before I have to live like this all over again. Everybody telling me what to do, which church, which concerts are correct to attend. Now, say yes and then we'll get started."

"And Mrs. Burch won't be angry?"

"Of course, she'll be angry until she can find another scullery maid, so you'll have to continue to help her for a few days until that happens. Then we'll be almost like sisters. And if anyone objects, I'll pay your salary from my own funds."

"Your own funds?"

My father left both Lily and me money as well as trust funds which become available when we each turn twenty-one. As I've had little need to spend my own money, I have more than enough to do what I please."

Annie mumbled.

"What's that?"

"Nothing, Miss, but I'll do it as long as Mrs. Burch won't fire me and your grandmother won't be yelling at me. Do I have to live in this house?"

Barbara hadn't considered that. "I think it would be helpful. There are three empty rooms on this floor. Pick one and fix it to suit yourself. There's plenty of furniture in the attics."

"Well, then." Annie smiled and smoothed her apron. "Perhaps I'd best get started. Do you mind if I bring two of my brothers to help me in the morning?"

"Not tomorrow morning. First, help me pack for New York."

"I had an idea you was going to say that." Annie sucked in her breath and bit her lower lip.

"You'll come with me so no one can accuse me of traveling alone. If I lend you my light cloak, you can even travel with me in first class. I'm actually not sure of the protocol of lady's maids when traveling, but that sounds all right to me. Go find a large valise and a small trunk. I don't know how long we'll be gone."

Annie remained still.

"Go!" Barbara snapped.

The girl rushed from the room. After she left, Barbara pulled open a bureau drawer and pulled out the silk purse where she kept her money hidden. After counting out five hundred dollars, she replaced the rest and tucked the cash into her hndbag. She then headed down the stairs to explain to Mrs. Burch she and Annie would be out for the afternoon. No sense in telling her everything at once, though she would hint at hiring a new housekeeping maid.

When she reached the ground floor, voices on the porch startled her. She slipped over to the open window, remained out of sight, and listened. Lily's voice sounded small and frightened. Barbara's first instinct was to rush out and confront whoever scared her sister, but on second thought, she remained still, first wanting to know more.

"I told you, Grandmother's not home, my mother's dead, and there's only me, the cook and the cleaning girl home."

Barbara's scalp crawled. Lily knew perfectly well Barbara was home. She held her breath, waiting to hear who would speak next.

A man's deep voice said, "You see, Miss Riis, we were supposed to deliver something special to your mother. We had no idea she had passed on. How long ago was that?"

"Five and a half years ago. And my name is von Bek. My father was Jacob von Bek. Grandmother makes me use her name."

A second person cleared his throat. "Sorry, Miss von Bek. So, you've lived here for five years?"

"Yes. But we take trips in the summer. This summer we're going back to France. It's nice there. Would you like me to get Mrs. Burch? She might be able to help you more than I. She might know more about my mother."

"How long she been here?" The deeper voice asked.

Barbara imagined Lily shrugging. "Six years."

"So she didn't know your mother."

"I'm going inside. If you want me to send Mrs. Burch out, let me know now."

Chair legs scraped on the porch floor. The screen door opened. Barbara pressed herself against the wall praying the men wouldn't follow her sister. Lily didn't notice her as she hurried straight down the hallway to the kitchen. A few moments later Mrs. Burch barreled toward the front door. Her eyes glanced toward Barbara, though she didn't stop to acknowledge her.

"What are you two doing on my porch annoying Miss Lillian?"

"How do you do, Ma'am. I'm Ernest Porter and this is my colleague, John Smith. We are private investigators working for a person seeking Mary Ellen Riis von Bek." He said the last name as if he had known it all along and hadn't just heard it from Lily.

"S'far as I know, the poor thing's been dead and gone these past five years. Next time you want a word, you call ahead and make arrangements with her grandmother, Mrs. James Riis. Now, go away." She sounded like she was chasing birds from the lawn.

"When do you expect Mrs. Riis to return?" The other voice sounded smarmy.

"Leave your calling cards and I will inform her of your visit."

A brief silence followed.

"It's urgent we confirm Mary Ellen Riis' situation, so please have her mother contact us immediately upon her return."

"I'll do that," Mrs. Burch responded in a tone implying she would do no such thing.

Mrs. Burch returned to the vestibule but did not appear in the hallway. Barbara waited.

The deep voice said, "New York apartment. Bet?"

"Let's go."

Footsteps thundered down the front porch steps.

Barbara peeked through the net curtains at the retreating figures. Two hulking men, one in a black suit, the other wearing a flashy plaid jacket, crossed the sidewalk to a waiting carriage.

~*~

When Mrs. Burch entered the room, she whirled to confront Barbara still standing near the front windows. "Why are those men looking for your mother?"

"I have no idea, but I think they're heading to the city to find Grandmother. Please find someone to help you for the next few days. I'm taking Annie with me to Grandmother's. She might be in more trouble than I thought."

She threw hands up in frustration. "Go! Take Annie. I can easily replace her. You're looking for any excuse to get out of here."

"Lily didn't tell those men she had a sister and they didn't seem to know," Barbara said, puzzled.

"As long as they did her no harm. I have their cards. I'll be asking Kevin O'Reilly about those two."

"What would he know? He's our street cop."

"Don't underestimate an O'Reilly."

Ten

Mary Ellen threw her arm over her eyes to ward off the daylight. Pausing a moment, she peeked out to see why her room was so bright. The weekly cleaning girl had strict instructions for the draperies to remain closed at all times. Mary Ellen certainly never opened them.

Through bleary, squinting eyes she studied the unfamiliar sunshine insisting itself into her room.

With a moan she rolled over and pulled a blanket over her head.

She heard whistling in the hallway. Whistling? Who would be in her apartment? She tried to think but her mind wanted to return to blank nothingness. Mother and Ledger. Mother and Ledger had arrived yesterday and said they were taking her home. But Mother didn't whistle; she didn't recall ever hearing Ledger whistle. He played the piano, he even sang, she couldn't recall whistling. Street children whistled. Boys in their teens whistled.

The doors to her room flung open. "Excuse me, Miss, there are two gentlemen asking for you."

She pushed the blanket down and peered over a pillow. A young girl in a fresh maid's uniform stood in the doorway.

"Nobody knows I'm here. Make them go away."

"If you'll excuse me, they asked for Miss Riis, isn't that your name?"

"You're mistaken. They mean my mother. I'm not here. Tell them you are mistaken. I'm not here. Shut the door and go away."

"Yes, Miss."

"Wait a minute. Who are you?"

"I'm Fiona. Mr. Ledger has hired us for the week. We're cleaning and preparing dinner for eight o'clock, I believe. Roast chickens, madam asked for."

"Uh." Mary Ellen rolled onto her back. "Wonderful. Tell the gentlemen to go away."

"I don't think they're going to like that, Miss, but I'll tell them."

Once the girl was gone Mary Ellen struggled to sit up. She should have asked the girl to close the draperies. She inhaled a deep breath, sighed, and then slid off the bed. She staggered to the window. Pulling the sheer curtains aside, she looked down at Park Avenue. Alive with traffic, people and vehicles going to and fro, it reminded her of ants swarming on a hill. The park across the way looked tranquil.

"I should go for a walk in the park. That would be special," she said, tripping across to her vanity. One look at her image told her she wouldn't be going anywhere until she cleaned up. "Looks like you had a good time last night, young lady," she accused her image. "Young lady? Middle-aged useless hag!" she spat.

With one hand she pulled her hair atop her head while reaching for hairpins from the vanity. Her head spun with the sudden activity and she collapsed with a thump onto the bench.

"You need a new man, that's what you need. Someone to take you away from all this. Someone like Lillian's daddy. He was good wasn't he? The rascal." She grimaced at the face. The reflection showed eyes smeared black, and cheeks pale as her bed sheets. "If you hurry, maybe you can see who the gentlemen are in the parlor," she told her image.

Holding the hairpins in her teeth, she tugged and pulled her hair into place, then balanced in front of her washstand and rubbed the cosmetics from her face. She plucked a clean white blouse and black skirt from her wardrobe and thrust her arms into the sleeves of the blouse, then squirmed her hips into the skirt as she fought to pull it up. Her fingers, feeling like swollen sausages, fumbled as she prepared to meet a new man for her life.

She threw open the doors, hesitated a moment as she surveyed the empty hallway, and then marched grandly toward the living room. The room sparkled with tidiness, the windows open to fresh air. It was lovely except no one was in the room. No men. She sank down onto the sofa. "Too late, old girl. Once again, too late."

Dinner would be served at eight o'clock. Where had Mother and Ledger gone? She looked at the mantle clock. Four fifteen. Daylight, so it was afternoon. More than three hours until dinner. She must find something to eat while she waited.

Once again, she pulled herself up and made an effort to look dignified. Pretending to have a book on her head, she walked through the dining room and pushed open the kitchen door. The heat of the ovens and the fragrance of baking bread assaulted her.

"I'm starving," she announced. Three strangers looked at her. "Bring me food. I'll be in the parlor."

She whirled around and then, unable to continue the facade, staggered to the living room and arranged herself on the chaise. She allowed her mind to wander over the man, or men, she'd missed. If they were looking for her, they would surely return. If their reasons were important enough, they might even come back today. She smiled at the thought as she heard the chatter and bustle of the servants. They began to set the table for dinner. The friendly clatter of silver and china, and the clinking of glasses soothed her. Maybe she wouldn't go out tonight.

Eleven

Barbara and Annie stepped down from the train into the hustle and bustle of the station. With Annie as her responsibility, Barbara had to appear to know what she was doing. "We'll have a porter bring our bags out to the sidewalk where he'll hail us a taxi to take us to Grandmother's. If you're nervous, feel free to clutch my arm. No one will pay the slightest attention to you. You look more like an Irish immigrant than someone born American."

"I feel like an immigrant, Miss, but may I confess to enjoying the train ride and the food and the excitement of it all?"

Barbara felt Annie's thin body shudder against her. "I'm glad. I thought there was more to you than a terrified little mouse."

"Yes, Miss."

They stepped through the doors to the street. Annie squealed. "Jesus, Mary and Joseph, what is that smell?"

"Annie! Watch your tongue."

"But that smell, like a giant disgusting stable."

"Never mind," Barbara said although she tried to avoid breathing too deeply.

"Miss! Miss! That's an automobile, isn't it? Oh, Miss, will we get to ride in one?" She pulled Barbara toward a waiting taxi.

"Wait a minute for our bags to catch up to us. Of course, we can ride in one. I've never been in one either. They're interesting looking. I wonder what makes them go. I've heard of steam engines but these are called electric cars, yet there are no wires."

Annie's face radiated such joy Barbara was glad of her decision to bring the girl along as not only a helper, but perhaps something of an accomplice.

Once arranged in the taxi with their luggage strapped to the back of the vehicle, she gave the driver Grandmother's address and the two of them sat on the edge of their seats expectantly. Barbara didn't know if she enjoyed Annie's excitement more than her own glowing feeling of sudden independence. Annie's presence made Barbara feel mature and sophisticated.

"Look at the ladies' hats, Miss Barbara. I feel quite the drudge in this plain boater."

"Your hat is perfect for your age. Besides, you are a working-class girl, you aren't supposed to look like the gentry."

"I feel like it in this cloak." Annie rubbed her hands over the linen wrap Barbara had given her to wear on the train.

"Don't get used to the feeling. You are still my maid, understand?" Barbara said, feeling a little guilt at having to remind the girl of her place.

"That's all right. I'll be the best maid in the world for you. Oh, how glad I am you forced me to come with you. Who would have guessed this six weeks ago when I came to work for Mrs. Riis?" She bounced with excitement as the taxi worked its way up Park Avenue and closer to the city apartment. "Won't they be surprised to see us?"

"I'm sure. Now, settle down. We're almost there. We have to have the doorman carry our bags upstairs for us. You'll be in charge of that."

"I will?" Annie gasped in awe.

The driver slowed as he maneuvered the taxi through traffic closer toward the curb in front of the building.

"Keep going, driver," Barbara commanded. "Move quickly. Forward, away from the house. I'll tell you where to go later. Drive!"

"Which one is it, Miss?" Annie said, her head trying to keep up with the passing facades.

"Turn your head. Look at the park across the street. Do it now!" Barbara said sharply.

"Yes, Miss, I was just wanting to see where we was going to be staying. What's happened?"

"Didn't you see them?"

"Who?"

"The two men who were at the house this morning. They must have been on the same train. They were talking with the doorman."

Annie sucked in a deep breath. "I never seen 'em."

"They were looking for Grandmother and asked Lily about our mother. They didn't seem to know Mother's married name, nor did they know there are two of us. I don't know what it was all about, but I heard them say New York as they left the house, only I didn't imagine they would be coming here so quickly."

"Where to now, Ma'am?" the driver called over his shoulder.

"A respectable hotel, driver," she called out, making a quick decision to avoid the apartment until she had a better understanding of what was going on.

The driver pushed the steering stick, changed their direction and drove them a few blocks to The Plaza Hotel, an enormous building that must have housed at least two hundred rooms.

"You'll be secure here, ladies," he announced as he helped them from the automobile. "Will you want me to deliver any messages?"

She and Annie exchanged glances. "That won't be necessary. We appreciate your time." She handed him his fare and a tip. He saluted and pulled away, leaving the two of them on the sidewalk with their baggage. A doorman blew a whistle and immediately two bellhops appeared, collected their bags and led them to the registration desk.

Annie tripped along behind them ogling the central staircase and the highly polished mahogany reception desk. "Oh, my. How grand. Have you ever stayed in such a place?"

"Don't be silly, Annie. Of course. I've stayed in plenty of hotels before. We've traveled much of the world, first with our mother and later with Grandmother and Ledger. Come, we'll bathe and then change for the evening." She leaned closer to the girl. "This isn't the fanciest I've been in, but we'll only be here one night."

"Excuse me, Miss. I got no clothes to be changing with the time of day. I'm the personal maid if you recall."

Barbara looked at her as if wondering what she might be talking about and then realized she'd been thinking of her little sister, not this cleaning girl she'd recently elevated to personal maid. "You're right. I was thinking of dinner at Grandmother's. Technically I should leave you to your own devices or let you eat with the servants."

"Is that what you do when you travel with Ledger? How does he ever find his way around new and strange places?"

"Ledger grew up in new and strange places. But you're right to say that. Grandmother always pretends he is some sort of dignitary so he can dine with us. I think she quite enjoys his company. You could wear one of my dresses and pretend to be my sister."

"Is that what you said on the register?"

"You were right there."

"I don't read, Miss."

The bellhop stopped at a grilled door and pushed a button. Within seconds the door slid open and the boy stepped back to let the ladies enter. Barbara saw the terror on Annie's face. She herself had never ridden in an elevator, but not wanting the poor girl to become hysterical, she assumed a relaxed attitude and stepped into the tiny room. Annie followed her, remaining close. A uniformed man slid a brass grilled gate closed and waited for the bellhop to say "five." The floor moved. Annie gripped Barbara's sleeve.

"It's only an elevator, Annie. Relax," she whispered to the girl, trying to comfort her even as her own heart pounded at the sight of the walls moving downward as the car slipped upwards past other doors.

When they arrived at "five," the bellhop led the way to their room. Thick carpeting and wide hallways lent an air of refinement to the hotel. If Grandmother knew where they were, she'd approve. Maybe.

After the boy opened the draperies and showed them the adjoining bathroom, complete with a bathtub, sink and a flush toilet, he tipped his hat and held it out. Barbara dropped some coins in it.

"When you want to go downstairs, you hit the button next to the elevator. The operator will come get you." He whistled his way out of the room.

"He's cute. Short, but cute." Annie said. "What do we do now?"

"It's getting late. I suggest we each take a bath and change before we go back to Grandmother's. I don't know about you but I feel dreadfully hot and tired after everything that's happened today."

"Right, Miss. Is this the place where I go and draw your bath and then freshen a dress for you to wear? Do I take care of your personal linens as well?"

Barbara laughed. "Sure. Go draw me a bath. I'll see what I want to wear and I'll even lay out a dress that might suit you. You're a bit smaller than I, but we'll make something work."

"Imagine this. The two of us in a room with two wonderful beds. What a lovely place. You were clever to think of this."

"It's a little small, but it'll do and at least we have our own private facilities. Not every room does."

Annie inched her way around the room with her hands behind her back until she reached the bathroom door. "What's that?" she pointed to an instrument on a small desk under the window.

"I believe that is a telephone," Barbara said, in awe herself. "I know they exist, but I've never seen one."

"Well, this is the most amazing day of my life. Electric cars, elevators and telephones."

Annie ducked out of sight and then Barbara heard water running.

"Ow!"

"What happened?" Barbara ran to the door.

"The water's damned hot!" Annie held up a red hand to prove her point. "We never got water that hot at your house."

"Make sure you mix some cold in with it. Drawing my bath doesn't include boiling me."

Annie laughed and Barbara quickly joined her. Even before her bath, the tension of the day began to wear off.

After some consideration, Barbara decided Annie would look good in the beige cotton with the dark piping around the hem, bodice and sleeves. She'd let her wear a small cameo that had been Grandmother's.

Once her bath was pronounced "drawn" she withdrew to the bathroom.

Annie sang as she emptied the suitcases, hung dresses in the closet and filled the bureau with their personal items. "What do we do with this telephone, Miss?" Annie called.

"Talk to someone else who has one, I suppose," she said. She tossed the washcloth in the air enjoying her newly found freedom. It reminded her a little of when she and Lily had been left on their own with the gypsies.

~*~

They returned to the apartment building shortly after six p.m. The two burly men who had arrived on the train with them had been replaced by two others. This pair stood outside the doors smoking cigars and conversing with the doorman. Though they appeared to be in conversation, their eyes continually scanned the cars, carriages and foot traffic as if they were searching for someone. Barbara turned her head as she directed the driver to take them back to the hotel.

Twelve

Ledger stationed the two Pinkertons outside to prevent strangers entering the building. He co-opted the door man to help identify the residents of the two lower flats.

Elisabeth climbed the stairs, weary from the day's sailing adventure on the ferry to visit the wonderful statue. She had waited while Ledger climbed up to the torch. He swore he had called down and waved to her and she responded, but she only remembered shielding her eyes from the sun when she looked up.

The fresh air, the salt water, an open-air lunch in the park combined to tire her in a most delicious manner. This was not anxiety, nor worry about her daughter, just physical tiredness. She looked forward to her bath, a quiet dinner and an early bed.

So it was with mixed feelings when she opened the door, she found her daughter fully dressed on the divan, a cup of tea in hand, looking fairly bright.

"Good evening, Mother. Did you have a nice day?"

Elisabeth stood in the entrance, surprised by her daughter's appearance and manner. "It was lovely. Have you been to see the statue for yourself?"

Mary Ellen laughed. "Mother, I live here. I'll get around to it someday. I'm waiting to speak with you on an urgent matter. Why don't you make yourself comfortable and join me for a cup of tea? Fiona tells me dinner will be at eight. We have time."

"Who's Fiona?"

"One of the new staff. Please hurry."

"Ledger will be right up. He's speaking with our new security guards." Elisabeth crossed the room. "I'll be right back."

"Security? How could you have heard already?"

The note of panic in Mary Ellen's voice stopped Elisabeth. "Heard what?"

"About the men who were here today looking for you – or me. Fiona couldn't be quite sure." She settled her cup onto its saucer on the table in front of her and then straightened. "I don't believe they have your best interests at heart."

"Why would that be?"

"You arrive and the next day two hoodlums are in search of you? What is it you're not telling me, Mother? Why are you so anxious for me to return to Albany with you?"

Elisabeth studied her daughter's face, trying to interpret Mary Ellen's story. Her daughter's drug-addled mind could be making the whole thing up. Then again, perhaps not. "Send the girl, Fiona, to my room. I'll talk to her while I freshen up."

Turning her back on her daughter she headed to her room. She sank onto her bed, sitting with her hands covering her face.

"All these years. Now he searches for his daughter. She's right. He can't mean anything good," she said.

Fiona tapped on the door and then stepped into the room. "You asked for me, Mrs…?"

"It's Mrs. Riis, dear. I did. Tell me everything about the men who came to the door this morning."

"It was this afternoon, Mrs. Riis." She stood with her hands folded politely at her waist, awaiting further questions or orders.

"Go on. When did they arrive, what did they look like and what did they say?" Elisabeth removed the lightweight jacket and her hat while waiting for the girl to reply.

"They were big men. They both were in need of a shave and a bath." She wrinkled her nose. "They smelled bad. One was wearing an awful plaid jacket. Their clothes were appropriate but not good quality. My father's a tailor and I know quality. They didn't remove their hats in the house. As I don't know your family, Mrs. Riis, I couldn't tell them anything. I thought the lady sleeping in here might be the Mrs. Riis they were looking for."

"She goes by the name of Riis, that's true."

"But then I got confused because it seemed like they were asking for a mother and a daughter both called Riis. I told them nobody was home and they should check back later. Mr. Evans came out at that moment. He's the butler and chef, a big man himself, and they left. Mr. Evans scolded me for answering the door. That's his job, but he was busy cleaning the chickens and bossing Maureen around. I'm new to this type of employment, Ma'am."

"Thank you. Go back to your work."

"Oh," the girl said, hesitating at the door. "Mr. Evans wants to know if you'd like sherry in the parlor before dinner."

Elisabeth waved her away. "Check with Mr. Ledger when he comes in. I'm going to rest for a little while before dinner. Please make sure Miss Mary Ellen doesn't leave the apartment, will you?"

"I can't do that, Mrs. Riis! How would I stop her?" The maid threw her hands over her mouth, recognizing she'd just refused an order from a new employer.

"Never mind. Pass the message to Mr. Ledger. He'll be here momentarily."

Fiona curtsied and left.

"Ledger will help. He always has; he always will," Elisabeth muttered. She pulled herself up onto the bed and rested against the large pillows. Her mind raced with the possibilities and probabilities. Someone else had come in search of Mary Ellen the same as she had. Sometimes a coincidence wasn't a coincidence; there was a reason the girls had decided to play a prank at the Albany Club. It gave her fair warning and now she had to act on their information. The newspapers had confirmed this morning that Justin Pembroke was set to oppose William Jennings Bryan at the Democratic convention at the end of the month. "We'll see about that."

She picked up a fountain pen and sheet of paper from the nightstand and began writing out a plan.

~*~

Ledger woke her at 6:30. "Mary Ellen is becoming agitated. I've asked if dinner can be pushed up a little earlier. We'll be eating at seven-thirty. She has a glass of sherry at the moment but is pacing in front of the fireplace talking about meeting friends again tonight."

"We can't have that."

He held up the paper. "I see you have some ideas."

"Ledger, until this past week, we never had any concern about Mary Ellen's escapades, nor did we worry about her welfare. Not very good parents, were we."

"Yes, I could agree with that."

She noted the lift of his head, an indication of his disapproval. Ledger had never supported abandoning Mary Ellen. His high smooth brow, the broad flat nose and high cheekbones did give him the look of a dignitary. He might have been an ambassador had he been left to grow and develop in his own country.

"All right. I know you didn't want to abandon her. But now, of a sudden, we have people checking on her. I've ensured Mary Ellen stayed out of the limelight all her life. She's no threat to him. Why would he now concern himself with her?"

"He is considering running for president; if knowledge of her came out, it would not bode well for him. Also, if I may be

79

so bold, my dear, what makes you think it is only the senator who has any interest in her? She travels amongst an unseemly group of people."

"We don't know who she travels amongst." Elisabeth gathered up the papers and set them aside. "Help me up, please. My legs are weak. That was quite a trip today."

"I enjoyed myself. Mrs. Burch will like to hear about the Statue of Liberty." He held out a hand. Elisabeth used it to pull herself to a standing position. Her legs trembled a moment before they steadied and let her stand independently.

"I'll wash my face and then be in for some sherry. We need to leave here. Trust that I am suspicious. It is the senator's men who would be after Mary Ellen."

"If you say so."

"I do say so. We are leaving here and going into hiding until we can get back to Albany undetected, do I make myself clear?"

"You are, as ever, the boss, Ma'am." He turned smartly and left the room.

Elisabeth took a sip of water and stared in the mirror. Her face glowed from the exposure to the sunshine today, but her eyes appeared narrow and mean, even to her. She slammed the glass into the sink, shattering it. The hell with it, she thought, let the girl clean it up.

She smoothed her hair, brushing it back with her hands and then headed to the parlor for the confrontation with Mary Ellen. She'd tell the story slowly so it wouldn't be complete until after dinner, by which time she and Ledger would have plied the poor woman with so much wine she would fall asleep shortly thereafter. Then they could follow through with her plan. When she entered the room, Ledger was coming in through the main entrance. He raised a reassuring hand toward her.

"I think we surely have time for a little sherry before dinner, Ledger. Mary Ellen, would you like to join us?" She knew full well Mary Ellen had a pretty good start on the sherry.

Ledger stepped up and poured for them. "To a wonderful day."

"You let him be far too personal, Mother," Mary Ellen said as she accepted her drink. "Why were those men looking for you?"

"We won't know until we meet with them, will we?" Elisabeth remarked as she took her seat in a comfortable overstuffed chair facing the sofa.

"There are things we have to discuss, Mary Ellen." Ledger spoke from where he stood near the fireplace.

Elisabeth raised a hand to stop him. "Not now, Ledger. Let's have our drink first. How are you feeling this evening, dear?"

The stunned look on Mary Ellen's face warned Elisabeth her interest was too sudden. "I'm still curious. Anxious. We haven't had any rain for weeks. Did you know that?" she added in a weak voice, hoping Mary Ellen would relax. She turned to Ledger for a lead. He smiled.

Elisabeth forced a smile on her face and continued. "Rain would be refreshing. We're having roast chicken for dinner. I remember how you used to like it served with roast potatoes and fresh green beans and parsnips. I've asked Ledger to select an especially nice white wine to accompany it."

Mary Ellen sighed. "I tried cooking for the girls a few times. They preferred when we had a cook. I haven't been very good at anything, I'm afraid."

"That would be my fault. I'm so sorry to have failed you."

Ledger cleared his throat. "But we can always try again, can't we? Perhaps we can have Mrs. Burch teach you how to make a fine cake to make your daughters proud."

"Lovely." Mary Ellen held out her glass, which Ledger immediately refilled. "Jacob used to tell me it was my bloody stupid Irish heritage that made me an incompetent and a drunk."

"He wasn't a nice man, then. It's best he died."

"Dinner!" a booming voice sounded from the dining room door.

With great relief, Elisabeth rose and held out her hand to Mary Ellen.

Mary Ellen's hand trembled as she accepted her mother's gesture.

Thirteen

Mary Ellen eyed her food listlessly. Ledger said grace then served a clear soup from the tureen along with fresh, hot bread rolls. As soon as the consommé was finished, the staff paraded in with serving bowls and platters, one filled with sliced chicken white meat, another with the dark meat, a bowl of roast potatoes and yet another of boiled parsleyed potatoes. Roasted parsnips, julienned carrots and fresh peas, all slathered with rich, creamy, fresh butter, finished out the main course.

Mary Ellen kept her head down, playing with her food, periodically taking a bite. She had to admit to herself, if not to her mother, the food tasted delicious. Had it not been for her tiredness, she might have eaten more. The choice of wine satisfied her and she was pleased to note no one showed any concern when she asked for more.

"You've had my girls for five years now. Will you tell me about them?" she said as they slowly made their way through the feast.

"Barbara is tall, smart but has no ambition. She did finish school in Albany," Elisabeth said.

"You didn't send her to Switzerland as you did me? Why not?"

Elisabeth took a deep breath and seemed to search her mind for the reasons for sending Mary Ellen away so long ago. "We lived much of our time in Europe when you were young. It made sense."

"You tried to keep me from my father. I think you were jealous of his affections for me." Mary Ellen waited for her mother's anger, but instead she watched tears well in her eyes. One slid down the right side of her face. "Was that it?" she added more softly.

"No. Jim was becoming more and more belligerent with his disabilities. I feared for your safety." Elisabeth held out her own wine glass for a refill.

"Liar!" Mary Ellen exploded. "You were jealous of us. I loved him and you didn't."

Ledger slammed his dinner knife on the table. "Silence! You will not speak to your mother in that tone of voice. Perhaps you'd like to excuse yourself until you can exercise some control."

Mary Ellen's eyes slid over the large, gentle Negro who had been so much a part of her life years ago. He's never raised his voice. *I need to get out of here. My friends. I'll tell them I must meet my friends.*

"I'll accept an apology, Mary Ellen," her mother said calmly.

"Yes. I apologize. If you'll excuse me, I do have an appointment with friends this evening." She began to push her chair back but Ledger raised his hand to stop her.

"Finish your dinner first, and then we'll talk about where you might go tonight. If you insist on taking opium, I am going to insist you eat a healthy diet."

"I'm thirty-six years old, Ledger, not the little girl you can boss around anymore. You're not and never were my father." She crossed her arms defiantly.

She watched her mother's face blanch and then turn bright red. "Dessert and cognac, Evans," Elisabeth said through clamped teeth. The words came out as a strangled hiss. Evans pushed the kitchen door open and disappeared.

Mary Ellen leaned against the back of her chair, finding herself satisfied for once she managed to make Elisabeth lose her composure. She watched Ledger for a cue. He appeared concerned but he did not move to help Elisabeth.

"Would you like to take your dessert in your room, Elisabeth?" Ledger asked.

"She needs to know if my plan is going to work. She must cooperate." Elisabeth's voice quivered.

Mary Ellen followed this exchange, trying to puzzle out a solution, but the wine had muddled her brain. Cognac was definitely in order. She did not want to hear what might be coming next. What could her mother want her to know? Why did she have to take her to Albany? Whatever the secret, apparently Ledger knew it. Her mother had a plan that included Mary Ellen and Ledger. Her stomach churned; she couldn't be sick right there in front of them. As she took a deep breath, a slice of apple pie appeared before her along with a snifter of brandy. Anxious to do something with her hands she tried to pick up her fork and the glass at the same time. She tipped the drink onto the pie, thinking she was cutting it with her fork.

The glass and pie were quickly replaced. A hand dabbed at the tablecloth to mop up the liquid that had dripped off the pie plate. This time she focused intently on taking a bite of pie before setting her fork down and picking up her drink. If she drank enough, she wouldn't worry about going out; if she drank enough she wouldn't have to hear whatever these evil people had to say to her. The girl, Fiona, hovered nearby. She'd have her help her to bed tonight. Yes, Fiona. A sweet girl.

"Justin Chauncey Pembroke," Elisabeth said, her voice now strong.

Mary Ellen's head snapped up.

Elisabeth held her head high, her eyes glaring down her nose toward her daughter. "This is something you should have known a long time ago. I never knew exactly how to tell you. Justin Chauncey Pembroke is your father which is why I never wanted to see you. I hated the sight of you."

Mary Ellen struggled to swallow the piece of pie threatening to choke her. Her right hand, which held the fork, fell limp onto the table. She pulled herself up straight, taking time to register what her mother had just said.

Fiona approached Mary Ellen's chair but Mary Ellen pushed her hand aside. Her eyes remained riveted on Elisabeth's face. "Why didn't you give me away? Go to a convent and give me to the nuns? Why did you let me love Father? Jim Riis, my father."

"My father wanted to send me to a convent in Switzerland, but then James Riis came along with his proposal. Mr. Pembroke had abandoned me. My father was only glad to get rid of me and so I married a useless cripple."

Mary Ellen's heart raced, feeling out of control. He held a hand to her heart. There had to be so much more to Mother's story yet she feared hearing another word.

"An Irish tramp. That's what they called me," Elisabeth continued. "Trying to work my way up in the world. Daddy blamed me for throwing myself at Justin. I did, but I didn't. I was so young and loved him so much. He promised he'd marry me if I would give in to him."

"And you had no mother to counsel you. Just like me," Mary Ellen said. She felt Fiona's hand on her shoulder and resisted the urge to scold the girl.

"I had no mother, but not just like you. Mine died in childbirth. I'd killed my own mother by the simple act of being born. You can't imagine the terror I felt when I realized I would be giving birth - maybe dying and there was no one I could turn to." The liquid in her glass rippled as she raised it to her mouth. "The fancy school, the clothes, everything he wanted so I could look like I belonged in the world where he wasn't welcome. He could have had all the money in the world and still he wasn't welcome in society."

"And Father? Where did he come from? What made him want to marry you?"

"We met at a picnic."

Elisabeth wiped her brow with her lace handkerchief. Mr. Evans remained at attention near the kitchen door as Elisabeth told of meeting Jim Riis for the first time. She'd been attracted to him, his frail, blond good looks, and charmed by his courtesy toward her; so different from Justin.

~*~

In late October, 1864, as Elisabeth prepared to leave the country, James came calling with his aides, who carried him to her front door.

When Father called her down to meet someone, she was shocked to see him sitting in the parlor with a smile on his face. He held out his hands to her.

"Mr. Riis?" She stared at him in wonder, ignoring his outstretched arms. Though her gown disguised her condition, she moved self-consciously to the farthest seat in the room. He was in the wing chair near the fireplace; she sank onto an old, overstuffed chair near the pocket doors that led to the dining room.

Father left them alone in the drawing room though the doors remained open.

"I've come, Miss Ackert, to ask your father for your hand in marriage."

She dropped onto the nearest chair, stunned by his bold proposal. Why would he suddenly appear like this? Her mouth trembled as she blurted out, "Marriage? You don't want to marry me. I'm going to Switzerland."

"Perhaps we can change that to a honeymoon." He paused for a moment and then added, "If you'll have me."

Dumbfounded, she sat feeling like one of her dolls, waiting for someone to give life to her. "W-why me? Why would you want to marry me?"

This time when he smiled, she noticed a dimple to the left of his mouth. The memory of another mouth jumped to the forefront of her thoughts and she felt herself blush. "Because I know you to be a charming and delightful person."

Did he know about her condition? Was that why he came? Why would a handsome and well-off man want to marry her? Unable to think of anything else to say, she choked out, "Thank you."

"I've had words with Mr. Justin Pembroke and if it were humanly possible I would have challenged him to a duel. Unfortunately, I cannot do that. I have admired you from afar since the first day I met you, Miss Ackert. I would be honored if you would accept my offer. We can marry as soon as possible and the two of us can set sail for Europe right away. Switzerland first, if you like. I've heard the sea at Biarritz is healthful."

"I'm still not hearing you correctly, sir. You know about Justin and yet, you want to marry me? You know what they call me?" She studied the kind face, wondering why God had chosen to bless her so. The nuns would have fallen into a dead faint if they heard this proposal.

"I know his travesty against your body was not of your doing. He is an evil man, Miss Ackert. And I confess to having my own selfish motives as well." Now he looked at the carpet as if appraising it.

"Yes?" she questioned tentatively. Could this really be her salvation? Marrying this kind gentleman?

"It might send you away from me forever, but Miss Ackert, should you accept my proposal, you should know I could never…" He hesitated. "I could never be a proper husband to you." His eyes now met hers. "Other than to worship, adore, respect and love you forever. If you'll have me."

Her breathing became labored. Perspiration broke out on her brow. Be married but not have to do that nasty stuff ever again? Justin told her she was wonderful, but all she remembered was his ugly thrusting and sweating and grunting. Afterward he collapsed on top of her and told her she was beautiful and how much he loved her. Before she could recover, he had her dress quickly so he could send her home.

"I'll – I'll get my father," she said. "Shall I send in tea?"

His eyes glowed. "If I may be so bold, perhaps something a little stronger to celebrate?"

~*~

A loud knock on the door startled the diners back to the present. Elisabeth signaled the girls to clear the table while Evans headed for the front door.

He returned a moment later and handed Ledger two calling cards. Ledger read them without comment and then excused himself from the room. He slid the dining room doors shut as he left.

Mary Ellen watched her mother compose herself after the telling of her story. She tried to imagine her as a young girl accepting a proposal for a sterile marriage with no hope of more children. She remembered her father as a warm and loving man. But then, as a little girl, she had no understanding of that part of life. Once she grew old enough to understand those things, she found herself as eager as the other girls at the boarding school to experience marriage and secret things of the flesh.

She held her glass out quickly before the memories of her first experiences could take over. Memories like floating shadows, drifted through her mind, never quite forming but always threatening with a heavy blackness. Like her mother, she had been grateful when a seemingly kind man wanted to marry her. The strong sweet drink slid down her throat, warming her belly. It helped her mother look young and lovely. "Thank you for the story, Mother. It's good to finally confirm what I suspected all these years is true. You never wanted me. You never loved me. I've been no more than an embarrassment and shame for you. I only wish you had let me love my father. My father, Jim Riis."

When Mary Ellen said the name, "Jim Riis," Elisabeth looked like she had been punched in her stomach.

She watched the changing expressions on her mother's face. Mary Ellen had loved him as a father and he had loved her. Too bad he died. Too bad mother never loved him enough to care for him. Ledger appeared to do his best to bring mother and daughter together, but Mother always thwarted his efforts.

Mother held her mouth pinched as she always did when about to scold. "I know you and Jim loved each other, Mary Ellen. We won't discuss it again. He's been dead and buried these twenty years. Let him – leave his name in peace."

"Now what is your plan? Will you introduce me to my real father? Is that the reason for wanting me in Albany? I am an adult and don't have to go with you, you understand." Mary Ellen eyed the doors, hoping Ledger would return soon so she could escape to her room.

"You'll find out soon enough." Elisabeth turned to the two maids. "Clear up and await further orders."

Fiona stepped forward. "Excuse me, Mrs. Riis, are we to spend the night? I was told we would be leaving following dinner."

"You'll be informed shortly."

The girl eyed Maureen nervously and the two of them joined each other at the kitchen door, looking unsure what to do next.

"Stop looking so put upon. Nobody is going to shoot you!"

"Yes, Ma'am," they said in unison.

Mary Ellen smiled inwardly at the girls' discomfort. Mother was so capable at intimidation. No wonder she never found anyone to love her.

Fourteen

Elisabeth sipped a glass of water. Mary Ellen sulked, twirling her brandy snifter. The girl never had any sense of responsibility nor cared for anyone but herself. Of course, she loved Jim. Jim fondled the girl incessantly. It disgusted her, but rather Mary Ellen than herself. She wished Ledger would return so they could get on with their business. She wanted to get back to Albany, to the security of her real home and protecting her granddaughters. The thought brought a smile to her face. Little Hooligans. Her father would have adored them.

"All set, Elisabeth. We can retire to the sitting room for after-dinner drinks and I'll explain the next plan of action," Ledger said as he entered the room.

Mary Ellen jumped up from her chair so quickly it rocked behind her. "I'm going to my room. I may join you later," she said stumbling from the dining room.

Ledger chuckled. "I don't think we have to worry about her tonight. She may have something to soothe her nerves in her room. It's too bad you believe she needs to be with us."

"You don't know my plan, Ledger. Where is Evans?"

Ledger pulled back her chair and helped her up. "I've explained things to him. He'll ask the women if they want to accompany us to Brooklyn or if they'd prefer to go home. He assures me he can find replacements."

"Brooklyn?"

"If someone really is looking for you, we need to relocate. We agreed."

"I suppose we did. So wearying."

He took her arm and escorted her to the living room. The new arrivals sat on the sofa, hats in hands. They stood as soon as Elisabeth entered. She waved them back to their seats.

"These two gentlemen have worked as my agents and secured new housing arrangement for us," Ledger explained. "We'll leave here at four in the morning. Miss Mary Ellen should be too sound asleep to object and anyone searching for her will not expect us to depart before dawn."

"You're very intuitive, Ledger. I thank you for your diligence."

He smiled. "I find my life as it is quite comfortable and don't want it disturbed unnecessarily. It won't be long before we'll be returned to the security of our routines."

"We promised the girls we'd take them to the south of France this summer," she reminded him.

"We shall. We shall. So, gentlemen, you are welcome to remain here until the witching hour or go on about your business and meet us at the location in Brooklyn at, say six o'clock? You will make sure the appropriate persons are present for the legal exchanges?"

Both men stood. The taller, a man who looked like a banker, not a person involved in intrigue, spoke. "It will be above board and legal. The owners are pleased you will be the purchaser, sir." He and Ledger shook hands.

"My pleasure, I'm sure. I like life's little twists of irony - the humor of the universe." Ledger smiled.

The two strangers exchanged glances, donned their caps and left.

"You're being mysterious, Ledger. What are you buying? Not one of those beautiful old Brooklyn houses near the water? We don't need another house." Elisabeth replaced the men on the sofa, stretched her legs out and reclined against the pillows. "I'll rest here until it's time to go. Will you have the girls pack our things?"

"I can do that, my dear, but you may want to change into more comfortable traveling clothes first." He lifted the lid from a humidor on the mantle, something she hadn't noticed before, and selected a cigar.

She watched him with annoyance as he took the time to sniff it, tap it, roll it in his fingers and then pull out a cutter to snip off the end before lighting the damned thing. Throwing her legs to the floor, she stood, swished her skirts, and headed for her room. Travel clothes. Her black wrap with the long cape would do. She didn't understand why she would have to change only to move from one house in Manhattan to another in Brooklyn, but over the years she'd learned to trust Ledger, even when she had no idea what he was up to. It was Ledger who'd helped build her father's fortune by investing in the stock markets, real estate, cash and gold so her grandchildren's grandchildren would never have to give a thought to money. And someday she might return to Ireland to see the thatched cottage where Father grew up.

As she changed, she considered her reasons why she'd never made the trip. As soon as she stepped off the boat, she would be inundated with poor relatives wanting to hang on to her skirts and suck the life out of her. Maybe someday she'd set up an anonymous fund for them, enough to keep them in food, but not enough to make them feel entitled to anything more. Yes, two hundred dollars a year to ten or fifteen of them wouldn't hurt her accounts. And they'd be grateful to their rich American cousin. Satisfied with her decision, she stored it away. She would ask Ledger to implement the program once she was finished with Justin Pembroke.

The girl, Maureen, bustled about the room filling her steamer trunk and carpetbag with her clothes and other personal items. "Evans asked that we attend you while you're in Brooklyn for a few more days, Ma'am. I don't mind, but I'd like to send a message to my people so they won't worry."

"Tell Ledger. He'll deal with that," Elisabeth snapped. "Hook this for me." She turned her back to the girl and waited for her to figure out what she wanted hooked. Secured in her corset, she pulled on a fresh blouse and continued changing, tossing aside the soiled clothing for Maureen to pick up.

When she'd changed, Elisabeth returned to the living room and settled herself on the chaise while the servants dealt with packing and preparing for the middle-of-the-night departure. She managed to doze so when Ledger shook her gently a few hours later, she awoke somewhat refreshed, though it took her a moment to remember what they were about to do. "Ah. Brooklyn," she said. "Via the new bridge?"

"*Certainmente,*" he replied while twirling her cape before settling it on her shoulders. "Once everyone is safely ensconced, I shall have our gentlemen bring Miss Mary Ellen to the coach."

And so, in the darkness, minus young Fiona, who'd insisted she had to be at home evenings, the entire household including the two Pinkertons and the two agents rode off to Brooklyn.

Covering her mouth as she yawned, Elisabeth pulled back the window curtain to see a faint glow in the distance – the sun about to rise. The start of a new day.

She heard seagulls and smelled the scent of salt water. Peering around the dark interior of the large carriage, she noted everyone else was either asleep or pretending to be. Ledger was the exception. He regarded her as she wriggled in her seat, trying to ease the aches of the long, confined ride. "The sea?" she asked.

He smiled and held a finger to his lips. "Not quite," he whispered.

Fifteen

Barbara covered her face with her forearm, trying to avoid the daylight streaming through the hotel window. They had left it open last night to get some air into the stuffy room. While small as the bedroom she shared with Lily at home, this hotel room was not nearly as pleasant. She should have insisted on something more elegant rather than agree to a hotel close to the apartment.

"It's morning, Miss," Annie said from the other bed. "We might as well get up and get washed. If you like, I'll go first."

"By all means," Barbara groaned. "Just don't use all the hot water."

"I don't believe that would be possible."

Barbara kept her eyes shut and listened while Annie rustled through her things and left for the bathroom to prepare for the day. First, they eat breakfast downstairs and then cross through the park to Grandmother's, then they would have a better idea of what was going on. Good of Annie to waken early and want to get up. Lily would never have agreed to arise with the sun. She tossed the light sheet aside and sat up. Stuffy though the room was, there was still the tingle of excitement of being on her own again, much like when they'd been abandoned by their mother as young girls. After Seamus left, life had become chaotic but far more interesting and fun.

Without him around she could play with the Gypsy girls and boys and no one bothered. Lily was a two-year-old when he left, or died, depending on who told the story, and so became her responsibility when Mother went away with one of her beaus.

Barbara stretched, yawned and leapt to her feet. "Don't take forever in there, Annie. I'm anxious to get to Grandmother's!"

"I know, Miss. I'm used to washing in a hurry, just not used to the luxury of the hot water ready and waiting for me. I'll only be another minute," she called from the bathroom.

By seven-thirty the two of them were dressed. While Barbara took the elevator to the main floor, Annie insisted on taking the stairs. They met in the lobby and, guided by a bell hop, went in search of breakfast. Palm plants decorated the corners of the room. Waiters moved silently amongst those already seated, mostly businessmen hidden behind newspapers drinking coffee.

"What would you like, Annie?" Barbara offered the girl.

"What are my choices?"

Barbara passed her the menu.

"I told you, Miss, I don't know how to read." She handed the board back to Barbara.

"Eggs Benedict! How's that? It's French bread toasted with ham, poached eggs, and Hollandaise sauce. It was invented by Benedictine monks. I've never had quite such a combination of food for breakfast. What about it?"

"What about fresh fruit with porridge?" Annie asked. "I don't know about Holland sauce."

"Hollandaise. It's lovely. Mrs. Burch makes it for asparagus and fish sometimes."

"We could have fresh fruit, if they have it, and also a poached egg on the French bread."

"And orange juice. It's the season."

"Good. Orange juice. I don't know as how Mrs. Burch is going to like me running about with you, acting as your personal maid and eating with you and all this." Annie looked around the intimate dining room as if Mrs. Burch might be one of the people hiding behind the papers.

"We'll take care of her later. I'd be more worried about Grandmother when she learns I've decided to take my place as a woman in the family and no longer a child to be told what to do every waking moment." Barbara laid the menu to one side and a waiter immediately appeared.

After giving their order they spent time speculating on what condition they might find her Grandmother in once they arrived at the apartment.

With the meal finished, they returned to their room to freshen up, gather the things they'd need for the day and then headed for the apartment. The air outdoors was still chilly and fresh as they strode purposefully through Central Park to the exit nearest the building.

As usual, a doorman stood under the canopy. Being June, the flower boxes overflowed with brilliant-colored pansies and geraniums with ivy trailing over the sides. The windows were shut tight behind ornate wrought iron balconies.

They walked up the short, curved drive to greet the doorman.

"We're here to see my Grandmother, Mrs. Riis," Barbara announced.

"I'm sorry, Miss. Mrs. Riis is not in residence," he said.

"Of course she is. She was here yesterday. Wasn't she, Annie?"

Annie nodded.

"I'm sorry. I was informed when I came on duty at seven that the Riis party has departed."

"Let me in so I can see for myself."

He moved to block her way. "I can't do that, Miss. I'm sorry and don't mean any offense, but I don't know you and am not permitted to allow entrance to anyone unexpected."

"How ridiculous," she fumed as she poked in her handbag to find a calling card. "Here. My name is Barbara Riis. I am her granddaughter."

"Them Pinkertons warned us people might come snooping pretending to be family members. There is no message to expect anyone, Miss. I'm sorry. I hope you didn't have a long trip."

"From Albany," Barbara said trying to stare a hole through his forehead.

"Always wanted to see Albany. State capitol, you know." He tipped his cap, dismissing them.

She grabbed Annie's wrist and nearly dragged her down the drive to the sidewalk. "All right," she huffed. "Back to the hotel. We'll send a telegram to Mrs. Burch to see if they've gone home and our trip was for naught."

"Not all the way back up to our room? That's a long climb," Annie complained.

"It wouldn't be if you'd come with me in the elevator."

"I'll wait for you downstairs, if it's all the same to you."

"We'll keep our room for two more nights in case we don't receive a reply right away. Come on. It's an adventure, remember?" she said, more to remind herself than Annie.

In the lobby, Barbara penciled a brief message for the concierge to send as a telegram to Mrs. Burch.

> *ANNIE AND I SAFE STOP*
> *NOTIFY HER FAMILY STOP*
> *HERE FOR THREE DAYS*
> *AWAITING YOUR REPLY*
> *STOP NO GRANDMOTHER*
> *HERE STOP PLEASE ADVISE*
> *BY RETURN MESSAGE STOP*
> *BARBARA RIIS STOP*

"That should elicit some sort of response. I also asked her to let your family know you're all right. So, shall we spend the day shopping? Maybe we can find you a book that shows you how to read. That is, if you want to learn to read." Barbara handed the message to the clerk and passed over the appropriate number of coins.

"It would be nice. I hear people talking about what they read all the time. My brothers read. Anthony, the priest, even reads and speaks in Latin. We don't see him often."

"If you don't need anything from the room, I'll go up and clean my teeth and fix my hair more securely for the day. You can wait over there in the lounge."

As the elevator slowly rose toward the fifth floor, Barbara thought about what the doorman had said. "Pinkertons." They were detectives and investigators. Why would Pinkertons be talking to their doorman about Grandmother? One more missing piece to the puzzle. Surely, Pinkertons would have nothing to do with Grandmother's health. Still, maybe she did want complete privacy if she was ill. Perhaps they worked as bodyguards as well. She'd have to ask.

Sixteen

The coach came to a stop. By now, it was clear to Elisabeth they were at a marina where several sailboats, yachts and other seagoing vessels stood along piers. Leave it to Ledger to come up with the idea of a boat to use as a hide-out. They had sailed on a yacht out of Monaco years ago and she recalled it as a luxurious affair. This would be a refreshing change of pace for everyone. Maybe the sea air would help Mary Ellen.

The coachman opened the door and Ledger jumped out, turning to hold out his hand for Elisabeth. The coachman scowled at the intrusion into his job but stepped aside. Evans and Maureen had been riding in the back. They dismounted and waited to one side for orders. One bodyguard exited and then the other, with much grunting and huffing, emerged with Mary Ellen slung over his shoulder. Elisabeth did not want to know how they had kept her so sound asleep through everything.

She breathed in the fresh morning air, suddenly feeling much younger, more like a girl waiting for the day to begin, for her father to bring out a surprise.

Ledger said, "Come along."

They followed him in single file along a wooden pier still damp with morning dew. Evans and Maureen carried their personal items, but nothing else. Ledger had told them everything would be taken care of.

As the sun broke the horizon, Elisabeth shielded her eyes against the glare. Water lapped at the edges of the pilings, seagulls called to one another, boat beams creaked in the morning swells.

"Which one is it?" she asked.

"Right at the end of the slip."

Straight ahead the silhouette of a three-masted yacht filled her vision. "My heart," she gasped. "That can't be. It's – it's huge. What kind of a boat is this?"

"Seaworthy and expensive, but don't worry, we can afford it. It's probably the most famous steam yacht in the world. Only came up for sale recently. I had my agents arrange the purchase through my private corporation with you and I as co-owners. We'll be signing the paperwork later today."

"A steam yacht?" she asked. She had stopped walking, holding up the rest of the party as she gaped at the massive boat.

"A ship to be sure. One stipulation in the purchase is we must rename her. I have chosen the Armbruster Legend. What do you think of that?" He turned to her proudly, a broad smile on his face.

"Armbruster Legend. Nice." How could she not let him name it whatever pleased him? "You couldn't have added an Ackert in there someplace in honor of my father?"

"If you recall, we are going into hiding for a little while. Your name on a famous yacht would hardly be hiding, would it? If it's still so important to you later, we can make other arrangements. Now come along and let me introduce you to your new home."

As they approached the ship, a crew assembled on deck. The captain stood tall, slender, and handsome in his crisp white uniform awaiting their arrival.

Ledger approached first and asked permission to come aboard. The captain saluted him and then held out a hand in greeting. Ledger took it.

"Welcome aboard, Sir," the captain said.

Elisabeth nudged him from behind. "It's our boat, Ledger, you don't have to ask anyone's permission."

He turned and smiled then spoke softly through his teeth. "Yes, we do. I'll give you guidance on certain shipboard customs, traditions and etiquette later. Meanwhile, follow my lead."

Feeling chastised, she stepped aboard with the assistance of the captain and a mate. The others followed. The captain introduced himself as Jonathan Alter, "Serving at your pleasure, Madam." Using a clipboard passed to him by the first mate, he explained the location of their staterooms. When he reached Mary Ellen's name, he cleared his throat as if what he was about to say was distasteful. "Miss Mary Ellen Riis, is placed in an interior steward's room below."

Ledger assured her, "We have three nurses coming aboard later in the day to care for her. There will be no drink, no drugs, no refuge for her here. By the time we are in Albany, she will be a daughter in whom you will take pride."

Elisabeth eyed him skeptically. "Thank you, Ledger. You do think of everything. Did you think of our money when you made this purchase? How much is it costing us in daily operating expenses? All this crew can't be cheap."

"The engine room men receive thirty-five dolars a month, uniforms and food. Most of them have been with the ship on its round the world cruise and know her better than any novice, less expensive crew, would. The rest are paid according to their ratings. You don't have to worry about running out of money. You won't. Now, look toward the stern." He pointed her toward the rear of the ship.

"She measures two-hundred-thirty-two feet overall, has a thirty-two feet beam and fourteen feet draught."

"What about living quarters?" Elisabeth asked, uninterested in the measurements of a boat.

"You should know it's built of steel throughout and has refrigeration, a complete electric plant and distilling machines." He held up a hand to an anticipated protest. "And I think you'll find there are an abundance of luxurious living rooms, state rooms, furnished to the meet the tastes of the most esteemed monarch. You need never be ashamed of inviting anyone aboard."

"Humph. Who would I invite aboard? Mrs. Burch and my granddaughters? Show me to my rooms."

"May I, Madam?" Captain Alter removed his hat to reveal a full head of sun-bleached hair. His tan face had the lines of a seafaring man, a handsome, sturdy man. He held out his arm.

"Once you are refreshed, we'll dine in the main dining room and then we can go ashore to purchase items we'll need for the next stage of our journey," Ledger said to her as she allowed herself to be led away by the captain.

It had been a long time since a man besides Ledger had escorted her anywhere. It felt nice.

"She carries nearly eleven thousand square feet of canvas," Ledger was explaining to the Pinkerton as she and Captain Alter stepped into the interior of the boat.

"We refer to her as a ship, Madam," the captain explained.

She took a deep breath. "It smells new. And what beautiful woodwork!"

"She was built in eighteen ninety-six but refurbished after her last voyage. That was a two-year jaunt around the world. The lady who owned the yacht was quite a sportswoman. We've been to nearly every port open to us in the world including China and Japan."

She heard the pride in his voice and was pleased for him while at the same time disappointed. "I'm afraid our adventures won't be taking us very far. Albany soon. And then perhaps Cannes."

"That suits me find, Madam, and if you'd like to keep me on as captain, I'll be delighted to take this ship anywhere and anytime you'd like to go."

As long as my money holds out, you mean. She smiled. "Thank you."

He left her at the cabin door, after opening it and stepping aside for her to enter. Ledger was right, any caliph, queen or emperor could enter this room and feel at home. A large parlor filled with velvet covered sofas and chairs, on vibrant Turkish carpets, surrounded by damask lined walls covered in fine artwork made her smile. As she entered the room, other details came into play. Ivory and gold figurines standing in little corrals, lest they slide off during a voyage, she supposed, stood on mantles and marble table. Heavy brocade draperies stood closed, but the room was alive with light from an electric chandelier hanging in the center of the ceiling. She grinned in secret delight as she leaned against the outer door and shut the world out. Crossing the carpet to a pair of gilded double doors, she opened them into a bedroom beyond her dreams.

With all their wealth, Father had never indulged in a single extravagance. Ledger had often tugged her along the road to fine things by encouraging her to purchase finer linens and silks for her and her daughter's clothing and sending the girls to private schools, but even he had never shown her anything like this.

A four-poster bed dominated the room. Gold framed seascapes covered the pale blue silk walls. Gold bed curtains dotted with small blue *fleur de lis* stood tied back to the bedposts. Only the slight sway of the chandelier indicated the room wasn't in the middle of a European castle. She ran to another door and found a luxurious bathroom with marble floors and gold fixtures. She pressed the light switches several times over, enjoying the control of turning lights on and off at will.

A knock on the outer door sent her back into the living room. "Enter," she called.

Ledger stepped into the room, beaming, proud of his achievement.

"This is beyond belief, Ledger. How did you ever think of it? Have you been planning this for a long time? Why didn't you say anything before? Come. Sit down. Do we have food on this boat? I mean, ship?"

"Cook's not aboard, yet. We've decided to eat at a restaurant before our meeting with the attorney's and owners. Are you sure you're all right with this purchase? Money is not the slightest problem here, Elisabeth, only your pleasure concerns me."

"Ledger, I'm touched." She reached out and placed her bare hand on his cheek. "If you did this for me, it is the most wonderful surprise of my life. And even if you did it for Mary Ellen, it's still for me, isn't it?"

His eyes lowered briefly before he replied. "Mary Ellen and Senator Pembroke are incidental to this purchase but it does turn out to be fortuitous. Now, let's go ashore, eat and make this yacht officially the Armbruster Legend."

"Why that name?"

"Using my British first name with the word Legend?" He tilted his chin, his eyes taking on a distant look. "One day this famous yacht will be sold again and someone will say, 'Who was Armbruster Legend?' The history will be available. The story of a small African slave who became a white family's pet for many years, but also educated himself and learned the ways of the world. He chose to spend his years in the pseudo service of a kindly white woman whom he worshipped from afar until his dying days. His entire goal in life was to remove troubles and cares from hers. For the most part he succeeded."

"Very romantic story, Ledger. Armbruster. How long since that name's been spoken," she said with a sigh. "I like your story, Ledger. Write it that way. You can leave out the part about Senator Pembroke and the misbegotten daughter. But you can add that the white woman also admired, respected, and loved him."

"Miss Mary Ellen is not misbegotten. She was a good girl with plenty of spunk and love to give. We'll find her again. Now, let's go." He stood and held out his hand for her.

Seventeen

Mary Ellen's eyes opened to dimness. Four walls surrounded her. No windows. The room felt as if it were rolling. She'd read about earthquakes. She might be in the middle of an earthquake. Her stomach threatened to heave, but without enough energy to move her arms and legs, she simply moaned and rolled over on a soft mattress. A cover settled over her upper body. A voice said, "Rest, dear."

The next time she opened her eyes, the room was a little brighter, but in a dark corner she saw the little Chinaman sitting with his fan cooling his ever-smiling face.

"I need a privy," she groaned.

Hands helped her to her feet while the Chinaman smiled. Someone raised her nightgown for her and set her on a porcelain toilet seat. When she finished relieving herself, the same hands passed her sheer paper and the voice from earlier said, "Clean yourself."

Like an obedient child, she followed orders and then the voice with the hands, wiped her brow with a cool damp cloth and led her back to her bed. "Rest."

The Chinaman had left his post. She closed her eyes. The room moved more now reminding her of what a cradle might feel like. The secure feeling lulled her into a deep, dreamless sleep.

Something crawled on her arm. She brushed it aside, but it returned instantly. A second one inched along the back of the hand that tried to remove the first one. She scratched at an itch on her neck, opening her eyes to see what was on her.

A large cockroach crawled across the bodice of her nightgown. She let out a shriek and brushed at it. The bug resisted and was joined by two others, three others, a swarm! Flailing her arms, Mary Ellen rolled from her bed, screaming.

"Get them off me. Help! Get them off me!" Rolling into a ball on the carpeted floor, she covered her head with both her hands and continued to scream.

Hands reached around her middle and pulled her upright, sending spasms of paralyzing terror through her body. "Make them go away," she screeched, but no one listened. The bugs swarmed over her head and face which now dripped with blood combined with her tears. Someone held her ankles.

Running water filled her ears along with voices. "Make it cold." "Get the gown off her." "No time. Get her into the shower quickly!"

Her feet landed on cold tile as icy cold water splashed over her body. She leaned against a slick, wet wall and then let her body slide to the floor while hands guided her downward slump. The bugs started to fade, to fall, to spiral down the drain below.

Huddled on the shower floor, soaking in her nightgown, Mary Ellen began to sob. "Help me. Somebody help me."

Her body shivered uncontrollably while two women pulled the wet gown from her body and began to towel her dry, rubbing vigorously in an effort to warm her. "You'll be all right now, dear."

"I'm sending Martha for soup. Let's dress in our nice clean gown and get back into bed. Come look. Martha's put fresh sheets on it for you. Doesn't that look comfy and cozy?"

Mary Ellen stumbled, feeling like a toddler as she allowed the stranger to lead her back to the bedroom. The bed did look comforting and welcoming. She wanted nothing more than to crawl back into it for an eternity of sleep—of nothingness.

"That's good. Yes. I want to sleep more. Can you keep those bugs away? Please, can you?" she begged, holding desperately onto the wrists of her caretaker.

"They'll be gone before you know it, my love. Let me fluff these pillows and tuck you in."

For the first time since waking, Mary Ellen focused on the woman who helped her. She appeared to be in her mid to late thirties, wore a white dress fitted at the waist with a large white apron covering it. On her head she wore a lace trimmed white cap.

"You aren't one of the maids," she said to the woman. "Who are you?"

"Constance Keating. I'm here to nurse you back to health. Martha Abbott works with me. You follow our instructions for a while and soon you'll be good as new."

Now perspiration formed on Mary Ellen's brow. "I'm ill? What happened? I remember Mother came to visit and wanted to kidnap me. She and Ledger wanted to take me back to Albany. Where am I? What is this room? Why does it move? Am I imagining that like the bugs?"

"No, dear. No one is kidnapping you and yes, you have been ill. For many years. But now you will be better than ever. Relax. Your soup will be here shortly. You can have that and some tea if you like with a little sugar. Later we can give you some soft foods." The woman finished her ministrations and returned to a chair near the bed.

"And the room?" Mary Ellen asked suspiciously, as she regarded the distance from the bed to the door.

"We're on a ship. But don't worry. We're not going anyplace. It's been storming for two days." She picked up knitting from the floor and began working on something green.

When the soup arrived, Mary Ellen discovered she was hungry and found herself quickly swallowing the clear consommé and then two cups of tea. The liquids refreshed her somewhat and she leaned back against her pillows, relaxed, prepared to learn more from the two women who hovered over her better than a couple of mother hens.

She didn't tell them about the Chinaman who had lurked in the dark corner. He must have taken a walk outside. Maybe he went to find something to refill her pipe.

Her breaths quickened at the thought of a fresh supply of opium and she smiled. "He'll be here soon, won't he?"

"Of course, dear," Constance answered. Martha nodded.

Constance knit while Martha read. Mary Ellen tapped her fingers on the counterpane. "Could we play a game of checkers?"

Martha set her book on a table. "I can see if we have a game if that's what you'd like."

"No. Checkers are boring. What about Canasta? Can we play cards?" Mary Ellen shifted in the bed, trying to ease a kink in her neck. "Can't we do anything besides sit here and stare at one another?" she barked.

Martha and Constance both jumped and turned their attention to Mary Ellen.

"I didn't mean to shout," she said, holding her hands out in apology. "I won't do it again. Just don't hit me."

"No one is going to strike you. Why don't you try to sleep some more?" Martha said.

"I'll do that," Mary Ellen answered as she snuggled down into the covers and sniffed the fragrance of the freshly aired sheets. "I'll sleep well here."

And she tried. She shut her eyes as the ladies turned down the lights and removed themselves to a far corner of the room where they could sit under a lamp to continue their work.

Her breath came in shudders. "A little cognac wouldn't come amiss right now," she sang out.

"Go to sleep. There's a good girl."

"The Chinaman will be back. He'll take care of me," she said in half a whisper, hoping she believed what she said.

She awoke drowning in a pool of her own perspiration. Her hair hung in damp strands around her neck and shoulders, suffocating her, strangling her. In a frantic burst of energy she threw aside her covers and pulled off her nightgown. Two women grinned like skeletal remains from one corner of the room while the Chinaman continued to fan himself and smile in the other. Her body longed for the Chinaman's soothing pipe. Rolling onto her stomach she slithered from the bed and crawled across the carpet but before she could reach him, the women stopped her and forced her once again into the unrelentingly cold shower. The water did nothing to soothe her; she needed her pipe. If they didn't provide one soon, she knew she would die. Life became simple for her. Pipe – live; no pipe – die. A high pitched voiced keened. Her voice. The Chinaman grinned at her from the ceiling of the shower, his face distorted by the running water.

Eighteen

"Barbara, if it rains one more day, I'm finding my own way home. How can you stand being stuck in here day after day?" Annie complained on the second day of the heavy rains.

"I'm quite enjoying the freedom and so should you. Look how much has changed in the last few days."

"What? We can't find your grandmother and Mrs. Burch is angry with us. She can't fire you, but she can fire me, and then what will my mam and pa say?" Annie stirred three teaspoons of sugar into her tea, clanging of her spoon against the cup.

"They'd tell you to appreciate what you've received. You look adorable with those spectacles and imagine how proud they'll be to find out you're learning to read." Barbara took pride in her discovery that Annie was nearly blind. Using her letter of credit, she'd gone to a bank and taken out enough cash to carry them through at least another week in the city, including shopping excursions. She first bought Annie the spectacles at an optometrist's office and then they found a bookstore where there were plenty of simple readers from which Annie could learn.

Annie proved a quick study, absorbing letters and then words as fast as Barbara had when a small child. She found Annie refreshing compared to her little sister, Lily, who resented reading or any form of learning. Lily made a good follower, but never a good intellectual companion.

"I'm going to finish my coffee and then we shall decide what to do today," she told Annie. "You can practice your letters until then."

Annie tossed her napkin onto the table and rose. "I'll go see to our laundry, if you don't mind, Miss. I still have to earn my keep."

Barbara laughed. "All right. I know. This afternoon, after lunch, if it's not pouring too hard, we can go have two dresses made for you."

"You've already bought me enough personal linens to suit a wealthy bride. I have three dresses plus the nice beige one you gave me. Why do I need more?"

"Because I enjoy your company and if you're going to be seen with me, you ought to have stylish clothes. Personal maids do, you know." Barbara wasn't exactly sure what personal maids wore but figured that would appease Annie. "I insist."

"You insist. All right, Miss. But I'm telling you, we need to buy you something special as well. Do you see how them men in here ogle you in the mornings and at dinner? With your fair skin and dark hair, you'd be a real beauty in a brilliant turquoise dress. Or maybe red!"

"Perhaps not red," Barbara said, smiling at the girl's enthusiasm. "So, now you're an artist."

"Oh, no. I like to look at fine ladies' fashions and imagine someday I could even wear such things. I confessed it to my brother one time and he told me to stop thinking above my station. He made me say so many rosaries I lost count!"

"You're not supposed to tell what your penance is, Annie! It's a sin."

Annie flapped a hand in the air. "Not when the priest is your brother; it doesn't count then."

"All right. Go do what you have to do with the laundry."

Annie stood and then leaned in to speak quietly to Barbara. "I do have to confess to enjoying having someone else make up our rooms, even changing the bed linens every day. I'll be so spoiled by the time we get back to Albany, you won't be able to stand having me around you. But I promise to learn how to do your hair and help you dress."

Barbara reached out a hand to Annie. "You might even begin designing some of my fall wardrobe."

"Go on. You never had no spring and fall wardrobes. I've seen your clothes."

"You haven't seen me since I've decided to become my own woman. I might even call myself Edna for a while until I get used to the idea of thinking."

"Who's Edna?"

"Never mind."

Annie headed out of the breakfast room and turned toward the stairs. Someday, Barbara thought, she might get over her fear of the elevator; meanwhile she would trudge up every single flight of stairs no matter how tired she got or how long it took.

Now alone, she returned her attention to the newspaper. On an inside page she found an article about a steam yacht that had changed owners two days ago. The previous owner, a wealthy sportswoman, had decided to sell it. The sale was remarkable because the price of it made it one of the most important yacht sales ever. The purchaser was a representative of an anonymous corporation, a Mr. Armbruster Slade. An odd name, she thought, though it sounded vaguely familiar. The article did not say how the company earned its money, but whatever it was, it apparently had no trouble meeting the asking price. The only stipulation of the sale of note was the new owner had to change the name. It would now be known as the Armbruster Legend. The reporter could only state that the purchasing agent was a Negro man of British nationality. She

115

reread the item several times searching for more clues, while the suspicion grew stronger with each reading. Armbruster Slade, a British Negro of some wealth. Could it be Ledger? He always said he had independent means and worked for Grandmother because she made life easy for him. As a purported long-time employee, he wasn't subject to the prejudices of the white people in Albany who resented the Negros, especially the Irish who believed they took away their jobs. She knew he and Grandmother shared some kind of special relationship, not an illegal one between the races, but a kinship of spirit.

Tebo Basin. Where the yacht was docked. Tebo Basin in Brooklyn.

She returned to the front page, sending the information about the yacht into the recesses of her mind for further examination. Senator Justin Pembroke, senior senator from New York, would be attending the Democrat Convention in Kansas City in July.

Slamming the paper down, she picked up her now cold cup of coffee and set it back onto its saucer. "Senator Justin Pembroke," she muttered. He'd only come to her attention a few nights ago and now his name popped up everywhere.

"Is there something wrong, Miss?"

Planning to send the waiter on his way she looked up to see a young businessman looking down on her with some concern. His blue eyes twinkled with humor. His sandy blond hair fought the hair cream that tried to keep its parting in the middle. A full handlebar mustache might have made her laugh, except he did look sincere. How could she laugh at a sincere young man with an overaged mustache? "No. I'm fine. I sadly read the political news and found myself drastically annoyed. Not important."

"But it is! Anything that disturbs such a splendid face should be banned! If you'll excuse me. I saw that your friend

116

has abandoned you and thought I might come and make your acquaintance before I head to my office. I am Alistair Rogers, insurance investigator, at your service." He bowed.

"And I am Barbara Riis of Albany. I'm in New York on my own kind of investigation. I seem to have lost my grandmother."

"How tragic!" He dropped to the seat abandoned by Annie, sitting tentatively on its edge, a bird ready to take flight. "Do you think I can be of assistance?"

"I'm afraid not. She's come here on a secret mission." Barbara relaxed, beginning to enjoy the conversation with the nice looking stranger.

"I'm an investigator." He pointed to himself proudly. "Perhaps we can meet this evening and discuss the matter. Your friend, of course, should join us."

"Annie will be delighted. As will I, if we're still here. Should I learn anything of significance during the day, we may have to leave in a hurry."

"I should be disappointed. However, if it proves to be good news for you, then I'll be pleased. Will you leave me a note at the front desk?" He reached into his waistcoat pocket and pulled out a business card.

"Pinkerton?" she read with surprise. "You look like the least likely Pinkerton I could ever imagine."

His eager expression dropped. He looked crestfallen.

"I'm sorry. I imagined them as bullies who carried guns and looked like gorillas in the circus. You know, thumping their chests." The image of this fellow behaving in that manner made her giggle.

"Some of us use our brains to work things out," he said with injured pride.

"I didn't mean to insult you. Perhaps I can make it up to you by inviting you to join us here for dinner this evening?"

How bold she felt, inviting a stranger to dinner. But it was a public place and Annie would be with them.

"I'd enjoy that," he responded eagerly. "It gets quite lonely here in the city when you don't know anyone."

"I hadn't even thought you might not live here. Of course, you're in the hotel the same as we are. Where is your home?"

"I live in Hartford, Connecticut with my parents, a younger brother and two little sisters. And you?"

"Albany since I was twelve, with my little sister and grandmother. That's my life." She shrugged.

He stood. "I do have to get to the office. I'm in a training program for the rest of this week. I look forward to seeing you this evening and hope you have good news."

Barbara wanted to grab his wrist and force him back onto the chair so she could tell him her thoughts about the yacht, but she reluctantly watched him twirl his umbrella before stepping out into the lobby. Smiling, she promised herself she and Annie would be here for dinner tonight, no matter what happened today.

She had the waiter bring her fresh coffee to the lounge where she picked up a *Saturday Evening Post* and searched first for the humor columns and then glossed over the current events. As she studied a political cartoon, a voice interrupted her.

"Telegram, Miss Riis."

The bellhop handed the folded yellow paper to her. Trying to appear mature, calm and composed, she accepted the telegram, "I'll call you if I have a response, thank you." She ripped open the message and read:

NO WORD STOP COME HOME
STOP MRS BURCH STOP

She crumpled the message and stuffed it into her purse.

Annie found her sitting there a little while later. "It's still pouring cats and dogs. I've brought my books and thought I might work on them this morning. Maybe we can go out after lunch if it clears."

"Mrs. Burch wants us to come home. And only this morning I met the most marvelously bright, handsome intelligent man in the world. He wants to dine with us tonight," Barbara said in a monotone to tease Annie.

"We can't go home. Oh! You mean you've had a message!"

Barbara nodded, waiting for Annie's further reaction, which wasn't long in coming.

"A man? What man?"

"His name is Alistair Rogers. He's an insurance investigator for the Pinkertons and he gave me his card and he lives in Hartford, Connecticut and I asked him to join us for dinner here tonight." Barbara could hardly contain herself with the news. Finally, something really new and different in her life. "Also, I have a feeling I know where Grandmother is. As soon as the weather lets up, we're going to Brooklyn with the hope we're not too late."

Annie dropped down on to an armchair across from her, placing her books on the round table separating them. "If you know she's in Brooklyn, why don't we go there today?"

"Do you really want to go out in such terrible weather? If she's where I think she is, she'll remain in place, too, until the weather lifts."

Annie scowled. "How would you know? Have you become one of those fortune tellers? A Gypsy?" She placed her hands over her head to suggest a turban and then dropped them to the table to "read" a crystal ball.

Barbara laughed at her impertinence. "No, things I remember from my childhood. Pleasure yachts not on a schedule won't go out to sea during storms. Doesn't make sense."

"I see. Your grandmother is on a pleasure yacht with Ledger. What are they doing on this pleasure yacht? Can you see that?" A waiter arrived with the luncheon menu. Annie nodded and held out her hand as naturally as if she had spent her entire life with servants at her beck and call. She glanced at it and then waved him away. "We'll let you know shortly."

"No. I'm afraid I can't explain it, unless it's a special trip they're planning for this summer. They did say we'd go to the South of France again. They know I have fond memories of Cannes, Nice and Antibes. Such quaint and colorful towns. Warm, vibrant colors. Blue skies nearly every day. Friendly people."

Barbara pictured the villa Grandmother usually rented for their holidays, felt the cold tiles on her bare feet, smelled the fresh sea air, and gloried in the warmth of the sun on her face. Grandmother always stuck a parasol over her face after only a few minutes of exposure, because of her extremely pale skin.

"And the food!" Barbara leaned forward, excited to be talking about one of her favorite places in the world. "Fresh seafood. Fresh fruit. Always! The cream is so rich, it's a crime. Yes. That has to be it. A treat for me."

"And Lily?" Annie added, reminding her of her little sister.

"I don't think Lily even remembers. I love her to pieces but she is so vague sometimes. Does she seem that way to you?"

"Miss, I'm still a new lady's maid, not your personal friend. It hasn't been my job to observe you or your sister's behavior so's I could form an opinion about you. She seems a nice little girl who worships you." Annie opened a book, making it look like an admonishment.

Barbara leaned back. "If we do go, as my personal maid, you'd be included. What would you think of that?"

"I think I like my new spectacles and am very pleased to be a member of your staff in whatever capacity, Miss."

"Then for the duration, let's do what Grandmother and Ledger do. When we're away from home, let's be friends." Barbara reached out with her right hand.

Annie stared at the hand, hesitated and then took it with her own right hand. "Just please understand how new this is to me. I'm not smart and educated like Ledger. I'd a thunk you'd want someone more your equal to be your friend."

"I'd have *thought*. No. I like *you*, Annie. So, let's be friends and see what happens."

Nineteen

Elisabeth paced across the front porch of the small hotel she, Ledger and the crew of the Armbruster Legend had been residing in for the past three days. The new servants, Evans and Maureen, were particularly pleased to learn they had no duties until they took their place on board the yacht. They spent their days reading and playing checkers, enjoying every meal and snack. The captain kept them posted, each day assuring them the foul weather couldn't last forever.

The first mate tried to entertain them with stories of the previous owner's adventures in Africa and Asia. He had a tale of excitement when they sailed between Japan and China that left him relieved to have survived, but his stories fell on deaf ears.

On Saturday morning Ledger raced into the lobby, letting the screened door slam behind him. He held up a newspaper so close to Elisabeth's nose she couldn't focus.

After pushing it back, she looked where he pointed. "He's getting serious, Elisabeth. Read it." A fire at their Park Avenue apartment had all but destroyed the building. Fortunately, no one was injured, but the fire, which started in the top apartment kitchen had left the building uninhabitable. Police suspected arson.

Elisabeth's first thought was of her father's portrait in the dining room. She clutched the paper to her chest. "Ledger, you have to go over there and see if anything is salvageable. Please," she begged.

"I'll take one of the guards with me. Hopefully, no one has figured out we are the new owners of the yacht. Few know of our connection, and even fewer know my full name. You remain in the hotel while I'm gone."

"What about Mary Ellen?"

"The nurses will report to you as usual. It sounds like she's coming along well. It isn't going to be finished overnight. She's going to require a lengthy recovery. Be patient."

"The convention is in less than three weeks. We have to be there to confront him," she said, scowling and wishing she could be anyplace in the world except stuck in Brooklyn during an extended summer storm.

"We'll make it to Kansas City on time, don't worry." He paused before dashing up the stairs to his room. "I'll speak with the captain about moving the ship out into the bay and anchoring there until we're ready to leave."

"You also have to notify Mrs. Burch to keep Barbara and Lillian in the house! Oh, Ledger, can you send someone to the house to protect them?"

"I can. I will. The Pinkerton offices are right on 57th Street, not far from your building. We'll stop there and see what arrangements we can make. Don't worry, we will get to him before he can hurt any of us."

In spite of the determination on his face and in his voice, Elisabeth had her doubts.

She carried the crumpled newspaper to a sofa and sat, weariness overwhelming her. She spoke the only thought that came to mind. "The dressmaker is coming this afternoon. I'm having a few things made up for the summer. Oh, Ledger, why can't we just sail abroad and forget everything? I'm frightened of what I've started."

"Keep in mind you didn't start it. He did. Thirty-seven years ago. Please choose some lightweight colorful costumes for the Mediterranean. You look so lovely in pastels." He dared a quick touch on her cheek.

She savored the all too rare human contact, closing her eyes and wishing it could be forever. "I will. And I want something jaunty and seafaring."

"That's my girl."

She heard him descend the porch steps and mount the carriage. The security man doubled as the driver. The horse's hooves clip-clopped down the street, splashing in the puddles. He should return in time for dinner with news of the apartment and father's portrait. No one left the gas on in the apartment, of that she was sure. Hopefully, the vandals had finished their work and wouldn't be waiting for one of them to show up. She knew it was a warning, but could not stop now, as much as she wanted to. She shuddered at the thought.

Mary Ellen had been four days and nights without opium, morphine, or alcohol. Another week and perhaps they could consider her free of the addiction.

She headed inside to see if Captain Alter would want a hand at cards. There was so little to do, she actually looked forward to the visit from the dressmaker.

When Ledger hadn't returned by dinner, she sat with the captain and first mate in the hotel's cozy dining room and shared a meal with them. The food, though edible, was nearly tasteless. Declining dessert, she removed herself once again to the front porch to watch the rain and wait for Ledger's return.

"Mrs. Riis." The captain broke into her reverie. "If you don't mind, I'm taking the crew aboard tonight to begin preparations for departure on Monday morning. The weather ought to be clear by then. We have a great deal to do. The cooks and stewards must see to it the supplies are in order..."

"Do what you have to do. I don't need to be concerned. While you're there, please ask one of the nurses to report to me before ten o'clock. I shall be turning in then." She waved a hand dismissively.

"Ma'am." He saluted smartly, raised his umbrella and headed down the steps. A couple of minutes later, the rest of the crew scrambled from the hotel like rats deserting a ship and scurried toward the marina.

She sighed. Come back, Ledger. Bring good news. Please, bring good news. She watched as the ship appeared to move by magic into the bay. Shortly after nine o'clock the innkeeper's wife came out on the porch in search of her. "Mrs. Riis, there's a telephone call for you. You'd best come quickly."

"A what?"

"Telephone call. We have a telephone at the registration desk. Mr. Ledger is calling for you. Please come."

Never having received a telephone call, Elisabeth had no idea what to expect. She'd avoided having one placed in her home, seeing no need. After being shown how to speak into the mouthpiece and hold the receiver to her ear she shouted. "Hello."

"It's Ledger here, Elisabeth. No need to shout. I can hear you perfectly fine. The house is a loss. A few pieces may be salvageable, but we won't know until it cools enough for us to get up there. The firemen and the police are still there."

"The other tenants? Are they all right?"

"It appears they've moved into the Plaza Hotel. It's not far from here. I wanted you to know I came across an interesting pair of young ladies when I went to the hotel to see to the tenants."

"Stop playing games with me, Ledger. What are you talking about?"

"Your granddaughter, Barbara, is a guest at the hotel."

"Barbara? With Lillian?" Elisabeth looked around the room as if half expecting to see the girls materialize before her.

"No. Annie Clancy is with her."

"Who the hell is Annie Clancy?"

"The cleaning girl. You should know, you approved hiring her."

"The Irish slattern?"

"You forget yourself. You weren't always Mrs. Riis," he said referring to the word *Irish* and ignoring *slattern*, she noticed. "Miss Clancy is looking quite respectable in some fine city clothes. Barbara bought her spectacles and is teaching her to read as befitting a lady's maid."

"Whose lady's maid?" Elisabeth demanded to know.

"Miss Barbara's. She is pleased with herself and so she should be. She's doing a fine job with the girl and in such a short time."

"What are they doing in New York? Why weren't they at the apartment?" As quickly as she said it, Elisabeth grabbed her heart, realizing they could have been killed.

"Barbara was worried about our disappearance. She searched through your powders and lotions and decided you have a bad heart and went to New York for treatment. Not a bad deduction, considering your health lately. As to the apartment, we left strict instructions with the doorman not to let anyone in. Apparently, our security also warned him people might try to trick him into letting them enter."

"And they're staying at that hotel? How are they managing? I don't give the girls any money."

Ledger cleared his throat. "I had provided Barbara with a letter of credit. It was my graduation gift to her. She's been using it for cash and to pay her bills. They're managing nicely. Shall I bring them along to the ship?"

She looked out toward the bay but it was too dark to see the Legend now. Lights twinkled in the distance, which she took to be from the yacht, but she couldn't be sure. Mary Ellen was on the yacht. She didn't want a confrontation yet. "I don't know. I'm not sure."

"She knows you're in the area. It wouldn't seem right to leave her here. Perhaps you'd like to speak to her on the telephone and reassure her it wasn't health concerns that brought you to the city."

"I could. And then I'll order her to return immediately to Albany. Her little sister needs her."

"And you believe she'll obey? There's more I haven't told you. Two men came in search of Mary Ellen in Albany. They spoke to Lillian and Mrs. Burch, who sent them on their way. Barbara saw them again at the apartment when she first arrived, which is why she went straight to the hotel instead of trying to get into the building."

"Men? What men?"

"I can only guess Justin Pembroke's thugs. I have our men on the watch for them. What do you really want me to do with the girls?"

"Barbara and her personal maid. You can't bring them here tonight, there are no more rooms available, we and the crew have … actually, Captain Alter has taken the yacht out into the middle of the bay for safety. I can have two rooms prepared for them. Yes. Bring them here," she relented. "Barbara doesn't have to know about her mother. Bring her and her maid. What do I do now?"

"You might as well get to bed. If we don't come over tonight, we'll be there first thing in the morning. Miss Barbara can verify that I am one of her household servants and I'm sure they'll find a broom closet for me here."

"That's not what I meant. How do I terminate this telephone call?"

"Oh. Hang the receiver on the hook on the side of the mouthpiece. Good night, Elisabeth."

"Good night, Ledger."

After disconnecting, Elisabeth fanned herself with her hands, flustered by this change of circumstances. Barbara and Mary Ellen couldn't see each other for at least another ten days. Preferably after the convention, after her work was done. Then, if Mary Ellen survived, perhaps she could introduce them and explain how she only meant to protect both of them from further pain by pretending Mary Ellen was dead. Surely, Barbara would understand and then be able to explain it to Lillian.

Twenty

Barbara, Annie and Alistair sat in the lounge enjoying after dinner coffee when she saw Ledger heading for the reception desk.

"That's our man, Ledger!" she exclaimed on seeing him. Setting aside her coffee, she jumped to her feet.

"Ledger?" Alistair said. "What an odd name for a Negro."

"Oh, he's not a Negro, he's our friend." She rushed to join Ledger at the counter where the clerk insisted he had no rooms available because of the fire up on Park Avenue.

"Sir, the two parties involved required only four rooms. As this establishment has well over two hundred rooms, I find it difficult to believe..."

"Of course they have a room, Ledger," Barbara said from behind him.

He whirled around.

"Ledger! I do believe you've gone quite white!" she said with glee. "You're surprised to see me?"

"Miss Barbara! Does your grandmother know you're here?"

"Do you know this man, Miss Riis?" the clerk asked.

"Of course, he's my grandmother's accountant. Please find him a room. What have you done with Grandmother?" She took him by the arm and led him into the lounge where she introduced him to an astonished Alistair who stood, looking unsure how to greet him.

129

"Shake hands with my grandmother's oldest friend and acquaintance, Mr. Rogers," she ordered gently.

Annie remained seated with her mouth hanging open. Barbara thought the poor girl expected Ledger to take a whip to her. To put her out of her misery, she explained Annie's presence immediately, adding more to Alistair's confusion about his new-found friend.

The four of them sat around the low table while Ledger explained how they had, indeed, purchased a yacht which would take them up to Albany and then later in the summer, to Europe and elsewhere.

"Your grandmother's health isn't precarious at this point, but the time has come for her to enjoy herself while she still can. I've made it my goal to ensure she has pleasure in her life. Once she accomplishes her immediate goal, we'll be free to travel. You and your sister are, of course, going to be a part of our company. You, too, Annie, if you'd like to see the world."

"I'm learning to read," she announced proudly.

"Hence, the spectacles," he said with a warm smile.

"She was nearly blind," Barbara said. "She's far too intelligent to remain a scullery maid for the rest of her life. I've made her my personal lady's maid. Once she can read and write, we might even send her to school."

"Further education wouldn't hurt you either, young lady," Ledger scolded Barbara. "You need a career, something to do with your life. Unless you have other plans for marriage and children."

"I saw enough of my own mother's marriages. No, thank you."

Alistair cleared his throat. "Perhaps I ought to excuse myself. Tomorrow is Sunday and I like to be up early for church." He stood and held out his hand to Ledger. "It was a pleasure meeting you, sir. And thank you, Miss Barbara, for your company at dinner. You too, Annie. I had a good time. Good night."

"Don't leave now, Alistair." Barbara turned to Ledger. "How big is this yacht? Maybe we could bring Alistair to Albany with us. He can take the train to Hartford from there. Wouldn't that be fun?"

"I won't be free until next Tuesday but thank you all the same.

"It's possible we'll still be here. It depends on the weather, according to the captain. We do have some other time constraints though. I have to check with your grandmother. If you'll excuse me, I'll telephone her and tell her about the building and about your presence here," Ledger said.

Before he could stand, the clerk approached them and handed him a message slip. He opened and read it then slipped it into a pocket. "It seems they've found a space for me. Excuse me while I use the telephone."

"You know, Barbara, I do investigations. Perhaps I can be of some assistance regarding the fire in your apartment. Would you like me to make inquiries?"

She studied the earnest face and wanted so much to remain in his company that she replied, "I'll ask Ledger to put you on the payroll immediately."

"Oh no! I couldn't. I work for Pinkerton. They're paying for my training and a salary and for my room here. Maybe your Mr. Ledger can ask them to assign me to your case. Or I can do my investigating after hours. How would that be?"

"But you heard Ledger, we're going to Brooklyn to stay on a yacht!"

"Do you think your yacht has a telephone?" he asked.

She smiled. "I certainly hope so. Apparently, they paid enough for it, I expect to see an entire carousel and a complete zoo! And if we're still here on Tuesday you can come to

Brooklyn and join us and we'll sail up the Hudson River. It'll be so much fun."

Ledger returned. "Your grandmother orders you back to Albany immediately."

"Don't be silly, Ledger. We'll go with you to the new yacht. You said it's going to Albany, so we wouldn't exactly be disobeying her, would we?"

He threw his hands up. "I told her you'd say something like that. In which case, we ought to turn in so we can get an early start. Good night, Mr. Rogers. It's been a pleasure."

Before they could separate, a page boy arrived at her side and handed her a telegram. "This just arrived, Miss Riis."

"Wait a moment, Alistair." She opened the yellow paper.

> *TELL MRS RIIS OFFICER*
> *RILEY REPORTS TWO MEN*
> *HIRED THUGS OF SENATOR*
> *STOP URGES CAUTION STOP*
> *MRS BURCH*

Twenty One

Mary Ellen opened her eyes to see a round, red-faced woman staring at her. "Who are you?"

"Johanna Lee. I work with Martha and Constance. I have soup with meat, hot tea with sugar and a fresh blueberry tart. Would you like to eat now?"

Mary Ellen rolled her head to one side. A blue-gray wall filled her vision. She turned back to the red-faced woman. "Can you move away a little bit, please? I'm not feeling so good."

"Of course you aren't. You need some nourishment. It's been days since you've eaten any solid food. We're here to help you regain your strength. Shall we sit up?"

Looking down at her body, Mary Ellen realized she was lying in bed. How long had she been there? Pulling her arms up, she pressed on the mattress and tried to push herself upright. The effort failed. She managed to move perhaps barely an inch.

Johanna didn't waste any time. Putting her arms under Mary Ellen, she lifted her up while someone else fluffed pillows behind her. Next thing Mary Ellen knew, she was sitting upright in bed, the sheets tucked tightly under the mattress so she remained held in place. A bed tray appeared before her bearing a bowl of steaming chicken soup with dumplings, an equally hot cup of tea and a tempting blueberry tart with a mound of whipped cream on top. Her mouth watered.

"I am hungry." Mary Ellen picked up the soup spoon and aimed it at the bowl with a trembling hand. The spoon clattered against the bowl. She tried again, but her hand quivered too much for her to be able to spoon up the soup. The spoon dropped again. "I can't."

Johanna picked up the spoon with one hand while she stroked Mary Ellen's brow with the other hand. "Not to worry, dearest. Let Johanna help you. Here you go."

Mary Ellen ate like an obedient child, but after several spoons of soup and only a bite or two of dumpling, nausea threatened to send it all back up. She fell back against the pillows. "I'm finished."

"Not yet, dear. Let's try again." Johanna took her time with Mary Ellen until she managed to down about half the soup. When she could eat no more, Johanna let her slide down in the bed to sleep again.

Mary Ellen dreamed vivid and frightening dreams. She drifted from the depths of the ocean to the lap of a nasty old man who played with her breasts and back to flying with bluebirds over apple orchards.

When she woke again, Martha escorted her to the bathroom where she used the toilet and washed her own face, rubbing the soft cotton cloth over her eyes, her neck and around her body. Martha stood by, arms folded. After the simple cleansing, Mary Ellen returned to the single bed where Constance had changed the sheets and waited for her with a clean nightgown. Without hesitation, Mary Ellen accepted the fresh garment and then slid back into bed.

"I think I'd like some food now," she asked the women. "Can I have something more solid than soup?"

"We're keeping you on a light diet for a few days. Enjoy it. Soon you'll be on your way to complete recovery and then you can eat all you like." Martha looked like a proud mother of a graduating student.

Mary Ellen sighed deeply, enjoying the luxury of feeling hungry, clean and cared for. "One more question."

"Yes?" Constance said.

"Why do I keep thinking the room is moving? I know I haven't had any drugs or alcohol for a while, but I have the sensation that I'm rocking in a cradle when I'm asleep. And movement of the water in my glass."

"We're on a ship," Martha said, "Though we're anchored. The weather has been terrible for the past several days. That would account for the motion of the ship."

"A ship?"

"Well, a yacht. I believe it belongs to either your mother or the man she calls Ledger."

Mary Ellen shook her head. "Leave it to those two to dream up keeping me prisoner on a yacht. I thought they'd come to the city to kidnap me and force me into a hospital. I never suspected they'd create their own hospital. Have I been horrible?"

"Not any worse than any I've worked with. A bit better, I'd say," Martha offered.

Constance leaned forward in her chair near the foot of the bed. "Don't get the idea this is over, Miss. This is a lull between the storms. It's good you're hungry and want to eat. That gives us hope, but drug addiction is never gone from your system or your psyche. After we free you from the physical addiction you're going to be going through some intense mental and emotional rebuilding with other people your mother has arranged to help."

Mary Ellen drew in her breath. These women couldn't be leaving her so soon! "What about you? I see your faces every time I woke up. You can't leave me now."

"We won't. We're here to see you through the entire process."

A knock at the door sent Constance off to retrieve a tray of food from the steward. The soup contained pieces of chicken with carrots and other vegetables, accompanied by a buttered roll, more hot tea with sugar and a small slice of chocolate cake. A more substantial dinner than earlier, though it could have been her breakfast for all she knew. She was hungry enough not to care.

After the first few spoons of soup, Mary Ellen gagged. The chicken pieces felt like hot lumps of coal. Her stomach objected violently to the food. She dropped the spoon, splashing broth onto her bedclothes and nightgown. "I can't. I'm sorry, I thought I was ready. Take it away."

"At least drink the tea. It has plenty of sugar in it. Maybe the tea will stimulate your appetite. You need to eat something," Constance dabbed at the spilled liquid with a napkin.

Mary Ellen pushed the tray away, sending it spilling off the far side of the bed. Constance tried to catch it before the entire contents hit the floor but was too late. After calling stewards for a fresh mattress and clean bedding, she spent the next half hour with Mary Ellen sick in the bathroom, Afterward, she and Martha cleaned Mary Ellen, who no longer resisted.

Constance tucked her back into bed and straightened the covers. Mary Ellen knew she had displeased the nurse, but all she wanted was to open a window for fresh air so she could sleep.

"Why aren't there any windows in this room?" Mary Ellen asked.

"You're in a steward's room on a lower deck in the center of the boat," Constance said.

"Boat. Yacht. Ah, yes. You did tell me a little while ago, didn't you?" She stretched and yawned. "I'm going back to sleep. Go away."

"Yes, Miss. I'll be right here in the room if you need me." Mary Ellen thought that was Martha speaking, but the three nurses became muddled in her mind. Sliding down in the bed, she curled into a fetal position and waited for sleep to return.

It didn't.

Within moments of lying on her side and savoring the smooth, fragrant clean sheets, something stirred in her chest. The feeling ebbed and flowed down to the pit of her stomach, curved around her neck, filtered down her back and returned to her chest. She drew a deep breath and turned onto her other side. Again she needed a deep breath. The feeling became more like an internal itch she couldn't scratch. She flopped onto her back and flung the top sheet off her body. Her nightgown clung like a weighty woolen blanket. Another deep breath and the itching crawled across her shoulder blades, then pushed into her breasts and armpits. Perspiration soaked her nightgown as she gasped for air.

The bugs returned. This time they had little Chinaman faces. They smiled as they emerged through the fabric of her nightgown and crawled relentlessly toward her face, but never quite reaching it. She screamed and clawed at them.

The nurses held her wrists and before she knew what happened, her ankles and wrists were tied down to the bed. She couldn't get away. The nightmare grew worse. Her dry throat burned, her voice failed, hoarse from screaming.

Twenty Two

First thing Sunday morning Annie had their bags packed before Barbara was ready to go downstairs for breakfast. Ledger signaled them from the registration desk to let them know he had already eaten and would be waiting outside with a carriage to transport them to Brooklyn as soon as they were ready.

While the girls waited for their breakfast to be served, Barbara took the time to write a note to Alistair telling him of the telephone number at the hotel where her grandmother was staying and promised to call him as soon as she learned whether they had a telephone on the yacht. The thought of using a telephone made her feel important and cosmopolitan. She told him she looked forward to him joining them on Tuesday. If he did have some free time in the evenings, she would be grateful if he tried to find out more about the fire and the identity of the men who had been to the house in Albany.

They rode through noisy streets cluttered with men and women dressed in church clothes. The journey took them past rows of new brownstone buildings. Bells rang throughout the city. Despite a lack of sunshine and a hazy mist that clung to the streets, the people chattered and greeted each other with great bonhomie. The scenes reminded her of Paris when she was younger. She felt a sudden sense of loss for those days when she and Lily wandered the streets while Mother sailed or rode with her gentleman friends. Strangers bought them treats and kind ladies let them play with their little dogs. Life was fun. After Mother died and Grandmother came to take them away, life became tedious. Study, work, read books, clean rooms. Neither she nor Lily were encouraged to invite friends to their house and soon, other girls stopped inviting them to theirs. She now felt newly independent after making her own decision to come to the city and elevating Annie to be her personal maid. She tossed her head and smiled, imagining she was telling her grandmother she was now an adult and intended to be treated as one.

"What are you doing?" Annie asked.

"Nothing. I'm watching people."

"You're having an argument with yourself. I can tell. Your face keeps changing expression and your head moves about as if in conversation."

"You are an observant little wretch, aren't you?" Barbara laughed to show she meant no ill will. "If you must know, I was having an argument with my grandmother."

"Who won?"

"I don't know. You interrupted. I remembered being in Paris and the pleasant life there." They passed a large stone church where the steps were crowded with people. Small children held their parents' hands while older ones pushed and shoved each other playfully, jockeying for position on the steps. Annie blessed herself as they passed the church.

"I ought to be at mass. It's a sin, you know, not to go the church on Sunday," Annie said, perhaps hoping they would stop the coach for her.

"I think it's all right to skip it when you're traveling, and we're traveling."

Annie turned her head and watched the church disappear as they rolled on along the street. "If you say so. Don't tell my mother, though, just in case."

As Barbara had never met Annie's mother, or even knew where Annie lived, it was easy enough to promise she wouldn't say a word.

The Brooklyn Bridge fascinated her as the horse's metal shoes clanged on the metal gridded surface. People flooded the raised walkways on either side of the bridge. She wondered where they were going.

The carriage moved into an area of single clapboard houses along a waterfront. A light mist turned to rain and soon they had to lower the water-proofed canvas shades to protect themselves from the weather. The interior turned dark and gloomy, though Annie remained cheerful. She decided it was time Barbara knew about her family starting with her oldest brother, the priest.

By the time the horse stopped and Ledger opened the door, Barbara's head was dizzy with the names of brothers and wives of brothers and little children who showed up at the house every Sunday for dinner. "Mam wouldn't have it any other way neither. You'd think we was millionaires the way she puts on the spread every week. I'm thinking my brothers must be providing her some help."

"I'm sure they would. It sounds like a lovely large family. Are you missing them?" It had never occurred to Barbara that Annie might have preferred to be at home with her family.

"I'll see them soon enough. I don't imagine they even notice when someone's not at the table."

Barbara stepped down from the carriage and dashed for the porch. Annie followed quickly while Ledger supervised the unloading of their luggage. Their possessions had increased since they had arrived in the city.

Barbara bit her lower lip and drew a deep breath before pulling open the screened door to the hotel lobby. Ledger had called it a hotel, and it called itself a hotel, but it reminded her more of a guest house, or lodging home. Lamps glowed on small wooden tables in a cozy lounge straight ahead. A large painting of a fully rigged sailing ship hung over the mantle. Red and blue flames glowed in the fireplace.

"There you are!" Grandmother's voice called from her left. "Come in here."

Barbara turned to see her sitting at a table with a cup of coffee in her hand. "Good morning, Grandmother. How are you feeling?" she said, heading directly into the breakfast room, a forced smile on her face.

"Never mind. What are you doing here and why did you bring that girl?" She pointed to Annie standing mute, in the lobby. Ledger's back was to them as he spoke with the woman at reception.

"I brought Annie because I needed a chaperone. You would have disapproved of me traveling alone." Barbara took a seat across from her grandmother without waiting to be invited to sit.

"I disapprove of you traveling at all. You might have sent a telegram informing me of your intentions."

"I didn't know where you were. I feared you were in poor health and were hiding it from us. Besides, you and Ledger needed to know about the men who came to the house. How was I supposed to tell you without trying to find you?"

"Then it strikes me as even more ridiculous that you took a train all the way into the city when you couldn't be sure we were here."

"I knew you were here. The man who returned the carriage told us he'd met you at the train station. Where else would you have gone? I went first to the house on Park Avenue, but the same two men were already there ahead of us. I became frightened and took Annie with me to a hotel."

"You're a foolhardy girl." Grandmother folded her arms; her lips pinched in disapproval.

"Maybe, but I was worried about you. Not that you care!" Suddenly tired of trying to please her grandmother, she stood and stormed from the room bumping into Ledger as he turned from reception. "Sorry. You said there's a boat? Can we see it? Can we go to it?"

"They're in the process of provisioning it for our journey. We can go over tomorrow, but I can certainly show it to you." He took her by the arm and led her to the front porch. Rain continued to fall, though more gently than the past few days. "If you'll look out there, to the middle of the bay you'll see her. We've named her the Armbruster Legend."

She pulled a handkerchief from her handbag and dabbed at her eyes. "It's lovely, Ledger. Very big."

Ledger gave her upper arm a gentle squeeze. "You might like to take a couple of umbrellas and walk with Annie down the street. There are several nautical shops as well as a charming little restaurant with a magazine rack. I'll arrange dinner for us at seven."

Grateful for the opportunity to escape Grandmother's displeasure, she stepped into the lobby to search for Annie when she heard someone coming up the porch steps.

"Good day, Mr. Ledger."

"Doctor."

"I'll have a quick word with Mrs. Riis and then go out to check on our patient."

Her ears tingled. A patient on the boat?

Twenty Three

Mary Ellen leaned against the cold tiles of the shower stall. The nurses rubbed her body vigorously but nothing made the pain in her stomach go away. The hot spray relieved some of the cramps in her arms and legs.

"Go away and let me die by myself?" she moaned as Martha threw a dry towel over her head and began rubbing.

"Doctor will be here shortly and then you'll feel better."

"I don't need a doctor. I need Shu Fen. He can help me." She tried to push the nurse away. In her weakened condition, she was as powerless as an infant.

"Come along. We'll put a nice hot water bottle on your tummy. That'll help until the doctor gets here."

Mary Ellen allowed herself to be helped back to the bed, trying to grasp a thread of reality. Something had happened to her, something she didn't like very much. And now she was sick. If they would only leave her alone, she could feel good again.

After she was settled back in bed, Constance applied a towel-wrapped hot water bottle to her abdomen

"I can't go on like this, you know," Mary Ellen told the nurses. "I don't know what you think you're doing by holding me captive here, but I'm sure there's a law about it and if I can get word out, I'm going..." She knew there was more to the sentence but it slipped away as a new pain gripped her stomach.

She was on her hands and knees in the bed wailing for relief from the pain when she heard a man's voice.

143

"Injection," she heard.

"Hypodermic," Constance said.

"Everything is ready, doctor."

The two nurses forced her to lie on her side. Someone lifted her nightgown exposing her behind and then she felt the sting of a needle. Her last thought was a hope she could sleep forever.

First came the nausea. She retched into an empty bowl, but nothing came out. The spiders and bugs returned. This time they crawled across the ceiling, but now they didn't seem so threatening. She watched them as from a distance, drifting in and out of consciousness, wondering what she might see next. At one point she and Lily played in the Tuilieries in Paris, laughing little girls in a Renoir painting. Then they were hanging on a wall, little girls in pink framed in golden sunshine.

Lily disappeared, replaced by Daddy. Daddy grinning. Daddy holding her. Daddy's foul breath too close to her. And then there was another injection and more sleep, fewer spiders, sweeter dreams. Meadows of mustard in France, seas of poppies in the Middle East and unending skies twinkling with diamonds in Egypt.

Someone wiped her brow. The hot water bottle burned her stomach and she screamed.

"I'm in here," she yelled. "See me. I'm in here. Let me out, please let me out." Her heart raced out of control while the women hovered over her, preventing her from getting up. She wanted to go to the door, to see the world again.

She felt the sting of another injection, not caring about her exposed bare bottom. She threw her arm around the nearest woman, maybe Martha, she thought. "Hold me. Make love to me. Help me," she begged.

Martha pried her hands free and placed them under the covers. Now they kept her too warm. But the cramps were gone. Definitely gone. She didn't have any more stomach pains. She could smile at the dreams. At the blue skies and fresh air. Sleep became a pleasure, a place she didn't want to leave.

And then she didn't dream.

"Breakfast is here!" a cheery voice sang.

Mary Ellen had her arm over her eyes to keep out the light from the lamps. Her sleep had been so deep, she had no idea where she was or who might be bringing her breakfast. Not anyone she knew. Carefully moving her arm so she could peek out without being noticed, she saw a stout, red-faced woman bearing a silver tray with a coffee pot and covered food dishes. Moving her arm further, she watched as someone else pulled down legs on the tray. The woman then turned to Mary Ellen, catching her watching.

"Up you go, my dear. You've slept enough. Doctor says now we feed you a full diet of good nourishing food. Come along. Sit up."

The woman speaking helped her to a sitting position and rearranged her pillows. "There we are. How do we feel now?"

"We feel like we've been sluiced down a sewer and out to sea. I am drained, hungry and bewildered." Her brain tried to catch up with the activity. The simple act of sitting up sent her stomach into another spasm as she eyed the tray set before her.

The nurse, she now recalled her name, Johanna, pulled off the lids like a magician showing off her surprise. Shirred eggs, slices of ham, fresh asparagus, and a basket of rolls with butter and jam accompanied by hot coffee, a full bowl of sugar, a glass of milk and a full glass of water with ice in it were on the tray.

"I'm sure you have plenty of questions. After you've eaten, we can have a nice hot bath."

"I can't," Mary Ellen answered. "Just tea. Hot, hot tea to burn away the pain." She tried to slide back down but the tray was in her way.

Appearing not to hear, the nurse continued. "Doctor will be here to examine us later today. We've notified him that we have responded well to the injections. Now take a bite of the eggs."

Hoping compliance would encourage the woman to remove the revolting tray, Mary Ellen picked up a fork and took a mouthful." The unexpected heat of the food gagged her. She spit it out onto the tray. "What was that? Water! Give me some water."

The nurse picked up the glass from the tray and put it in her hand. "It's what the doctor prescribed. Good nourishing food with lots of cayenne pepper to help rid you of your addictions. Now, eat your food and soon you might be allowed to leave this room."

Mary Ellen drank most of the glass of water at once. "How long have I been here?" She wiped her mouth with the back of her hand. "I'm an adult. This has to be against the law. You can't keep me against my will."

"Today is Wednesday. You've been here five days today. And believe me, if you feel like it's been a long time, I feel as if it's been a month. You've been a naughty girl."

Mary Ellen gaped at the woman. "Naughty? Is that what you call it?" She then laughed, shaking the bed and threatening to spill the food from her tray. Johanna grabbed the edge of the tray and steadied it.

"I'm a naughty girl." Her tongue felt large in her mouth and she wondered if her words were even coming out coherently. "From now I'll be good and I'll go find myself a nice husband. I had one once, did you know? But he's gone now. We have a daughter named Barbara."

"You need to eat more," Martha said and sat back to watch.

There was a knock at the door. From the look exchanged by the nurses, they weren't expecting anyone. Mary Ellen looked toward the door anxious to see who would enter.

Twenty Four

Barbara leaned over the deck railing and watched men bring the last of the supplies for their journey up the Hudson River to Albany. The sun shone for the first time in nearly a week.

"I expect we'll leave tomorrow," Barbara said.

Annie, who stood beside her, mumbled. "Mmm-hmm."

"Are you still sulking about Grandmother?"

"I felt like a small bug. It weren't me who decided to make me a lady's maid or to learn how to read. What's wrong with me learning to read anyway? That's what I want to know."

"Grandmother can be harsh, but you'll see, once she gets over it and hires a new cleaning girl, she'll forget the entire matter."

"I'm scared whenever I see her coming near. If she fires me, where would I go?"

Exhausted with the girl's constant complaints about her grandmother, Barbara thought about firing her herself, but then remembered how much fun they had together while staying in the city with no Grandmother Riis to order them about. She, too, was weary of the constant admonitions and threats. If Grandmother were to be believed, Barbara could be locked in her room for the next twenty-seven years without food or water.

She drew a deep breath. In spite of agreeing with Annie she said, "That's enough, Annie. Grandmother is not going to beat you, she's not going to shoot you, nor is she going to fire you. You work for me now. She is my grandmother and you will show respect. In the end our welfare is in her hands. Is that clear?"

Annie's face turned red. "Yes, Miss. I'm sorry. Say!" she suddenly pointed ahead. "Isn't that your friend, Mr. Rogers?"

Barbara turned her head. It was indeed Alistair Rogers dressed in a brown business suit, hat in hand hurrying along the pier toward the yacht, sidestepping buckets and ropes strewn about. She raised a hand and waved. He used his hat to wave back and then broke into a run, passing Evans moving slowly under his burden of luggage.

By the time Alistair reached the gangplank, both Barbara and Annie stood waiting for him.

"Alistair! I didn't think you'd come. I'm so pleased. Annie, please let Grandmother and Ledger know that Mr. Rogers will be joining us for dinner this evening." She reached out to shake hands with him.

Flushed from the exertion, Alistair wiped his hand on his trousers before taking hers. "I have news for you and your Grandmother. Is there someplace we can speak privately?"

"Of course," she responded, alarmed at the seriousness of his tone. "Come into the lounge."

She led him into the lounge on the main deck, self-conscious about the extravagant luxury surrounding them. They sat on blue silk damask upholstered chairs.

A steward appeared immediately. "May I bring you something, Miss?"

"Iced tea with sugar, please."

"Iced tea?" Alistair said, his eyebrows raised.

"We have electric refrigerators on board. We have ice and cold milk. The food can stay fresh for weeks! It's like an amazing dream. Would you like a little lunch? We've already eaten. The steward can bring you sandwiches or an entire

149

meal. Between Evans and the ship's cook, this is going to be a fattening cruise up the Hudson."

"A sandwich wouldn't go amiss, thank you," Alistair said to the steward.

"Thank you, sir." He left.

"So, what news have you?" Barbara asked once they were alone again.

"Perhaps it ought to wait until your grandmother arrives."

"Oh. I didn't ask Annie to summon her. Let me ring her room." Barbara picked up the telephone on the desk. When there was no response from her grandmother's stateroom, she tried the bridge. She told Elisabeth about Alistair and asked if she would mind coming to the main lounge to meet with them. He had news of interest.

"For someone who never saw a telephone a few days ago, you appear remarkably comfortable with it," Alistair said.

Barbara laughed. "I am also becoming comfortable with this luxury and I've only been on board two days. I don't know why Grandmother never installed a telephone in our house. She mentioned the possibility of putting electricity in the Park Avenue building, but now, since the fire, I don't know what her plans are. She's old fashioned, as you've probably figured out."

"She may be old fashioned, but not so much that you aren't afraid to defy her on occasion."

"True enough. Here come our drinks." She waited until the steward set their drinks and a small plate of lemons on the table between them before speaking again. "Will you be free to travel to Albany with us?"

"I think I ought to. I've had your man bring my luggage aboard. I can then take the train from Albany to Hartford. This tea is good. What a nice drink for a hot day!"

"Thank Ledger. It was his idea."

"What is the meaning of this? Summoning me?" Grandmother said from behind Barbara. She'd entered silently from an interior door at the far end of the lounge.

Barbara and Alistair stood up and waited for her to join them. Once they were seated, Barbara made the introductions.

"She told me about you. You work for the Pinkertons?"

"I do. But I also did a little investigating on my own at Barbara's request. It's important you know that the men Senator Justin Pembroke --"

"Barbara has shown me the telegram."

"Please, if you'll let me explain. Apparently your two granddaughters went to his club one night disguised as maids. They didn't get away with their little game. One of the members realized they were not regular employees and had them followed to your house. He reported to Senator Pembroke that you, Mrs. Riis, had sent your parlor maids to spy on him."

"Parlor maids?"

"He hadn't bothered to note you had granddaughters living with you. He believes a daughter you had is deceased, but he worried about why you sent the spies." Alistair stopped at the rattle of silver on a tray as the steward entered the lounge.

The steward placed a tray laden with small sandwiches, bowls of condiments and fresh strawberries on the table before them. "Shall I bring more for the ladies?"

"Thank you, no." Mrs. Riis waved her hand, dismissing him. "Now, explain yourself, young man. How did you come by this information?"

"When Barbara received the telegram, I went directly to our main office and did a great deal of research. I know something of his background. It wouldn't be polite for me to give you the details, but if I were you, I'd move away from this position as soon as possible. When the fire was set in your apartment, those villains didn't know it was empty. They broke in through the kitchen door and used the gas stove to ignite the flames. I would say you have done something to irritate Senator Pembroke, though for the life of me, I can't imagine what it could be." He leaned back and folded his arms.

Barbara automatically picked up a sandwich while waiting for Grandmother's reaction.

A summer breeze played through the room teasing the ribbons on Grandmother's hat. She sat on the edge of her chair, her face pale but her back ramrod straight. She brushed a pale blue ribbon from her face. "Did you notify the authorities?" she asked.

"I have no viable evidence, madam. Only my suspicions."

Using both hands to push herself up from the chair, Mrs. Riis stood and faced Alistair, who had risen with her. "Thank you for your information, young man. I'll have Ledger take care of your fee. I understand my granddaughter has invited you to join us on our trip upriver. The steward will assign you a suite. I only ask you, like my granddaughter and her friend, follow my rules and remain on this level of the ship. We have a sick crew member below."

Without waiting for a response, Elisabeth left the room. When she was out of earshot they started talking at the same time.

"Sick crew member?" Barbara said.

"Sounds odd to me, too," Alistair said.

Barbara sat down again and helped herself to another of Alistair's sandwiches.

"I meant what I said about leaving here as quickly as possible. I hope your grandmother took me seriously."

"I'm sure she did, but you'll never know what her next move is. Your investigation should have revealed how wealthy she is. Although she has people running the corporations for her, there is no doubt who is in control when it comes to any final say."

Twenty Five

Elisabeth sought out Ledger and found him on the bridge with the captain.

"I'm glad you're both here. We must leave as soon as possible, Captain. Ledger, I need to have a few words with you in private."

Captain Alter saluted and turned to his charts.

"You don't look well. What is it?" Ledger took her by the arm and led her outside along the deck to a pair of deck chairs. "Sit here."

"I only have a minute. I plan to visit Mary Ellen this afternoon. The doctor has reported she's coming along well with his treatment. They tell me fighting this addiction is nasty business."

"Shall I come with you?"

"No." She paused, then looked directly at him. "This is something I have to do by myself. I want Mary Ellen and I able to face the senator together as a united team and if I am to gain her confidence and respect, I need to start now."

Ledger remained silent.

"I want to talk to you about this young man who has appeared in Barbara's life. Did you know he is working for the Pinkerton Agency?"

"He told us, yes." Ledger nodded. "He is in a trainee position."

"He's bright."

"I have that impression. He's also fond of our Barbara."

"That's neither here nor there."

"And she's fond of him," Ledger added.

"He said the fire was deliberately set and it is Senator Pembroke might be trying to kill me. Do you think him capable of such crimes?"

"Possibly. He wants to be president of the most powerful country in the world."

Elisabeth once again thought about the brief acquaintance with Justin Pembroke and how it dramatically changed her life. "Leave me for a few minutes, Ledger. Go check with the nurses to ensure Mary Ellen will be up to receiving me before dinner. Our dinner, not hers. And make sure the young man joins us at our meals. He'll be traveling with us." She gave a wave of her hand, implying she was in no mood for his fawning over her.

Ledger stood, bowed briefly, and left her alone. Within moments a steward appeared with a blanket and pillow. She smiled and made a note to thank Ledger once again. Why couldn't she have ever found a man like him to marry?

At one time I thought I had. Eighteen sixty-four, you were a sixteen-year-old wide-eyed fool. All the other girls knew what he was like and stayed away from him, but not you. You knew better than anyone.

Justin, then a handsome man of twenty-seven, had arrived at her school in Albany to collect his younger sister for their summer break. Elisabeth did not know Caroline Pembroke well, but when Justin entered the building, she dashed to Caroline's side to embrace her and wish her a happy summer, her eyes on the handsome brother.

Justin smiled at her and held out his hand. "How do you do?"

She pulled at her skirt and curtsied. "Sir."

Caroline looked with suspicion at Elisabeth but introduced the two of them anyway. She knew her brother well and had already warned several girls about him. Elisabeth held out her gloved hand; he took it, bowed and kissed it.

She felt heat rush to her face as she looked into his dark green eyes rimmed with the thickest lashes she'd ever seen on a man. He sported a wicked little beard and a thin mustache which gave him the air of a devil.

"Perhaps your friend would like to join us on our picnic, Caroline." He spoke in a deep and delicious voice.

Elisabeth's heart raced. She knew her face had to be red as a beetroot. She waited for Caroline to agree.

"She's not able, Justin. She lives here in town and will be going home shortly." Caroline turned to Elisabeth. "Isn't that right, Beth?"

Astonished at Caroline's rudeness, Elisabeth turned away, planning to leave, but Justin's hand on her arm stopped her.

"Perhaps, Miss Ackert would join us later. I can send my carriage if you think your parents would approve?" His smile melted her heart.

"Yes. Thank you. I'll ask Father when we get home. Will – will you be coming with the carriage so he can meet you?"

He laughed. "I'm afraid not, but I will send a note explaining that you are attending a picnic with your friend Caroline and her brother. Will that suffice?"

Elisabeth beamed her brightest smile. "I'm sure Father will approve. What time shall we expect you, Mr. Pembroke?"

"Please, call me Justin. Will two o'clock give you enough time to get ready?"

"Yes, thank you. Justin," she said before turning away. She couldn't hide her glee at being invited to a picnic with the Pembroke family. Father would be so proud of her.

"Irish tramp."

She pretended she didn't hear what Caroline muttered.

~*~

With her head high, she entered the house in time to catch her father at lunch, tiptoed up behind him and covered his eyes with her hands. "Guess what, Daddy?"

"Let me see," he said. Holding his fork in the air, he said, "The Queen of England has proclaimed all of Ireland a free and independent country?"

"Guess again." She giggled.

He dropped his spoon to the table. "What could it be?"

She removed her hands from his face and stepped to his side so he could see her.

"Whatever it is, Lass, it has surely made you one happy young woman."

Elisabeth lowered her eyes and smiled shyly. "Caroline Pembroke has invited me to go on a picnic with her family this afternoon." She hurried to add. "Her brother is going to send his carriage at two o'clock. I don't know what I have to wear."

Joseph Ackert shared his daughter's joy. "There's no time to have a proper gown made, but not to worry, Lass, you could wear a feed sack and outshine any young woman." He gave her a quick hug and invited her to sit with him while he finished his lunch.

"Imagine, after all these years, an Ackert being invited to socialize with the upper crust. I knew sending you to a fancy finishing school would help." Her father, with his balding head and bandy legs, sat at the dining room table dressed in his waistcoat, jacket and tie with a white linen napkin tucked under his chin. He slurped his soup.

Elisabeth loved her father but felt embarrassed whenever she had to go out in public with him. He tried so hard to be a "gentleman." If he only could understand he was perfect as he was.

After waiting a respectable amount of time, she excused herself and dashed upstairs to search her closet for an appropriate picnic dress. She pulled out half a dozen summer dresses before she settled on a white muslin with pink and green ribbons woven into the hem, sleeves, and bodice. Holding it against her, she spun in front of her mirror. This dress required a hoop. Shoulders slumped, she sat on the edge of the bed and wondered how to get into a carriage while wearing a hoop. She had never tried but knew other girls did it.

"Petticoats!" She sang out. "I'll put lots and lots of petticoats on then it won't matter if they get crushed in the coach." Holding up the dress again, she smiled at her image. She would tie her strawberry blonde hair back in matching ribbons and then wear the matching bonnet. Thank heaven it was a warm and beautiful day so she wouldn't have to worry about covering up with a heavy cloak.

"Amber!" she shouted down the back stairs for the servant. "I need you!"

She began layering her underskirts while waiting for Amber to appear. Her heart sang as she whirled around the room with each addition. Maybe they would go to the park where a band would play in the gazebo and she could dance with Justin Pembroke. She covered her face with delight as she imagined his touch.

"You're supposed to pull the bell, Miss," Amber said as she entered the room. "You know Mr. Ackert doesn't want you shouting down the stairs."

"Who cares about him? I'm going on a picnic with Justin Pembroke, Amber. Can you believe it?"

"Pembroke? Them high–faluting people? Why would they want you at a picnic?"

"Don't be mean. I'm friends with Caroline Pembroke at school." If she lied about it enough, it might become true. "Her brother asked me when he saw we were friends. Now, stop being rude and help me lace up this dress."

"It is a pretty dress, Miss, but shouldn't you be wearing a hoop instead of so many petticoats? You'll be awfully warm."

"I prefer them to a hoop," Elisabeth said while watching herself in the mirror as she tried to achieve the proper sense of haughtiness to mingle with the Pembrokes and their friends.

"Seems to me like they want you there for the entertainment, not to be a part of their circle." Amber tugged at the laces and secured the dress. "Want me to fix your hair?"

"If you don't mind, but please stop saying those ugly things. I'm scared enough."

"Well, you've been taught your manners. You'll be fine. Make your father proud. And remember, your dear mother will be watching." Amber made the sign of the cross at the mention of Elisabeth's mother. Elisabeth followed suit, knowing Amber would be upset if she didn't. For all her church upbringing, Elisabeth found it difficult to believe her mother, or any other dead person, could actually be watching her. The thought made her shiver.

"Gloves! What gloves should I wear to a picnic?"

"White lace ones, I should think."

Amber worked on Elisabeth's hair.

"Do you think they'll talk about the war?" Elisabeth wondered out loud.

"Those people are getting rich because of the war. I expect they'll be more worried about who brought the fanciest basket and best food."

Elisabeth shrugged. "Right now I don't even care what's in anybody's basket. I'll eat anything. I'm starving!"

She was rewarded for this comment by a light whack with the hairbrush. "I suggest you have a bowl of soup before you go off making a pig of yourself in front of those people. Remember, you're supposed to be a lady."

"How do you know so much about being a lady? Certainly Daddy hasn't taught you."

"I talk to the other ladies' maids in the park. Doesn't take much to learn, they're all eager to show off how much they know."

"Amber, do any of them give you a hard time because you're Irish?" Elisabeth looked at Amber's eyes in the mirror.

"No, Miss. Most of them are Irish themselves, though they do feel sorry for me having to work for an Irish family. I tell them I love my family, especially because they're not snobs like the rest of them around here."

"And what do they say?"

Amber smiled. "They agree with me. Some of those families have maids and grooms and gardeners – servants all over the place. Can't imagine how their families ever get any privacy. There you go now, Miss. Beautiful."

Elisabeth stood and held out her hands so Amber could button her gloves. When her maid finished, she turned to examine herself once again in the full-length mirror to the left of her vanity. Pleased with what she saw, she turned and gave Amber a quick hug. "I'll go wait downstairs. They should be here soon."

"You have a good time. I'll tell cook you won't be wanting much supper tonight. She'll be happy to hear you've gone out with friends."

Father had to return to his offices before her ride arrived, but he kissed her on the forehead and admonished her to be a good girl.

"You're going to wear a path in that carpet," Amber said as she came down the main staircase carrying loads of laundry.

"Do you think they forgot?" Elisabeth asked anxiously.

"The clock hasn't struck two, Miss." Amber huffed her way to the back of the house and the kitchen.

"Do you think I should have worn earrings?" Elisabeth called out.

"No, Miss. You're looking lovely as is," Amber shouted back.

Elisabeth pulled the curtain aside and watched the road, looking for a trap or any type of carriage slowing to turn into their drive. All she saw was an empty street in the shade of the Dutch Elms bordering it. She dropped the curtain and chewed her lower lip. The thought popped into her mind that the invitation had been contrived as a nasty joke. Tomorrow at school, Caroline and the other girls would point at her and ridicule her for thinking she had really been invited to join the Pembrokes at a family affair. Her face burned at the idea.

The heavy petticoats under her dress weighed her down. She didn't want to go anyplace ever again. This humiliation was too unbearable. Afraid to face Amber, she began to tip toe up the steps. When she reached the first landing, she heard the clip clop of a single horse and then the crunch of wheels on gravel. Like a lightning flash her mood lifted. She hurried back down the stairs and raced for the door as the bell rang.

Amber scurried from the back of the house in time to prevent Elisabeth from opening the door herself. "You go sit in the parlor like a lady. I'll announce whoever's at the door. Go on." She shooed her into the parlor to her right.

Elisabeth listened as Amber opened the inner door then entered the vestibule to open the outer door. She heard a man's voice, probably the driver, and then Amber appeared in the archway and announced, "Mr. Justin C. Pembroke to see Miss Ackert." Her usually rosy cheeks burst with color and her eyes twinkled as she tried to keep from giggling when she stepped aside to permit Justin to enter the parlor.

"Hello, Mr. Pembroke. I hadn't expected you to call personally. How kind of you." She held out her hand.

His eyes sparkled as he took it. "My pleasure, Miss Ackert. Are you ready to go?"

"All ready. I'll just pick up my bag from the hall." Her heart pounded in her throat as she took his arm and allowed him to escort her into the hall and out the front door. A horse and buggy stood waiting for them under the portico. A white-haired Negro driver waited patiently, reins and whip in hand. As soon as he saw them come out the door, he jumped down to open the small carriage door. Justin helped her into the buggy and then climbed in and sat beside her.

"We're off."

"This is exciting. Where are we going? To Washington Park?"

"No, my dear. I've chosen a quiet place near the river. Too much talk of the war at the park."

"Excuse me, Mr. Pembroke, but Caroline will be there won't she?"

"I asked you to call me Justin. May I call you Elisabeth?"

"Yes, of course," she answered with a dry mouth. "Um, what about Caroline?"

"She begged off, claiming a headache."

Elisabeth hands made fists in her lap. Her heart raced precariously. She couldn't think what to say.

Her concern must have shown on her face because he immediately said, "There will be plenty of other girls there."

She blushed. "I was a bit worried."

He laughed, a soft gentle sound, and reached out to cover both her hands with one of his. "You needn't fear me, Elisabeth. We're going on a picnic and we're going to have fun."

The carriage bounced along the main street for a little while before turning onto an even rougher side street which led to a bridge across a creek. They traveled in silence. The trees in full bloom created tunnels of shade along the lanes. The air, pure and clean, overcame the odors of the city as the horse trotted downhill closer to the Hudson River.

They pulled up to a gazebo in a clearing by the river where several young men and women chatted. Others played a variation of lawn tennis on the grass, and in another group a young man dressed in white trousers and a striped jacket with a boater on his head, played the banjo. Perhaps she would have a good time after all.

Justin helped her down from the carriage. His hand on hers gave her a little thrill made her blush.

"How many damned skirts do you have on under there?" he said with a grin on his face.

Embarrassed to be caught out, she lowered her eyes. "I didn't want to wear a hoop." And as soon as she said it, she knew it was wrong to speak of such intimate things with a man, a man she hardly knew.

"Sensible girl," he said.

Startled by his reaction she looked up at him. Her eyes met his and a shiver ran through her body. "Thank you."

The driver retrieved a large wicker basket from the back of the carriage and carried it to a picnic table to one side of the clearing. Justin led her into the middle of the recreation area and began introducing her to his friends. He knew all of the men, but hardly any of the girls.

"This is Frederick Bill; his father hopes he'll someday be the mayor of New York City. I told him, first he has to move there."

"Have you been to New York City?" she asked Frederick with wide-eyed wonder. She had often begged her father to take her there.

"Before the war," he said. "I don't dare go down there now. They're recruiting for the effort all over the place. Even dragging men in who are unwilling to serve."

"And you are unwilling to serve?" she said.

"I'm planning to serve my country with my brains, not by getting my body blown to bits. We'll win in the end and I'll be there for the people."

Elisabeth looked at him as if trying to see him from a different perspective. He was only as tall as she, with soft, mushy features. His cheeks were too round, his mouth too cherubic. Clothed in a light woolen three-piece suit, the trousers fashionably high-waisted, the coat cut like a morning coat, his collar with a perfectly knotted tie, he looked like a stuffed doll ready to be placed on a shelf. She decided she didn't like him.

"Can you ever shut up, Bill?" a man called from the other side of the gazebo. "Jim Riis is right over there."

Elisabeth looked where he pointed. On the lawn, an area opposite their own picnic table, lay a young man, blond and pale, his lower body covered in blankets. He reclined against a pile of pillows with a glass of lemonade in one hand. He had his other hand over a book on the blanket. Another young man sat on the edge of Jim's blanket.

Justin's demeanor changed instantly. "Jim!" He leaped down the steps of the gazebo and strode over to him.

Elisabeth, unsure what to do, followed. As she approached, Jim's eyes never left hers. She smiled at him and he smiled back, a warm expression that made him beautifully handsome.

"Jim Riis, may I introduce my friend, Miss Elisabeth Ackert? She is of the Ackert Lumber and Building Yards. Her father owns them."

She extended her hand and leaned down so he could comfortably reach it. "It's a pleasure Miss Ackert." He kept his hold on her hand and she feared she would collapse beside him. "You are a lovely addition to our little soiree."

"Thank you, Mr. Riis."

Justin laughed behind her. "Be cautious around old Jim, Elisabeth. He takes great pleasure in stealing my women."

Elisabeth looked from one man to the other and considered how to respond. Before she could decide, Jim spoke up.

"Have a seat." He patted an empty space on the blanket. When she hesitated, he added, "We're not formal here. Come on, join us. This is my friend Andrew – his family is coal and railroads."

Justin held on to Elisabeth's hand as she lowered herself to the blanket beside Jim Riis. Riis beamed as if he had been bestowed a huge blessing. "How do you come to be in that roué's company?"

"Do you mean Mr. Pembroke?" She glanced at Justin. "His sister, Caroline, is my friend at school."

"Lucky girl. Tell me about your school. What do you study?"

"If you'll excuse me, I see someone I need to speak with. I'll be back in a little while," Justin said, though neither Elisabeth nor Jim took any notice.

She explained about finishing school, all the while wondering why he would not or could not get up. When she finished her brief description of the school, she turned the table and asked him about himself. "Where did you go to school?" she asked instead of asking what she really wanted to know.

"I attended Yale College of Arts and Sciences. Though it doesn't do me much good." He stopped and looked around. No one remained except him and Elisabeth. He leaned toward her as if to convey a deep secret. "I joined the army as a medical officer and was promptly shot and invalided out. So here I lie, waiting for beautiful young maidens to come sit beside me."

Elisabeth didn't know what to say.

He laughed, bringing a touch of color to his cheeks. "You're blushing. Not many girls do anymore, at least not the ones Justin invites to these affairs. How did you really get yourself invited? You can't be a friend of that little snob, Caroline."

She lowered her eyes in embarrassment. "I'm not. Not really. But when I saw Mr. Pembroke yesterday, I was dying to meet him. He's so handsome and strong looking and-"

"And you couldn't resist him. I understand all too well. There was a time I might have behaved the same as he. Now, from this perspective, I can see what a rogue he is. Please don't permit yourself to fall under his spell." He reached out and placed a hand over hers.

"That's no way to speak of your host," she murmured.

"I was thinking of you, not of him." He removed his hand.

Justin cleared his throat. "Shall we lunch, Elisabeth? I've invited Martin and his friend to join us."

Startled by the interruption, she looked up to see Justin silhouetted against the sun. He loomed over her, and for a moment she felt a frisson of fear, but brushed it off as being spooked by Jim's comments. "I'm ready," she said as she held her hand up to him.

The servant pulled out cold chickens, seasoned boiled potatoes, tomatoes, which he sliced, a variety of pickled vegetables, including her favorite, cucumbers, and several bottles of wine. A second basket contained dinner plates and glasses.

Martin turned out to be another peacock, sandy haired, full beard and a jaunty tilt to his bowler hat. The girl with him appeared a bit old for this crowd. He called her "Bebe from France."

Bebe spoke barely understandable English. Elisabeth had the impression Bebe had come to America to do something for the war effort. Bebe wore powder on her face, had sharply penciled eyebrows and rouged lips and cheeks. She looked like one of those women the girls at school giggled about – a fallen woman. But what would a fallen woman be doing in such a group of upstanding men? Bebe ate her lunch as if she had not seen a meal in a month, all the while pressing her body close to Martin's.

As lunch went on Elisabeth became increasingly uncomfortable. Unused to drinking wine, her head swam. Food passed before her eyes as if in a dream – fruit and cheeses followed a rich dark chocolate pastry. She hoped tea would arrive to end the meal because she was ready to go home.

"Shall we take a walk?" Justin whispered in her ear.

"I'm not sure I'm up to a walk right now. I've eaten too much food and drank far too much wine."

"A walk will do you good." His lips brushed her ear and she shivered.

She cleared her throat. "If you insist."

He helped her to her feet and then kept one arm around her waist, steadying her, as he led her toward the woods. She took a last peek toward Jim who sat in his chair watching, a frown on his face. Did he shake his head or did she imagine it? Was he warning her not to go for a walk with Justin?

She turned back and leaned into Justin's strong body, telling herself she needed his support to walk on the uneven path. His arm felt nice around her waist.

When they reached a clearing a few minutes later, she was surprised to see Justin spread a large blanket over the leaves and grass. "We can rest here if you like."

"Rest?" Her voice felt tiny. "Where did everybody else go?"

"They've found their own secluded spots for an afternoon nap. Come, join me." He lowered himself to the ground.

With no one around to tell her what to do, she had to make up her own mind. Sit with Justin alone in the woods or go back to the picnic grounds. He smiled at her, his hand extended. "Come, my lovely maiden."

She returned his smile. He was handsome. Sinking down on to her knees, she kept herself separated from him as far as the blanket would allow.

"Are you afraid of me, Elisabeth?" his voice crooned.

"Not really," she said, her eyes downcast as her fingers fiddled with the ribbons on her gown.

"Does anyone call you Beth?"

"No."

"May I?" His fingers stroked her wrist softly, gently.

"Of course," she said more brightly. "But I might not answer, not being used to it."

"Excuse me, I thought Caroline called you Beth."

Her mind raced through those few moments when they first met. She had been so excited to meet Justin, she didn't remember Caroline calling her anything. Generally, the two girls rarely spoke except when necessary in classes. "Did she?"

"Doesn't matter. Tell me, what do you prefer?" As he spoke his fingers caressed her hands and he inched closer to her.

"My name is Elisabeth Anne. Father calls me that when he's annoyed with me." Something about names niggled at the back of her mind, something unpleasant.

"No one could be annoyed with anyone as lovely as you, Elisabeth Anne."

Now it was his voice caressing her ears. Jim's warning flashed through her mind, but how could anyone with so soft and enticing a voice and such gentle hands be anything but wonderful? She allowed her body to relax into his as he slipped his other arm around her shoulders. Closing her eyes, she sighed with the delightful new feelings surging through her body. Her stomach tingled and her heart raced. Could this be what her father meant about men taking advantage of her? If so, this felt too comforting and nice to stop.

Justin's hand moved from hers and reached up to turn her face toward his. When she looked into his eyes, so close to hers, his mouth inches from hers, an urge to press her body to his overwhelmed her. Before she could move, he eased back onto the blanket. "You're so young and so beautiful. Forgive me."

"Forgive you? For what?" she asked, thinking she had done something wrong to make him pull away from her.

"I have no business being here with you, after all you are the friend of my youngest sister. This is wrong." He turned his head away as if in shame.

She placed her hand on his shoulder. "I'm sorry, Justin. I - I thought you liked me." The memory registered. His sister, Caroline, had called her an Irish tramp. Well, a fine man like Justin Pembroke wouldn't invite a tramp to a picnic.

"It's not you, it's me. I'm no good. Bringing you here with these people was the wrong thing to do. Let's pack up and go now." He said the words but didn't move.

She leaned her body against his back and whispered in his ear. "It's not wrong to be here, Justin. Not wrong at all. I believe I feel the same way as you. It's...well...I have no experience. I've never been on a picnic like this." Her breasts pressed against his back, Her bodice felt too tight, constricting her breath. All she wanted was to be as close to him as humanly possible.

Without warning, he turned to her, placing his hands harshly on her shoulders. "You mustn't say those things. You don't know me."

"Jim cautioned me you're a rogue," she said looking up into angry eyes that inflamed her passion. "If this is being a rogue and a roué, I have to say I am enjoying it." She pulled back, untied her bonnet, tossed it aside and waited.

He leaned close so his forehead touched hers. His devilish smile seemed more of a smirk when he said, "So, it's true what they say."

Before she could ask what he meant, his mouth was crushing hers. She didn't know what to do. "Damn you girl. Don't you come off teasing a man like this," he said in a throaty whisper. He pulled back briefly and then the next time his mouth came down on hers, her lips parted a enough so his tongue could slip into her mouth.

She savored the coppery taste of her desire as her body took control of her mind and actions. Her body moved with his and then they were lying on the blanket facing one another, his kisses sending her deeper and deeper into a frenzy of desire. But a desire for what, she still did not understand; she only knew she had a need which had to be satisfied.

He kissed her throat. She nibbled on his neck. He loosened his tie as she tore off her gloves.

"This is too wonderful, too lovely, Justin. Oh, Justin, don't ever stop holding me."

"Never, my love. Never." His hands were running over her bodice, feeling the curve of her swelling breasts. He sank his face into the center and licked at the bare skin above her neckline. Things were happening to her body. She was a flower opening its petals. No one could have explained these feelings. No one could have ever felt like this before.

He struggled with the laces at the back of her dress. She tried to reach behind to help him but he brushed her hands away. She reached forward and began to unbutton his waistcoat and then his shirt. "That's right, my darling," he murmured into her neck, his breath hot.

"I don't, I don't know what to do," she choked.

"You're doing fine," he breathed.

She ran a hand through his hair and found it damp with perspiration. She wanted to press her face into such wonderful hair. Her skirt loosened and then his hands were tugging at a petticoat ribbon. "Damn! What the hell have you done?"

The anger in his voice brought her up sharply. "What have I done? What do you mean?"

He pushed her hand away from his head and pulled back from her. "That tangled web of ribbons!"

Stunned at the sudden anger, she stopped working on the shirt buttons. His anger dissolved and a smile appeared as his hands reached for the bottom of the dress and petticoats. "There's more than one way to do this." He groped for the fastening on her underpants.

Her stomach began to roil. She rolled away, leaned over, and grabbed her middle. "I'm going to be sick."

"Don't. Not in front of me. Go behind those bushes. Good lord, I hadn't realized what a child you are."

She scrambled for the bushes, managing to remove herself from his sight just in time. Careful not to soil her skirt, she rid herself of the unsavory mess. When she returned to the clearing Justin stood, his clothing in order, the blanket folded over his arm, staring into the distance.

"Is there any water nearby, Justin?" she asked weakly.

"Down there." He pointed.

Embarrassed, she moved down a narrow path to the edge of the river and then knelt down to scoop up water to rinse her mouth. Barely refreshed, she joined him for the walk back to the picnic grounds. How was she going to face those people? With her bonnet tied securely, and her gloves tucked into her waistband, she hoped she looked decent. If not, what would they think of her? Her face burned with shame at what she had nearly done.

The first person to greet them was Jim sitting in his rolling chair, his legs still covered with blankets. "Did you have a nice walk?" he asked her, ignoring Justin.

Unable to look him in the eye, she nodded. "It was fine."

Justin took her arm to lead her toward the carriage, but Jim grabbed her wrist tightly, hurting her, and he wouldn't let go when she tried to pull away. "May I have a word with Miss Ackert?" he called to Justin.

"Have whatever you want. I'll be waiting." Justin strode toward the carriage.

"Miss Ackert. Elisabeth. Are you all right?"

She nodded but tears threatened.

"I don't know you well, but I do know him. Do you like him?"

His voice sounded caring and gentle. She nodded again. "Very much, but he's angry at me for something. I don't know."

Jim scowled. "Hmm."

"I think it was the wine. I've never had any before and it tasted so good and then I was practically throwing myself at him." She gasped and covered her mouth with her hands.

"Your skirt is soiled."

"I became ill and had to go down to the river to tidy up. This is so terrible. He'll never speak to me again."

"Unfortunately, I believe he will. Next time he wants to invite you on an outing, make sure it is dinner at his parents' home, will you?"

She looked at him in horror. "Oh, I couldn't be so rude!"

"If you want to play grown up games, then it's time you behaved like a grown up. Do you have any idea what these picnics represent?"

"Represent? An afternoon of play and fun, I imagine."

"And were you playing in the woods with Justin?" His voice took on a tinge of hostility.

She turned her back on him. "I need to leave now. It has been a pleasure meeting you, Mr. Riis. I do hope we'll meet again." Head high, she tried her practiced walk to the carriage.

Jim Riis chuckled behind her.

Twenty Six

The loud blast of the ship's horn startled Elisabeth out of her reverie. Grateful for the blanket protecting her from the early evening breezes, she opened her eyes to see the city disappearing on the horizon.

She hurried along the passageway, found the stairs to the lower decks, and made her way to Mary Ellen's room. Finding it locked, she rapped on the door and waited, still unsure what she would say to her own daughter, the daughter of Justin Pembroke.

Constance opened the door. "What a nice surprise, Mrs. Riis. Mary Ellen has been waiting to see you. Martha and I have her prettied up. Come in, won't you?"

Elisabeth looked with disdain at the flustered nurse. The simple room had blue-gray walls, white furnishings, and a polished floor. An open door offered a peek into a bathroom. She had been told Mary Ellen was in an empty steward's room. Nice, she thought. Stewards received forty dollars a month, good food, and such a pleasant room. Not a bad job.

Her daughter looked younger than Barbara. She wore a white nightgown with a high lace collar, a blanket wrapped around her legs. Her hair fell in shiny waves down her back. Though her skin was pale, her eyes appeared clear, the green color of Ireland, reminding Elisabeth of her father. But there was no denying the coloring, the nose, so straight and perfect, and the beautiful full lips of Justin Pembroke. Elisabeth shuddered at the memories and tried not to hate her daughter. "So, Mary Ellen," she said.

"Hello, Mother," Mary Ellen answered. "I understand it's been a week since we last met."

"I hear you are doing well in your recovery. How are you feeling today?"

"Not quite so fine as they tell me. What do you want?"

The question startled Elisabeth. "Why should you think I want anything?"

"Because you went to so much trouble and expense to cure me." Mary Ellen smiled broadly exposing yellowed teeth in what Elisabeth might have called a grimace.

"You are my daughter."

"And a disgrace to you. I know. Come, now. Tell me. I don't want to think I've suffered through all this for nothing."

"I was ashamed of how I abandoned you and took your daughters from you. I thought it was time for you to see them again and get to know them as the lovely young women they've become."

"Of course. Are you tired of caring for them? Did they do something to embarrass you? Have they turned out to be too much like me?" Mary Ellen laughed. "Please, don't lie to me, Mother. I have always known you disliked me from the moment of my birth. I am glad I at least had Ledger in my life. Too bad you took him from me, too. "

"I never took Ledger from you. He belongs to me. You left to marry Von Bek."

"So I did. The only good that came from him was Barbara."

"And Lillian."

"Barbara," she said bluntly. "He was long gone by the time I had Lillian." Mary Ellen tilted her head. Her lips twitched at the corners as she watched her mother take in this information. "Gone as in dead."

Elisabeth bristled but stopped herself from saying anything. She looked over at the two nurses sitting on the other side of the room pretending to be interested in their knitting and reading. She waited for Mary Ellen to continue.

After a moment, Mary Ellen said, "I think I know who Lillian's father was, but when one is overwhelmed by alcohol most of the time, it's difficult to remember. The best I can come up with, based on her appearance and my vague memory of my travels, is a delightful Irishman named Seamus O'Connell. We gathered dried cow flops to heat his cottage. How long did I stay with him? I don't know. But I can tell you, he was fun, amusing and loved to share his whiskey." She closed her eyes as if remembering and then added. "I may have some of the details wrong, but he's the best bet. I paid for the whiskey, by the way. Jake left me well off."

She winced as if in pain but continued to speak. "When I tired of him, or he of me, whichever way it happened, I took my two little girls and moved on. Barbara had formed an attachment to Seamus, but I never allowed her to call him Daddy. What else do you need to know?"

Elisabeth felt the heat rise in her face. She had not asked for nor did she want so much information. "I can only think it is fortunate there were no more children. And so you roamed about Europe. What made you return to New York?"

Mary Ellen shrugged. Perspiration formed on her brow. "I thought the girls ought to know America and they needed an education. Barbara learned to read on her own, but poor little Lillian wasn't so quick. I enrolled them in school. Then you showed up and took them away."

"They weren't in school when I collected them. There were no servants in the house; and you were not to be found. What would you have had me do? Leave them unattended? A twelve and an eight-year-old on their own?"

Without looking at her mother, Mary Ellen said, "Certainly you never believed them about my nursing course. You did the right thing. I'm appropriately ashamed. Are we finished? Now, will you tell me now why you really sought me out? Why do you care if I'm sober?"

"All in due time. I'm pleased with your progress." Elisabeth stood up and turned to the nurses. "Carry on. By the time we reach Albany, you should be free to take the train and return to the city. Miss Riis is to continue to remain in her cabin until then. Thank you."

Without looking back at her daughter, Elisabeth left the room. She needed to rest now in order to be fresh for dinner with Barbara's new friend as well as Captain Alter.

~*~

Retiring to her stateroom she pulled out one of the new dresses to wear to dinner and then, in her dressing gown, reclined on the bed to consider the best way to approach Senator Pembroke. Should she bring along a plate of muck and rub it in his face so when the press tried to photograph him, he would look as if he had literally fallen face first into the mud? She liked the picture.

She still burned with shame when she remembered what Justin Pembroke did to her. At her insistence, he had invited her to his home for dinner, but only the servants were present. After that, they met in secluded places, places where no one knew them. When he finally took her to his bed, it wasn't his bed but a flea-infested bed in a rundown rooming house. And then when she confronted him with the pregnancy, he completely denied it, accusing her of being nothing more than an Irish tramp who would sleep with anyone who asked.

It wasn't enough he refused to admit he could be the father of her child. The morning she had gone to his house where two of his sisters, his mother and his father sat finishing their

177

breakfast in the dining room, he rose politely as good manners dictated and offered her a cup of coffee.

"No, thank you. May I speak with you alone, Justin?" she asked, her knuckles white from gripping her purse.

"There's nothing you can't say in front of my family, Miss Ackert. Please sit and join us. I insist."

A servant pulled out a chair for her. With her heart pounding furiously and her cheeks burning, she took a seat at the end of the table. All eyes were on her. "I'd prefer to speak to you alone. Please," she pleaded.

"Miss Ackert," the woman she presumed to be Justin's mother spoke. "My son tells me you have been badgering him for some time."

Mr. Pembroke patted his wife's hand. "Now don't be harsh, my dear. These girls can't help themselves. I'll excuse myself. You can find me at the club later, Justin." The older man left the room. The remaining three women and Justin kept their eyes on Elisabeth as if she might suddenly strike.

Caroline smiled at Elisabeth and for a brief moment she hoped the girl would be on her side. After all, it was her brother who had taken advantage of her. Elisabeth offered a tentative smile in return.

"I've already spoken to my father, Justin. He's disappointed and angry at both of us, but he's willing to forgive if you'll marry me in the church."

Justin could not hide his astonishment and he let out a huge guffaw. Caroline, Victoria and their mother also began to laugh until Mrs. Pembroke wiped tears from her eyes.

"Oh, my poor darling girl. Do you think you're the first girl who's threatened our boy? Oh, they come, they go. How much do you want? Mr. Pembroke will see to it your father is properly paid," his mother said.

Elisabeth kept her eyes on Justin who remained amused, though he had stopped laughing aloud. "I want my child to have his father's name, Mrs. Pembroke. The same as yours do. Justin promised."

Victoria covered her face with her napkin and tittered. "We've heard that before."

Elisabeth ignored the birdlike waste of a woman.

"Nevertheless, he did promise me. My father wants for nothing, just that his only child marry the man she loves and bears his children. That would make him happy."

"And why should my son care whether or not your father is happy?" Mrs. Pembroke asked. She rang a small bell next to her plate and a maid appeared. "Show this woman out."

Elisabeth remained seated. "Justin, why won't you speak to me? Why are you hiding behind your sisters and mother? What happened to loving me? Europe? Our own home? You wanted to make a home with me and raise sons."

The servant who had seated her now stood behind her with his hands on her chair. "If you will, Miss," he said in a not unkind voice.

"I will not. Mr. Pembroke has an important decision to make and I shall remain here until he tells me for himself what he wants to do, not what his parents and sisters want him to do." She clutched the edge of the chair as if the man might bodily lift her from it.

Caroline whooped with glee. "Oh, how delicious! A stand-off. Wait until I tell the girls. I knew you were no good the first day you two met. Why do you think I introduced you? You think a nice girl would have gone off with him into the woods the first day meeting him? I knew you would. I knew it!"

"I didn't!" Elisabeth protested.

"You did." Justin smirked.

"You said it was to be a family picnic!"

Justin smirked. "I lied, but when I arrived alone, you came with me anyway. Your social climbing father was only too eager to have you lay your trap for me. How could I know what you had in mind?"

Stopped dead in her tracks, Elisabeth leaned against the back of the chair as if she had been punched in the stomach. So that was the story he told. She remembered Caroline's comment when she walked away from them that day. "Irish tramp." She had hoped it was only a stupid phrase the girl had heard at school.

"And as I recall not long after you came here into my home, unescorted, to dine alone with my son. Do you want to tell me what decent girl does that?"

Unable to comment to comment without crying Elisabeth looked at the faces surrounding her and clamped her mouth shut. Tears stung her eyes.

Her knees weak, her body trembling, she at last rose from the chair and headed toward the hallway. The manservant remained by her side until she reached the door, opened it, nodded to her and let her pass through.

As she took the first step down from the porch Justin flew out the door and grabbed her about the waist, picked her up and carried her straight down the steps, across the sidewalk to the street. As he opened her carriage door and tried to maneuver her into her seat, she slipped from his grasp and, to her horror, landed in the gutter between the carriage and the sidewalk.

Her gloved hands hit the water first, splashing it on her face and clothing. Stunned from the fall, she pushed herself onto her knees and looked up at him.

"My apologies, Miss Ackert. I was anxious to help you make a hasty retreat before the women in my family could be further tainted by your presence."

By then, her own driver had reached her side and assisted her to her feet. He did not look at Justin, but made sure Elisabeth was secured in the carriage before he whipped the horse and raced down the street. She fell back against the cushions, unable to fathom what had happened. Although she knew and understood the words, none of them made sense. Justin loved her. He said so. Using a clean piece of her dress, she wiped her face.

She could not go home. No one should know of the shame she had experienced. She asked the boy to take her down to the river but he refused. He drove her around Albany most of the day until finally, in desperation, he said, "Miss, the horse's gotta be fed and your father will be home from the office by now. Surely, he'll be waiting for you."

~*~

Elisabeth angrily shoved her thoughts aside and wiped her eyes. Too many years had passed for the pain to be as raw as that day, yet it was.

Twenty Seven

Alistair declined Barbara's offer of a stronger drink but did ask for a cup of coffee.

"What happened to Annie?" he asked while they waited for it.

"She's gone exploring. She can't believe Grandmother assigned her a stateroom on the same deck as the family. I still can't believe she gave me nearly as fine a room as her own."

"Why shouldn't she give you a nice room? Though I am surprised she'd have a servant in a proper stateroom and not on a lower deck with the rest of the crew."

Barbara studied Alistair's face, not sure what she searched for, but wanting to know she could trust him. She took the chance. "When Grandmother first found us living in the Park Avenue apartment, she believed Mother was missing. She took us home with her to Albany."

Alistair opened his mouth to speak; she raised her hand to stop him. "Let me tell you this because somewhere in our history is a reason Senator Pembroke wants to destroy her and possibly all of us.

"When we arrived at the house in Albany over five years ago, I was surprised to find it a modest place considering the immense wealth the family controls. It was large, with plenty of rooms, but contained few amenities. Turns out it is the home where Grandmother grew up and, for sentimental reasons, she refused to make any changes to it. We still live without telephones or electricity though Grandmother could probably build her own power plant right there in Albany. Anyway, she escorted my sister Lily and me up to the third floor where the cook sleeps and gave us a room. It's a nice enough room, but plain as you'd expect in a servant's room."

She grabbed the arms of the chair as the ship lurched.

"Not knowing Grandmother at all, we were both terrified to say anything to her about our accommodations. Whenever we had traveled with Mother, if she went First Class, so did we. Sometimes she forgot us altogether, but when she remembered, we were important and equal to her.

"I know, and I think Lily understands, we're no financial burden to Grandmother, but I certainly have felt like an albatross around her neck. She makes it clear she has gone out of her way to take care of us, educate us, and holds herself responsible for our morals, our behavior and physical well-being.

"When she left home last week, I was concerned and checked her rooms. From what I found, I was sure she had become ill with a heart condition, which could only have come from worrying so much about us. I never connected it to our visit to the Albany Club."

"Stop. What trip to the Albany Club?"

"Lily and I went on an adventure one evening. I was bored and had been reading about the upcoming presidential election. Our Senator Pembroke suggested he planned to throw his hat in the ring and I was curious to know more about him. The newspapers said he had some things to clear up before he could make his commitment."

"Why would you care? You can't vote."

"That doesn't mean I can't be interested. Someday, maybe women will be able to vote. I might marry and I ought to be informed so I can carry on an intelligent conversation with my husband. I doubt any man would want to hear about a woman's shopping trips or the latest fashions from Paris all the time." She got up and stood behind her chair as the steward brought the coffee for Alistair. "Also, recently I've had this secret desire to become a reporter."

She caught the smirk on the steward's face when he heard her last statement. Choosing to ignore it, she continued. "That night she and I had Ledger drive us downtown to the club and drop us off. He's a good sport as long as he believes we're safe. We entered through the rear of the building into the servant's hall and donned aprons and caps, making us look like the help."

Alistair laughed. "Pinkerton's could use you. And you went undetected?"

"We thought so. Until you told us he thought Grandmother sent her parlor maids to spy on him. What we learned was he has a connection to Grandmother. He spoke about Mrs. Riis. He referred to her as 'that Irish Ackert bitch.' I never told Grandmother. I never even repeated the phrase until now. He said he'd like to have her silenced permanently, but another man spoke up and said as she'd never talked in 'all these years,' what made him think she'd be any kind of threat now. The senator said he didn't want to take any chances. He'd think about it. That's when we left the premises."

Annie burst into the lounge. "You won't believe what I've heard!"

"Annie! If you're going to be a lady's maid, then you must learn to behave properly. Running into a room shouting is not proper. Now, sit down and catch your breath."

Annie obeyed though obviously itching to relate her news. Barbara took her time seating herself. "Now, what did you hear?"

"They say there's a sick crewmember on board but it's not true. One of the stewards told me everyone is accounted for, and the nurses and your grandmother and Ledger brought a woman on board several days ago and locked her in an empty room below." She stopped to take a deep breath and waited for Barbara's reaction.

Barbara tried to puzzle out the meaning of this. "A woman? What woman? Did they say what she looks like?"

"No, only that she looked near to death. They're asking why they didn't take her to a hospital."

Alistair crossed one leg over the other and sipped at his coffee, a slight frown on his brow. "It didn't make sense to me earlier when she claimed a crew member had taken ill. The normal procedure would have been to replace him and send him home."

"They said a woman," Annie reminded him.

"I heard you. I'm thinking." He set his coffee down and checked his pocket watch. "It's nearly seven o'clock. What time did your grandmother say dinner would be?"

"Eight. Come on, Annie. We have to change. Dinner with the captain and maybe the first mate. Who knows who you might meet?"

Annie's eyes opened wide. "Do you mean you're going to have me dining with Mrs. Riis? Oh Lord. I don't think I've learned enough about all those knives and forks yet. Please don't make me."

"Just watch what I use. You'll be fine."

Alistair cleared his throat. "Excuse me, Barbara, but I hope I don't have to wear formal attire. I didn't bring any with me."

Barbara stopped and studied Alistair, quickly dismissing the idea of him borrowing anything of Ledger's, which would be far too large. "Wear a dark suit and don't worry about it. I won't wear a tiara or my jewels." His expression told her she had gone too far. She laughed so he would know her comment was meant to be a joke.

He reacted with a weak grin. "I'll see you at dinner. Meanwhile, you don't mind if I look around for myself?"

"Not at all. Maybe you can investigate our mysterious patient and tell us about her at dinner."

"It means disobeying your grandmother's specific directive to not go below."

"I'm sorry, I didn't hear such a directive." Barbara gave a small wave and then left him standing alone in the lounge as she took an inside passageway to her cabin.

As quickly as she shut her door, there was a knock. Annie entered in a rush, crossed the room to the vanity and took a seat on the upholstered bench. "Barbara, I've had fun with you these past few days, but please let me eat in the kitchen – galley – with the crew. I don't belong in such posh company. I really and truly don't."

"If you're going to be in here anyway, unlace me, please. What should I wear to dinner? You're wearing your new blue dress, right?"

Annie tugged at her laces and helped pull her dress and petticoat down. "You aren't listening to me. My Mam tells me all the time you can't turn a sow's ear into a silk purse."

"You can if it's really a silk purse in the first place. Have you looked at yourself in the mirror? You belong with us. We're neither better nor worse than each other. I won't hear of you leaving yourself behind when I'm trying to help move you forward."

"But all those forks and knives and glasses!"

"You wear your blue and I'll wear the gray and ivory. I love the smooth line of the skirt. Can you imagine Grandmother's time, wearing those large hoop skirts? Will you do my hair? I found a picture in a magazine here. It's very modern." She bent over and picked up the photo to show Annie.

Annie took it and studied it for a minute. "I can do it as long as we got enough hairpins. Your hair should stay nicely.

Very smart and grown up looking. Are you wanting to impress someone?" she teased.

"The captain, of course."

"Pearl gray and ivory. Wear your pearl earrings and I'll put the pearl broach in your hair. He'll be sure to notice." Annie fussed so much over helping Barbara with her bath and then fixing her hair, she would have forgotten to dress herself until Barbara sent her away.

"You have fifteen minutes," Barbara warned Annie, watching her face in the mirror.

"You've been right about everything so far." Annie's eyes met hers in the mirror. "If you're willing to trust me, I'll be honored to join you."

Barbara studied her own face in the mirror and then pinched her cheeks to give them more color. She hoped Alistair would be comfortable at dinner. She wondered if she had told Annie the truth about whom she wanted to impress.

Twenty Eight

When Barbara returned shortly before eight o'clock Elisabeth sat at one end of the lounge holding court like a queen. The captain stood nearby with a drink in his hand talking to Alistair and the first mate.

Barbara beamed at the sight of Alistair dressed formally in white tie and tails. He looked stunningly handsome as he stood with his feet slightly apart, steadying himself against the gentle sway of the ship.

"...boilers of the Scotch type. She measures two hundred thirty-two feet overall and has a thirty-two-foot beam. She's bark-rigged and carries ten-thousand-nine-hundred-thirty-five square feet of canvas," Captain Alter finished. His eyes lit up at the sight of Barbara and Annie entering. Alistair turned to see what caught his attention and he, too, smiled broadly.

Barbara blushed and took Annie's hand to draw her forward with her. "Captain Alter, may I present my friend and assistant, Miss Annie Clancy? Annie, this is Captain Alter, and of course, you know Mr. Rogers."

Annie held out her hand as Barbara had taught her and allowed the captain to bend over it, offering a passing kiss. "Charmed, Miss Clancy. May I present my first mate, Charles Corwin? Mr. Corwin, Miss Riis and Miss Clancy."

Barbara was sure she heard her grandmother sniff, but so enjoyed the attention of the men, she chose to ignore her.

"The captain has been telling me about this yacht. It is one of the largest in the world and one of the few to have traveled around the world. Did you know the previous owner was a woman? A lady sportswoman," Alistair said, obviously impressed. "She's been to Japan, China, India and Africa as well as Europe. I would have loved to know her."

"She sounds an impressive person," Barbara said.

"I traveled most of those places with her-the ship, I mean," Mr. Corwin announced proudly. "I'm pleased to be serving on her again."

"Should we not go in for dinner?" Grandmother asked.

"We have about ten minutes, Mrs. Riis," Captain Alter said. "Time enough for the ladies to have a little sherry. Shall I?" He picked up a decanter and held it over the crystal glasses.

"Please," Barbara said. When Annie didn't answer, Barbara gave her a nudge with her elbow.

"Yes, me too, please," Annie said.

"I'd be delighted to take you on a tour of the electric plant tomorrow, provided the weather is fair," Captain Alter said to Alistair.

"I'd love it. The engine room, too?"

Barbara listened to the men. "May I join you?"

Captain Alter looked taken aback by the request. "Well, Miss Riis, it could be difficult. Skirts are not made for clambering up and down the ladders nor for walking on catwalks. You see," he covered his mouth for a moment, searching for words. "You see, the catwalks are made of steel grates. Skirts are most inappropriate. I'm sorry."

"I'll be happy to tell you about it afterward," Alistair offered.

"Thank you," Barbara answered. "I'll be happy to sit in my skirts on deck and listen. Perhaps I can sip my tea while I catch some fresh air for my delicate complexion." She moved away to a separate circle of chairs and sat down, hoping Alistair would catch her sarcastic tone.

He followed her with the decanter of sherry. "May I offer you a little more?"

She held up her glass. "Of course, what else have I to do?"

"Barbara, I didn't design the ship. What if your skirt became caught in a piece of machinery? That could be disastrous. Anyway, I wanted to speak to you privately so this is a good opportunity."

Peeved once again at being separated because of her sex, Barbara wanted to remain annoyed if not downright angry, but she liked Alistair too much, besides she didn't care about engine rooms. "Did you learn something this afternoon?"

"One thing I learned is Annie makes a good detective. I didn't learn any more than she did. I confirmed a female, who appeared half dead, was carried aboard and secluded below in one of the steward's rooms. Three nurses are sharing a nearby room, and Evans and Maureen have been assigned to provide food specially for them and their patient. A doctor was left behind in Brooklyn. It must mean the patient is not in any danger of dying, whoever she is."

"That's next on our list, then. Find out who she is and if she is the reason Grandmother came to the city in the first place. I thought the trip was for Grandmother's health."

"I will caution you. In my conversations with Ledger, he has let on that your grandmother's health is not ideal. She has a lot of fatigue and her temper has been shorter than usual, according to him. I wouldn't know as I have no history to compare it with."

"She's always been grouchy and short-tempered," Barbara said, but paused to consider Grandmother's behavior recently. More testy? Maybe. Ledger would know as they spent so much time together hovering over her investments and bookkeeping. She'd check with him after dinner and keep a closer eye on Grandmother.

"Speaking of Ledger, here he comes now. Would you look at him?" Alistair stood to greet Ledger who arrived wearing a tuxedo with white tie. With his dark complexion and suit, he made a stark contrast to the captain and first mate in their dress whites.

"And look at Annie. I think she's in love with Mr. Corwin. See how she ogles him," Barbara added. "What a wonderful evening. And, by the way, where did you ever find the suit?"

"Ledger brought it for me. I didn't ask. I think the man's a magician."

"You're probably right. Shall we rejoin the others?"

"I saw a backgammon board earlier. Would you like to play after dinner?" Alistair asked as he took her arm to escort her back to the group.

"Only if you'll teach me. I've never heard of such a game, much less played."

"They look so serious. I think we have to rescue Annie," he said.

"The New York governor? Are you sure?" Grandmother was saying.

"Theodore Roosevelt. I don't know anyone else by that name. It was on the news wires this afternoon," Captain Alter said.

"Imagine, Teddy Roosevelt is going to become the vice-president of the United States," she said to Barbara and Alistair as they approached.

"I think it's time we go into dinner," Mr. Corwin said. He then turned to Annie and held out his arm.

Annie looked at it and then glanced over to Barbara who still had her arm in Alistair's. Annie hooked her arm around Charles Corwin's and placed her hand lightly on his wrist all the while grinning widely. Captain Alter escorted Grandmother, leaving Ledger to follow up the rear.

The dining room nearly overwhelmed Barbara. Stewards stood behind elaborately carved wood chairs, waiting to seat the guests. The table was laid with fine white linens and gold trimmed China. Candles and flowers ran down the center of the long table, which could have seated twenty comfortably. She smiled as broadly as Annie and was sure she felt equally as giddy.

Once seated, the dinner service commenced. Starting with a clear consommé and finishing with platters of fruit and cheese, Barbara hardly heard the conversation, catching snippets about people called Boxers being shot in China and Germans building up their navy, matters which didn't concern her. She only knew this past week had taught her new ways to live that her grandmother had denied her and her sister the past six years. She enjoyed sitting beside Alistair and was pleased to note he did not have to wait to see which utensil to use for each course. He knew a fish knife from a butter knife and a water glass from a white wine goblet. Annie did herself proud by being sly, watching for her cues from Barbara, so overall, the dinner looked to be a success.

When the wine steward brought in the after-dinner port, the men stood.

"If you'll excuse us, ladies," Captain Alter said, "We'll have our port in the library."

Barbara explained to Annie he meant the men would be smoking cigars with their port.

Before they could leave, Grandmother raised her hand to silence everyone. "I'd like to tell you what my plans are for the next few months. Captain, this concerns you and your crew, if you don't mind waiting a few minutes."

"Of course not, Mrs. Riis." The men returned to their seats.

"As soon as my business is finished in Albany, I shall gather up a small party of people, including my granddaughters and Ledger, and we are going to take this wonderful yacht on a worldwide cruise. We will most likely be gone for at least eighteen months if not two years, according to Captain Alter. He has helped me make up the itinerary."

"Eighteen months?" Ledger asked with some surprise.

Barbara, too, was surprised Ledger did not know about the plans. She assumed Grandmother did nothing without consulting him.

"And exactly how will you operate your business being away for such an extended period?" Ledger held out his right hand, palm up as if displaying the office.

"Don't fret, Ledger. You've seen the radio room and the communication system on board. We can be in daily contact with everyone, anywhere in the world. Now, let's raise our glasses to celebrate a real holiday for all of us."

Barbara felt Alistair's indecisiveness, but he raised his glass as did she. Her going away for so long would end any hopes she had of furthering their relationship. She held up her glass. "To a holiday."

Annie's eyes teared as she raised her glass. "A holiday," she whimpered quietly.

Wanting to reassure her she would bring her along, Barbara could do nothing but watch the girl's misery. Though the first mate was far too old for her, he was the first man to ever treat Annie as a first-class young woman and not a scullery maid. Barbara was sure the girl believed herself completely in love with him.

"Going someplace?"

All heads turned to the entrance to the dining room.

Twenty Nine

Mary Ellen leaned against the door jamb, her cotton nightgown outlining her naked body beneath, her hair long hair hanging wildly about her face.

Before she could say another word, Evans and Maureen appeared, followed closely by two women.

Evans separated himself from the group and stood with his mouth agape as he watched the two nurses grab Mary Ellen by the arms and pull her forcefully from the dining room and across the lounge. Mary Ellen let out a string of expletives, which Elisabeth was sure even the sailors had never heard.

When they were out of sight and could no longer hear Mary Ellen's crude words he turned, red-faced to the party in the dining room. "I beg your forgiveness, Mrs. Riis. She skipped out from her room as Maureen and I were bringing her dinner in. It won't happen again."

Elisabeth, stunned by the intrusion, clamped her jaw shut and felt her muscles twitch, only vaguely aware Barbara appeared equally stunned but unaware who the intruder might be. "See that it doesn't," she commanded.

Evans scooped Mary Ellen up into his arms while Maureen clucked over her. When the group was out of hearing, Elisabeth turned to Ledger.

"When we reach Albany, send them back to New York. Their services will no longer be required. We will deal with the nurses in good order."

Ledger nodded.

Now she had to deal with her granddaughter. Turning her attention to Barbara, she said, "I hope this hasn't upset you, my dear," and then waited, hardly daring to breath, to hear what her granddaughter might say.

It took a moment for Barbara to take her attention from the doorway and when she did, she looked to her grandmother with a puzzled expression. "Who is she? She reminds me of my mother, well, not exactly, but she can't be." She looked again at the doorway as if seeing the woman again. "Mother's dead."

"Now dinner is over, I shall retire. I'm not as young as I used to be and I need my rest." Elisabeth stood, hoping she could escape any further questions. She looked to Ledger who seemed as puzzled as Barbara. "Ledger, if you don't mind, would you please escort me to my cabin?"

"Of course, Mrs. Riis."

Apparently, Ledger was feeling somewhat out of his element in this grouping, she thought, wishing once again she could simply fall into his arms and ask for his comfort and protection. As that was not to be, she turned to the captain. "Thank you so much for a wonderful evening, Captain Alter. Dinner was delicious and the company most enjoyable. I apologize for the intrusion."

Captain Alter took her proffered hand and said, "Madam, it has been my pleasure. I am delighted to hear your plans are confirmed. While you are about your business in Albany, I shall see to it the ship is outfitted for our travels. Good evening."

He bowed and she noted the beginnings of a bald spot on the top of his head. "Good evening."

She accepted Ledger's arm and began to leave the room when Barbara stood and said, "Who is she? Why did she remind me of Mother?"

Elisabeth tried to pretend she had not heard the words but Ledger stopped next to Barbara. She had no choice but to acknowledge the girl. "Perhaps because she *is* your mother."

Barbara collapsed back onto her chair. Her young man caught her and kept her from falling to the floor. "You said she's dead. You told me and Lily she died," she said, her voice choking with sobs.

"So I did. It was for your own good. Now it is for your own good to not ask me any further questions. Good night. Ledger, I want to go to my stateroom."

"Madam," Ledger said and then led her out of the room.

"I'm having a hard time breathing, Ledger. Don't walk so fast." She heard Captain Alter offering Barbara water.

Ledger slowed and said, "That was unkind of you, Elisabeth. Could you not have spoken more sensitively to the girl?"

"And said what? Your mother is a habitual user of heroin and other drugs? Your mother was completely incompetent to parent you? She's a dead loss as a human being? Barbara and her sister have every opportunity with me to grow up and become sensible and mature women. With their mother they were like the wild Indians out west."

"You told them their mother was dead and now you want Barbara to pretend she didn't see what she just saw? You're cruel, Elisabeth. I've loved you for so many years and I've attributed your hardness to the heartbreak you suffered at the hands of your husband, but now I cannot be a party to the pain you're causing Barbara."

Elisabeth listened to Ledger as her head pounded with pain and her chest could not suck in enough air. "I need to rest. Get me to my cabin."

"You need to explain yourself to Barbara," he said, his hand too tight on her arm. Her corset suffocated her.

"I can't breathe," she said as she leaned on Ledger, her support and her love for so many years.

"Yes, ma'am," she heard him say as she felt his arms pick her up.

He carried her to her stateroom and laid her on her bed. While she gasped for air, he undid her laces and helped her out of her gown and then her corset and other undergarments. While she lay there covered by a light sheet, he brought her a nightgown and then left to get her peppermint schnapps and the box containing her medications.

"I need the digitalis. I need to sleep, Ledger. Please sit with me."

"Elisabeth, what game are you playing? I know you want Mary Ellen cleaned up from her drug use, but to what end? How is she going to help you with Senator Pembroke? What are you going to do?"

"Go away, Ledger, unless you're prepared to lie down beside me and comfort me while I suffer."

To her surprise, his voice became strong and harsh. "Not until I know. I've learned to love your daughter and your granddaughters and I will not see them harmed any further. What do you have in mind?"

Elisabeth closed her eyes and tried to imagine the scene she did have in mind. Ledger could never understand. He never had a family. She swallowed another sip of her schnapps and tried to take deep breaths, but her chest still hurt. How much longer did she have? She only wanted enough time to ruin Senator Justin C. Pembroke. "Go away, Ledger. I'm sorry to disappoint you. I can't see anyone right now, so tell Barbara whatever you want. I don't care any longer. I need to sleep."

She felt him cover her with a blanket and heard him go out the door easing it closed behind him. "My darling Ledger. My beautiful girl. I'm doing it for you. Please believe me, I am."

A knock at her door surprised her. The clock beside her bed showed it to be after eleven. She could pretend she was asleep and not answer it, but the unknown guest knocked again.

She finished her drink and called out, "Come in."

Exhausted though she was, Elisabeth sat up and poured another glass of liqueur. As she thought about the evening, she considered the one pleasant aspect of it Barbara's presence at the table, participating as an adult. A beautiful child matured beautiful woman. Perhaps it was time to start her education in the family businesses. Ledger would be her first teacher and later, when he advised her the girl was ready, they would offer her a position. She smiled as she imagined the girl's delight at finally having something to do with her life.

Barbara entered. She paid no attention to finding her grandmother already in bed, the lights lowered, looking ready for sleep. She stormed across the room and leaned over the bed, her face inches from Elisabeth's. "Explain it to me now, Grandmother.

Thirty

Barbara's anger at her grandmother left no room for compassion or care about her. "Explain why you led us to believe our mother was dead! Who gave you the right to take us away when she was alive all along?"

Elisabeth raised a hand and placed it on Barbara's shoulder, pushing her back. "If you'll pause for a breath, I can explain."

Barbara brushed the old woman's hand away. "Tell me why she's locked up like a prisoner on this boat."

"It's a yacht or a ship, not a boat, so they tell me," Elisabeth answered. "She's not a prisoner; she's a patient."

"You want to play word games? Then explain why you treat Lily and me the same as the servants yet call us family. It was only through Ledger's generosity on my sixteenth birthday I began to understand our financial position in the world."

"You are talkative tonight. I'm not feeling well, Barbara. Can we discuss this in the morning?"

"No." Barbara was not going to let her get away with her stingy, mean ways any longer. She pulled a chair close to the bed and took a seat. "Start with Mother. What is she doing on this boat? For how long did you intend to keep her in hiding?"

"I planned to reintroduce you once her nurses assured me she was in full recovery from her illness."

"What illness? What's wrong with her?"

199

"Not a disease. I didn't want you to know. Heroin. Opium. She has a serious addiction."

Grandmother's pallor confirmed her earlier statement that she didn't feel well, but Barbara was too angry at being told lies to let it go now. "How can I believe you? How did you know? Why did you decide to 'cure' her now?"

"I – I can't explain it now, dear. Please, let me sleep."

"Why should you be allowed to sleep when I won't be able to until I know the truth. The real truth. Shall I call Ledger to explain?"

"Ledger doesn't know the entire story. Give me time, Barbara. We'll be in Albany soon and then you'll understand what I've been doing for you all this time. I have one final duty to perform to ensure your success."

"My success. My success at what?"

"I have plans for you, Barbara. I was waiting for the right time."

"I'm leaving and moving back to the city with Mother as quickly as possible. I don't care what you have planned."

"Water. Please bring me some water." Grandmother held out her empty water glass.

Barbara snatched it from her hand and headed for the bathroom to fill it. When she returned, she set it on the table rather than hand it directly to Elisabeth.

"First, let me explain something to you. You are not free to do as you please until you are twenty-one years old. I am your legal guardian and I don't believe it's in your best interest to live with your mother yet. Maybe someday, when we know she is able to care for you again…"

"I no longer need caring for. And you must have lied to gain legal custody, telling whoever it was Mother was dead."

"No, dear. I did not tell the court Mary Ellen had died. I had two doctors testify to her addictions. The judge agreed you and Lillian would be better off with me." She picked up her glass with a shaking hand and sipped a little water. "You have been well fed, clothed and educated."

Barbara sniffed. "We had plenty of food and clothes with Mother."

"And no supervision."

"We were doing fine."

"It's obvious you've hardened your heart against me, Barbara, but in a few days you'll understand everything. I promise you. Now, please leave me in peace. Go find your new beau and talk to him about it, if you must. He seems a bright young man."

"He not my beau, he's my friend." Barbara noted the blueness around Elisabeth's lips. "I'll leave now and see you at breakfast." She couldn't bring herself to kiss her goodnight, though she feared she might not last the night. She rose from her chair.

"Goodnight, Barbara."

"Goodnight."

She left the room, shutting the door far more gently than when she had entered. Looking up and down the passageway, she wondered where to find one of the nurses who tended to her mother. Unsure, she chose to head for the bridge to ask whoever was in charge. They should know who was where.

It took a while as she wandered through passageways to get to the bridge. The low lighting inside the room allowed the view outside under a full moon to appear as if it were midday. The night was still so the engines hummed making the corridors sound like a beehive.

Charles stood at the helm with Alistair beside him. The two of them watched ahead, neither of them speaking. Alistair had changed back into his own clothing and looked at home, comfortable. She wished she could have time to get to know him better, but he would have to leave for Hartford as soon as they arrived in Albany. She cleared her throat to get their attention, though they must have heard her open the door.

Charles turned first. "Good evening, Miss. Would you like a cup of coffee?"

"No thank you." She watched the back of Alistair's head, wondering how she could bring up the subject of her mother in front of him.

Alistair shifted his weight and said, "Would you look at the Palisades, Barbara? Have you ever seen anything so beautiful?" His right hand stretched out behind him as if to draw her close.

She moved to his side and looked where he pointed toward the left. Sure enough, steep cliffs, rocky in places, covered with trees and shrubs in others loomed over the river, everything appearing mysterious in the moonlight.

"If you keep watching you'll see homes of the Cornells, the Rockefellers, and other industrialists. They have lawns running right down to the river. Magnificent estates. The Astors are further up beyond Poughkeepsie, but before Albany," Charles said in a quiet voice as if he were speaking in a church.

"It's beautiful. I've never sailed on the Hudson River. We've been on European rivers but I was too young then to appreciate the travel." While she spoke, she wondered how she could get rid of Alistair to ask Charles Corwin about Mary Ellen.

Alistair took her by the arm. "May I take you out on deck to see the view?"

She hesitated. As much as she wanted to be with Alistair, she wanted to learn more about her mother.

"I expect you had quite a shock this evening, Miss Riis. I don't think I'd be able to sleep after learning such monumental news in such a way."

Her tongue was tied. He was so correct, so polite. "Yes, it was. I couldn't sleep. I want to see her, to talk to her."

"Do you think that's a good idea?"

"I went to see Grandmother. She says Mother is an addict. I don't know what to think."

Alistair took her hands in his. "Perhaps the first mate can tell us what stateroom she is in and we can walk there together. You can decide then whether you want to knock on her door. She could be asleep, you know."

Charles gave them the directions to the stateroom without hesitation.

Barbara responded with a warning, "You haven't worked for Grandmother before. I won't tell her you told us where to find my mother. She would be most displeased. You heard what she said about the couple who were supposed to be in control of mother. They're out of a job. I've never seen them before, but I expect they were only recently hired. She doesn't tolerate mistakes."

"Thank you, Miss."

Barbara looked up at Alistair and found herself attracted to the set of his jaw, the strength of his features. Funny how only a few days ago she found him to be slight and perhaps a little too bookish for her taste, and his mustache silly, but as the days went on, she found she looked forward to seeing him in the mornings for breakfast before he left for work. And now, on the yacht, she could see him all the time. He put an arm on her waist to guide her through the passageway to the inside staircase to the lower level.

The ceilings below were lower, the hallway narrower. Before they reached the designated room, she saw the man sitting on a chair effectively blocking off the narrow hallway.

"Do you think he's one of your security men?" she whispered to Alistair.

"I'd have no way of knowing. There are thousands of us. Come along, he's no doubt making sure she doesn't escape again. He's no threat to us."

Skeptical, she allowed herself to be guided up to the man who rocked back on his chair so it rested on two legs. His head was against the wall. "Excuse me," she began, "I'd like to visit with Mary Ellen."

"Sorry, Miss. Orders are no visitors." He dropped so the chair now stood on all four feet.

"The woman in there is my mother."

""I'm sorry. She's asleep now. The nurse gave her an injection. After tonight's unfortunate incident, I'm not leaving this spot and no one is going in without Mrs. Riis' specific permission."

"What is your name?" Barbara demanded.

"Evans, Miss. And my employer is Mrs. Riis."

"Come along, Barbara. It's probably for the best. We can speak to your grandmother in the morning and arrange to see your mother. It wouldn't be fair to show up unannounced in your mother's room."

"Not polite, either," Barbara said followed by a derisive laugh. "Above all, we must observe the proprieties." *After all these years, even though Grandmother told us she was dead, there was nothing to stop her from trying to find us.* Barbara wasn't sure if she wanted to cry or strike out at someone. "I'm going to bed, excuse me."

"May I show you the way?"

She paused. Her mind made up, she allowed Alistair to escort her to her room.

Thirty One

Barbara waited behind her door until Alistair had gone. When she peered out and saw no one, she slipped out and retraced her steps to the lower deck, careful to hold the rails to avoid making noise. At the sound of voices, she stepped into the shadows beneath the stairs and watched. Her heart pounded. She was convinced the nurse who passed could hear it. The nurse stopped at a cabin door and pulled a key from her apron pocket. As she opened the door, Barbara hurried to her side.

"Good evening. My name is Barbara Riis, may I speak with you a moment?"

Although the nurse appeared startled, she stepped aside and allowed Barbara to enter before her. Once inside the tiny, cell-like room, Barbara hurried to explain her circumstances. The nurse introduced herself as Martha Abbot. She was close to Barbara's size, though a bit shorter.

Within the hour, a new nurse, Constance Keating, arrived. Martha explained the scheme to her and although Constance pursed her lips and shook her head, she reluctantly went along with it.

Barbara felt reassured by the two women's trust. They reinforced her decision that she was doing right. Both nurses expressed belief it would help their patient more than any injections would.

Constance said, "In a little while we can go to the room together. She was sleeping quietly when I left her. Johanna won't mind an early break. We tried to explain to Mrs. Riis six nurses for this type of around the clock care would have been better, but she insisted on only three of us."

"Grandmother does have her own methods," Barbara said, not wanting to sound disloyal. "I hope you're right about Mary Ellen. I'd hate to make matters worse."

Martha said, "My dear, I don't think they can be any worse for her. She's been in despair for a long time. One doesn't become so wasted overnight."

"I noted how thin she is. I remember her as rosy-cheeked and a little plump, rather a taller version of Grandmother."

"Never," Constance said and then covered her mouth. "I mean, certainly not in appearance. Your grandmother is short and very high strung. She looks like she could use a little nursing care herself."

"I was in her room earlier, after dinner. Her lips looked bluish," Barbara told her.

"Bluish?" Constance asked in some alarm.

"She was agitated about me, I'm afraid."

"Does she have any powders she takes regularly?" Martha asked.

"She takes a lot of heart medications. I saw them in her rooms at home. I imagine she would have some with her as well."

Martha spoke up. "While you two go see to Mary Ellen, I think I'll go up and look in on Mrs. Riis. I could say I'm there to report on her daughter."

Close to midnight Barbara, dressed as a nurse wearing a cap and a pinafore over a dark cotton dress, entered her mother's room with Constance. When they entered Evans never looked up from the magazine he was reading.

Once they were in and Johanna had left, looking bewildered, Constance checked on Mary Ellen who still slept quietly.

"What do we do now?" Barbara whispered.

"We sit and wait. She'll wake up soon enough to go to the bathroom or wanting water or she might start screaming at imaginary insects. We never know, but each time she wakes up, she seems a little more clearheaded."

Barbara stood over the bed and studied her mother's face closely. Blue veins stood out on her forehead and around her eyes. Her skin appeared thin as tissue paper and nearly as white. She resisted the urge to stroke her brow, not wanting to disturb her. "Mommy," she said softly to the sleeping form. "I've missed you so much."

Constance took her by the shoulders and led her to a chair. "Just sit and relax. Nap if you want. I'll alert you when she wakes up."

Barbara sat and waited, hoping and fearing the moment her mother awoke. As the minutes ticked by her eyelids grew heavy. Periodically, her head nodded and she would jerk awake. Eventually she fell asleep.

"It's four a.m., dear. Your mother's been asleep for the longest stretch since we've been here. That's a good sign. She's waking now."

Shaking her head and trying to remember where she was, Barbara opened her eyes to see the nurse, Constance, standing in front of her. "My mother? She's awake?"

"She's coming around. I'm going to call for some food for her. If you'd like, you can sit on the edge of the bed and comfort her if she is upset when she fully awakens."

Barbara yawned and then stretched. "What will I say to her?"

"You'll figure it out." Constance backed away and returned to her chair in the corner and picked up her knitting.

Mary Ellen rolled onto her side and opened her eyes as Barbara approached the bed. She closed them and then opened them again. "Who are you?"

"I'm Barbara, Mother." Barbara's hands trembled as she reached out to touch her mother's face.

"I'm Mary Ellen. I had a daughter named Barbara, but she went away." A tear slid down across her nose and dripped onto her pillow. "She was so pretty. Like you."

"I am your Barbara."

"My daughter is much younger."

"I'm grown up now, Mother."

Mary Ellen groaned. "Go away. You remind me of her. There was another little girl, too. Her name was Lillian but we called her Lily. She was so sweet with her red hair and freckles. Barbara liked to take care of her."

"No, I didn't, Mother. I took care of her because you wouldn't." Barbara knelt down beside the bed so she could look Mary Ellen in the eyes. "Can you see me? Do you understand I'm your daughter?"

"You have the same eyes as Barbara but look at your hair and your clothes. Has it been so long? I don't feel well right now. Maybe you can come back another time. They're keeping me prisoner here, you know."

"I know. I don't know why, but I know you're a prisoner and Grandmother wants you cured of your habit. Do you want to be cured?" She resisted the urge to wipe the tears now flowing freely.

"No!" Mary Ellen shouted. "I want a shot. I need something right now! Someone bring me a needle." Her body shuddered and she rolled over, turning her back on Barbara. "Help me. I need the toilet again."

The nurse came and helped her to her feet. Barbara saw the soil on the back of her nightgown before she smelled the odor. Backing away from the bed she took the other chair in the corner of the room while the nurse tended to Mary Ellen in the bathroom. From the noises coming through the door, Mary Ellen was also busy throwing up. She heard the shower running. After a while the nurse returned with Mary Ellen dressed in a clean gown.

"I'm sorry, dear. She is going to have a sedative shot and then will probably sleep again for several hours. Soon she will be free from the heroin and the opium and all the evils she has put into her body, but for the rest of tonight we must leave her in peace. I will remind her in the morning that you were here. She will remember and she will be pleased." She sat Mary Ellen in a chair and then pulled the soiled padding and replaced it with fresh before helping her into bed.

"You'll give me a shot now, Constance? Please?" her mother whimpered like a small child.

Barbara wanted to cry again.

"Yes, my dear. You'll have a nice shot and then you will sleep. In the morning your little girl will come to see you again."

"My little girl? Barbara or Lillian? I want to see my babies again. I loved them so much. Where did they go?"

"Hush."

Barbara's legs trembled as she stood up and eased toward the door. Evans snored softly in his chair in the hallway. She wiped the tears from her face and, stumbling over her own feet, headed toward the stairs.

Thirty Two

"Another hour and we'll be in Albany, Ma'am," Captain Alter told Elisabeth as she entered the dining room for breakfast.

She'd slept soundly last night after taking her medications and the schnapps though she fretted about Barbara's questions. The gentle rocking of the boat soothed her.

So many years to get to this, she thought as she sat at the head of the long, table. It seemed no one else would be joining her for breakfast this morning. The chef explained that her guests had asked for breakfast to be brought to their rooms, including the young Miss Annie. Ledger had already taken his meal. *So, that's how it is. Alone again. I handled it before and I can handle it again.*

She sighed. *Almost over. And none too soon.* Thirty-seven years of agony and shame since the night she told her father. She knew she killed him. It couldn't have been anything else. She broke his heart and killed him the same as she'd killed her mother by being born.

~*~

"No, Daddy, it's not school I'm missing. I need to go away, Daddy. Far away where nobody knows me." She looked at the sandwiches on the platter and thought she'd throw up. Not here, not in front of Daddy.

"Where would you like to go? I really don't have time to get away from work. With the war nearly at an end, the railroads are creating so much development across the country, there is a huge demand for supplies. Can't it wait for a few months?"

"No. I want to go to Switzerland. I know a place to stay and you won't have to worry about me." She kept her arms folded across her chest, her hands tucked under her armpits. Her right foot tapped uncontrollably.

"Switzerland? What place?" His face told her he was beginning to understand.

"A place where some girls go when they want to get away for a while," she answered.

"A while?"

"Until they are fit and ready to come home again."

"Are you telling me what I think you're telling me?" His face turned red, his lips nearly disappeared.

She nodded as the tears began to flow. "I'm sorry, Daddy."

"You're...?"

"With child. I'm going to have a baby." Now she'd said it, the relief overwhelmed her and she began crying more heavily. "Will you help me?"

Her father lunged from his chair to shake her by the shoulders. "Who? Who did this to you? I'll kill him with my bare hands, do you hear me? I'll kill him!"

So startled by his reaction, she couldn't respond.

"Tell me. Tell me now or get out of my sight." He released her so suddenly she fell back against the cushion like a rag doll.

"I - I -" Her mind raced for a response. He couldn't kill Justin, not until she'd had a chance to talk to him. What could she say? The truth? "Daddy, let me talk to him first. We've been talking about getting married though we wanted to wait until I turned eighteen. Please. Then I'll tell you. I promise."

Her father stalked behind his desk and sat with his head in his hands. "What would your poor mother ever be thinking now? She's going to come down from heaven and kill me before I get to that blackguard of yours. When she was dying, I promised to watch over you and care for you." His hands slammed palm down on the desk blotter. "This is not to be tolerated. Have you been to confession?"

"Confession?" The change of direction again caught her off guard. "No. I - I hoped to say I was officially engaged to be married. I thought it would make it seem less disgraceful."

"Why do you want to go to Switzerland if this person claims to want to marry you? Tell me that." Now his face turned pale, his eyes squinted at her.

"I – thought…"

"You thought just in case you're wrong. You're lying, aren't you? No one's asked for your hand in marriage. He already had what he wanted! How could you do this to your poor mother and me?" He dropped his head onto the desk and sobbed, repeating, "I'm so sorry, my love, so sorry."

"Do this to you?" Elisabeth watched him, all the while her heart grew harder. "Fine. I'll deal with this myself. Good night, Father." She forced herself from the chair and managed to leave the office and climb the stairs to her room.

The next evening she went to Justin's house.

After that humiliating experience, she knew she had to put on a brave face in front of her father and pretend things were working well. She told him she'd be married soon but it wouldn't be a large wedding nor in a church. After the wedding they planned to leave immediately for Europe. They would return after the birth of her baby, though she didn't know for how long they'd be gone.

With Amber's help she packed her clothes in steamer trunks, the whole time her mind racing with possibilities, possibilities discarded nearly as quickly as she thought of them. Then one afternoon a week later as she sat on the front porch, she saw an open carriage pass by the house. In it sat Jim Riis and his caretaker.

Without thinking, she jumped up and waved. "Mr. Riis. Hello!"

The carriage moved on past the house and then turned around, pulling up into the driveway.

She skipped down the steps, a smile on her face, her hands stretched out in greeting. Jim's face reflected her apparent joy at seeing him. "I asked Decker to take a different route today for my prescribed 'airing.' How delighted I am to see you again."

"And I, you," she responded with the appropriate amount of shyness. "You were so kind when we met at the picnic."

"You looked like a lamb being led to the slaughter. I was glad not to see you there again. Justin is a wicked womanizer. Good you weren't completely taken in by him, though I was worried that afternoon. Would you like to ride with us?"

"Why - yes, I would. I'll go let the housekeeper know I'll be away for a little while." She skipped happily into the house, picked up a light wrap and shouted to Amber, "I'm going out and I may not be back for dinner."

~*~

She hadn't returned for dinner. Later that evening she came home and announced her engagement to Mr. James Riis. They planned to be married on board ship as they traveled to Southampton and then on to Europe for at least the next eighteen months. She did not explain the bargain to her father. In exchange for giving her his name, Jim expected her to become his nurse and companion. Had she had any idea how difficult the task would be, she might not have agreed. She was grateful when he retained his personal caretaker a full six months following the birth of her daughter.

For the next six years she became a drudge, bathed him, pushed him around in those god-awful chairs, as he became more and more ill-tempered. And sat with him while he fondled little Mary Ellen. Then Ledger came into their lives.

She looked around the empty dining room. "Let them all go to hell. I will finish this by myself if I have to." She wiped away a tear as she recalled the last time she'd said those words. The morning she and Jim boarded the ship she received a telegram announcing her father's sudden death from a heart attack.

Married in sorrow, she gave birth in anger and bitterness. The shell around Elisabeth's heart thickened.

"The launch is ready to take you ashore, Mrs. Riis," First Mate Charles Corwin announced.

"You must learn not to sneak up on people, young man," she scolded, trying to give herself time to recover her composure.

Leaving orders Mary Ellen was to remain on board until sent for, Elisabeth went on deck. Barbara, Annie, Ledger and Alistair joined her, prepared to go ashore. While she knew what she had in mind, the others talked cheerfully about a dinner party, which Ledger apparently planned for the evening. "We can invite Captain Alter and Mr. Corwin as well, if you like," Ledger suggested.

That did not meet with Elisabeth's plans, but she agreed, not wanting to give away her hand.

"What a wonderful idea," Barbara said.

Annie blushed as she smiled gratefully at Ledger.

As soon as they stepped ashore, Elisabeth took the first carriage, stopping the others. "You take the other carriage. I have something to do before I come to the house."

Thirty Three

Once her grandmother's carriage was out of sight, Barbara told Captain Alter she would be returning to the yacht. "I want to spend time with my mother."

Annie gaped at her. "Your mother? What about our party?"

"You go on to the house. I'll be there later. You can entertain Mr. Corwin. Ledger will most likely be there."

"But he went with Mrs. Riis," the girl said.

"Just go! I won't be long. Tell Mrs. Burch to prepare rooms on the second floor for guests."

"Guests? You want me to boss her around?"

Charles Corwin stood by a carriage waiting to help Annie into it. He smiled at the exchange between the two young women.

"She's not going to believe we're having guests any more than she'd listen to orders from me."

"They're orders from me, not you," Barbara said. "And send a carriage back for me."

Alistair remained by her side. "Do you want me to come with you?"

Barbara hesitated and then said, "That would be nice, but I don't want you to come to Mother's cabin with me. I want to speak with her by myself."

"I want to be there if you need me."

She drew a breath, comforted by his words. "Thank you."

Once aboard, she asked Alistair to help her find her mother's room again and explained how she'd gone back last night to talk to her. She still didn't understand completely how ill her mother was, having no experience or awareness of the seriousness of drug addiction.

As she described her mother's condition, Alistair remained quiet. He left her at the door but reassured her he would be waiting alongside the new guard, a steward reassigned from his regular duties to replace Evans. The steward had apparently not been provided with any instructions about visitors. At Barbara's request he knocked on the door.

Martha let her in. "Good news, she's feisty today, Miss Riis, and she remembers you were here last night. I think it won't be long now, she'll turn the corner and you'll have your mother back, good as new."

Barbara snorted at Martha's comment. "You didn't know my mother before, did you? I wouldn't recognize 'good as new.' Mother has always done what she pleased. I want to see her happy without the drugs."

"We have the same objective. As does your grandmother."

"We won't talk about my grandmother, Martha. Would you please wait outside while I talk with my mother?"

"I'm sorry, no, Miss Riis," she answered in alarm. "You don't know what'll happen. She might be fine, but she might also become sick again. You won't be able to handle her."

"Wait outside. If I need you, I'll call you. Don't worry, I know I'm not a nurse and I won't try to be one." Barbara stepped aside so the nurse could leave.

Left alone with her mother, Barbara suddenly felt unsure of herself. Mary Ellen lay asleep, snoring lightly. Her face looked peaceful, the dark lashes accentuating the pale skin. Barbara took a seat beside the bed, set her hat and handbag on the floor and waited for her mother to stir and open her eyes.

Memories of Mary Ellen filled her head. She saw her dancing, splashing through the shallow water on the edge of the beach in Malaga, her hair flying wildly in the stiff breeze. She wanted to see that mother again, the one who was careless with her children but fierce if anyone or anything threatened them. Her chest shuddered as she held back tears of mourning for the mother she'd lost. Would she find her?

Mary Ellen opened her eyes as if in response to her thought. "You're Barbara grown up, aren't you?"

"I am," she managed to choke out. "Are you all right?"

"I don't think so. It seems like I've been in this bed all my life and then I think I just arrived. I know it's not a hospital but there are nurses around me all the time." Mary Ellen didn't move. Her voice came out as a soft croak.

"It's Grandmother's yacht. Well, hers and Ledger's. She told us you were dead."

Mary Ellen shut her eyes again. "I heard."

"But you're not. I'm glad. I've missed you so much." Barbara leaned forward in the chair aching to reach out to her mother.

"I'm sorry. She was right. I've been a bad mother. I deserved everything that happened to me."

"What's going to happen after you're cured?"

"My mother, your grandmother, seems to have plans for me. I don't know. I don't know if I want to know. I feel so edgy and ready to jump every second when I'm awake. I like sleeping. Can you leave me for a while? I'll take a nap. Where is the nurse? I need another shot." Her mother's eyes watered.

"I'll get her," Barbara said, disappointed they couldn't have more of a conversation. She stood up, went to the door and stepped into the hall.

Before she let Martha return, she asked, "What shots are you giving my mother?"

"They're to help her get over the opium. It's called hyoscine." Constance stood, ready to tend her patient.

"I don't want you to give her any more injections until I have time to speak to a doctor."

Constance bridled. "Excuse me, Miss Riis, but I don't work for you. It's one thing to let you sneak in to talk to your mother, it is quite another to disobey doctor's orders."

Alistair stood up when Barbara came out, but he didn't interfere in the conversation.

"I don't know a lot about addictions, but I do know it doesn't make any sense to give her something that knocks her out and makes her want more when she wakes up. Sounds like another addiction to me." Barbara slipped back into the room and shut the door before the nurse could enter. She locked it from the inside and returned to her mother's side.

"Martha will be here in a while. In the meantime, do you think we could talk? I want to know what happened to you after we left. What you've been doing for the last six years. You can't have been out of your head with drugs the entire time."

"I really want my shot. Please let me have it and then I can tell you everything." Mary Ellen had not moved other than to turn her head.

"It won't be long. Tell me about the opium. Is it true you went to opium dens? Are they really places where you did terrible degenerate acts?" Barbara had read about them in the newspapers, but still had no concept of what went on in those places. Barbara's eyes focused on her mother.

Mary Ellen smiled. "You heard wrong," she began. "I have frequented them and I have done things of which I might not be proud, but I did I try to change my life."

Her mother closed her eyes. A small smile touched her lips. "You know I enrolled in a nursing program. I left you in good hands. I was only gone for six weeks." Tears slipped out from under her eyelids. "When I had my first break, I came home to find an empty house. The woman I hired gone. And both of you. I went to the police but they couldn't tell me anything. I tried to return to school, but my mind was always on you and your sister."

"Why didn't you check with Grandmother? Didn't it occur to you she had us?"

Mary Ellen drew a shuddering breath. "We hadn't communicated in years, why would I think of her? I thought the woman I hired took you away."

"I told her you were in nursing school, but she said you still abandoned us. And I was glad to go to her house. I wasn't good at cooking. Lily was getting very thin."

"I couldn't understand what happened. The doorman said you'd left with an older woman. I never dreamed it could have been my mother."

"The woman you hired was a drinker. From the first day, once she found the liquor cabinet, she kept at it day and night. I screamed at her and then hid the bottles. But she'd find them again. So I poured the drink out. She gave up and left us. I wrote to the school where she said you were, but we never heard from you. We didn't mind. We used the money you sent for her to buy food and I took good care of us." Barbara recalled how she and Lily explained to the doorman they went to the green grocers for the exercise.

"One day a letter arrived addressed to you. It was from Albany. I opened it. It was from Ledger. From the manner in which he wrote, I understood you two had kept in touch. So I wrote to him and told him what had happened with the nanny you hired. Next thing we knew, Grandmother showed up and didn't believe a word of what we said about you. She was convinced you were in Europe with another man." Barbara shrugged at the memory. "We came to live in Albany and hoped you'd come for us. We never received responses to any of our letters. Then one day, Grandmother told us you died."

"The old bat."

Unsure she had heard her mother correctly, Barbara ignored the comment and continued. "She did send us to school and made sure we had good food, though she made us live upstairs on the third floor in an empty servant's room. I'm so glad we found you. Tell me, Mother, what happened? I know you liked to drink, but what made you turn to heroin and opium?"

"When I thought I'd lost you forever I couldn't handle it. I never answered Ledger's letters. I threw the letters away. Life meant so little. I drank more and then I met a man who gave me my first taste of opium. It made me feel so good I never wanted to stop using it. Never." She gasped for breath, slid her arms from under the covers and reached out to Barbara. "I loved you so much. Now, please, please let Martha come in with my shot."

"I don't think that's a good idea. Heroin, opium and now something else, which seems like the same kind of thing. Please wait a little longer." Barbara took her cold hands in hers and held them like a mother tending her child. "Try to sleep now without the shot. I'll stay with you."

Mary Ellen looked as if she would acquiesce. She closed her eyes again and took a deep breath. Pulling one hand away from Barbara, she put it over her head. Barbara watched her breaths become more even; the hand relaxed in hers.

Sure her mother was asleep, she stepped out to summon Alistair to sit with her. Martha could wait in the hall.

As soon as the door opened, Mary Ellen's voice reached out to them. "Martha! Help me! I need you now."

Before Barbara or Alistair could react, Martha pushed past Barbara, knocking her into Alistair. This time, it was Martha who shut the door and locked it from the inside. Barbara banged on the door and shouted, "Don't you dare give her an injection!"

Alistair joined her in banging on the door until the steward tapped them both on their shoulders. Barbara turned, ready to strike him, but when she saw the grin on his face and the key in his hand, she stood aside to let him unlock the door. She rushed into the room followed closely by the two men as Martha reached for her medical bag on the other side of the room.

Barbara went to her mother while Alistair and the steward confronted Martha.

"Miss Riis asked you not to give her mother any more injections. I suggest you honor her request until such time as either she or her grandmother rescind the order," Alistair said.

Martha looked around him at Barbara who sat with her arms crossed defiantly, protecting her mother. The woman backed down. "I'll remove myself from the room but I will not abandon my patient, am I clear? She's not a well woman and it's my duty to care for her. Constance and Johanna will be here shortly and they'll feel the same way." She exited the room in a huff.

The steward followed her out after once again saluting Alistair.

"Thank you for your help," Barbara said.

"My pleasure," he responded with a wink and smile.

~*~

Mary Ellen watched the activity from her position on the bed, hoping Martha would win the confrontation and stay with her, but the cowardly nurse left the room with her precious medication.

"I wanted that shot," she said to her daughter. "You have no business keeping it from me. It's supposed to cure me." She felt the moisture on her brow and under her arms as her body began to shiver. The shot would let her sleep.

"You're alive and I want you to remain so. I want my mother back. Can I order some food for you? Tea? What can I get you?"

Her daughter looked so beautiful and young, so anxious to please, but Mary Ellen couldn't focus on her right now. "You can get me my nurse, you stupid child. Just bring her in here! Now!"

"No. I'm going to put some clothes on you and take you home. You can finish your cure in your own bedroom. There's no point in shouting. If you don't cooperate, I'll have to ask Alistair to help me."

The girl looked serious as the young man's face turned bright red. "I don't think I have any clothes. Those Amazons keep putting me in nightgowns."

"Then we'll wrap you in a blanket to cover you. Can you get out of bed yourself?"

"I could if I wanted to. What will be different at the house? You'll lock me in a room and keep those watchdogs on me, that's what. I don't even remember having a room in a house."

"We're in Albany. Your mother's home, where you were born."

"I was born in Switzerland. I think we came to Mother's house once for a short while when I was ten years old. It was cold and musty. No one had lived in it for years." Mary Ellen remembered her mother explaining about Grandfather Ackert who'd died before she was born. "She and Ledger took me to an office and then in a few months we went back to France where we'd left Father. He was in the care of nurses when he died. He was so unhappy."

"Stay with her a minute, will you, Alistair? I'm going to speak with the nurse."

Mary Ellen watched Barbara leave while the young man backed further away from the bed, nearly pressing himself into the far wall.

"Do I make you nervous?"

He shook his head. "No, ma'am."

"I'm not going to have any fits. All I want is something to help me sleep. You'll help me, won't you?" She struggled to pull herself to a sitting position, cocked her head to one side and fluttered her eyelids. The eye thing, along with a smile promising more, had worked on so many men over the years.

"That's exactly what Miss Riis has in mind for you."

"She's a child; you're a man. You know about life." She ran her fingers through her unkempt hair, pulling the long strands down the front of her bodice, letting her hands linger over the swell of her breasts.

He stood to attention, observing her as if she were a specimen.

She dropped her hands to the covers and grabbed her middle, her face twisted in pain. "Ow! Oh no. Help me," she cried.

Thirty Four

"It's too late," Ledger repeated. "Whatever you had in mind won't work."

"Don't tell me it's too late. Explain yourself," Elisabeth commanded, her anger and frustration building. She had been waiting for a message in the office for over five hours. How long could it take to find out if a man as important as Justin Pembroke was in town? She glared at Ledger, who stood on the opposite side of her desk looking unperturbed. *Damn him, anyway. It was all meant to be finished tonight.*

"I don't need to explain myself to you. Senator Pembroke has already left for Kansas City. Apparently, he made his decision to run. Now, if you'll excuse me, I'll finish my work and return to my dwelling. I have need of some quiet. And you are having a dinner party, if you recall. You invited the captain and first mate." He turned his back on her and left.

"Jealous bastard," she muttered as he shut the door. It was a rule they both observed from the first - when they were in Albany, a city populated with far fewer than the three million who lived in New York City, they would maintain separate residences. They would also keep up the facade of employer/employee. After so many years, she wasn't sure they fooled anyone, but it had become a habit. She invited the captain, but not Ledger, to her dinner party.

An accounts book lay open before her on the desk. She found the numbers incomprehensible at this time of day. The best she could figure is everyone had been doing their jobs and all appeared to be in order. She signed letters authorized by her manager and written by her two male secretaries and then slammed the book shut. "Next," she said as she summoned the elder of the two, "more travel."

"Arrange a private rail car to leave Albany as soon as possible. I want to travel to Kansas City. See that it has ample accommodations for me, Ledger, at least two servants and my granddaughters. Notify Mrs. Burch she'll be traveling with us then see that the galley is fully stocked and equipped for her and a cleaning girl."

"Yes, Ma'am," the old man, Thomas Carter, replied with a bow. "Anything else?"

"No. I'll have Ledger make any other arrangements. Be sure it's done before the end of today," she said to his retreating back. She noticed ink stains on the sleeves of his shirt in spite of the protective cuffs he wore. Shaking her head at his sloppiness, she made a note to herself to see how Edgar Sullivan, the other secretary, managed to remain so neat and tidy.

Leaning back in the chair she considered her original plan. How could she adapt it to a different venue? "Senator Justin Pembroke at the Democratic convention humiliated by scandal, resigns before he is chastised and run out of office by his colleagues in the senate," she said, reading imaginary headlines. "Senator Pembroke has disappeared from Washington, Albany, and most importantly, the presidential race. It is rumored he has run off to Mexico." Elisabeth smiled as she rang the bell for Mr. Sullivan to retrieve the ledgers from her desk. By the time he entered her mood was greatly lifted.

"Place these back in the safe and then you may leave. I'll be going home now. Carter has his orders and will lock up when he's finished. Say hello to your lovely family from me."

Sullivan raised his bushy eyebrows. "Thank you, ma'am, I shall. And may I welcome you home?"

"Thank you." She dismissed him with a wave of her hand and then gathered her bonnet, gloves, and wrap. Now, she thought, how to get Mary Ellen on the train without too much fuss. A good thing those nurses had whatever it was they used to inject her. Perhaps they could transfer her from the yacht to the train during her sleep. The addicted fool would never notice. Elisabeth closed the office door behind her and headed through the outer office, past clerks still diligently writing in large volumes.

Out in the fresh air, she looked around for her carriage. The driver stood smoking and talking with a stranger nearly half a block away. He knew she always left her office at five o'clock. What was he doing over there?

Folding her arms, she tapped her booted foot on the sidewalk. The day was warm and she became uncomfortable waiting for him to notice her standing in the late afternoon sun. It was nearly five minutes before he turned his head and saw her. Tipping his cap to the stranger he quickly leapt onto the carriage and whipped the horse into action.

"To whom were you speaking?" she demanded when he arrived and jumped down to help her into her seat.

"An old colleague, ma'am. Sorry. I expected you to be longer in the office seeing as how you been away for a while." He bowed and backed away once she was settled.

"You will be docked for this."

"Yes, ma'am," he said as he took his own seat and whipped the horse into motion.

She worked on the logistics of a trip to Kansas City. With Ledger in charge, it ought to run smoothly. He was always good at getting tasks done in a timely and efficient manner. The thought of Ledger by her side again as they traveled west comforted her.

~*~

When she arrived at the house, she found a state of chaos. Mrs. Burch shouted at someone called Bridget in the kitchen, followed by a scream of pain and a clatter of falling pots. As she stepped into the foyer, she found a boy dragging her trunk up the stairs while a smaller boy, about eight years old, pushed at it from the lower end. The two of them had a counting system going. "One, two, to you," called the older lad. "Three, four, heave! To you," said the smaller one as he gave a shove to the trunk. It can't be that heavy, she thought without amusement. She needed to get past them in order to get to her rooms to bathe and change for dinner. The stairway was wide enough, but she did not relish the idea of coming in contact with their sweaty little bodies.

"Mrs. Burch!" she called.

The woman hurried from the back of the house wiping her brow with a kitchen towel. "There you are, Mrs. Riis. Please excuse us. That is, welcome home. Don't fret, everything will be in order by eight. I'm trying to teach the new girl some cooking; she's fairly useless at cleaning. Do you want me to send her up to run your bath?"

"Stop chattering and send the useless girl here. And find someone to help these two. I'm going to need everything washed and freshened. I'll be leaving again in a day or two. And don't stand there gaping at me. There's work to be done!"

"Of course." The large woman's face flushed from rushing about.

Elisabeth thought Mrs. Burch ought to be able to manage better. She'd had a nearly empty house for over a week, which left her little to do. Lazy woman.

She waited for the boys to reach the landing and then ordered them to stop while she mounted the stairs, using the banister to pull herself up each step, holding her skirts when she passed the boys.

There were people talking upstairs as well as below. What was going on in her home? It used to be quiet; the invading voices annoyed her. She paused, winded from the climb, at the open door that led to the upper floors and called, "Who's there?"

Barbara appeared at the top of the stairs. "Lily, Annie and I are here, Grandmother. We're finding dresses to wear for tonight. Do you need something?"

"I need that useless girl to go down to the kitchen and find out what Mrs. Burch has for her to do." Her heart raced. She needed to rest. "See that she does," she finished lamely.

Digitalis. She needed to get to her digitalis to slow her heartbeat. Crossing the hall to her room drained her. Time to nap. The bed looked so far away. Instead of the bed, the soft, overstuffed armchair near the window would do. She collapsed onto that and waited to catch her breath so she could make it to the cabinet containing her medicines.

~*~

"Oh, Miss Barbara, what should I do?" Annie cried.

"Stay here with me and Lily. Mrs. Burch has the new girl, Bridget, and two others are supposed to be along any time to help with serving and clearing up tonight. We can prepare the rooms for the guests. You know where the linens and things are kept, so you'll be working by anybody's definition, even Grandmother's." Barbara heard the thumping on the staircase and stepped out to look downstairs again. Two young lads had reached the top of the steps with Grandmothers trunk. They had yet to deliver hers.

"Come on, Annie, find pinafores for me and Lily and we'll play housemaid with you. We want Mr. Rogers and our other guest to be comfortable."

"But, where is he? And why is the other guest a secret?" Lily asked for the fifth time.

"He said he wanted to go downtown and would arrive early enough to change for dinner. I suspect he might be embarrassed not to own his own dinner clothes. Maybe he's gone to find a haberdasher."

"Come on. I'm not going to help unless you tell me who the other person is."

"It's a surprise. One I hope you'll like. And you'll feel really, really bad if you haven't helped fix her room." Barbara hoped keeping their mother a secret from Lily was a good idea. She wanted her sister to be surprised and happy to see her. By the time Mother arrived, the sleeping drug ought to have worn off enough so she would be coherent and able to speak with them.

"Her room? A lady? Who?"

Giving up on her sister, Lily turned to Annie. "Do you know who she is?"

"I do and I'm not telling either."

"All right, then, tell me more about Mr. Rogers. Is he handsome? Did he make love to Barbara? Does he recite poetry?"

Annie laughed. "He's a fine-looking lad, but I didn't hear any poetry, Lily. Time enough for that." She headed out the door to the linen closet across the way and began pulling out sheets and blankets. "Come along, Lily. I'll show you how to make up a proper bed."

"I don't know why I have to help. I'm never going to be a housemaid and he's not my friend anyway." She held out her arms to collect two pillows and clean, pressed scarves for the bureaus and nightstands.

Barbara tied her pinafore behind her back and followed the girls down to the next floor. Grandmother's bedroom door stood open so she peeked in to see if she was resting. Surprised not to see her on her bed, she peered into the dim room until she caught sight of the sleeping form in the chair to her right. "Grandmother?" she whispered, not wanting to disturb her, but wanting to be sure she wasn't ill.

Grandmother didn't respond. Barbara pulled the door to, gently shutting it so the noise wouldn't disturb the older woman.

"She's resting," she cautioned Lily and Annie. "Let's try to be quiet."

"What're we supposed to do with this?" the boy at the top of the stairs said.

"Set it to one side. Mrs. Riis is resting. Go back and bring up the rest of the luggage. And be quiet about it, she's exhausted from traveling."

"I heard she came here in a huge ship! Right up the Hudson River!" the smaller boy said, his eyes wide with wonder. "Is that true?"

"We all did. Now hush."

In spite of her warning, the two boys clattered down the stairs. She rolled her eyes and shook her head. No sounds came from Grandmother's room.

The next trunk thumped up the stairs as Lily and Annie helped Barbara air and her grandfather's old room for Alistair. It looked like a man's room with its dark wood paneling, and heavy green velvet draperies. Lily started the cleaning by sweeping the carpet and then used a damp mop to clean the exposed floorboards. Next, Annie and Lily took down the curtains and draperies and hung them out the windows to shake the dust from them. There was no time to hang them out in the sunshine, but with the windows open, at least the room would lose most of its musty odors before Alistair arrived.

Annie used lemon oil to clean the mahogany furniture and wiped down the bedposts. The three of them turned the mattress and then made up the bed.

"Strikes me as a futile exercise in moving dust," Barbara observed when they finished, though she did feel a sense of pride in their accomplishment. Fresh candles stood on the mantle, the fireplace was made up and a filled oil lantern stood on a bedside table.

"Come on, one more room. We'll do Grandmother's old room. It's light and airy. Our guest will love it."

They marched in with their cleaning supplies and did the same as they had in the other room, sweeping, dusting and waxing so everything sparkled. Barbara removed the oil lamp and the candles, without explaining to Lily.

"Can we get dressed now? We need a bath!" Lily exclaimed once they finished.

"All right. You two go first, I want to check on Grandmother." Barbara watched them trundle back up to the third floor and then as she headed toward Grandmother's room, she heard Ledger downstairs asking for Mrs. Riis.

"She's resting," she called over the railing. "I was about to wake her so she could get ready for dinner."

"I need a minute of her time," he said as he came up. "We're off on another journey in two days."

Barbara felt her shoulders sag. Exhausted from the heavy work, she did not want to face the prospect of traveling again. "Back on the yacht?"

"This time a train," he said when he reached the top of the stairs.

"Let me go in and wake her gently," Barbara said, stopping him from knocking on her grandmother's door.

"What happened to you?" Ledger asked as he looked over her clothing and mussed hair.

"We've been fixing rooms for Mother and Alistair. He's staying for dinner and expects to leave tomorrow."

"I plan to have your mother remain on the boat until our next trip."

"No! You can't do that, Ledger. I arranged to bring her here so I can look after her. I don't like the way those nurses keep giving her injections to put her to sleep. Every time she wakes up, she begs for a shot and they give it to her."

"That is the prescribed treatment, according to the doctor who made the arrangements."

She looked at the oil lamp and the candles in her hands. "I removed these from her room so she wouldn't have any accidents." She leaned on the hall table and tried to absorb the new information. Mother would remain on the yacht receiving injections, and she, Barbara, would have to pack again for another trip. All that work for nothing.

She glared at Ledger. "Well, I'm going to find a doctor for her myself. One I trust. Wait a minute and I'll let Grandmother know you're here. Let's see what she has to say."

Thirty Five

After she received her digitalis from Barbara, Elisabeth felt far better by the time Ledger entered the room.

"Take a seat and tell me about the train car. Were you able to secure one?" she asked him.

"It'll be here in two days. I've dealt with Evans and Maureen. They're on their way back to the city with their pay. What do you want to do about the nurses?"

"We should have at least one of them with us. Choose one and pay off the others. Tell Mrs. Burch we'll all be going and then make sure Barbara and Lillian pack for the journey. They won't be going any place special so there's no need for fancy clothes. They can remain on the train while I conduct my business. And see to it the girl, Annie, comes along to help Mrs. Burch."

"Barbara won't like that. The two of them have become close this past couple of weeks. Barbara's teaching the girl to read."

"Too bad. She is hired help and I pay her wages; she'll do as I say." Elisabeth couldn't understand this bossy attitude Barbara had suddenly taken. "What makes Barbara think she has the right to take over my employees?"

Ledger's annoyed Elisabeth. "Barbara is a bright girl. She has money in her own right and I suppose, as there is no more slavery, hasn't been for a long time, Annie can work for whom she chooses."

"Not in my house."

"It isn't technically your house either, though Barbara doesn't know that. No point in creating too much of a fuss about it. Mrs. Burch has a new girl. I'm going to retire to my rooms and spend the evening catching up on some reading. It's been a busy couple of weeks for all of us. And I suspect the next couple will be even busier. Good night."

She watched him stand up and wished she could abandon her plans and remain ensconced in this house forever, but she could no more give up her plans for revenge than she could force herself to stop breathing. "Send one of the girls. I don't care who shows up to help me dress for dinner. Thank you."

~*~

"Should I go?" Annie asked Barbara.

"Lily can. She gets along well with Grandmother, don't you?" Barbara ruffled Lily's hair as if she were a small child.

Lily pushed her hand away. "Stop it. I need you to fix it so I look nice tonight."

"Go help Grandmother and when I'm done bathing, I'll fix it for you while Annie does my hair. How's that sound?"

"Fine," the younger girl grumbled. "I wish I'd gone to New York and been able to buy new clothes. It's not fair. Besides, Grandmother doesn't even like me."

Barbara rolled her eyes. "Are you going to say that all summer? If you are, then I'm leaving again and taking Annie with me."

Lily threw her hands in the air and stormed from the room, slamming the door behind her. Barbara and Annie laughed at her.

"I really don't want to be crammed into a single rail car with Grandmother and everyone else for weeks on end," Barbara said.

"Nor do I, but I think I have to go where I'm told. Two days to get ready. We'd better get busy with the laundry." Annie plucked clothing from Barbara's luggage and separated it into piles for laundering and airing.

"Give it to the new girl. If she asks, tell her you're my companion, that sounds better than lady's maid. I've been thinking about it and lady's maid sounds too pretentious, like I'm trying to be royalty or something. You are now officially my companion. But you'd better hurry up and learn to read. I learned a new game from Alistair called backgammon. I'll teach you that, too."

"You're making my head spin with all the new things you want me to learn. I can read and write my name and make out the letters of the alphabet. Soon I'll be able to read to your grandmother in the evenings." Annie continued working as she talked. "And with the new wages I receive, I can send some home to my family. Life is getting better, isn't it?"

"It seems to be," Barbara answered half-hearted. Her plans to introduce Lily to Mother had been thwarted. Maybe she would have to wait until Kansas City. And now, there would be no time to find a doctor and take him out to the yacht.

Barbara studied her glum expression in the mirror as she considered the next few days. "I have an idea," she said in an effort to cheer herself up. "Let's find out the train schedule and then buy First Class tickets so we don't have to stay with Grandmother. We can have our own sleeping room and eat in the public dining car. Another adventure. What do you think?" Barbara twirled around in the pale blue dinner gown. Annie's face reflected confusion rather than approval.

"About what? Traveling in a train with a bedroom or the dress?"

"Both, you goose."

"The dress suits you. I'm not so sure about the train. All the way to Kansas City? That's way out west, isn't it?"

"You were afraid to go to New York, too, remember? And look how that turned out."

"That's what I'm thinking of. Someone tried to kill us by burning down the house."

"Nobody got hurt and I met Alistair," Barbara corrected. "Now, see what you can do with my hair. Lily ought to be back shortly and we can go down to dinner. I wonder what's keeping Alistair?"

She went down to the front porch to wait. With her elbows on her knees and chin in hands, she stared, unseeing, at the trees at the front of the property, not quite shielding the house from passersby. Birds sang their evening songs to one another in the treetops while Barbara brooded over her mother.

"You're looking awfully glum," Alistair said, walking up to the right of her, carrying his valise.

"Oh! Where'd you come from?"

"I took the omnibus from downtown. They let me off at the corner. Are we still having dinner? You look awfully pretty." He stopped about five feet away from her, his hat in one hand as he set down the suitcase and waited for her reply.

"Dinner's still on as far as I can tell. Mother won't be joining us as I'd hoped. Ledger ordered Martha to keep her on the boat."

She reached up to the railing in order to pull herself up right. Alistair dropped his bag and rushed to her side. "Let me help you. So, this is your house, where you live. It's much larger than I imagined from the way you described it."

"Come inside. Grandmother should be nearly ready to come down. Lily is helping fix her hair."

"I'm sorry about your mother."

"What happened?" Barbara stopped in the vestibule to ask him.

"What happened when?"

"I left you with Mother when I went to talk to the nurse."

She knew right away something happened when his face turned red from the roots of his hair down to his neck. "Tell me."

"I rolled a cigarette for her. It seemed better than an injection and she enjoyed it."

"Oh, no. She's a tobacco fiend as well?"

"I don't think so. Your mother wasn't completely in her right mind."

"Did you talk with her at all?"

"I did."

"And?"

"Your mother flung her arms around me in despair. She was crying for her opium and I tried to comfort her."

Barbara felt her heart sink. One minute Mother talked like any normal person and the next she begged for drugs. Relieved when there was no more to the story, she relaxed. "I'm sorry you had to see her that way. I'm even more sorry we can't surprise Lily. Come in. I'll get Bridget to show you to your room. Annie, Lily and I made it up for you," she added with a feeling of pride.

"I went to the train station to secure my seat for tomorrow. I'll be sorry to leave."

His eyes reflected her own sadness to see him depart; she had come to rely on his company. "I understand. You have your work."

He nodded.

~*~

Dinner, though a sumptuous meal, turned out to be a glum affair. Grandmother ate little, complaining of indigestion; Annie was nervous and dripped soup on her new dress; Alistair, dressed in his new dinner attire, asked after Ledger.

"Is he unwell? I hoped to talk with him at dinner," Alistair said.

"Ledger has his own lodgings over the stables," Grandmother told him.

Not understanding, Alistair continued. "I thought you were business partners, Mrs. Riis. He's an interesting fellow, quite a background."

"Ledger knows his place in this household. What you may have observed elsewhere is of no consequence here. Are you quite finished with your soufflé? I'll have Mrs. Burch send in the main course. Lily, stop swinging your feet under the table."

Lily sat up straight her eyes wide with surprise. "How did you...?

"You're jiggling."

Lily turned her head toward Barbara and smiled a shy, embarrassed smile at being caught.

"After dinner, I'll explain the arrangements we've made for Kansas City. Meanwhile, I'd like to ask you, Mr. Rogers, if you would please come along in your role as a Pinkerton operative to protect our little troupe. We'll be in a private rail car."

"That wouldn't be up to me, Ma'am. You might want to wire the Hartford office and request my services but there are far more experienced men available."

"Ledger has already taken care of everything. He tells me they said it is your decision. You will be on their payroll, but I will be your employer."

His eyes turned to Barbara, who wanted him to be on the same train with her, but also didn't want him subject to Grandmother's whims. She lowered her eyes without giving him any hint of her position on the matter.

"Well," he said. Fortunately, he didn't have to say more because the two temporary helpers brought in the main course, making several trips to serve everything. When they had placed the bowls and platters on the table, they poured fresh glasses of wine.

They ate mostly in silence with occasional compliments on the food. Annie even managed to stammer out, "This is the best roast pork I've ever tasted."

Barbara couldn't imagine that she'd tasted many roasts but was pleased that her protégé paid attention to her table etiquette. She did not receive one reprimand from Grandmother.

"My compliments to your chef, Mrs. Riis," Captain Alter said, raising his wine glass in a toast.

"My chef, as you call her, is a cook and housekeeper." Though her words were sharp, Barbara could tell by the gleam in her eyes, she was pleased with the compliment. "We'll be back before the end of July. Will you have the Armbruster ready for a lengthy journey?"

"I will, indeed."

After desert, coffee and tea, Elisabeth announced they would have their port in the living room. There would be no gentlemen's cigars in the library this evening. "We have important matters to discuss."

Once they were settled with their after-dinner drinks, Lily limited to lemonade, Barbara waited to hear how Grandmother would handle explaining who their passenger was.

"Captain Alter, our guest will remain on board until Wednesday, when Ledger will come to collect her and the nurse for transport to the train. Now you and Mr. Corwin are free to return to your ship."

Annie jumped up. "I'll be happy to show you to the door, gentlemen," she said with her eyes on Charles Corwin.

Having been summarily dismissed, the two men stood and bade everyone a good evening and a safe journey. Annie escorted them from the room.

"Now, as to you two," Grandmother turned her attention to Barbara and Lillian. "I will not be making the mistake of leaving you behind again, therefore tomorrow you will spend the day preparing your clothes for our trip."

"We're already aware we're traveling on the train to Kansas City, Grandmother," Barbara said. "Annie and I have made our own arrangements to have a private sleeping compartment on the main train. I thought it would keep the private coach from being too crowded. If you have Alistair, Lily, Mrs. Burch, and your guest along with you, there will hardly be room for us."

"You will have Lillian stay with you as well." Grandmother's lips pinched indicating she was about to say something important. "Lillian, you may go begin packing. I wish to have a private word with your sister."

Lillian eyed Barbara with a mischievous grin.

She thinks Grandmother is about to scold me! Barbara watched with amusement as Lillian skipped from the room.

"You do understand, Barbara, under no circumstances is Lillian to know about Mary Ellen."

"It doesn't seem fair."

"I will brook no disobedience from you, young lady. Would you really want your sister to see your mother in her present condition? You can tell her once we leave Kansas City. And you'll keep your sister with you in your private drawing room. Ledger has assigned a guard for you."

Barbara didn't want her little sister with her, but if she stayed with her, then she'd be less likely to find out about their mother. She nodded, blinking back tears at having to deceive Lily.

"May I be excused now? I also have packing to do. Annie hasn't quite got the hang of it yet."

Grandmother raised her eyebrows. "You may."

Barbara's heart raced as she climbed the stairs to their third-floor room. It looked so small and shabby after the yacht. Lily sat on the bed examining stockings.

"I have good news for you. You and Annie and I shall be sharing our own private drawing room on the train."

"Great! It'll remind me of when I was little and we were on our own."

"Except we'll have Annie."

Annie knocked on the door and then strolled into the room without waiting for a response. "They are the nicest two men I think I've ever met." She sighed as she took a seat without asking permission.

Lily cleared her throat. When Annie looked at her, Lily tilted her head toward Barbara.

"I meant nicest I've ever met since we met Alistair in New York." She smiled to show she meant no offense. "That reminds me. Mr. Alistair Rogers requested your presence on the front porch, Barbara."

Wondering what that could be about, Barbara set aside the stockings she had been rolling for Lily and headed downstairs.

She found him standing at the porch railing, breathing in the fresh night air. She stood beside him. "I hope you realize you didn't have to accept this trip because of me." She awaited his reply, eager to hear his explanation.

"I didn't. Ledger is paying the company well for my services, far more than I would have expected on my first professional job."

Her mind and body deflated. "Oh."

"But I do want very much to talk with you, if you have a few minutes now. We can talk more on the train, of course."

"Now is fine! Shall we sit here?" She pointed to the wicker chairs.

Once seated, he began the conversation. "What I need to know from you is what your mother was like before. When you and your sister lived with her?"

Barbara turned her face away from him, hoping he didn't see the disappointment in her face. "What difference does that make now?"

"I need to know the real reason I was hired to come along on this trip. Ledger has hired guards, but your grandmother wants me to protect your mother and keep Lily from knowing about her until we reach Kansas City. She said I could leave once her business was finished. I tried to find out about asylums or sanitariums in Kansas City where she might be seeking treatment for your mother, but so far, I haven't learned anything."

"The Democratic Convention is being held there."

"What does that have to do with your mother?"

"Nothing as far as I know, but it all goes together. Grandmother hates Senator Pembroke and he's going there to run for president." She heard the wicker creak as he rose from his chair. She turned to face him.

"I'm sorry if I offended you, Barbara. Will I see you tomorrow?"

She looked up at him, his face shadowed in the moonlight. "You haven't offended me."

"I had the feeling I said something. You've become so aloof."

If only she could see his face clearly, see his eyes. "No. Perhaps we'll meet at breakfast. If you need anything, there's a bell pull next to your bed. Good night."

"Good night, then." He pulled open the screen door and then paused. Perhaps he would turn back to take her hand and kiss it.

His face, partially lit by the inside light, looked too serious. He nodded once and then went inside.

She flung herself onto the nearest chair with an annoyed groan. "Ignorant idiot!" she grumbled at the door.

Thirty Six

The transfer of heavily sedated Mary Ellen to the private coach was completed by noon, long before the scheduled hook up with the main train. Mrs. Burch and Ledger saw to the baggage. Annie, Lillian and Barbara remained on the platform after examining the elegant furnishing in the coach. Elisabeth thought she glimpsed a wisp of envy in Barbara's face, perhaps regretting her rash decision to ride in the main part of the train. She couldn't concern herself with that at the moment. Mary Ellen's sedation had begun to wear off Ledger and Martha were trying to calm her in the servant's room where she had been placed.

Elisabeth seated herself on the red and gold brocade chaise, rested her head on a soft pillow, shut her eyes and closed out the sounds of her daughter. Mary Ellen wanted to remain on the yacht to be transported back to New York. She wanted no part of Elisabeth, Ledger or the stalwart nurse, Martha. "I only want to see my little Lily. Please."

Now Mary Ellen fluctuated between screeches and sobs. One minute she demanded something, anything to drink and the next she wanted a cigarette. To Elisabeth's relief, she didn't ask for any opium or heroin. Maybe the cure had worked.

"I should have requested a separate car for her. I hope this isn't the way she's going to be the entire trip," she said to Ledger when he came through to collect a pitcher of water.

"She'll settle down. Martha will give her another, stronger, injection before we pull out. Do you want me to send Mrs. Burch into you?"

"No. I need some peace and quiet so I can take a little nap."

"Won't be long," he said.

~*~

Barbara, Lily and Annie inspected their surroundings in the reserved drawing room while the porter stored their luggage.

"It's more cramped than Grandmother's car, but if all three of us were in there as well, it too would be crowded."

"Makes me feel grown up," Lily said. "Traveling alone."

"Ledger will be in here every hour, you wait and see," Barbara warned her. "Plus guards are on the train to protect us."

"Protect us from what?" Lily asked.

Barbara realized she should not have said anything about their safety. She shrugged. "Oh, you know how Grandmother is. She was so worried when I went to New York with Annie, she's afraid of what we might do next."

"So? I don't want to do anything different or bad, I just like the idea! Remember the Riviera when Mother left you in charge of me? This is like that."

"The Riviera?" Annie said. "I know you were there, but it's still amazing to hear you speak of it as if everyone just happened to be there. 'Oh, yes, dahling, when we were on the Riviera and we met the Sultan of Arabia'. You two could probably tell so many stories."

"What should we do first?" Lily asked. "Do you think we can get lunch?"

"We have food in the basket," Annie said. "Mrs. Burch gave it to me this morning. She didn't believe me when I said they have a buffet available on the train."

"I thought that was more of your baggage," Barbara said with a little laugh indicating the wicker hamper. "What have we got?"

The three of them plunged their hands into the basket and pulled out paper-wrapped packages of food.

~*~

Mary Ellen couldn't breathe. The room was far too hot and cramped. Stifling. She wanted to rip her clothing from her body. Martha's bulk took up what little floor space existed. Curtains framed a large window to her right. Mary Ellen kept them closed while the train remained in the station. People on the raised platform gathered around the private car trying to peer inside, eager to gape at the people rich enough to afford such luxury. She knew they were envious. If they understood the agony and misery of this wealthy family, they wouldn't be so jealous. She focused on seeing her youngest child, Lily. Her Lily flower. The little Irish beauty.

A shot. Soon, Martha promised. Mary Ellen closed her eyes and felt the perspiration drip from her brow down the sides of her face to her neck. Her soaked scalp wet her pillow. Praying that once the train was in motion, some cooler air would pass through the car, she forced herself to dwell on Lily. Lily playing on the beach, skipping stones across a mountain creek. My little Lily. She's nearly grown up now. I *will* see her.

~*~

Barbara and Lily sat opposite each other looking out the window at the people gathered around the private car behind theirs, trying to catch a glimpse of those inside.

"Why are they so interested?" Barbara asked as she lowered the shade.

"They're probably waiting to get into their third class coached. They never seen the insides of private rooms. Leastwise, I sure haven't," Annie said. "I'm gonna go wanderin' to see the rest of the train. See who's our traveling mates." She left.

Lily had a tendency to bounce up and down on the seat. "Will we get off the train in Chicago when we change engines? Is everybody in this car going to Kansas City?"

"I don't know. I would guess they'd put us all in the same car, but I don't know. We'll find out together. I'm kind of sorry we can't have our own private car attached behind Grandmother's," Barbara said while thinking that their own mother was locked in a compartment in that private car. She wanted to tell Lily but was afraid of the consequences. Watching Lily's innocent young face as she stared out the window, she had an idea. First, she'd have to find Alistair to watch over Lily while she went to talk with their grandmother.

"I'm going out for a minute. I want to talk with Alistair. I think he's in Grandmother's car. Lock the door after me."

Lily waved at her. "I will. When you come back maybe we can both take a tour of the rest of the train like Annie is doing."

"A fine idea," Barbara answered, "But for now, come lock this door."

She stepped out into the passageway. People were still boarding. The train should be pulling out of the station any minute. She worked her way amongst the oncoming passengers and then made her way through the doors separating the two cars. The private car door was locked. She knocked on it and waited.

The train shuddered as she stood on the open platform between the cars. She held on to the handles on the side of the door to keep her balance as the cars began moving. Picturing herself crushed between the cars, she banged harder on the door until Ledger pulled back the curtain over the window and looked out. He smiled and slid the door open.

Falling into the posh sitting room, she let him help her to a seat. Grandmother rested on a chaise, a small liqueur glass at her side. There was no sign of anyone else.

"Grandmother."

Elisabeth opened her eyes and studied her granddaughter. "What is it? Why are you in here? I thought you chose to ride in a public compartment."

Feeling the chill in Grandmother's tone, Barbara answered, "Only to help make your trip more comfortable. The three of us in here would have made it far too crowded."

Grandmother harrumphed and sipped her drink.

"I came to ask about Mother. I'd like to let Lily know she's alive but I don't know how to present it to her. I think it's time she knew."

"There's no reason for her to know. Once our business is finished in Kansas City, I doubt anyone will want to know your mother, including you." With one hand over her brow and the other holding her drink, Elisabeth reminded Barbara of an actress she'd seen once on stage. Even her words sounded as if they had been written by a stranger.

"What do you mean? You mean the heroin? I know about it and I still love her."

"She abandoned you."

"She didn't. She went away to nursing school and you took us away from her."

"She'd say anything to make me look bad. Drug addicts are like that. Go back to your sister and enjoy the trip. Don't worry about your mother."

"May I see her now?"

"You may not."

Barbara rose, unsure whether or not to press the issue. We have nearly a week on the train. I'll find time to bring Lily back here. She needs to know. "We'll be here for dinner later. What will Mother do for her meals?"

"She'll be served in her room, the same as she was cared for on the Armbruster Legend. Please let me rest now. I do so enjoy the cadence of train wheels on tracks. It lulls me to sleep."

Barbara pinched her lips and said, "Enjoy your rest."

Ledger had been sitting at a small deal table the entire time reading a newspaper. When Barbara stood, he rose and escorted her to the door. "Please listen to your Grandmother. I promise to keep an eye on your mother. I see signs of improvement."

"Thank you, Ledger," she said with a small smile, knowing that he had practically raised Mother and would be attentive to her care.

He assisted her across the platform to the next car and opened the door for her. The train swayed sending her lurching into him. He grabbed hold of her to steady her as a man stepped from a nearby compartment. The spectacled old man stared at the young girl and old Negro in the odd embrace. He scowled as his face turned red and he scurried away in the opposite direction.

When he reached the end of the car, he turned around. Ledger bent over and kissed Barbara on the top of her head. "Go on. Now we've created a scandal and you'll be notorious."

She gave him a playful slap on the sleeve. "You're terrible, Ledger."

"See you at dinner. Mrs. Burch will be cooking."

As the train passed into the countryside and on toward Schenectady, Barbara found her footing and returned to her compartment where, obeying orders for once, Lily had locked the door.

"Annie hasn't returned?" Barbara said when Lily let her in.

"Not a sign of her. Look out there. It's so wild! I've never been in this part of the country. Did you know? Are there still

Indians roaming in the forests?" Lily had removed her hat, gloves and jacket and made herself comfortable on the plush seat that stretched the length of the small compartment.

Barbara took her seat opposite. "I doubt it. If the settlers didn't kill them in the last century, they've probably all moved west. We might see some in Kansas City."

"That would be exciting! Cowboys, too?"

"I suppose. Why don't we rest until dinner? Did you bring books to keep you entertained?"

Two hours later Lily dozed while Barbara watched the landscape pass by. She found herself curious about the lives of those who lived in the few houses alongside the railroad tracks. At some, barefoot children waved at the passing train. She waved back, but too late for the children to notice.

The compartment door flew open and Annie tumbled into the room. "You'll never guess what I've been doing!"

Thirty Seven

Elisabeth sat at the writing desk with Ledger at her side. Once Barbara had gone and Martha assured her Mary Ellen was sleeping, she announced her plans. By the look in his dark eyes, she knew he disapproved, but she was determined.

"There's no evidence that Mary Ellen ever married that Irishman, therefore Lillian is not entitled to inherit a penny."

"That does not stop you from leaving her a bequest." He set his pen aside.

They had been working on her Last Will and Testament for over two hours. Elisabeth had not changed Ledger's bequest though she had to change those of the servants as so many of them had come and gone since she wrote her last will five years ago. Mrs. Burch was the only constant in that period.

"How much effort have you made searching for a birth certificate that would prove her parentage?" She didn't wait for an answer. "You wrote a few letters, that's it. And that is because you know as well as I that Mary Ellen hasn't a speck of moral fiber in her body. I'm only surprised that she married Barbara's father."

Ledger sighed and picked up the pen. "I'll make the appropriate adjustments, Elisabeth. You really ought to rest before dinner."

Agitated by his disapproval, Elisabeth shrugged her shawl more tightly around her shoulders and hunched over the papers. Besides the will on which Ledger worked, she had deeds to several properties to consider. "Not before I deal with these."

"Why would you bring all these documents with you?"

"There are things which must be dealt with before it's too late. Tell me what you know about the girl, Annie, whom Barbara is so fond of."

"I know nothing about her. She appears to be diligent in her duties, cheerful, and intelligent. You should ask Mrs. Burch as she did the interview and hiring." His pen continued scratching across the vellum.

"I thought about giving her one of the smaller houses to get her away from Barbara. What do you think of that?" she asked as she held up a title deed.

"I think it would be a cruel slap in the face for your granddaughter, Lillian. Now, let me finish one thing at a time. We'll need two people to witness your signature. As soon as I'm finished, I'll call in Mrs. Burch and one of the porters. That should do it."

"I want to know what you think of my giving that girl a house." She shoved the deed under Ledger's nose so he had to pull back. In doing so, a large spot of black ink fell onto the will.

"Just like Mother to ruin everything, isn't it, Ledger?" Mary Ellen said from the entrance to the parlor.

Elisabeth turned. "You're supposed to be asleep. And look at you. You look like you've been at war with the devil himself. Go back to bed. Ledger, go find her nurse now." With her right hand over her aching heart, Elisabeth drew several deep breaths as she waited for Mary Ellen to obey.

Instead, her daughter came further into the room, catching at the backs of chairs to keep from falling as the train sped along the rails. "What girl are you giving a house? My Lily?"

"Not your Lily." Anger edged Elisabeth's voice. The strain of seeing her disheveled daughter made breathing difficult. "Ledger, go find that nurse now. We can fire her when we reach Chicago. Wire ahead and let them know we'll need someone else."

"Martha's been fine, Elisabeth."

Mary Ellen came within five feet of her mother before she eased herself onto a straight-backed chair. "Martha is excellent, Mother. She gives me shot after shot, but I don't like that they make me sleep so much. I'd rather be awake. Can you believe that? I want to see my daughters. I've already met with Barbara, now won't you let me see Lily?"

"Get back to your room," Elisabeth ordered, hoping she would behave and obey her. She didn't think her heart could take much more torment. She pushed herself up from her chair. "Go to your room, now."

"No, dear Mother, I won't. When Martha returns, I plan to ask her to help me dress. I would like to join everyone for dinner tonight. And I *will* behave." Mary Ellen sat upright, her hands folded on her lap like a schoolgirl though her hair fell in limp strands across her shoulders and down the front of her nightgown. The nightgown showed perspiration stains under the arms. Her feet were bare, the toenails in need of clipping.

Elisabeth stared at the mess that was her daughter. The sight of her had never become easier as the mid-wife had promised the day she was born. "We'll see whether or not you will join us for dinner. I've yet to prepare Lillian for the shock of seeing you. She might not remember you."

"I remember her, such a dear little child. And Barbara is a wonderful young woman now. Nearly eighteen years old. I've missed them so much."

"You could have changed your behavior. I told you when I took them that you would be able to see them if you chose."

"Need I remind you, you never contacted me at all? When I didn't hear from the girls or the nanny, I returned home to find everyone gone. The police were of no help. Ledger eventually wrote to let me know they were safe with you. What was I supposed to do? I went to Europe for a long time." She gripped her folded hands so tightly the knuckles turned white.

"So I learned. Well, now we're together again and you are in the process of becoming cured. I expect by the time we reach Kansas City, you'll be able to come out with us and meet the public again as my daughter." Elisabeth forced herself to smile, hoping her message was received as sincere.

"Kansas City? What's in Kansas City?" Mary Ellen leaned forward, curious.

Elisabeth kept the smile fixed on her face. "You'll soon learn. Now go back to your room. At least bathe, I can smell you from here."

Ledger rose and headed toward the exit door at the front of the car. "I'm going to see to the girls," he said, his demeanor and voice stiff.

Elisabeth watched him leave and then turned back to her daughter. "Will you go now?"

Mary Ellen dropped her head so her chin rested on her chest and her hair covered her face. "I will, Mother. But you won't get rid of me so easily this time. You wanted me cured; I had no interest, but in spite of myself, it's working." She used both her hands to push herself up from the chair. Tossing her head so her hair swung back from her face, she stared at her mother through clear eyes. "You may be sorry."

The shock of her statement brought tears to Elisabeth's eyes. They weren't tears of joy at her daughter's improved health nor of love for a daughter recovered; they were tears of sorrow for herself because her plan might now backfire. She didn't know what she would do if Mary Ellen caught on to her scheme too soon.

Turning her back on Mary Ellen, Elisabeth studied the deed to the small house on the river in Albany. She would sign it over to the girl, Annie. one more item out of reach of Mary Ellen and the bastard, Lillian.

She glanced over at the will Ledger left on the desk. Perhaps she could ask Mr. Rogers to make copies for her. He was educated and should have a good hand.

The deed to her own home caught her attention. Would Barbara want it? She planned to leave the bulk of her estate to Barbara with Ledger managing it until she turned twenty-one. Now she wondered about Ledger. He seemed to have changed in the past few years. Not quite so agreeable anymore.

Thirty Eight

Barbara and Lily followed Annie forward through the train eager to see what she'd discovered. In the coaches, men and women sat with picnic baskets between them, remnants of their lunches visible on the floor and seats around them. It was obvious the porters were kept busy in these cars.

Grateful for their first-class drawing room, Barbara wondered where Annie might be leading them.

At the fourth car forward, Annie pushed open the door and held it for Barbara and Lily to pass through ahead of her. The noise shattered her eardrums as an entire car full of young children clamored, arms outstretched, for more food from a skinny young man at the opposite end of the car.

"This is it!" Annie screamed into her ear. "Can you believe this?"

"I don't know," she shouted back while trying to keep Lily in check behind her. She didn't need her little sister contaminated by whatever diseases these urchins might be harboring. "What are they doing here?"

"They're orphans from New York City. Right from where we were, if you can be believin' it."

"But what are they doing here?" Her head was beginning to ache from the noise. She wanted to retreat into the previous car where she could at least hear herself think.

Instead of answering, Annie took her by the hand and began leading her down the aisle toward the young man. As they passed, children sat back and became quiet, watching the well-dressed strangers moving amongst them. By the time they reached him, most of the car was quiet. One little girl said, "I told you she'd come back."

"This is Herbert Meecham," Annie said proudly introducing the man who had been feeding the children. "He's in charge."

"I'm Barbara Riis." She didn't hold out her hand. To Annie she said, "Why did you tell them you'd be back? You aren't supposed to be in the third-class coaches."

"I said you be buyin' them food at the next stop, if you don't mind. The agency that's sending these children out for adoption don't seem to know the size of the country or the length of the journey." Annie reached out and patted a young boy on the head.

Herbert grinned at Barbara. He appeared to be nineteen or twenty years old. Bushy red sideburns emphasized his youth, though he did have kind eyes. He held out his hand to her. "It's kind of you. We're given very little money to supply the children. Anything at all will do."

"I want cookies," a little girl behind her said.

"Bread with butter!" another called out.

"Warm milk with honey, please."

"Quit yer beggin'," a more mature voice called from the corner of the coach. Barbara turned toward the voice. A girl wearing a plain bonnet and dark cotton dress, the same as the other girls, glared with a sullen face at Barbara and Annie. When she realized the two were watching her, she pulled herself up straighter in her seat. "We was all told only last night that we're going to Kansas City. They took us away from our families and said we'd have new ones on farms. The little brats ought to be happy about it instead of complaining about the food. Ask them what they were eating before they were plucked off the streets, why don't you?"

Astonished by the outburst and remembering how she'd been taken away from her own home, Barbara turned back to Herbert. "What does she mean, 'plucked from their families'? That can't be true, can it?"

He took a step back.

"We know what that's like," Lily said in a low voice. "We were taken from the only mother we ever knew."

Herbert's eyes moved from girl to girl as if seeking rescue. "I didn't do it. They were living on the streets or were so neglected they were starving. "Agnes," he pointed to the one who'd spoken, "was a street singer. She and her little brother lived down by the docks. God only knows how she survived without being dragged out to sea on one of those cargo ships."

"But, what about their families? Do they know what happened to their children?" Barbara asked.

"Certainly, they do. At least most of them, the ones the Children's Aid Society could find. They sign papers giving us permission to give their children a new life. And Agnes isn't nearly as hard as she makes out to be. At the Foundling Home where they were gathered last night for the journey, she even sang songs to the little ones to comfort them." He held on to the back of a seat to steady himself as the train rounded a curve with a screech of wheels on metal.

He looked much like an orphan himself dressed in the ill-fitting black suit, the string tie too tight around his neck.

Barbara relented. "I don't know where our next stop is, however, I'll be happy to send Annie onto the platform to see what she can purchase."

She gripped Annie by the lower arm. "Come along now. It's nearly time for us to get ready for..." she hesitated, seeing the children watching her, "...ready for a rest."

Lily, who had been quiet during all this, spoke up. "May I stay? I could tell stories to them until we get to a stop."

"Please-a, Missy. You letting her stay. We be good," a curly headed waif begged.

"It's not up to me. Our grandmother would be upset."

Annie leaned closer to her so she could whisper, "When did you start caring about what your grandmother thinks?"

"Miss Riis, Lillian, Annie!" Alistair Rogers called from the other end of the car.

"See?" Barbara said. "She's sent Alistair after us. Come along. We'll do something about food later, hopefully before they go to sleep." She looked at Herbert. "Where *will* they sleep?"

"They'll sleep in their seats. It's only for a few days and then they'll be with their new families."

Barbara turned to view the children again. At least twenty-five pairs of eyes watched her, faces with circles under hollowed eyes. "Do they all know?"

"Of course, it's going to be grand for them. They'll have fresh air and plenty of fresh wholesome food. Ministers and town leaders are arranging interviews before we get to each town. And the children have the right to refuse to go with anyone they don't like." Herbert sounded as if he believed what he was saying. Barbara had doubts about a bunch of farmers making good homes for homeless orphans from the streets of New York City.

"Perhaps we'll talk later," she said. "Come along, Annie. Lily! Don't touch them. You don't want to get lice, do you?" She shooed the two girls down the aisle toward Alistair.

"Your grandmother was concerned when Ledger didn't find you in your compartment," Alistair said.

"Where have you been?" Barbara asked, wishing he'd opted for staying in a compartment in their car instead of in the lavish private car with Grandmother.

"I was sleeping until Ledger came to wake me. Between last night and preparing to leave this morning, I've barely had a moment's rest. What are you doing with these children?" he asked as he held the door for them to cross to the next car.

"Annie wants to adopt them all and bring them home with us," Lily said as she skipped past him.

"I only want to give them a little food. You saw them, poor things. Even my Mam can manage to feed our lot with what little she gets. I can't imagine her giving any one of us up no matter how hard life was."

"Not all mothers are as good as yours, Annie," Barbara said, thinking of her own mother confined to a compartment until the effects of using narcotics for so many years could wear off.

"Herb told me how they rounded them up off'n the streets and told them they was going to go live on farms. He never mentioned looking for mothers and fathers. Just a bunch of do-good social women with nothing better to do than rid the streets of unsightly brats."

"Watch your language, Annie," Barbara warned. "Remember your position."

"Not sure I want a 'position,' beggin' your pardon, Miss," Annie grumbled.

They reached their compartment and Alistair left them with the warning to clean up and dress for dinner. "You grandmother wants you to arrive at seven-thirty for dinner at eight. She has some things she wants to discuss with you."

Barbara looked at him sharply. Since when had he become Grandmother's toady? He was supposed to be her friend, not a clerk under Grandmother's thumb. She frowned at him but answered, "Thank you, Alistair. We'll be there. I'm assuming Annie is included as well as you?"

"We are included as there are no acceptable alternatives. I'll see you in a little while." He pulled the door shut, leaving them to wonder at the change in his demeanor.

"I'll bet Grandma is paying him thousands of dollars to work for her. Now she's got him, he'd probably crawl on the ground in front of her and pick up pebbles and mop puddles dry with his handkerchief so she shouldn't ruin her old shoes." Lily pulled a fresh dress from the closet.

"Now, that's what I call rude," Annie said. "I think Alistair is making himself useful to your grandmother because he's sweet on your sister."

Thirty Nine

"Get me a book," Mary Ellen demanded of Martha.

"What kind of book?" The nurse's eyebrows shot up.

Mary Ellen sighed. "I don't know. It's been so long since I read one, I don't really care, but I need something to distract my brain."

Martha hesitated. "I'll see if anyone's brought anything along. Maybe I can buy you a magazine at the next stop."

"That would be fine. Who's going to be at dinner tonight? Everyone?"

"Oh, ma'am, I wouldn't know about everyone. Mrs. Riis, of course, and Mr. Ledger for sure. I imagine the three young ladies and the young gentleman would be included."

"Who are the *three* young ladies?"

"Misses Barbara and Annie and the younger girl. I'm going to see about your dinner now. You be good and stay in here."

"The younger girl is my daughter, Lillian. Barbara and I call her Lily. I don't know an Annie." Mary Ellen leaned back against the sofa. "All dressed up with no place to go."

"You do look a sight better than when I first saw you. If you keep it up, you may not need any more injections." Martha beamed a warm smile at Mary Ellen.

"You don't know the reason for this trip, do you?"

Martha stood up. "As I said, I'll be checking on your dinner. If you want to know what's going on, you might ask your mother after she's finished her meal."

As the woman left, Mary Ellen drew a sigh of relief. Alone at last, perhaps for the first time in weeks. She had lost track of the days since she first saw Mother at the apartment. How bad she had been. Her skin crawled at the thought of her behavior in front of Mother and Ledger. She pulled the curtain aside but saw only her own reflection. A gaunt woman with her hair piled neatly on her head, a prim white blouse with a black satin bow at the neck. Leaning close to the window, she shielded her eyes from the light and tried to see out. Dark as a cave.

She wished her father could be with her now. He had always been so good to her; he never struck her as some fathers did their children. He liked to tell the story of meeting Mother at a picnic with all those men who were destined to become important, though other than Senator Pembroke, she could not recall any who had made a name for themselves. Perhaps they were important in other states. He didn't like to talk about the war or how he'd been injured, but she knew he lived with a lot of pain. They had traveled the world in search of a cure for him, but in the end, he died anyway.

A pipe. She could use a pipe right now. Taking deep breaths, she forced herself to try to make out shapes in the night. The rhythm of the wheels on the track hypnotized her as they moved steadily westward through the darkness.

A tap on the door startled her. Smoothing her skirts as she stood, she hoped it would be Martha with an armful of books; she really needed distraction. Pulling it open, she was even more pleased than if it had been Martha. Barbara stood in the hall, a finger to her lips.

"Hush. May I come in?" she asked as she stepped through the entrance into the cramped room.

Mary Ellen stepped back, nearly falling onto Martha's chair. "Of course. Why are you whispering?"

"Grandmother told us we weren't be permitted to see you until after Kansas City. I wanted to see how you're getting along. You're looking much better."

Mary Ellen felt her heart tingle at the unexpected words of praise from her daughter. "I'm feeling stronger. We have Mother to thank for this." As she made the comment, part of her still had doubts about her mother's motives.

"Lily's upset tonight. She still doesn't know about you, but we met a group of orphans being transported from New York to live on farms with strangers."

"I don't understand. What orphans? Why are they upsetting Lily?" Mary Ellen took her seat on the sofa and patted the cushion beside her for Barbara to join her.

"She's concerned for the orphans. I don't have much time, Mother. Martha told me she was going in search of books for you. I told her I had two in my valise she could take. I hope you haven't read *Little Women* sixteen times or *A Journey to the Center of the Earth*. I have it in French, though I've already read it in English."

"Well," Mary Ellen said, impressed and pleased by her daughter. "I haven't read *Little Women*. Will I find it too soppy and romantic?"

"I enjoyed it, but I read it first when I was around eleven years old. I'm finding different things in it now. Perhaps the Jules Verne in French might be more appealing. It'll challenge you."

"You sound more like my professor than my daughter. French always came easy to me. Perhaps I'll read it while we are on the train, only please tell me the center of the earth isn't really Hell. I've already been there."

Barbara's hand rested on Mary Ellen's and she wanted it to remain there forever.

"You needn't worry, Mother. It's a Jules Verne adventure. The monsters might frighten you, but if they do, you can always pick up Louisa May Alcott."

Tears gathered unexpectedly in Mary Ellen's eyes. She didn't know why she should cry, but the tenderness of her daughter overwhelmed her. "I hope Martha brings them both. I shall stay up all night reading."

"Maybe not all night, Mother. You still need to regain your strength. I have to go into dinner now, but I wanted you to know we're here and I, for one, am happy to see you looking so well." She leaned over and kissed Mary Ellen on the cheek.

The warm soft lips completely melted her heart. *So many years wasted, lost in self-pity and wayward behavior. If only I'd* – Mary Ellen stopped her thoughts. *No use crying about the past now.* "Come back when you can. And please, help Lily. Maybe if you bring her to me…"

"I can't. It'll be hard enough on everyone if Grandmother learns I've been in here to see you. Remember, she did say that after Kansas City, she doesn't care what happens."

"A strange thing to say." Mary Ellen stood up with her daughter and took the few steps to the door with her. Feeling shy, wanting desperately to hold her child, she offered a faint smile. Barbara smiled in return and then held out her arms for a hug.

Forty

"Let's go visit the orphans," Lily said as they returned to their room following dinner.

"You heard what Grandmother said when you told her about them. She's afraid we'll get head lice and worms." Barbara found herself sounding like their grandmother.

"Oooh. Head lice. I had them once a long time ago." Annie reached up to scratch her head as if remembering. "Mam cut my hair nearly all off. Everyone laughed at me until they caught 'em too."

"You see?" Barbara opened their room door to lead them inside.

"Yes, but Herbert said everybody got brand new clothes and baths before they left this morning. They're all clean," Annie added.

"Oh, now it's 'Herbert.' Two days ago it was the first mate. You are a fickle girl."

Lily pushed past them into the room and pulled her dinner dress over her head. "I'm going anyway. We can help Herbert and cheer those kids up."

"Why are you changing?" Barbara asked.

"Are you dim?" Lily tossed her dress on the bed and then pulled on a plain cotton day dress.

"Them kids has got only one set of clothing, Miss. We ought not to be parading around in front of them with dinner clothes and jewelry." Annie followed Lily's lead and removed a pair of pearl earrings Barbara had loaned her for dinner.

"So, you're going in spite of what Grandmother said?" Hands on her hips, her head tilted, Barbara studied the girls as they changed clothes.

"It's a lot safer than you and I going to a gentlemen's club pretending to be maids." Lily's voice came muffled through a pinafore she was pulling over her head.

Throwing her hands in the air, Barbara sat on the sofa and unclipped her own earrings. "I suppose I'll join you. No point in sitting in here and staring out at the dark all night."

As Annie was helping tie Lily's pinafore in place, someone knocked at the door.

"Probably a porter wanting to make up the beds. Let him in," Barbara ordered, glad she hadn't begun changing.

Instead of a porter, Ledger and Alistair stood out in the hall. Alistair held onto a window ledge as the train rounded a curve. "Barbara, I'd like a private word with you," Ledger said.

"That's all right. We were just going out anyways." Annie inched her way around Ledger into the hall.

"Where are you going?" Alistair asked.

"Me and Lily are going to visit the orphans and help Herbert. Barbara's coming, too. You want to join us?"

"Sure, I'd be delighted. Mrs. Riis has dismissed me for the evening. The security guards are in place; there's nothing left for me to do." He leaned into the room. "Will you join us later, Barbara?"

Barbara raised an eyebrow in Ledger's direction. "Depends on what Ledger has to say."

"We won't be long," Ledger said. "But didn't your grandmother forbid you to go to the orphans' car?"

"She didn't actually forbid us. She said we might catch head lice, but we won't." Lily said as she bobbled up and down, anxious to go.

Ledger smiled and shook his head. He waved an arm to dismiss them and then shut the door. "Those two girls could pass for a pair of orphans the way they're dressed."

Barbara eyed him anxiously, still holding her earrings and necklace on her lap. "I was about to change and join them. If you'd seen the children, you'd know Lily and even Annie are far too healthy looking."

Ledger moved the discarded dresses from the other sofa and then sat across from her. "I've had a conversation with your grandmother you ought to be aware of, Barbara. She wanted to update her will—"

"I knew it. I knew she was sick. What's wrong with her?" She tossed the jewelry onto the small table next to the sofa and leaned forward, eager to hear what Ledger had to say.

"If you know she's unwell why do you give her such a difficult time?"

"I don't. I haven't. Not since I found out about her bad heart."

Now his eyebrows shot up. "Her heart? What do you know about her heart?"

Barbara feared she had said too much. She shrugged. "I looked up her medications and tonics. The most serious one is the tincture of digitalis. I read up on it."

Ledger sat with his forearms on his knees, his hands clasped as if in prayer. He didn't look at her when he said, "I see."

Tears stung. She wanted to run to her grandmother immediately and ask her so many questions. First, she wanted the truth about her mother. But Ledger's expression when he finally faced her, made her stay in her place.

"You know about your legacy from von Bek."

She nodded.

"Elisabeth wanted to be assured you would never want for anything. I explained you have more than enough in trust from your father. At the moment Lillian has no prospects of any income other than what you may choose to generously provide." He stopped and watched her.

He's waiting for an answer from me. Why would I have to provide for Lily? "I'm not clear what you're talking about. Neither Lily nor I have ever wanted for anything, except maybe some heat in our bedroom in the winter." She thought she made a joke but Ledger jumped back as if he had been slapped.

"Elisabeth believes your characters were better shaped by depriving you of too much comfort. It wasn't from a lack of generosity."

"If you say so." Barbara's neck muscles tightened. Her jaw ached. With a sudden need for air, she stood up. "Was there anything else you wanted to say before I join my sister and friends?"

"It's this. She named you her sole heir. Your mother and your sister have been left out of her will. She specifically states it so there can be no questions later." He, too, got up and put a hand on her shoulder. "I thought you ought to know now so you'll be better prepared when the time comes."

Barbara leaned against the door and shut her eyes, feeling the motion of the train, hearing the clicking of the wheels on the tracks. "Her own daughter and granddaughter?" A tear slid down her cheek as if Grandmother had already died.

"I beg your pardon? I didn't hear you," Ledger said.

"Why?" She waited for Ledger's answer, but when he didn't respond, she opened her eyes. "Maybe I can understand about mother. Maybe. But her granddaughter? What did Lily ever do to her?"

Now Ledger shrugged. "I'm not at liberty to explain her reasons. She does love all of you, I'm sure."

"No, Ledger. I think *you* love all of us and wish she did as well."

He reached around behind her and twisted the doorknob. "Your friends are waiting. I'll leave so you can change. I believe you were about to when I came."

She'd forgotten. "Thank you. And good night, Ledger. I don't think we'll be in to say good night to Grandmother."

"Shower and wash your hair when you return from your excursion."

"If you have the opportunity, tell Mother I'm thinking about her." She shut the door before he could see the fresh tears.

Dressed in a plain dress minus the pinafore, Barbara made her way through the train to the orphan car. She pulled the door open to hear fiddle music and hands clapping mingled with the sounds of the train racing along the tracks. Inside the car it looked like chaos reigned. Three girls danced with abandon at the far end of the car while the children stood in the aisles and on the seats clapping in time to the music. She paused a minute to watch.

Lily, Annie and the orphan, Agnes, held hands with one another raised above their heads as they danced to the lively jig played by Herbert. Their faces were flushed with excitement, making them look most unladylike. Barbara smiled at the sight of them.

The music stopped. The girls bowed and curtsied as the children cheered, shouting encouragement for more.

Lily shouted above the din, "Everyone grab a partner and we'll dance together!"

Before Barbara could move forward the aisles were crowded with laughing children. Herbert started the music again as young bodies released energy stored up from sitting all day. *Money has nothing to do with anything.* Lily, a disowned heiress, and Annie, a common working girl were having as much fun as any one of these abandoned children. The only one not dancing and playing with them was Barbara, the heiress. She perched on the arm of a seat, trying to absorb their pleasure.

The door at the far end opened. Whoever it was would have a hard time trying to move through the car. She stood to see who had entered. By the size and shape of them, the two men had to be the pair of security guards Ledger mentioned. But, no! It wasn't. She recognized the awful plaid jacket worn by one of the men on the porch in Albany.

She needed to warn Lily about them before the mob cleared the aisle. Heads bobbed as the music continued. Four younger boys near her climbed back into their seats looking spent from the effort.

When the music stopped most of the children scrambled back to their seats still laughing and chattering. A few remained in the aisle begging Herbert to play more. Annie and Lily, having befriended Agnes, walked with her as she returned to her seat. Without noticing Barbara three rows further on, they slid into the seat next to Agnes and continued talking.

The two men, paying no attention to the orphans, pushed past Herbert. They stormed down the aisle focused on the door leading to the next car.

Barbara ducked her head and hoped Lily had seen them in time to turn her face away from their view.

Forty One

Mary Ellen finished her dinner and, resigned to being locked up for the duration of the trip, asked the nurse for a deck of cards so she could entertain herself while waiting for the promised books from Barbara.

Martha left to find cards and to check with Barbara about the books, leaving Mary Ellen alone in her compartment. She had dressed in hopes of being invited to join everyone for dinner. Now she watched herself in the window as she removed the pins from her hair and let it fall around her shoulders. What a ridiculous color, she thought. Did I really do that to myself? She wondered how long it would take to grow out for surely Mother wouldn't allow her out to purchase more products to recolor it.

Martha brought the books but no cards. "Your mother insists cards are tools of the devil and refused me."

Surprised at her mother's reaction, Mary Ellen accepted the books and set them aside. "I'll change for bed now, Martha, and then read until I sleep."

"I'll come back to give you your injection."

"No. I don't want any more injections. Please trust I no longer need them. I have the love of my daughter – that's all I require. Now go and have a good night for yourself."

Martha appeared hesitant, looking from Mary Ellen to the door as if Mary Ellen might dash past her. "All right, Miss, but if you need anything during the night, you only have to knock on the wall. My room is right next door. I'll just bid good night to your mother."

Smiling at the nurse, Mary Ellen said, "If it makes you feel better, you may lock the door and keep the key with you."

"Yes, Miss. Sleep well."

Relieved that the nurse finally left her alone, she changed her clothes, drank a large glass of water and then settled into her bed leaving the light on. She enjoyed the rhythm of the train's movement as she opened the Jules Verne book. Instead of reading, she lowered the light and tried to make out the landscape passing by. Her mind drifted to happy moments with her daughters.

The coziness of her compartment reminded her of a stormy night in Ireland when she and Seamus and the girls snuggled together in bed. Seamus told stories, fantasies much like the book she had laid to one side. She smiled and began humming a lullaby as rain began to streak the window. *How appropriate for it to be raining.*

The train slowed. She wondered if they were coming to a station or about to cross a bridge. With no sense of the geography of New York west of the Hudson River, she leaned closer to the window, her nose almost touching the glass, in an effort to see outside.

Her door rattled, startling her. A hard thump followed the rattle. Men's voices raised in anger outside her door. Martha's voice joined in the mix. With fear for her own safety, Mary Ellen pulled on her dressing gown and approached the door. With her ear against the panel, her hand automatically reached for the handle. It turned. Her breath caught in her throat. Martha was supposed to lock the door.

"Put that gun away!" Ledger's voice rose above the others.

~*~

As soon as the two men passed through the door to the next car, Barbara jumped up from her seat and went to Lily and Annie. "We have to go!"

"I don't want to," Lily said. "We're having a good time."

"Didn't you see those two men? They're the ones who were at our house in Albany, they followed us to New York. They mean harm to m – grandmother."

Lily scowled. "I saw them but they didn't see me."

Annie reached out for Barbara's hand. "If I may, Miss Barbara, it's better if we stay here, wouldn't you be thinking? If they didn't see Lillian, then they might not know she's here. And they never did see you."

Barbara considered Annie's comment. "All right. I'm going to Grandmother. You stay here with Lillian. Don't let her out of your sight."

Annie jumped up and grabbed her arm. "You can't go back there alone, Miss. Them men don't know me anymore'n they know you. And I know how to handle myself. I'll come with you. Agnes can take care of Miss Lillian." She turned to the orphan who sat near the window, open-mouthed.

"Wot? Me?"

"Yeah, you. You been living on the streets. Surely you know how to be taking care of yourself. You can look out for Miss Lillian for a little while."

Agnes' jaw slammed shut.

"We'll pay ya handsomely."

Barbara's eyes widened at that last comment, but when Annie looked to her, she nodded. "Of course we will. The two of you can help Herbert settle the younger children for the night."

"In that case, I'd be honored to help and to watch out for Lillian." She clutched on to Lillian's hand to prove her point. "You go about your business and we'll be right here when you return."

Not completely convinced, but unable to think of any objections, Barbara turned and led Annie through to the next car where travelers were settling themselves in for the night. Windows, open in the daytime, now were shut to ward off the cool night air, the shades drawn.

"Doesn't your grandmother have her own security guards on the train?" Annie said softly from behind Barbara.

"She said she does. Hopefully they'll have taken care of those two by the time we reach her car. Porter and Smith's their names as I recall." The train lurched and Barbara fell against a well-dressed middle-aged man who had his hat pulled down over his eyes. She quickly leapt up with an apology.

The man grumbled but turned to lean his head against the woman sitting beside him. The stout woman had been asleep but now she glanced at the man before looking up at the girls. "You two keep away from my husband and go back where you belong before I call a porter." She pointed back to the orphan car.

Barbara put a finger to her mouth. "Shhh. You don't want to wake him, do you?" She covered her mouth to keep from laughing.

They made it through the rest of the car without any more incidents and then crossed to the next car. Annie tugged at her dress.

"Miss. What if they're in there with your grandmother?"

"Remember, Alistair and Ledger are there as well. They'll look after grandmother."

"Mrs. Burch, too. She scares me when she's angry. If they wake her, I shudder to think what she'll do to them. I'd say my prayers if I was them."

Annie huddled close behind Barbara as Barbara slid open the door to the platform linking the cars. No one stood guarding the entrance. The door to Grandmother's car slid back and forth in rhythm with the train's motion.

Skin prickling with fear, her heart thumping so hard she knew Annie could hear it, Barbara stepped across the threshold. Annie slid into the parlor behind her and gently shut the door, latching it securely.

Before Barbara could move, the sounds of a struggle came from the hallway. She stepped to the side, pulling Annie with her, and then edged her way around the room, hoping to reach the sofa against the wall where the two of them might be able to duck down out of sight.

She heard Ledger shout, "Put that gun away!"

"Oh, Lord save us, they got guns," Annie gasped as she hunkered down next to Barbara in the corner of the room.

Barbara squeezed her eyes shut and hoped the bodyguards would show up quickly. She held her breath waiting for the explosion of a gun while Annie whispered muffled prayers. Either her mother or her grandmother must be in danger, their lives at the mercy of those thugs. She wished she had a weapon in her hands right now; she'd march down the hallway and hold it to their heads and make them get off the train, moving or not. And where was Alistair? He was supposed to be staying in the private car, sharing a room with Ledger most likely.

"Stupid old woman!" The man from the porch sounded like he was in the parlor. Barbara was afraid to peek over the arm of the sofa. She crouched down and leaned back as far as she could go. Annie grunted softly behind her.

"I'm not going anywhere with you, you fool. Do you think the authorities will let you off the train pointing guns at our heads?"

"Quit blathering, woman. You should be quiet like your daughter here."

Perspiration poured down Barbara's face as she considered what she could do to stop them. With no weapons, and unsure where the guards might be, she froze in place. She could scream and give Ledger a chance to take a gun away from one of them, but if they both carried weapons, screaming wouldn't help anyone. She couldn't think.

The movement of the group caught her eye as they passed further into the room. She could see a little of them from between the sofa and the chair that stood at right angles to it. Praying no one would look behind, she watched them moving closer to the door. As she watched Grandmother sank to the floor.

"She's fainted!" Mary Ellen cried.

"Pick her up and carry her." The plaid jacketed man's arms came into her vision.

"Now, sir, you will please drop your weapon," Alistair's voice came from out of her line of sight.

Grandmother fell unceremoniously back onto the carpeted floor. This time she faced the sofa. The scowl on her face suggested she had not fainted at all. It was a ruse to slow the men down. Barbara wanted to jump up and cheer but waited to see what would happen next. Alistair sounded so self-assured. Did he also have a gun?

Barbara caught Grandmother's eye. Did she imagine it, or did her grandmother just wink at her? Now, she felt faint from being cramped into such a small space with Annie.

"You know how to use that, little boy?" The deep voiced man growled.

"Try me," Alistair replied.

"You wouldn't dare. What if you miss and hit one of the ladies?" The sneering man then ordered Plaid Suit to pick Grandmother up again. "He's not going to shoot anybody."

A shot rang out. Barbara instinctively covered her ears.

Grandmother once again landed on the carpet. Barbara watched in fascinated horror as feet moved in and out of her vision in total silence. Terrified the shot had deafened her, she started to rise in order to get help when two more shots rang out further hindering her ability to hear. Annie clung to her shoulders from behind.

Barbara grabbed the edges of the sofa and chair to pull herself up. She dragged Annie to a standing position as she rose. People's mouths moved but she couldn't hear the words. Grandmother remained on the floor, the man in the black suit beside her looking very dead.

Slowly the ringing in her ears subsided and voices became clear again.

"...You shoulda killed me, too. This ain't the end. Now it's personal, see. Before we was working for someone; now I'm on my own. You better not close your eyes at night." The man in plaid held his upper arm while backing toward the door.

"Where do you think you're going?" Alistair said.

"I'm getting outta here, ya damned hooligan."

"You're going to get on the floor and put your hands over your head. Ledger, would you check on that fellow."

"I'll do it," Mary Ellen said. "I'm right here."

Grandmother remained still. Mary Ellen wore a dressing gown and her hair hung down below her waist. Barbara thought her mother had never looked more beautiful as she bent over the fallen man and felt for a pulse.

"Dead, I'm afraid."

"Better him than us." Alistair replied.

"I'll take the gun now," Ledger said. Alistair rushed forward and picked Smith's gun up from the floor and handed it to him.

Her mother had her arms around Grandmother, helping to steady the older woman. Grandmother's complexion appeared gray, her lips blue.

Mary Ellen was the first to notice Barbara. She gasped. "Barbara! What are you doing here?"

"Traveling to Kansas City, like you." Barbara's eyes went from her grandmother to her mother to Alistair, who wore a pair of trousers but otherwise had bare feet and only an undershirt on his upper body. She was surprised to see a broad chest and well-muscled arms.

"Yer ears are turnin' red, Barbara," Annie said as she nudged her from behind. "Never seen a half-dressed man?"

Ignoring Annie, she squeezed her way between the sofa and chair. Until now she had thought of Alistair Rogers as something of a milquetoast. Annie was right, her face was probably as red as Grandmother's was gray. Turning her attention from Alistair, she crossed the room to Elisabeth. "Grandmother! Are you all right?"

"Of course she's not all right, you silly goose!" Mary Ellen said. "We need to get her to her room."

Grandmother hung limp in Mary Ellen's arms. Barbara rushed to them. "Where's your nurse?" she asked Mary Ellen.

"Gone. I have a feeling we won't be using her services any longer." Mary Ellen glared meaningfully at the body on the floor.

Ledger said, "She has digitalis in her nightstand. The directions are on the packet. Mr. Rogers, if you'd be so kind as to help me dispose of these two." He nudged the standing villain with the barrel of the gun and pointed with his booted foot to the man on the floor.

Mrs. Burch appeared from the hallway dressed in a flowing flannel nightgown with a lace edged nightcap askew on her head. "What's going on in here? Brigitte and I were trying to get some sleep. Who's that on the floor?"

Everyone stopped to watch the impressive bulk skim quickly across the floor to the body. "Why, it's Mr. Ernest Porter. And that one's John Smith. They're the ones who came to the house in Albany. What did they do?" She placed her hands on her hips awaiting an answer as if she were in charge of the company.

Ledger obliged. "They had the misfortune to choose the wrong employer. They are now being discharged from their duties. Come along, Smith." He nudged the man.

"Whatcha think yer gonna do?" Smith growled at Ledger.

"What did you do with our guards?"

Smith stopped. "We didn't shoot them, if that's what yer thinkin'. We pushed them off the platform." He chuckled at the memory.

"You killed them?" Barbara shrieked, ready to charge him and shove him off the train by herself.

"Not likely. We wasn't going that fast. It'll take 'em a while to get back to a station though." He laughed.

"Well, thank you for the suggestion. Let's go." Alistair opened the car door.

The train whistle echoed in the night as they raced toward Chicago.

Forty Two

Mary Ellen sat on a chair by the head of Elisabeth's bed while Barbara sat near the foot. Elisabeth rested quietly, her color better, though Mary Ellen believed she ought not be left alone, yet.

She studied her daughter who had quickly regained her composure and helped tend to Elisabeth. Barbara, nearly eighteen years old, had conducted herself far more sensibly than Mary Ellen would have at the same age. At eighteen she was already married to Jacob and expecting her first child. After leaving the boarding school in Switzerland, she felt alone and abandoned, her mother and Ledger had been traveling in the Far East. Mother claimed to be unaware of her graduation from the all-girls' school. When Jacob Von Bek found Mary Ellen beside a pool in the Austrian Alps, she was hungry for attention from anyone.

His concern for her well-being, sitting alone in the wilderness, warmed her heart. She had been contemplating jumping into the frigid pool fed by the mountain streams. Grateful for his attention, she yielded within days to his amorous advances. She was fortunate Jacob was wealthy and able to care for her. Disappointed in the intimate aspect of marriage, she found herself quickly bored. Jacob had no occupation other than to travel from casino to casino, gambling. He spent so much time away from home that eventually, Mary Ellen realized she could do as she pleased as long as she showed her face occasionally at whatever residence they maintained at the time. She had no illusions about his faithfulness to her. She took a great deal of pleasure and delight in her beautiful little girl, refusing to discipline her or allow her to hear a harsh word. This left little Barbara willful and disagreeable by the time she reached the age of six.

By then Jacob had died of wounds received in a duel in France. She had no doubt the fight had been over a gambling debt. Happily relieved of his presence but not his money, she and Barbara had moved to Ireland where she met Seamus. He encouraged sending Barbara to a boarding school where she would learn not only reading and arithmetic, but also the meaning of discipline. Against her better judgment, she made the arrangements. Barbara resisted the nuns' strict rules. After several letters of complaint about her daughter's antics, they brought her to live with them in the Irish countryside.

Then Barbara gave birth to Lillian. To her delight, Barbara took to the baby instantly, even scolding and disciplining her when necessary. Though she loved her daughters dearly, the tedium of caring for children bored her. Relieved of those burdens, Mary Ellen once again took off for places unknown and adventures she hoped would fill the emptiness in her heart.

"I thought your door was locked."

Mary Ellen, jolted back to the present, faced her now grown daughter. "What was that?"

"The nurse was supposed to stay with you and keep the door locked. How did they get to you?"

"I told Martha to leave me alone. I didn't want any more of her injections. She agreed."

"Too easily, I'm guessing," Barbara said.

"Much too easily. I wanted to read the books you sent to distract myself...my mind had been in such a fog. I was unsure how I even came to be on this train." She wiped her forehead as if that might stir her memory.

"Do you remember the yacht?"

"What yacht?" When she saw Barbara's look of disappointment, she turned her face to Elisabeth, trying to hide the shame she felt from her daughter. She had been on a yacht but had no recollection.

"Grandmother is sleeping soundly. Perhaps I'll go find out what I can about the nurse." Barbara stood.

"No!" Mary Ellen said, "You've been through enough tonight. I'll go." Barbara appeared startled. "I'll be fine. As long as no one tries to give me any more of those injections. Honest, Barbara. You sit here and lock the door behind me."

Looking doubtful, Barbara nodded. "Find out what Alistair and Ledger are doing, will you?"

"I'll be back shortly."

"And Annie? ... No! Never mind. Lily doesn't know about you, yet and Annie's probably with her. Grandmother wanted to wait." Barbara half rose from her chair as if to stop Mary Ellen.

"This entire thing is too bizarre. I'll be right back. If Mother wakes up, comfort her until I return." Mary Ellen shook her head as she exited the ornate bedroom. She wondered who owned the rail car; certainly Mother had never spent money on such luxuries. And where could they be going? Her head ached with unanswered questions.

No one was in the hallway or the parlor. She pushed open the door the heavy woman had come through during the disturbance earlier. It led to a small dimly lit kitchen with a door at the far end. She crossed the room, using the counter tops to steady herself as the train lurched along the rails. The boy, Alistair, she remembered meeting him someplace else, but could not recall where. Were he and Barbara seeing each other romantically? The young man had proved himself by helping Ledger remove those two evil men.

The next door was locked. She tapped on it, not expecting a reply, imagining it was a pantry, so was startled when the fat woman opened the door. She was still in her nightdress and sleeping cap though she didn't appear to have been asleep. Barbara smelled whiskey.

"What is it?" the woman said.

"I was wondering what happened to the nurse, Martha."

"Martha? Is that her name? She won't say a word to us. You're Mary Ellen, the cause of all this trouble, aren't you?"

Mary Ellen, forced her face to remain impassive as her feelings fluctuated between shame and annoyance at the woman's attitude. "Perhaps. And you are?"

The woman stood straighter and said, "I am Mrs. Burch. I've been caring for your girls for going on six years."

"I'm grateful to you, but what about Martha? She was my nurse." The smell of the whiskey made her hands tremble. She made a fist to keep them still. "In spite of her disobedience, I still have need of her."

"We're holding her here until we stop in Chicago. We'll set her out there. She can find her own way back to New York City. You'll have to be doing without her, Miss."

"Who is it, Mrs. Burch?" a voice called from inside the room.

"It's herself, the infamous Mary Ellen. The one who was reported as dead."

Mary Ellen bristled at being spoken about in such a derogatory manner, especially by a servant.

"As you have apparently learned, I am very much alive," Mary Ellen said. She turned her back on the woman and started back toward the parlor, but when she heard the door behind her click shut, she stopped. In the soft light of the kitchen, she replayed Mrs. Burch' comment in her head.

"...the cause of all this trouble...the cause of all this trouble." The fragrance of the whiskey remained with her. "The cause of all this trouble."

She no longer had a nurse with a shot to soothe her. A glass of brandy would help. Her hands shook as she pulled open the cabinet doors, slamming each one shut when she couldn't find a bottle. Moisture soaked her brow. The room suffocated her; she needed to get out of it. "They must keep the liquor somewhere in the parlor. Just one drink. That would do it," she muttered as she continued to open and close cabinets.

Forty Three

Barbara yawned. It was late and she ought to be getting Lily and Annie back to their own compartment for the night. Grandmother snored softly so there was no reason to remain by her side. She eased herself up from the chair and tiptoed out the door, careful to shut it gently behind her. The hall lights had been dimmed.

If her mother had gone in search of Ledger and Alistair, she should not have had to go far. They planned to put the body and the other man off the train. How long could that take?

The parlor was empty. Blood stained the carpet where the dead man had fallen. She shuddered at the sight. Lifting her skirts, she gingerly stepped over the stain to reach the door. After shoving it aside and finding no one on the platform between cars, she moved into the next car. Annie and Lily were not in their room.

In the hall, she paused, wondering where her mother might have gone dressed in her nightgown. "Leave it to her to create a mystery around herself," Barbara mumbled as she headed forward, toward the orphan car. At least she could get the younger girls to their room and tucked in for the night.

She walked through the darkened coaches. Men and women in the coaches slept wrapped in their coats, their heads pillowed on their partner's shoulders or rolled up shawls. She moved through the cars trying not to disturb anyone, but the sounds of the train invaded each car with a blast when she opened the doors. Feeling guilty, she bunched her shoulders together to make herself less conspicuous.

She reached the orphan car and stepped into the dimness. There were no children in sight. At the far end of the car, Herbert sat with his violin playing a lullaby. Agnes and Annie sang softly, their voices angelic against the background of the clacking wheels and the roar of the train. Lily sat beside Herbert, gazing up at him as if entranced by his playing. Barbara moved forward and realized right away why she had not seen any children. They were sleeping, little ones stretched across the seats, the bigger ones curled up with dark woolen blankets covering them.

The picture of Annie with Agnes and Herbert warmed her heart. Their youthful innocence glowed. She hoped Annie hadn't told Lily about the men and the shooting.

Leaning against the door and knowing she stood in the shadows, Barbara closed her eyes and listened to the soft music. She wondered how Agnes had come to be on the train with the much younger children. The girl was nearly Annie's age with no family to take her in. She found it hard to believe not one family in all of New York City wanted such a nice girl as a daughter, or even a maid, for that matter. Maybe it was because of the little brother. The train swayed rhythmically, almost in time to the music, or maybe the music played in time to the motion of the train. Whatever was happening, Barbara enjoyed the serenity.

A raucous squawk from the violin interrupted her daydreaming. Ledger and Alistair hurried past the trio of entertainers and rushed along the aisle toward her. She stepped aside, wondering what could be happening now.

"Barbara, collect the girls and go to your compartment now," Ledger said as he drew up to her. "Mr. Rogers has arranged to have new security meet us in Chicago."

Her eyes went from Ledger to Alistair. Alistair seemed to have grown into his mustache. Her heart fluttered. *Mr. Rogers arranged....* She felt proud of him as if his bravery earlier and his take-command attitude were somehow connected to her. Alistair's eyes met hers and she lowered her lids, lest he see how much she admired him.

She cleared her throat. "I'll get Lily and Annie right away."

~*~

Mary Ellen, having exhausted hiding places in her search for a bottle, sat on the floor leaning against a cabinet. Convinced she smelled the lingering aroma of whiskey coming from the cook's room, her mind tossed around the idea of getting a drink from her. As she considered pulling herself to her feet, she heard Ledger call her name. If she remained quiet, maybe he would go away. His primary concern was for Mother now.

"Ugh." She reached for the countertop to pull herself to her feet.

The door to the parlor opened. "There you are, Mary Ellen. What are you doing in a dark kitchen? Do you want some food? I can put something together for you. Mrs. Burch and Brigitte have gone to bed. They've got custody of Martha until we reach Chicago." The entire time he spoke he turned on the lights and began poking around in the cupboards, pulling out cheeses and fruit.

"I was looking for a drink," she said, knowing she sounded sullen and disagreeable. She didn't care. "Martha never gave me my shot."

His hair might be turning white, but his dark brown eyes were sharp as ever. "I think fruit and cheese with a glass of milk ought to do the trick. Come along."

"Where?" She held back, not wanting to be locked up again.

"To your room. You've demonstrated to my satisfaction you're fully capable of taking care of yourself at least for the next few days. You'll need to have your wits about you." He held the door for her while balancing the tray of food in his other hand.

Eying him skeptically, she headed back to her room where the book lay open on her bed. After settling in she held a hand out to Ledger. "If you want the truth, I told Martha I didn't want any more shots, but I'm finding it difficult. Will you sit here and read to me and share my snack?"

"I'll be happy to read to you until you fall asleep."

"Like when I was little." She smiled and tucked her blankets snugly around her waist. Leaning against her pillows, she munched on the late-night snack, drank her milk and listened to Ledger's musical French accent as he read. It didn't matter she couldn't understand all the words; his voice was so elegant and soothing.

"I shall bid you good night, Mary Ellen. Please, remember to trust me when we get to Kansas City."

"I've always trusted you, Ledger."

Forty Four

Elisabeth rested comfortably, receiving her meals in bed for the duration of the journey. She insisted on being kept up to date on Mary Ellen's behavior, which Ledger continued to report as improving.

The girls, Barbara, Lily and the newly promoted Annie, spent their days playing with and entertaining a bunch of orphans. Elisabeth insisted the girls' clothing be washed daily and they bathe every night before retiring. Though they complained, they obeyed.

The changing of the private car in Chicago took far longer than anticipated causing her to worry they might not make it to Kansas City in time. Ledger reassured her they would be fine.

"We have two new men on board for security," he reported as the train set out for St. Louis. "I warned them about the sudden departure of the previous men so I think they'll be far more alert. Alistair Rogers is an asset. I'd like to offer him a permanent position with Ackert Industries, if you don't mind."

Elisabeth sighed. She was too tired to worry about industries and business. "You've always made the right decisions, why would I object now?"

He smiled. "Because I believe he and young Barbara are attracted to one another."

She flicked a wrist, dismissing the idea. "She's too young to be worrying about men."

"She'll turn eighteen in two weeks."

"You know I've been thinking about her future, Ledger. I'm not well and she stands to inherit a great deal of money and responsibility..."

"Now hush. You are simply tired from the excitement of the past week."

"I'm thinking about how my father wanted nothing more than for me to be accepted into society. I want more for Barbara. Will you look into Vassar College?"

"Vassar? You do realize what an upper-class school that is, don't you? The status of the young women who attend? That would be doing the same thing to Barbara your father did to you."

"Barbara can handle herself. But she'll wind up in trouble; too much brain and not enough to keep her occupied. With an education, she'll be able to cope with the world. She'll have to, you know. Life is sure to change in the twentieth century; she should be prepared." Elisabeth watched for Ledger's reaction.

He sat with eyes downcast, lost in thought for several minutes before he spoke. "You intend to give her the education you refused Mary Ellen."

"Speak up! I can barely hear you. What about Mary Ellen?" Her hands trembled. She hid them beneath the covers so he wouldn't notice. She wanted to be rid of thoughts of Mary Ellen once and for all. How many different ways could she explain it to him?

"I think a college education would be excellent for Barbara. Now you need to take a nap. I'll wake you in plenty of time for dinner." He stood to leave.

"We have five days before we must be in Kansas City."

"I've told you, we'll be there in plenty of time. The convention begins in five days. It will last at least a week."

She watched him leave, wondering if he told the truth. "I'll find out soon enough." Turning her head, she stared out the window as the train moved through the countryside.

~*~

On July 1st, 1900 the train left St. Louis for Kansas City.

"What do you suppose Grandmother is going to do once we get there?" Lily asked while she helped pack her luggage.

"All I know," Barbara answered, "is we'll be staying in a hotel for a few days. Maybe a week." Barbara wanted to tell her sister about Mary Ellen being alive and living in the private car with Grandmother. She hated being sworn to secrecy. "Now, let's get busy, we'll be there in a few hours."

Annie, dressed in the beige suit, having finished her packing earlier, deposited neatly folded linens into Barbara's case. "My head is spinning with all we've done these past weeks. How can we ever go back to Albany and be the same people again?"

Barbara laughed. "That's an interesting thought. Ledger spoke to me yesterday about the possibility of going to college this fall."

"College!" Lily shouted. "Where? Why? I thought you might take up with Alistair. How could you leave him?"

"Hold on. We're talking about Poughkeepsie. It's only a few hours from Albany."

"All the snooty girls go there," Lily said. "What does Grandmother think of that?"

Barbara didn't care what Grandmother thought; she knew her mother would approve. She was still unsure she wanted to follow through and take so much time out of her life, but then she thought about Mrs. Burch and Edna in *The Awakening*. If she attended college, the education could open a whole new world for her. The idea frightened her at the same it time gave her shivers of anticipation. She would ask Ledger to take her there as soon as they arrived home. Her mind raced with all she would have to do to prepare. "New clothes. I'll need new clothes if I'm going to school there. I wonder if I'll have time to shop? You don't suppose they wear uniforms, do you?"

"I wouldn't have no way of knowing, but I do know my brother had to wear a cassock when he went to the seminary." Annie's voice sounded angry.

"What's the matter, Annie?" Barbara stopped tying the bow at the neck of her blouse to look at the girl.

"What'll come of me if you go off to college? Mrs. Riis has Brigitte to work now. I'll have no place to go."

"Oh." Barbara sank onto the sofa, dismayed at her thoughtlessness. "I don't know, Annie."

"Can she be my personal maid?" Lily piped up.

Barbara considered her mother and wondered if Annie could be her maid. She should have kept her mouth shut until she had it worked out; now Lily and Annie would be pestering her every moment. "Now that Annie is learning to read, maybe she'd want to attend classes when we return home."

"Annie go to school?" Lily scoffed at the idea.

"She's right, you know. I don't have money for school. You don't think I'm working just for the fun of it, do you?" Annie began folding and packing, slamming items as if they had offended her.

"Let's not talk about this right now. I don't even know if I really want to go to a college. Ledger made the suggestion. Come on, the porters will be around soon to collect our luggage."

"Yeh, well, if yer decidin' to go away to school yer might be givin' me a little notice," Annie grumbled at the latches as she secured them.

"Why don't you go see if you can help Herbert with the children? Lily and I can manage the rest of our packing. We'll see you on the platform later." Barbara was in no mood to deal with the unhappy girl. She was more concerned with how

Grandmother planned to keep Lily from seeing their mother when everyone disembarked from the train.

Forty Five

"I've told the girls to wait inside the station for me. You stay here and rest while I see about the hotel. I wired ahead, but I never received a reply." Ledger fussed around Elisabeth trying to tuck her blankets more snugly around her middle.

She slapped his hand away. "Haven't you noticed it's about a hundred degrees in here? You go do what you have to do and I'll have a bath before we run out of water. What does happen with a private car left on a siding?"

"I've arranged for water and power. You and Mary Ellen will be fine until I return." He stroked her forehead like a father moving a strand of hair from her eyes. Like her father used to do.

"Go along then."

He hesitated in the doorway. His eyes bored into hers. "Are you absolutely certain you want to go through with this? It could backfire, you understand."

"I haven't traveled all this distance to quit now. I've waited thirty-five years for this opportunity."

He sighed. "Eat a good lunch. I'll do the rest. The guard will remain outside on the platform." He placed his hat on his head and left.

When she heard the outer door slide shut, Elisabeth removed her covers and called for Brigitte.

~*~

295

Barbara had their luggage stored and then went into the station and sat with Lily on a long bench while they waited to see Annie and Herbert with the orphans. People flowed around them, shouting to one another. A baby cried behind them. She turned to see a frantic young woman, perspiration dripping down her face. The yowling infant dangled over her shoulder, its red, toothless little face in Barbara's direction.

The stink of the stockyards permeated the enclosed space.

"There they are!" Lily jumped up and pointed as the line of somber, well-behaved children paraded into the station. Each one carried a small cardboard suitcase. A group of about a dozen adults who had been sitting opposite the girls stood up. A stout woman wearing a prairie bonnet and a plain homespun dress applauded their arrival. The others soon followed with applause. Barbara thought this a good omen for the children. They were welcome. She had imagined gruff farmers hauling them off as slave labor and felt pleased by this civilized reception.

"Agnes! Annie!" Lily dashed to the end of the line where the two girls shepherded the last of the orphans through the entrance. Barbara's attention returned to the adults who looked over the children. Something about their manner seemed familiar. She watched as the men and women moved amongst the children, who stood still. A man directed a young boy of about five to open his mouth. He studied the boy's teeth. He then wrapped his beefy hand around the child's upper arm. *The grocery and the butcher shop.* The adults looked like people inspecting meat and vegetables. Now the reception didn't feel as friendly as she'd first thought. The children waited patiently. Eight of the smaller children were led away within minutes; the rest continued to suffer the humiliating examinations in silence, some with tears in their eyes. No one looked at Agnes, and Barbara wondered if it was because she was too old. But then Herbert signaled for her to come forward, separating her from Annie and Lily. Agnes stood, head high, cheeks burning as three men approached and prodded her. Barbara wished the girl would strike out at them.

A group of finely dressed young men stood idly by, watching and laughing as Agnes underwent inspection. Finally, Barbara could stand it no longer. She rose from the bench and strode toward Herbert, who was in conversation with one of the women.

"Herbert! Make those men stop molesting Agnes. Immediately!"

"Don't be upset, Barbara. They are checking to make sure she's fit for farm work. She'll be fine." He turned back to the woman.

Angered, Barbara approached Agnes. "That's enough! If you haven't figured it out by now, you can leave!" she barked at the men who mauled Agnes. "If this is the way you treat young ladies, then you don't deserve to have her in your homes."

"Please, Barbara. Leave it be, for the love of God," Agnes begged.

Stunned by this reaction, Barbara clamped her mouth shut and stared at Agnes.

"If I don't get picked now, I have to go to a place where it will just keep happening. If one of these gentlemen wants me for their farm, and will take my little brother, then I'm happy to go."

"You got a brother? Which one is he?" the tallest and skinniest of the men said, turning to look over the other children.

"John Joseph! C'mere!" Agnes shouted.

The little boy separated himself from the crowd and ran to her, clutching her skirt with one hand and staring in terror up at the faces of the men.

"This is my brother, Johnny. He stays with me."

"My wife told me to get a girl to help her with the chickens and the garden. She didn't say nothing about no boys," the second man said. The other two mumbled agreement.

"If he can't come with me, then you can't have me. That's the rules we were told. We have to agree to the folks as wants us." Agnes had dropped her suitcase and now folded her arms belligerently in front of her chest.

The skinny man bent down and prodded Johnny, who giggled. "That tickles."

"Ah, what the hay. He ain't gonna eat much. Come on, girl. What's your name?"

Agnes lunged toward Barbara and grabbed her in a tight hug, squeezing the air out of her. "Thank you for making the trip so much easier. I'll remember you forever."

"You have my address. Write to me some time and let me know how you're doing."

Agnes released her. The two girls wiped their eyes and then Agnes turned toward her new "father." "My name is Agnes, but if you want to change it, that's okay with me. I never liked it anyways."

"Agnes will do just fine. If the missus likes you, it don't matter what your name is."

Barbara watched the two children follow the man out of the terminal, feeling like she lost a sister.

In less than an hour, sixteen children remained. Herbert waved to the girls as he led the children out of the terminal to go to the school building where they would once again be examined and prodded. Those who were left behind today would then be returned to the train and go on to another town.

"Come along, Lily. Annie. Let's go see if we can find a cup of tea. A place this busy must have a café."

Forty Six

Mary Ellen sat in the parlor playing checkers against herself. A cup of cold tea sat on the table beside the board.

Ledger returned to the train car late in the afternoon. He hesitated at the entrance.

"Hello, Ledger. Is everything all right?" She moved her hands to her lap so he wouldn't see the slight tremors.

"Alistair is at the station waiting to see Martha Abbott on the train. The girls are in the depot waiting for my return and I have secured two rooms at a hotel for them and Alistair. How are you feeling?"

"I'm doing well, thank you. I've won three games already." She dare not tell him about her struggle since she found herself alone. With Mrs. Burch and Brigitte busy in the kitchen, she had wandered through the parlor pulling open cabinet doors until she discovered where they kept the alcohol. She sank to the floor and studied each label, remembering the taste and the feel of it sliding down her throat and warming her insides. Then she remembered the spiders and the Chinaman and her lovely pipes. Her stomach churned and she had to race to the bathroom where she lost her lunch. After regrouping, she cleaned up and prepared herself to go out later, hoping Ledger would find rooms in the city for them.

"Before you go in to see Mother, can we talk, Ledger?"

His eyes focused on her face. Looking for the signs of alcohol, she knew. She deserved it. Satisfied, he sat across from her and moved a red checker. "Your move."

She jumped the red checker, knowing full well he had deliberately put the piece in jeopardy. "Do you know exactly what she has in mind? Why we're in Kansas City?"

"I have an idea, but I'm not exactly sure how she intends to accomplish her goal."

"Which is?" They continued exchanging checkers.

"She wants to destroy Senator Justin Pembroke."

"The man she claims is my father."

"That's right."

"Do you believe it's true?"

"I was not present during that time of her life."

Reminding herself to keep calm, she drew a deep breath. "I was six years old when mother hired you."

Ledger raised his eyebrows. He picked up his crowned checker and proceeded to wipe the board clean. She realized too late the man who had always protected and cared for her had been hurt by her statement. Ledger had grown to be a part of the family, not like a hired man at all.

Ledger stood. "I win."

"I know you're more than an employee, Ledger," she tried to apologize. "It's been so long…" He disappeared around the corner, heading toward her mother's room.

Disappointed in her behavior, she forced herself to replace the checkers neatly in their box, folded the board and then carried it across the room as if bearing precious gems. She pulled open the drawer to replace them, but instead, a sudden rage overwhelmed her and she threw the board and the box across the room. Red and black scattered in all directions as if happy to be freed from confinement.

"Damn all of you!" she screamed. "I want to see my children and I want to see them now!" Her heart raced in fury;

tears ran down her face. "I've been through hell for you," she shouted at the empty hallway.

A movement to her right caught her eye. Brigitte, the serving girl peeked out from the kitchen door. "What are you staring at?" Mary Ellen picked up a heavy glass ashtray and made as if to throw it. The girl retreated.

"Mary Ellen." Ledger's voice came from the hall.

"I'm leaving," she said. "I'm going to find my daughters." Before she could change her mind about heading out into an unfamiliar city and before Ledger could stop her, she pushed open the door to the car and jumped down from the platform onto the gravel rail bed.

Pausing a moment to get her bearings, she spotted the depot and ran toward it. The pebbles and stones made for awkward footing. At one point her ankle twisted, but she did not care. All she wanted was to see her daughters. Mother had no right or reason to keep them from her, or her from them. It wasn't fair.

She held her skirt pulled up nearly to her knees to keep from tripping as she raced for the building ahead. Not daring to take time to turn around to see if Ledger chased her, she took the steps to the platform two at a time. At the top of the steps, she stopped. People on the platform turned to stare at her. There couldn't be anything wrong; she was dressed in her traveling clothes; her hat remained in place. What could they be seeing? Then she heard the footsteps behind her. They were watching a colored man running after her.

Her mind searched frantically for an escape. The alarmed faces around her provided the answer she needed.

"Will someone help me? I need to get away. That man is following me!" Without waiting to see what would happen, she dashed to the entrance .

A gentleman yanked the door open for her. "You get inside, Miss. We'll take care of this."

Darting through the entrance, she glanced back to see several men gathering outside the doors. They would stop Ledger and give her time to find her girls. She scanned the interior of the depot, not seeing either one of them. With another nervous look at the doors, she then moved through the large room searching more closely. Still no daughters. They must have left already. Most likely Ledger had arranged rooms for them in the city. She was surprised he let them go alone, unescorted by a male companion.

She wondered where the guard was that Ledger said would be protecting their private car. No one stood outside when she left. As she passed the street exit, she made the sudden decision to walk into the city to find the girls. Ledger would have put them up in a first-class hotel. How many of those could a cowboy town like Kansas City have? She pushed out into the open air and felt free for the first time in weeks. The sunshine hit her face. At that moment she wanted to fall back and let it warm her. But she had to find her daughters first.

"Wait, Ledger said they were waiting for him in the depot." She turned around as if by doing so she could see the interior of the train station. "But they weren't there."

"May I help you, dear?"

Startled, Mary Ellen turned to see a tall, stout woman dressed totally in black smiling the way people smiled at mad men, or women, in her case. She held a lorgnette in one hand and carried a large carpetbag in the other. Mary Ellen backed away. "I'm fine. Fine. My little girls are lost. I'm looking for them."

"You were talking to someone, dear." The woman continued to smile. "Perhaps you'd like to come with me and have a nice cup of chamomile tea?"

"I was talking to myself," she explained, and then realized that would make her sound crazy. Living alone for so many years, she had become accustomed to speaking aloud when trying to resolve an issue. Her only social life of late had been when she was drinking or using dope. No matter what other motives her mother had in mind, she had helped free her of that mad cycle.

The woman waited patiently.

"I realize how that may appear, but I assure you, I truly am fine – and fit. If you could please tell me the name of the better hotels in this city, I believe I shall find my daughters in one of them." There, she had spoken clearly and sensibly.

The woman's eyebrows raised and her lips pinched in disbelief. "Why should they be at a hotel?"

"Because my mother and the rest of my party are staying in their private rail car. Our man has found rooms for the girls and their bodyguard at a hotel, but I forgot to ask which one." Still believing herself to sound reasonable, she waited for an equally reasonable response.

"Perhaps we ought to call a policeman. There are plenty of them on the streets because of all the dignitaries here for the convention." The woman looked around, then dropped her lorgnette which was attached to a chain around her neck. Mary Ellen felt a shiver of fear and stepped back but not before the woman took her by the upper arm. "Seeing none, perhaps you'd like to come with me. I can show you to very nice lodgings. It isn't safe for a woman to wander the streets unaccompanied, especially this week."

The woman's fingers clasped her arm with more strength than necessary.

"My name is Mrs. Oats. It is my journey in life to help lost women."

"I'm not lost. I've never been to Kansas City and I need to find my daughters. Must you walk so fast?"

"Out of condition, are we? Some calisthenics will help you. I have my girls do them every afternoon. It helps maintain their stamina." Mrs. Oats guided her around a corner where a brougham stood waiting. Two horses with feed bags attached, stomped their feet and switched their tails to chase flies. "Here we are. Jump in and we'll soon be home."

Mary Ellen pulled against Mrs. Oats' firm grip. "I am not jumping into anything! Let me go. I'll scream."

"You may scream. Matthew! A little help, if you please."

The driver leapt down from his perch. The last thing Mary Ellen saw was his beefy hand holding a black sap.

Forty Seven

Elisabeth struggled to get into her corset. No matter what Ledger thought, she would go into the city to learn everything she could about Senator Justin Pembroke. She first needed to know at which hotel his party was lodged. If she could find a convention schedule, that would be most beneficial.

Frustrated at her inability to fasten the hooks, she pressed the button that would call one of the help. While she waited, she added a little brandy to her coffee. That would soothe her nerves.

A commotion in the parlor made her grab her dressing gown. After covering herself, she opened the door and stepped into the hallway.

"Good Lord, what have you done to him?" Mrs. Burch's voice came from the parlor.

"I rescued him from a mob, that's what. Go get water so we can clean him up," Alistair Rogers ordered. "And bring some tincture of iodine."

"What did you do with that nurse?" Elisabeth demanded as she entered the room and saw Ledger sitting in a straight-backed chair with Alistair hovering over him.

"For God's sake, woman, this man is injured!" Alistair snapped.

Ledger's condition had not registered with Elisabeth. "Ledger? What happened?" She rushed across the space to him, kneeling by his side. The sharp pain in her joints reminded her of her age.

"Mary Ellen," Ledger mumbled through swollen lips, the lower one split and bleeding. Alistair mopped at the blood with his own handkerchief. "Mary Ellen ran away."

Rocking back on her heels, furthering her discomfort, Elisabeth let out her breath. "I might have known. Why wasn't someone watching her?"

"I left her for a moment. When I returned, I saw that she had gone and went in search of her. She was running toward the depot. As I chased after her, she said something to the crowd on the platform and suddenly I was being attacked and called the most horrific names." His eyelids drooped and his body sagged as he related his story.

Mrs. Burch appeared with a basin of hot water and clean towels. Pushing Alistair aside, she began dabbing at the bruises and cuts on Ledger's face.

"I heard tell of colored men being hung for lesser offenses. Why didn't you call me?"

"I never thought…"

"Don't talk. Let me fix that cut," Mrs. Burch admonished.

Elisabeth turned to Alistair. "We have to do something about Mary Ellen."

Muffled sounds came from Ledger. Mrs. Burch stopped administering to him so he could speak. "If it hadn't been for this young man, I most likely would have been hung. That was one angry crowd. I'd like to know what Mary Ellen said to them. I'll find her, believe me, I shall."

"You won't be finding anyone for a while, so just be quiet and let me work," Mrs. Burch said.

Alistair helped Elisabeth to the divan and sat beside her. The partially hooked corset pinched at her fleshy hips, but she dare not show signs of discomfort; that would be too embarrassing. She tightened the belt to her dressing gown and leaned toward Alistair, speaking in a soft voice. "What about that nurse?"

"I gave a man five dollars to see her onto the next train going anyplace." His eyes lit up with amusement.

"Good for you. What did you see? Did you see Mary Ellen?"

"No, I'm sorry to say. I did hear a woman's voice call out, but not the words. Next thing I knew, men were in a huddle, pummeling on someone. When I heard Ledger's voice I explained who he was and asked them to leave him alone."

"I see," she said, observing his red knuckles and the beginnings of a bruise on the left side of his chin. "You must have a very convincing manner of speech."

"Yes, ma'am."

"I want you to go out and find a carriage for us. We must find Mary Ellen as soon as possible."

"But I'm supposed to take the girls to the hotel Ledger secured for them. They're waiting in the depot."

"They can wait a bit longer. This is far more important." She pushed herself up from the sofa. "Mrs. Burch, send Brigitte into me immediately. I must dress."

"Right away, ma'am."

"Baltimore," Ledger said.

"Baltimore what?" Elisabeth asked.

"The Baltimore Hotel. I managed to book the last two rooms." He paused to smile at a memory. "They were anxious to have me leave quickly lest people think I was planning to stay there." He held a wet towel to his cheek as he spoke. "Money talks."

Mrs. Burch left the room with the bloodied water, assuring him she would be right back; he dare not move from the chair.

"We brought her this far, I'm sure she'll be fine, Mrs. Riis." Alistair placed a hand on her shoulder.

Elisabeth leaned away from his touch. "Two security men and Ledger and not one of you could manage to keep track of one woman. A lot of good you are. Just go see if you can manage to find a carriage. I'll be dressed if that girl ever makes an appearance." She stood up, feeling lightheaded for a moment. Her partially fastened corset already felt far too tight. She would have to adjust the laces before they went through the process of hooking it again.

Alistair also stood up, raising his hands to support her, but she shunned his help.

"I'll find a carriage and return shortly," Alistair said. "Ledger, will you remain with Mrs. Riis until I return?"

"Don't worry about him, he's staying right where he is until I say he can go," Mrs. Burch said as she returned with fresh water and towels. "The other guard is out back on the platform smoking a cigar. You could give him something to do."

"That is his job, Mrs. Burch," Ledger said. "Will you ensure that he is still at his station, Alistair?"

"Right away, sir." Alistair nearly ran from the room, disappearing down the hallway. "I'll be back!"

Elisabeth crossed in front of Ledger to take a closer look at him. She cringed at the sight of the broken skin on the swollen lip and the bruise developing around his right eye. Afraid to ask him where else he was hurt, she folded her arms and watched Mrs. Burch tend to him.

"He needs to rest, Mrs. Riis."

"We haven't time," Elisabeth answered. "Ledger, when Alistair returns with a carriage, I want you to go with me to find Mary Ellen. She can't have gone far. Most likely she'll have gone to wait with the girls in the depot."

"We'll check there first. Did you make the appropriate hotel arrangements?"

"I did. The Royal Hawaiian party canceled their reservations. They'll be staying in their private rail cars. Their party will only be here for one day," Ledger said.

"Good for us. This car is far too confining."

"I could only get two rooms. I made the reservations for the girls in one room and Alistair Rogers in one adjoining." He held a hand up to stop Mrs. Burch from further ministrations. "If you're prepared, then I suggest you collect your hat and gloves while we wait for Rogers."

Without hesitation, she headed back to her room for the items, as well as a packet of digitalis. Not long now and she would have her revenge. She smiled at the thought, ignoring the rope tightening around her chest when she raised her arms to fix her hair.

Forty Eight

Elephants danced a tarantella in her head, waking Mary Ellen to the odors of dirty linens, sweat and cigars. Her stomach churned. She groaned.

"About time you woke up. It's near on to seven o'clock and you ain't had no dinner, yet."

Mary Ellen kept her eyes shut; she didn't want to see where she was nor who was speaking. She rolled from her stomach to her back.

"Gawd, you're old! What's she planning to do with you? Save you for some blind man?"

Now Mary Ellen did open her eyes enough to peek at the speaker who turned out to be a tart who might have made her sixteenth birthday, just. "Where are we?"

"We're at Mrs. Oats' establishment. In the posh end of town." The girl giggled at her own joke. "Leastwise it's where the posh gentlemen come when they want a little fun and games."

"A brothel?"

Sally ignored her comment. "There's also roulette and blackjack in one of the rooms. Wanna get up so we can eat?"

"No. I want to get back to my family."

"Sure you do. That's why you was running away."

Mary Ellen lay the back of her hand across her forehead. "I wasn't running away; I was looking for my daughters."

"Not what Mrs. Oats told us. She said you were wandering the streets talking to yourself. Over by the stockyards."

"We just arrived by train."

She heard the girl's skirts ruffle. "Name's Sally, what's yours?"

Pausing for a moment, Mary Ellen answered, "Mary Smith."

"Huh! I'm just trying to be nice. Mrs. Oats told me to keep an eye on you. If I do, I can get out of a couple hours work tonight. Want some water?"

Reluctantly Mary Ellen opened her eyes. The girl, with black hair drawn tightly back from her face, stood not three feet away looking down at her. She wore a brightly colored Mexican peasant's skirt and a loose-fitting cotton shirt. The natural shape of her breasts, including the nipples, showed through the sheer fabric. Embarrassed for the girl who was younger than Barbara, she closed her eyes again. "Cover yourself and, yes, I am indeed extremely thirsty. What happened to me? Did I fall?"

"Probably. Be right back." Sally left.

Mary Ellen tried to sit up but fell back before she could raise herself more than a few inches from the disgusting mattress. Her life seemed to be one completely out of her control. In spite of the black hair, Sally's fair complexion, blue eyes and mid-western accent belied the Mexican attire. A brothel with themes? What a mess she'd made of her life. Now she had to try to get out of this place in order to find her girls.

She rolled to her right and saw a lace-curtained window. If only she could get up and look out, she might figure a way to escape. Trying once more to ease herself upright, she managed to slide her feet onto the floor and then, push herself halfway to a sitting position. She was stuck leaning on her elbow, her head throbbing, but the sight of a porch roof made her pull up straight. Managing to stagger the few feet to the window, she was able to assess the possibility of leaving via the window. Satisfied with her discovery, she once again positioned herself on the bed to wait for whatever came next.

Sally reappeared with a tray containing a pitcher, a glass, and a sandwich.

"Mrs. Oats said to feed you something and she hopes you're feeling better. I made a chicken sandwich." She placed the tray on the bedside table and then poured a glass of water for Mary Ellen.

"Thank you," Mary Ellen managed. "Did she send anything for a terrific headache?"

"I'm sure we got something here. Eat your supper and I'll go see what I can find." She turned to leave and then added, "Mary Ellen."

Mary Ellen's headache ratcheted up two notches. Her scalp crawled, reminding her of the days and nights when she didn't know where she was. Sally sauntered out the door. For some reason it pleased Mary Ellen that the girl had added a bright red, green and yellow poncho to her costume, covering the upper portion of her body. She closed her eyes and willed the pain in her head to go away. Sally and, most likely, Mrs. Oats knowing her name frightened her. What could it mean?

Forcing herself upright, she managed a few sips of water.

Sally returned with a small packet. "Don't know what's in it, but it's what Mrs. Oats gives the girls when they complain of headache." She tossed the small, folded paper on the bed. "You take it with water."

Mary Ellen eyed it with suspicion. How long had it been since she had ingested anything except wholesome food and drink? She took a deep breath. "Could you please find out what this is before I take it?"

"Just trying to help you a bit. If you want, I can get you a cup of coffee," she offered eagerly. "I don't let on when I have a headache 'cause I don't like the way the girls act after they've had these powders." Sally rushed around the bed and planted herself in a wooden rocker. Her eyes went from the window back to Mary Ellen. Her mouth twitched, like a child trying to keep a secret. "If you're thinking about leaving, I wouldn't recommend it. They have ways of catching you and the punishment is none too nice."

"How do you know my name?" Mary Ellen decided against the powder but slipped it into her skirt pocket just in case she needed it later. Though it couldn't have weighed more than an ounce, the envelope felt like it weighed five hundred pounds as it rested in the darkness of the pocket.

"Mrs. Oats. Guess you must have told her. Want me to get the coffee?" She rocked, again reminding Mary Ellen of a child, a child about to propel herself out of the chair.

"I never had a chance to talk to anyone. I do remember the woman who offered to help me, but I didn't want any help. Then something hit me on the head." Her hand reached reflexively to the lump just above her right ear.

"That would be Matthew and his sap." She rubbed her own head in sympathy. "Glad I never got it. Mrs. Oats doesn't like him using it too much."

"Perhaps the coffee." Mary Ellen wanted the coffee; she also wanted time to recover enough to form a plan. She offered a wan smile.

Once the girl left, Mary Ellen, head throbbing, struggled to the window. Her view presented an easy descent; however the porch roof covered the main entrance to the establishment. The movement aggravated the pain in her head and caused her right eye to water. Using furniture for support, she placed herself on the rocker, too weak to make it back to the bed.

Did I tell that woman, Mrs. Oats, my name? Madame Oats. If my head would stop hurting, I could figure a way out of here. Why would anyone want me in a brothel? I'm far too old and skinny. Sally, with her fresh face, blue eyes and plump curves is what the men want. Now, what do I want? She shut her eyes and tried to concentrate on not taking the powder that lay so heavily in her pocket.

Sally returned with a tray bearing a porcelain coffee pot, matching cups, and polished silver cream and sugar containers. "If you don't want your sandwich, you might want to try these pastries." She set the tray on a table across the room from the bed. "That's some lump on your head. Are you sure you ought to be up?"

"It hurts either way," Mary Ellen answered as she removed her hand from her pocket. She would wait to see if the coffee helped her headache.

Sally moved a small round table to Mary Ellen's side and set a cup of coffee on it, adding a monogrammed linen napkin and a small plate of delicate pastries.

"I am sure I did *not* tell Mrs. Oats my name." Mary Ellen watched Sally for a reaction.

She only shrugged. "Maybe you forgot after the cosh on your head. Eat something; you're skinny as a rail."

Forty Nine

Barbara, Lillian and Annie had long since finished their tea. Announcements for arriving and departing trains kept them apprised of the time. They had been sitting in the café for a little over three hours.

"We'd best go back to Grandmother's car," Barbara said.

"But if Ledger's looking for us, he won't know where to find us. What if he's on his way to the train station right now?"

"We'll pass him on the way, you silly goose," Barbara said to Lily. "If we sit here any longer, the staff is going to become suspicious of our motives."

"Why?" Lily asked.

"Never mind. Come along. If Ledger hasn't been able to find a room for us, we might have to sleep in Grandmother's car." Barbara thought about her mother being in there and wondered how Lily would react to seeing her. It had to happen soon. How long could she keep such a secret from her sister? It just was not fair of Grandmother to impose that on her.

"It's almost time for dinner already," Annie said. "Do you think we'll be eating on the train?"

"I have no idea what we'll be doing. At least we won't be stuck in a public place looking like a group of runaways." Barbara felt anger surge through her as she led the way out of the station and on to the path to the rail car. What had begun

315

as an adventure two weeks ago had turned into a marathon of nonstop traveling and deception.

As they stepped from behind the station, she was surprised to see several private cars along the sidings.

"Which one is ours?" Lily asked, gaping at the array of private train cars in the yard.

"I'm not sure," Barbara said. Dismayed and embarrassed to not know, she led them amongst the trains, hoping Alistair, Ledger or one of the private guards would notice them and come to their rescue. She felt lost in the maze of train cars when she heard Alistair's voice from behind.

"Miss Riis! Where are you going?"

Barbara and Lillian whirled about to see him running toward them. Barbara instantly rushed to meet him, while Lillian remained beside Annie.

"Alistair! What's going on? We were told to wait at the depot but no one came."

Alistair took her by the arm and led her away from the other two girls. "We've lost your mother. I went to get a coach to take you to the hotel. Ledger was watching her, but somehow, she got away. I looked for you in the depot."

Barbara gasped. "What do you mean you lost my mother?"

"Keep your voice down. Your sister doesn't know about her, yet."

"I don't care who knows what anymore! I want to know what is going on with my mother!"

At that, Lillian rushed forward, followed closely by Annie. "Mother? Whose mother?"

"*Grand*mother, Lily. We were speaking of your grandmother," Alistair said, with a warning look toward Barbara.

Ignoring him, Lily turned to Barbara, who stood still, afraid to say a word. Lily's face turned red and tears threatened. "I heard you say Mother! Tell me what's going on? Is Mother alive? Why are we in Kansas City? Is she living here? Is that why we came?"

The questions rattled so quickly from her that Barbara had to shout to be heard. "Yes, Mother is alive. You weren't supposed to know until she was well."

Lily's face went white. Annie reached for her to keep her from falling. Tears flowed down Lily's face. "Mommy's alive? Really alive?"

Barbara's heart ached at the evidence of her sister's pain. She reached out and took her in her arms. Lily fell into the embrace, sobbing but within seconds, she pushed away and glared, once again red-faced, at Barbara. "Why did you keep it from me? It's not fair! She's my mother, too. Where is she now?"

"Grandmother wanted to protect you. No one wanted to see you upset," Barbara tried to pull her in, but Lily jerked her body out of reach.

Annie stood next to Alistair, a handkerchief to her mouth as if to stifle her own words.

"I'm not a child!" Lily shouted. "Tell me where she is! Now!"

Barbara, desperate to calm Lily, turned to Alistair. Without her having to say a word, he stepped forward. "She left the train about an hour ago. Your grandmother is upset, so why don't you calm yourself and we can go talk to her."

"I don't want to talk to that nasty old woman! I hate her! She told us Mommy was dead!"

Though Barbara had felt the exact same way when she learned her mother was alive, she wanted Lily to calm down so they could go to Grandmother without upsetting her. As it was, she must already be in distress about her missing daughter. She had done so much to help Mother get well, then Mother ups and runs away. Barbara didn't know what to feel.

"Alistair, please take us to Grandmother. Lily needs to hear the truth from her."

Alistair shifted his weight from foot to foot, glanced to his right then dropped his head, looking at the gravel as if searching for lost gems. He mumbled something incoherent.

"Alistair." Barbara barked at him. "Speak up."

"Your grandmother isn't well right now. Perhaps later. I have a carriage to take you to your hotel. We can see Mrs. Riis later." His right hand gestured behind him.

"If you won't take us, I'll find the car myself."

He grasped her by the wrist. "No, Barbara. Believe me, she is not well. Mrs. Burch is tending to her. Ledger has gone in search of your mother. It's best if we get you settled in the hotel. I've already sent your luggage ahead. Please," he pleaded.

She looked from him to the alley of private rail cars. Suddenly feeling like a small, lost child, she held out a hand to him. "Take me to Grandmother. Annie can wait with Lily outside, then we'll go with you." With tears in her eyes, she added, "Please."

"I won't wait outside. I want to go in with you," Lily cried.

"Stop acting like a child. Grandmother isn't well. You heard Alistair. And Mother has slipped away."

"There's more," Alistair interrupted. Before Barbara could say anything, he continued. "When your mother left, she set a gang of men on Ledger. He's been badly beaten." He took her by the arm. "I'm going to insist the younger girls remain outside on the platform under the watchful eye of the guard until we come out."

"Ledger?" Barbara felt her eyes well with tears. She had a difficult time seeing and was glad for Alistair's guiding arm. "Is he...?" She couldn't finish.

"Nothing appears to be broken. Mrs. Burch is tending to him while Mrs. Riis dresses. They'll be going to the Baltimore as soon as your mother returns."

"None of this makes any sense to me."

"It obviously has to do with Senator Pembroke."

"The man is running for president, but I don't see what this has to do with Grandmother."

"Careful. We cross these tracks and our car is right there." He helped her step over the rails and led her to the car where the guard stood in place on the platform. She checked to make sure Lily and Annie were behind them.

"You two wait out here. Annie, keep your eyes on Lily. She is not to come inside and upset Grandmother any further than she is already upset. I can't imagine what she thought when she saw Ledger injured." Barbara shook her head, feeling overwhelmed with all that had happened since they arrived in Kansas City.

Alistair placed his hands around her waist and helped her up the high first step onto the platform. Alistair's hands on her waist sent a shiver up her spine. The guard reached down and took her hand to assist her the rest of the way up. He opened the door and she passed into the cool interior of the rail car.

She took a moment to let her eyes adjust to the dim light. Ledger sat on a straight-backed chair. Mrs. Burch wrung out a cloth over a dishpan on the table beside him. Barbara watched as Mrs. Burch tenderly ministered to the side of Ledger's left eye. She glanced up at Barbara briefly but returned to her work without a word.

After taking a deep breath, Barbara said, "Is Grandmother in her room?"

"She is," Mrs. Burch answered without looking up. "I'm going to put a couple of stitches in here. The bleeding won't stop unless I do. Would you like some whiskey?"

Ledger groaned something sounding like "yes."

Barbara cringed at the sight of his bruised face but felt a shred of relief that at least he was upright. She headed around the corner to her grandmother's room and tapped on the door. Without waiting for a response, she entered the compartment. Grandmother sat on the cushioned chair next to her bed. She appeared pale though red blotches lent color to her cheeks.

"Grandmother?" she whispered when Elisabeth did not respond to her entrance.

Elisabeth's right hand rose and fell. "It's almost over, Mary Ellen. Almost over."

"I'm Barbara, Grandmother. Where is Mother? Do you know?"

"We need to go to the hotel now. Tell Ledger to stop whatever he's doing and come help me. He's become too independent lately." Her eyes lifted to Barbara's.

Barbara was appalled at the blue tinge to Grandmother's lips. Elisabeth needed Mrs. Burch and Ledger immediately. They should be taking her to a doctor. She shuddered at the thought of Ledger being ministered to by Mrs. Burch for cuts and bruises to his face. "I'll get him," she whimpered and left the room.

Trying to conceal her panic, she backed from the room, shut the door quietly and then dashed to the parlor where Bridget stood next to Mrs. Burch with a fresh bowl of water. Ledger's head was bowed as Mrs. Burch dabbed at his exposed neck.

She cleared her throat. "Grandmother doesn't look well. She wants to see you, Ledger. I think you and Mrs. Burch need to find a doctor for her."

Mrs. Burch stopped dabbing and looked up. "Bad, is she?"

Barbara nodded.

Mrs. Burch turned back to Ledger. "Are you up to it?"

Ledger's shoulders heaved. Barbara heard a deep sigh. Without speaking, Ledger took Mrs. Burch's hand and let her help him to his feet.

"Is Rogers close by?" he asked Barbara.

"He's outside watching over Lily and Annie. He's waiting to drive us to the Baltimore Hotel."

"Then go with him. We'll meet you there shortly." Ledger leaned on Mrs. Burch's shoulder with one hand as she led him away. "I'll see to your grandmother. Remain in your rooms at the hotel until we arrive."

With tears in her eyes, Barbara nodded, wondering if she would ever see her grandmother alive again.

Fifty

"Someone told her your name," Sally said to Mary Ellen, "How else would she know who to look for?"

Mary Ellen rocked slowly in the chair thinking about that very thing. How did Mrs. Oats know her name? She remembered events of the past few weeks in small pieces. So many gaps existed. Someone tried to burn her apartment. Barbara knew she was alive. Did Lily? Was someone trying to kill her? Then why keep her alive – and in a brothel, of all places?

Her hand reached reflexively for a small pastry. She nibbled at the edge of it. As the sweetness filled her, she realized she was hungry.

Sally sat on the bed across from her and waited for her to finish the pastry. When Mary Ellen reached for the coffee pot, Sally jumped up and took it from her. "Perhaps you don't really want coffee. You know it'll keep you up all night."

Mary Ellen glowered at her. "Of course I want coffee. Do you think I want to fall asleep in this place? I intend to remain awake until I can meet with Mrs. Oats and clear up this ridiculous misunderstanding. There is no reason in the world I can think of where a madam of a brothel would incarcerate me. Now, give me the coffee."

"No!" Sally's demeanor had changed in the last few moments to one of strength and control. "You can't drink the coffee. I won't let you. Please, Miss Riis, trust me." Tears filled the girl's eyes.

"My name is Von Bek. Mary Ellen Von Bek. Mother made me revert to my maiden name."

Sally threw up her hands. "I don't care a fig for your name. I heard Mrs. Oats tell the senator that she would release you after the convention. She has no intention of harming you, but I don't want to see you drugged for the next week. Let me bring you a fresh glass of water." She eased the coffee pot from Mary Ellen's hands.

"Drugged?" Mary Ellen said, stunned by the news that she was meant to be held for an entire week. "Why?"

"So you won't try to leave. Mrs. Oats is taking a chance trusting me. If I ask you nice, you'll behave, won't you?" The eyes pleaded with Mary Ellen.

Exhausted, Mary Ellen relented and agreed she would not bring Sally any distress. "I'll not cause any trouble provided you tell me what this is all about. What senator?" As she asked the question, the answer loomed from the center of her being. It would be Senator Justin Pembroke.

"Senator Pembroke," she and Sally said in unison.

Sally gasped. "How did you know?"

"He's my father."

"Your father? And he wants you held in a brothel?" Sally appeared to forget about the coffee and set the pot on the table. "Why would he do that?"

Mary Ellen's head spun with possibilities. Senator Pembroke. Justin Pembroke. Her father, according to Mother. She squeezed her eyes tightly shut and pushed away the impending headache. "I don't know. I was in search of my daughters and now I'm here. Is there any way you can find out for me? I'll be able to pay you once I'm free."

Sally's skirts rustled as she rose from the bed. "You don't need to pay me. I will find out and whenever I learn something, I'll come tell you. You got to promise to stay here until I do, right?"

Peering at the girl through one eye, Mary Ellen agreed. "I'm in no condition to go anywhere at the moment. Bring the water. I'll drink that."

Sally departed leaving the door slightly ajar.

Mary Ellen rocked as she pondered the unlocked door. Should she leave the room and seek a means of escape? Should she run after Sally and force her to let her out? What made Sally change her mind about drugging her?

Before she could come to any conclusions, Sally flew back into the room. "Say," Sally said, breathless, "How is Riis your maiden name if the senator is your father?" She stood with one hand on the doorknob and the other on her hip.

"You can figure that out," Mary Ellen said, rocking faster. While the girl took a moment to puzzle through her answer, Mary Ellen pushed hard so the chair rocked as far back as it could without tipping over and then shot forward sending Mary Ellen to her feet and across the room where she grabbed hold of Sally.

Sally staggered under the sudden weight. The blood drained from Mary Ellen's head and she wobbled, faltering in her hold on Sally. While Sally worked to support her, Mary Ellen caught her breath and felt her strength returning. She placed a death grip on Sally's arms and pleaded, "Get me out of here and to the Baltimore Hotel. I'm sure that's where my girls are. I must see them. Both of them."

"If I do that, Mrs. Oats'll kill me. I'm really afraid of her." Sally's eyes teared up.

"I'll see to it that you're well taken care of. Help me out of here. Please." Mary Ellen knew if she did not convince this girl to help her, then all would be lost. Desperate to get to her daughters, she begged. "Please, I want to see my daughters again. I need to know they're safe. They could be alone in this city. I don't know why Senator Pembroke wants me out of the way, but I haven't had any drugs for weeks. I wouldn't do anything to embarrass him."

Mary Ellen released her grip on Sally and folded her hands under the girl's chin. "Please?"

Sally studied her for a moment then slammed the door shut behind her and folded her arms. "You might as well go to bed. There's nothing else gonna be happening around here until tonight."

Mary Ellen drew in a deep breath and thought about the last time she had seen Barbara. The child, now a woman, had looked at her with tenderness and compassion. Barbara should be with her now, by her side. Sally bore no resemblance, other than her age, to Barbara. Mary Ellen owed this girl no favors.

Without giving anything away, she sat on the edge of the bed and posed in what she hoped looked to be a defeated manner. Shoulders slumped, she said, "You win. I'm far to weak to fight you. You offered me drugged coffee a while ago." She sighed. "I suppose they told you that I'm a drug fiend, addicted to heroin."

"They did. That's not so bad. Most of the girls here are."

"They told you to keep me drugged? Perhaps you should. I'll even take the headache powder." Mary Ellen reached into her pocket. "That should rid me of this terrible headache."

Sally eyed her with suspicion. "You mean it?"

Mary Ellen nodded. "Will you bring me more food as well? Some meat and cheese, perhaps?"

The girl hesitated before answering. "I'm locking the door. You fooled me before. You won't again."

"I shan't even try." Mary Ellen raised a hand to her forehead and closed her eyes. "I'll lie down until you return. Thank you."

When she heard the door lock, she sat up, unwrapped the powder, placed the contents under her pillow and then laid her head down.

She then dropped the paper wrapper that had contained the headache powder.

Fifty One

Barbara sat with Lily and Annie in the ladies' waiting room while Alistair registered them at the hotel. The three young women had entered the lobby of the Baltimore Hotel, their mouths agape at the splendor of the marble columns, floors, and magnificent plush draperies surrounding arched entrances to various dining and sitting rooms.

Their luggage and hatboxes awaited them on a polished brass carrier. A uniformed colored man stood guard beside it. The sight of the man brought Ledger to mind and Barbara wondered how he would present himself with Grandmother. She chewed her bottom lip, contemplating trouble in spite of the fact Ledger had traveled successfully all over the world. She hoped whoever had beaten him had done so for reasons other than his color, though she could not think of a single reason to assault him. He and Grandmother piled more concern and responsibility on her shoulders. She wanted to know what happened to her mother. Where could she have gone? As far as she knew, Mother had never been to Kansas City so would know no one to call on.

"What's wrong?" Lily asked.

Startled by her sister's voice, Barbara turned to her. "What makes you think anything's wrong? Grandmother drags us halfway across the country into the wild west and then we're abandoned at a hotel."

Lily laughed. "At least it's a nice one. Mommy used to do this to us all the time."

Barbara scowled at her little sister. "Grandmother isn't Mommy. And we're not exactly little girls that kind strangers will care for; I'm a woman now and you and Annie are my responsibility. And stop swinging your legs. Behave like a young lady."

"I need to go."

"You'll have to wait."

"Are you in love with Alistair?" Lily asked.

Annie snickered.

Barbara could feel her face turning red. "Of course not. I like him the same as you do. And he is Mr. Rogers to you."

Another snicker from Annie.

Barbara kicked her ankle just as Alistair returned to escort them to their rooms. She was furious at her sister because Alistair caught her behaving like a child.

"We have the last three rooms, the best ones in the place." He dangled the keys in front of them. "Well, almost the best. I think a couple of senators have the best ones, but we have the suite of rooms that were reserved for the Hawaiian prince and his entourage. Ledger had reserved two, but fortunately their reservation included a third room."

"What happened to them?" Lily asked.

"They chose to remain in their private rail cars. They're on a business trip and this was only an incidental stop. They hadn't planned on the Democratic convention being here at the same time."

"How could they not know?"

Alistair shrugged and signaled the bellhop to bring their baggage. "Hawaii is a new territory; I suppose they have a great deal to learn. Once you are settled, I'll go back and help Ledger with your grandmother."

Barbara took him by the arm when the elevator arrived and stopped him from getting on with the girls and the luggage. "Let them go first. I need to ask you something." With a quick look at Lily and Annie, who giggled in the corner of the elevator, she added, "Something private."

Alistair passed the keys to the bellhop. "I'll be right up."

"Do you know what's happened to my mother?" she asked him once the elevator doors closed.

"She ran off through the train station. When Ledger followed to stop her, she shouted that he was trying to kidnap her and the men on the platform grabbed him. Lucky I was there to stop him from further injury and to explain the situation. He could have been killed."

"You saved Ledger's life?" She eyed him with more respect. Did she love him? She smiled and thought it could certainly be possible.

"I'm no hero. It was only luck that I was there." He hit the elevator call button several times. "Great inventions, these things, but it would be quicker to run up the stairs," he grumbled.

"Grandmother looks unwell. Do you have any idea what she has in mind?"

"She doesn't confide in me. She wants me to look after you and your sister."

"And Annie."

"I suppose, though she never mentioned her." He fidgeted with his hat in his hands, appearing eager to be parted from her company.

"You could go back to her now. I can find my own way to my room. What is the number?"

"Oh, no! I couldn't leave you alone! This place is crawling with men…" He stopped and bit his lips.

"I noticed." She smiled at his discomfort. "Well, hit that button again and let's get upstairs to our room if you're in such a hurry."

She heard a gasp behind her and turned to see a middle-aged couple also waiting for the elevator. After thinking about what she just said, her face suddenly burned with embarrassment. Alistair took her arm and escorted her into the elevator, leading her to the back so the other couple would be in front of them facing the door. The elevator operator checked which floors they wanted and they began the slow climb upward. They were going to the fourth floor; the other couple to the fifth.

"Lily hasn't said another word about Mother since I told her she's alive."

Alistair raised a finger to his lip and then mouthed the word, "Later."

They found the three adjoining rooms as the bellhop was leaving. Barbara entered first. The massive room contained two canopied beds, nightstands, bureaus, rocking chairs, electric lamps with ornate shades and near the windows, a table surrounded by four dining chairs. Lily draped herself across the far bed. Annie had disappeared.

"She's checking out the bathroom. It has the biggest tub I've ever seen. This room makes the rail carriage seem like a dollhouse," Lily said.

"Don't look so excited," Barbara commented. She felt a pang of pity for Lily. "I'm sorry I didn't tell you the instant I knew Mother was alive. Grandmother insisted we keep it quiet until Mother finished her course of treatment." Barbara removed her gloves and tossed them on the nearest bed.

A moment later Annie emerged from the bathroom with a broad grin on her face. "You ought to see this, Barbara. It's...it's *massive*! We could all three of us bathe in there at once and not get in one another's way."

Barbara, annoyed at the girl's cheerfulness in the face of Grandmother's obvious illness snapped at her. "See to our luggage. I'm sure we shall meet Grandmother and Ledger for dinner. Find me an appropriate dinner gown." She then whirled on Alistair. "The shops are bound to be open, perhaps you can go find yourself something presentable to wear to dinner."

He took a step back as if slapped in the face while Annie picked up a small valise and began unpacking Barbara's personal items and laying them out on a dressing table.

"I'll go check on my room and see you in half an hour. If we haven't heard from your grandmother by then, we'll dine together," Alistair said as he backed out of the room.

Barbara glared after him and then turned to Lily. "It's no good pouting. It won't change the past. Why don't you go bathe first? You must feel awful after all that time on the train with those miserable orphans."

Lily remained still and silent, her lower lip pushed out in a pout.

"Fine. I'll bathe first. You can stay here and sulk while the rest of us go have our dinner," Barbara said when Lily didn't move.

She opened her steamer trunk, pulled open the drawer containing her underclothing and pulled them out. "I'll be out in a while, Annie. Let me know immediately if there is any news of Mother."

"Yes, ma'am," Annie said, her voice sullen.

Fed up and exhausted, Barbara stormed into the bathroom and turned on the water in the tub. Half an hour later she returned to the room, once again calm and feeling in control of herself. "Your turn, Lily," she sang out.

Lily clomped into the bathroom without a word.

Barbara turned to Annie. "Will you help me fix my hair?"

331

Annie dropped the dress she was about to hang in the wardrobe and picked up a hairbrush. "Of, course, Miss."

"What is wrong with you two?"

"Everyone is overtired, Miss. Lily has just learned her mother is alive but is now lost. She's upset, Miss. Will yer be wearin' the small green hat what matches yer gown?"

"You're angry about something." Barbara turned her head left and right to study the hairdo in the mirror.

"Yer actin' like one a them rich people I told ya about. It's not very friendly-like."

"And you are speaking like an Irish kitchen maid. You can do better than that."

"I can, if I want to be seen sitting with you at dinner in this fine hotel. There, you look suitably rich." She plonked a small disk of green velvet with colorful birds' feathers attached on the top of Barbara's swept up hair.

"Ouch!" Barbara spun around. "I'm going to see Mr. Rogers. You and Lily should wait here until Ledger and Grandmother arrive.

"You're not supposed to leave the room either."

"I have a few things to attend to before they arrive."

She left before Lily could put up an argument. Out in the hallway, she contemplated going down to the lobby to watch for Grandmother or going to Alistair's room next door to speak with him. The elevator stopped and disgorged four men, all loudly proclaiming their ideas for the party.

"The damned Republicans are imperialists. We need to emphasize that in the platform."

"Against imperialism, indeed."

"What do you think, Mr. Truman?"

"I'm not allowed to think, sir. I'm here as a page."

Barbara backed up to Alistair's door and tapped on it, afraid the rowdy men might approach her.

When Alistair opened the door, the four men in the hall noticed her, paused long enough to tip their hats and then carried on with their discussion, focusing now on the Hawaiian prince who would speak in favor of free silver.

Alistair covered his mouth and coughed. "I'll – um – leave the door open.

Barbara stopped short of crossing the threshold, glanced back at the men, lowered her eyes,and then stepped demurely into the room. "Thank you," she whispered.

Fifty Two

Mary Ellen waited until no sounds came from the interior of the house. She peeked into the hallway and then crept down the back staircase of the brothel and slipped out the back door. With no idea where she was, she decided to head downhill. The train station was near the river. Going that way, she should eventually find their train carriage. Though the sun was low in the sky, she still had light for a while and then, she hoped, streetlamps would light her way.

The avenue she walked along appeared to be a major thoroughfare, so she followed it east, careful to stay close to the street to avoid dark alleys. She hurried, hoping to reach a well-lighted area with plenty of people around. As she walked, she heard footsteps behind her. She slowed; the footsteps slowed. Panicking, she picked up her skirts and began to run. The footsteps increased their pace.

"Mary Ellen. Mrs. Riis. Wait!" Sally's voice gasped behind her.

Out of breath, Mary Ellen grabbed a lamppost to stop her forward motion. She turned to see the girl running toward her carrying a bundle of clothing.

"You'll need a cloak, Mrs. Riis, if you're going to be out at night. It gets very chilly. Here I've brought one for both of us."

"I'm not going back with you. I'll tie myself to this post if you try to force me." Mary Ellen searched the darkening avenue hoping to find help.

"Take the coat. I knew you weren't sleeping when I saw you on the bed. That was a good trick to leave the packet open as if you had taken the powder. I waited in the shadows to see what you would do."

"Why didn't you call for help?"

"You offered me money; how you going to give it to me if I'm not with you? And you showed me a way out." She held a cloak open.

"I thought you said it wasn't so bad there," Mary Ellen said as she slipped the cloak over her shoulders and found the holes for her arms. "What will you do now?"

"Right now, I'm following you to make sure you're safe. Let's go before Mrs. Oats figures out we're both gone. She'll have Matthew combing the streets for us. You don't want to meet up with an angry Matthew."

"He's the one who struck me." Mary Ellen's head still hurt from the blow. "My family would most likely be at the newest or best hotel in the city. Which one would that be?

"Baltimore Hotel. It's huge. Takes up all the space between Eleventh and Twelfth Streets. Are you scheduled to meet your family at a certain time?"

"They're not expecting me. I was supposed to remain on the train – in our private car. A nurse has been taking care of me."

"Are you ill?" Sally moved several steps away from Mary Ellen.

"Not that kind of sick," Mary Ellen said with a smile. "I managed to get myself addicted to heroin and have been on my mother's treatment program for a couple of weeks. For the most part, I do believe it's working."

Sally moved back in beside Mary Ellen. "Wow, am I glad you didn't drink the coffee. It was laced with laudanum. That's pretty strong stuff."

"Did you know about my addictions before I arrived?"

"Nope. Didn't even know you were arriving. All's I knew was Mrs. Oats needed to do a special favor for Senator Pembroke for a night or two by keeping you away from him. Do you know why?"

"I didn't come to Kansas City to see him, but my mother did, I'm sure of that now."

"There it is. It's the biggest and nicest hotel outside of New York City, so I've heard. I've never actually been to any real hotel."

Mary Ellen took Sally's hand. "Will you come in with me?"

"Scared to go in alone?" Sally asked but kept her hand clasped in Mary Ellen's.

"A little bit."

Holding her head high, Mary Ellen strode, with Sally in tow, into the grand lobby and reception area of the Baltimore Hotel. Looking neither left nor right, she approached the long, elegantly carved marble reception desk and waited for a clerk to acknowledge her. Sally tried to remain out of sight behind her.

"Madame?" A man wearing a morning coat and a pince nez looked down his nose at her.

"I'm here to meet the Riis party."

He raised his eyebrows. "Are you indeed? If you will kindly have a seat in the ladies' waiting room, I shall notify them of your presence. Whom shall I say is calling?"

Mimicking his attitude, Mary Ellen answered, "Mrs. Jacob Von Bek and party."

She heard a giggle behind her.

"Please send in a pot of tea for us while we are waiting."

He slammed his open palm onto a bell. Immediately a bellhop appeared and stood at attention. "Bring tea and refreshments for the ladies, William."

The boy saluted and rushed off.

Mary Ellen, feeling safe in the hotel and knowing she had found her family, collapsed onto a dark green velvet chair. The luxuriousness of the hotel was not lost on her. She had been to many of the grand hotels throughout Europe, but this had to be the most extravagant she had seen. Sally teetered on the edge of a chair opposite her.

If she could hold herself together for a few more minutes, she would finally see Lillian with Barbara. With the three of them united, she could face anything, even her mother.

The boy brought a tray filled with a steaming teapot, cups, a plate of sandwiches and another filled with cookies. As she bent to serve, her eye caught sight of two familiar people entering the lobby. They approached the reception desk and the same aristocratic looking clerk approached them. She knew immediately what would come next.

Her mother and Ledger turned to face the waiting room.

Mary Ellen's hand trembled as she tried to pour the tea. When she splashed it into the saucer instead of the cup, Sally took the teapot from her and poured.

"One lump or two?"

Mary Ellen turned to the girl. "What did you say?"

"Sugar. One lump or two?"

"Four." Mary Ellen watched as if hypnotized as Elisabeth Riis, supported by a battered looking Ledger, came into the waiting room.

"We can meet in the lounge next door, Mary Ellen. Ledger is not allowed in the ladies' waiting room."

"He's probably not allowed in the lounge either," Sally said.

"I don't know who you are, young lady, but Ledger can go where he pleases."

"Ledger?" Sally grinned. "Is that really your name? How odd. Well, don't say I didn't warn you."

"I beg your pardon, Miss, but are you a friend of Miss Mary Ellen?" Elisabeth spoke up.

Sally easily mimed her accent. "But of course. I have recently saved the lady from a fate worse than death."

Ledger raised his eyebrows. "Mary Ellen, where did you find this girl?"

"Ledger, she found me and she's right, she did save me. Now we have to save her." She wanted to ask him what had happened to him, but feared the answer.

"I'll call for Rogers and the girls to come down. I've reserved a table for us." He went to the reception desk.

Sally gawked at the marble and onyx pillars, the plush fabric of the furnishings and draperies, all green, ivory and a deeper green. The marble columns, topped with gilt capitals, supported a balcony. "I've never been in such a place. It's fancier than the cathedral in New York."

Elisabeth cleared her throat. "If you will go sit in the ladies' waiting room, I will have a word with my daughter. Rest assured you will be adequately rewarded for helping her."

"You think maybe enough so I can get back to New York?"

Elisabeth sniffed. "More than enough."

Mary Ellen turned Sally by the shoulders and pointed her toward the lounge. "I'll make sure you have enough to care for yourself for a very long time. My daughters will be arriving shortly. You will stay in the waiting room, won't you?" She kept her voice deliberately low.

"Sure. I know you don't want me meeting your fine girls. I know what I've become."

She looked so forlorn Mary Ellen wanted to hug her. Instead, she said, "You remain out of sight in there and I'll see to you after dinner. Perhaps the girls have some clothes more suited to a young lady traveling to New York."

In spite of her effort to cheer the girl, Sally's shoulders remained slumped as she left the party.

Mary Ellen turned to her mother. "What happened to Ledger?"

"You." Elisabeth turned to watch Ledger at the desk. "In all the years I've known him, no one has ever dared attack him. How did you manage it?"

Mary Ellen couldn't remember. One moment she felt fine and the next her heart and mind raced out of control. "I left the train to find the girls. He tried to stop me. That's the last time I saw him."

"How did you get away? And where did you go?"

Three bearded men in business suits barreled their way through the lobby, laughing loudly. Mary Ellen waited until they passed by to speak. "I was kidnapped by a woman named Mrs. Oats on the order of Senator Pembroke. Sally was supposed to keep me drugged, but she let me go."

Elisabeth gasped. Her right hand went to her heart as she staggered and grabbed Mary Ellen's sleeve with her free hand. Her purse fell from her arm. Ledger appeared in time to prevent her from falling to the floor. Together he and Mary Ellen led her to a nearby chair.

"Tell me. Tell me all about it," Elisabeth ordered Mary Ellen.

"What's going on?" Ledger looked accusingly at the younger woman.

Mary Ellen explained what happened after she left the train depot in search of her daughters. "I'm truly sorry for what happened to you, Ledger," she concluded.

"Senator Pembroke, you say?" he responded, ignoring her apology. "And that girl knew all about it?" He indicated Sally who sat watching them from the ladies' waiting room.

Ledger signaled her to come to them and, after hearing her story, he sent her back. "The girls should be down any moment with Rogers. Are you recovered sufficiently to dine, Elisabeth?"

"Ledger!" Mary Ellen's voice shook with alarm. "Can't you see Mother is ill? We should take her to upstairs and call a doctor."

Elisabeth held her hand out to Ledger, ignoring Mary Ellen's comment. "Let's get this over with."

Fifty Three

Elisabeth held out her hand for Ledger to help her to her feet.

"Mommy!" a child's voice shouted.

Mary Ellen swayed as Lillian rushed from the elevator and threw her arms about her. She held Lillian tightly. "Is it really you?" she sobbed.

Elisabeth watched this scene as if underwater. Nothing existed outside this small circle of people. Her daughter, granddaughters, Alistair, Annie and most importantly, Ledger.

A formally attired, slightly balding gentleman approached their group. "Excuse me, perhaps you would like a private room for this reunion?"

Ledger pulled a chair around so both Elisabeth and Mary Ellen could sit. "We're fine, thank you. We'll be going in to dinner in a few minutes. We reserved for six, but now we will be seven, thank you."

"Excuse me, sir, but may I have a private word?"

"Concerning?" Ledger said.

"As the manager, it is my duty to uphold the company policies. If you please." He extended his hand toward the rear of the lobby.

Elisabeth watched this exchange while Lillian, along with Barbara, Alistair and Annie formed a semi-circle around Mary Ellen. She feared the next move – Ledger being asked to leave. Not now, she thought. I need him more than ever tonight.

Alistair watched Ledger depart with the manager then bent to speak with Elisabeth. "I'll return shortly. We may have to go to dinner without Ledger."

She heard the words but refused to accept them. "You tell that bald headed bastard that Armbruster Slade is amongst one of the wealthiest men in this country; he is an ambassador, and he is dining with us."

"Yes, ma'am," Alistair said. He then took Barbara aside and for brief word with her before departing.

Come along, Grandmother," Barbara said when she returned. "We'll settle you with Lillian in the lounge and then I'll take Mother and her new friend upstairs to change for dinner. Alistair won't be long. Annie, you'll help me, please?"

Elisabeth permitted herself to be led by Lillian into the lounge where the two of them sat side by side, not speaking. Sally had managed to clean up most of the delicate sandwiches but hot tea and three cookies remained. Lillian picked up a cookie and nibbled around the edges.

"You'll spoil your dinner." Elisabeth did not look at her granddaughter.

"I won't."

They sat in silence for several minutes.

"Can I pour some tea for you?" Lillian asked.

"I can pour my own, thank you." Elisabeth wished the girl would go away although she felt more secure with her nearby. "Maybe half a cup. Everyone should be here soon. If you'll excuse me, I am a bit anxious about dinner."

"Strange group of people you have assembled, Grandma."

"I suppose they are. I have a pill box in my purse. Will you get it out for me, please?" Elisabeth held out her arm with the small handbag hanging from it.

Lillian took it. "Maybe after dinner you would like to see my sketch book? I drew pictures of you and Ledger and Barbara. I'll do one of Mommy, too."

"Very nice, dear," Elisabeth said distractedly as she spilled a powder into her tea cup.

"I'm happy to see Mommy."

"That's nice."

"You told us she died and I hated you."

"You mustn't talk like that. I did what I thought best for you and your sister."

"I think you did what was best for Barbara, maybe. Not me."

Elisabeth felt perspiration on her brow. Her eyes still watered though she had no desire to weep. "Go find Ledger or your sister. I'm not feeling well."

"Can I get you something? Do you want me to ask for a doctor at the desk?" Lillian stood up, her young face ashen with worry.

Elisabeth tried to see her clearly. She looked so much like someone from her past. Who could it be? she wondered. "Just find your sister. Ask the desk to call her room."

"It's my room, too, Grandmother," Lillian said in a soft voice before turning away.

Her red curls bobbed as she hurried to the desk.

Elisabeth drew in several deep breaths and closed her eyes to rest for a moment while she waited for someone to come to her aid. The child's blurred face and bobbing curls appeared like a moving photograph. She knew who Lillian reminded her of. She was herself at that tender age, full of innocence and trust, believing everything would be right in the world as long as she had her Daddy. She sighed again and told herself Ledger would have to be notified to rewrite her will one more time. Something they could take care of in the morning.

The hum of activity surrounded her. Voices of other women in the lounge waiting for their dinner companions spoke of children and husbands, of prospects for their daughters, and with fondness of sons. She listened as she played the memories of her life. How fortunate she felt the day Jim drove by her house for the first time. How much did these women know of life and heartache? Perhaps she ought to open her eyes and explain it to them. Then again, perhaps not.

"Grandmother?" Someone shook her shoulder.

Reluctantly opening her eyes, she saw Barbara standing beside her. Lillian, Mary Ellen and two other young women hovered nearby. "Where's Ledger?"

Barbara exchanged glances with Mary Ellen. "He won't be joining us for dinner but will meet us later at the train."

"Nonsense. Send the hotel manager to me immediately." Elisabeth felt as though she had rested for hours instead of moments. "Help me up from this chair. I want to clear this up at once."

Lillian and Barbara both assisted her in rising. As a group they left the lounge reserved for ladies and found Alistair lurking in the lobby, waiting for them. He was dressed formally for dinner.

Elisabeth approved. "What have you done with Ledger?" she asked Alistair.

"Nothing, Mrs. Riis. He has left and will meet us later."

She shook off the girls' hands. "In all my life we have managed to overcome such circumstances." She scowled and looked around at her entourage. "Am I to do this alone?"

"Do what alone, Mother?"

Elisabeth snapped a sharp turn and headed toward the dining room. "Let us take our places for dinner. Alistair, give me your arm."

He rushed to her side and held out his arm. "What can I do for you?" he said as they waited for the maitre d' to lead them to their table.

"I will let you know at the appropriate moment."

She allowed the maitre d' to seat her and then asked him to point out the senator's table.

No one was at his table, but the settings indicated eight diners. That suited her just fine. The more, the merrier. She was beginning to feel much better.

The girls giggled amongst themselves while Alistair took his place beside her. He alone appeared nervous.

She smiled. "It's good to see the girls with their mother again. I do believe Mary Ellen is doing remarkably well, don't you?"

"Shall we read our menus?" he countered, picking his up. "Perhaps you'd like to start with something light? A consommé?"

Elisabeth ignored Alistair. A large party of men entered the dining room. There was no mistaking Senator Justin Pembroke. The tallest of his group and the obvious leader, he laughed as he followed the maitre d'. Her heart stopped as she gaped at the man she hated for so many years. Even if he looked her way, he would neither notice nor recognize her, she had changed so much. Except for gray hair, he looked the same. How unfair life could be. More than ten years her senior and still fit and trim. *Enjoy yourself, Justin. I'll see you after dinner.*

Turning her attention back to Alistair, she smiled once again and then joined in light-hearted conversation with the young women. Even the new addition now looked more like an acceptable member of society than a runaway orphan.

~*~

Barbara laughed at Annie's version of how they captured the villains in the train but kept an eye on her grandmother.

She had not liked the pallor of her complexion when they arrived at the lounge after dressing. Mother, thus far, seemed in control and, hopefully, would be able to make it through dinner without causing a scene. Sally seemed a little awkward but fit in well with Annie at her side to teach her about forks and knives.

Grandmother said little during dinner, appearing distracted. Whatever they had come to Kansas City for, might be about to happen. She wished Ledger could be here to support Grandmother. With so many hundreds of diners in the room, it was remarkably quiet. Their table stood near the right side of the room next to a fountain that looked like it came straight from Egypt. Potted palms helped separate the tables.

"Are you really going to go to college?" Sally, Mother's new friend was asking. Barbara had been so caught up in her surroundings and watching Grandmother, it took a moment to realize Sally spoke to her.

"It is something Grandmother, Ledger and I have discussed."

"I'm all for it," Alistair blurted. When all the girls turned to him and laughed, his face turned red.

Barbara admired the way he took control and helped Grandmother when they learned Ledger could not be with them. If she did go to college, she would study the workings of governments so maybe someday she could help change things like segregation. For now, she enjoyed her lemon meringue pie.

"I think it's time. Alistair, if you please. Mary Ellen, will you join us?"

Barbara felt the hairs on the back of her neck stand up. Her mother pushed back her chair and a waiter ran to help her. On impulse, Barbara folded her napkin and also rose. "I'll come with you, Mother."

Barbara and Mary Ellen followed behind Grandmother and Alistair. She had no idea where they would be going. Her heart raced. She bit her lower lip.

The party stopped at a table not far from theirs and Grandmother turned to Mary Ellen and held out her arm, gesturing Mary Ellen to come to her side. Alistair took a step back, and Barbara reflexively took his hand.

"Senator Pembroke." Elisabeth's voice rose above the din.

A gray-haired man sporting a small mustache and a Van Dyke beard, looked up inquisitively. "Madam? We are enjoying our dinner. If you have business with me, you can make an appointment through my secretary." He turned away, dismissing her.

"Justin!"

He turned back. Recognition dawned as he studied her face. "You?"

"You know very well it is I. Your thugs were unsuccessful in stopping us."

"This is outrageous. Leave and meet me privately later if you must." He scowled.

The gentleman standing next to the senator nudged him and said, "Senator, this lady is Mrs. Riis. She runs the Ackert Industries and is head of the Ackert-Riis Foundation, the philanthropic group that does good works."

Barbara studied the senator; he was the man in the Albany Club who talked about getting rid of somebody.

Grandmother spoke up. "If you are making plans for the White House, Senator Pembroke, I wondered if you had plans to bring your daughter and grandchildren with you."

"My wife will, of course, join me. My *son*," he emphasized the word, "has his own family business in New York and isn't able to join us."

"I'm speaking of your daughter, Mary Ellen Pembroke, whom I have the honor of introducing to you now."

Barbara watched her mother's body sway and moved to support her, but Alistair held her back. So this is what Grandmother had in mind. She didn't care about getting Mother well, she just wanted her upright long enough to humiliate everyone in the family. Her lower lip trembled.

"You can't ignore me, Justin. I wouldn't be surprised to learn some of these very men at this table were party to your scheme when you lied and seduced me."

"I don't know what you're talking about. It is Elisabeth, isn't it?" He stood and smiled at his colleagues, taking his time, enjoying himself.

"You know my name very well. As does at least one member of your group." She faced the men at the table who had also risen from their chairs. "I was sixteen. Elisabeth Ann Ackert, the Irish tramp, I believe your sister called me. Gentlemen, this is the man you want in the White House? A seducer of young girls? A man who denied his responsibility to his daughter?"

Barbara thought most of the men appeared decidedly uncomfortable; only one seemed curious. "I know you're the one who sent those men to murder us by setting the apartment on fire! And then when that didn't work, those men came on the train. I heard you the night you talked about it at the Albany Club." She knew she had not heard exactly that, but enough to realize he was the perpetrator of the scheme.

"Pardon me," Justin said to his friends. "I'll settle this quietly if the ladies will step into the lobby with me."

"The ladies will not," Elisabeth said.

"Mother," Mary Ellen murmured.

Justin took hold of the lapels on his dinner jacket like a man prepared to present a speech. "All right then, if you want to air your dirty linen in public, I'll explain. This girl's father," he pointed to Mary Ellen, "is the late James Riis, an impoverished friend of mine, who was injured in the War

Between the States. I paid him to seek you out and marry you, my dear. I suggested with your Irish background, you would make a grand helpmate and servant to him." He laughed. The rest of the men either hung their heads, or their eyes scanned the dining room as if seeking rescue. "He received an allowance every month."

Barbara watched Elisabeth's back stiffen. "You knew very well he was a cripple and–and unable to father any children."

Alistair gripped Barbara's hand more tightly. The senator *paid* someone to marry Grandmother? Did Alistair want her to remain quiet while this old man tried to ruin their family's reputation in public? And why did Mother stand there so quietly?

She leaned closer to Alistair so she could whisper in his ear. "We need Ledger here for Grandmother."

"He's behind the building near the service entrance. Send Annie and Sally for him. I don't think I should leave your grandmother."

"What do I tell them?"

"Say your grandmother needs him and could he please take on the role of servant for a short while. He'll do anything for Mrs. Riis."

Barbara eyed him gratefully, squeezed his hand and ran back to their table where Lillian, Annie and Sally had been watching them. She passed along the message ending with, "Hurry! Lily, you wait here."

"I won't," Lily said as she stood up and placed her folded napkin on the table. "I'm coming over to find out what's going on."

Barbara eyed her determined little sister and then shrugged. "Suit yourself, but you won't like what you'll hear."

Lily followed behind Barbara as they headed back to the senator's table where the senator stood regaling his thoroughly shamefaced, embarrassed colleagues with his tale of picnics at the riverfront with assorted wanton women, Elisabeth being one of them.

As they approached the table, one of the men, slightly younger than the rest, separated himself from the group. "I'll say good night, gentlemen and will see you in the morning. We have much to discuss."

He nodded acknowledgement to the women and left the table. Within seconds of his departure, two more men excused themselves.

A bald, potbellied man harrumphed loudly, and left without saying farewell.

Two more followed suit, making their excuses to the ladies.

The last man remaining whispered something to the senator and then stepped around him to approach Elisabeth. Alistair dropped Barbara's hand and moved to Grandmother's side.

"Mrs. Riis, I offer you my sincere apology for your years of grief. I had not known of the depth of your relationship with Justin. I was at that first picnic when you met Jim Riis and am ashamed to say," he lowered his voice, "I behaved badly. Rest assured the morning's papers will announce that Tammany Hall will support Richard Croker as our candidate for the president of the United States following the sudden withdrawal of Senator Pembroke. I bid you good night." He bowed slightly from the waist and, without looking back at the senator, left the room.

Senator Pembroke stared after him briefly but when Lillian stepped forward to stand beside her mother, the senator's jaw dropped. He looked as if he had seen a ghost.

Mary Ellen took her youngest daughter's hand and smiled down at her. Elisabeth turned to see what had upset the senator.

"She looks just like you," Senator Pembroke said, pointing a finger at Lillian.

In a weakened voice, Elisabeth said, "And why shouldn't she? She is my granddaughter. Have you not recognized yourself in Mary Ellen? Her height, her coloring. The slender build? How – how dare you deny her?"

Mary Ellen's arm went around her mother's waist to support her. Elisabeth staggered and regained her footing.

"Do you think those men care about this? They left because they were bored. Don't you think they've had their share of harlots over the years?"

"Enough, sir!" Alistair spoke. He stepped in front of the women. "Their private affairs are not in question here. I doubt any of them ever molested the young daughter of a highly respected businessman. I don't know why Mrs. Riis chose to keep your name from her daughter for all these years, but I do know you will not speak to her in such a manner. In fact, you will not speak to her again. Ever. Do I make myself clear?"

"Who the hell are you?"

"Mind your language in the presence of ladies."

Barbara watched, wide-eyed with respect, gratitude and love as Alistair defended their grandmother.

"Well, well. Young pup. I suggest you remove these women from the premises before I call the police and have you up for disturbing the peace."

"Go ahead and call the police. You were the one tried to kill Mother and Grandmother," Lillian said.

Elisabeth, who now leaned heavily on Mary Ellen's shoulder, drew Lillian close. "Bless you, child, you do get right to the point." With that remark she slid gracefully to the floor.

Ledger burst through the group with a team of waiters and the maitre d' chasing after him. Annie and Sally ran behind him, blocking the men from catching up.

"Elisabeth!" he called out as he reached her and knelt by her side.

"That's no way to address your mistress, boy!" Senator Pembroke said, a note of authority returned to his voice.

"This is Mr. Armbruster Slade, late of the United Kingdom, and more recently a citizen of the United States, manager of Ackert Industries, and owner of *The Armbruster Legend*. I suggest you show respect, sir." Alistair moved to help Ledger lift an unconscious Elisabeth from the floor

Mary Ellen stepped gingerly around her mother and approached the senator. "Father," she said with disdain, "I agree with my friend, Mr. Rogers. Look around and see who is surrounded by people displaying love and respect. You, sir, are unworthy to be in the same room with my mother."

Justin Pembroke threw his napkin to the table and stalked from the room. Barbara heard a whisper of hisses and murmurs of "scoundrel" as he passed tables.

With Elisabeth's limp body in his arms, Ledger sent Alistair for a carriage.

Fifty Four

Elisabeth heard voices. Though extremely tired, she opened her eyes. A group of people crowded around her bed. The room felt suffocatingly close. Her breaths came in short, uneven gasps. Finally, her eyes rested on Ledger.

She tried to lift her head but he stroked her forehead and said, "You're not to move."

"Who is that man?"

Ledger smiled before answering and then placed a kiss on her forehead. A murmur of approval flitted through the room. "He is a physician. A priest is on the way."

"Ledger," she whispered so he would have to lean closer. "Are you telling me I'm ready for Extreme Unction?"

"Last Rites? No, he's coming to bless you and give you hope."

She coughed bringing the doctor to her side. He held a stethoscope to her chest. She realized someone had changed her into her nightclothes. They'd put her to bed in her private rail car, not in the hotel.

"Try to take a deep breath," the doctor ordered in a gentle tone.

"I can't seem to catch my breath at all. I feel like a weak kitten."

"We're doing all we can for you. Your car will be attached to the next train heading east."

"Ledger. I need to tell Ledger some things."

"There's no need, Elisabeth. I understand. Your Lillian will be cared for appropriately. I explained to Barbara what I believe you wish done."

"Ledger," she gasped. This would be her last opportunity. She knew it as sure as she knew she would not see the next sunrise. "I do love them."

His ear was so close to her lips she could bite it off had she the energy. Was she whispering so softly? "I love them all, Ledger. But I loved you most of all. I wish..." She couldn't finish the words she longed to say for so many years.

He stroked her brow. His hands felt cool. "My darling, Elisabeth, I love you as well. You will remain in my heart forever."

"Why?" So many words she wanted to say but her mouth didn't seem to want to work. *A doctor of letters at Cambridge or Oxford. A highly respected lecturer. You could have had it all, but you chose to stay with me. You suffered at James' highhanded manners. You worked more like a slave than any slave ever worked. You became my heart, my reason for living.*

"Mommy? Is Grandma dying?" Lillian's weeping voice reached her ears.

"Hush, darling."

"But I told her I hated her for saying you were dead. I wanted to tell her I really love her. She can't die until I tell her."

Barbara spoke. "She knows, sweetheart. Look at her face. How peaceful she is."

A deep baritone voice then took control. "The Lord is my shepherd..."

The End.

About the Author

Veronica H. Hart

Veronica Helen Hart is an award-winning author and playwright. She is a member of The Florida Writers Association, Carrollton Writers Guild (Georgia), and Sisters in Crime. She moderates two local critique groups. Recently, she founded Paranormalice Press, LLC in order to publish paranormal murder mysteries. In addition to print and ebook, several of her books are now available as audiobooks.

Other Titles by
Veronica Helen Hart

*The Knife
Elena – the Girl with the Piano
*Escape from Iran
Silent Autumn
Release date, 1/15/2021: Boy Comes Home

The Blenders Series featuring Doll Reynolds
The Prince of Keegan Bay
Swimming Corpse
Safari Stew
Midnight in Mongolia
Soon to be released: The Bridesmaid

Short Fiction
Speculative Fiction
Storey's Orphans: Masters Reimagined Volume 2
Annie Karenina: Masters Reimagined Volume 1
Recovery: Return to Earth

* Available as audiobook at Audible and ACX